HUMAN RESOURCES

HUMAN RESOURCES

A novel

BY MARGOT MARTIN

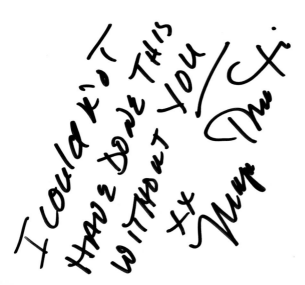

I could not have done this without you / Cxi

tt Mxxe

Charleston, SC
www.PalmettoPublishing.com

Human Resources
Copyright © 2020 by Margot Martin
#TXu002201669

This is a work of Fiction. Names, characters, places, and incidents either are the product of the author's
imagination or are used fictitiously. Any resemblance to actual persons, living or dead, events, or locales
is entirely coincidental.

ISBN-13: 978-1-64990-524-6
ISBN-10: 1-64990-524-6

GRATITUDE

I have been fortunate throughout the process of writing and editing Human Resources. I stumbled my way into an extraordinary support team as well. My far more than just an editor, Dr. Charles T. Brumfield, Jr., our son, Chuck Field, my son, Nick Falzerano, our friend Sean Lynch, my friend, Diane Fenn, my friend, Don Surath, all had great suggestions I used which greatly enhanced the final story. Thank you.

Also, much gratitude for the illustrators who brought my concept for a book jacket to life, Colton Starley and Joseph Cabungcal of Sketch Soup. Wow! What a cover! And to the hard- working Kate Derr, my social media maven, thank you for helping me in the race to the finish. I could not have done this without any of you.

Many thanks to my cheerleading squad of lifelong friends, Barbara Wells, Ingrid Hills, GB Buchanon, Terry Higgins, my daughter by another mother, Nini Le Huynh, and my first cousin, Helen Greenwood, who over a span of 40 years have listened to my sorrows, shared in my triumphs, cheered me on and believed in me. This life of mine has been better because you are in it. And to my newest friend, cheerleader, eagle eye editor and former business associate, Amy Nachman, who, like Barbara Wells and GB Buchanon, is a fellow Southern Belle and all that means, welcome to the club. We share a lot.

Dr. Patricia Frisch, my therapist of 16 years in Mill Valley, CA, thank you for reconstructing me and making me whole. You know what you have done for me!! I would not be here without you.

And finally, to my dearest of friends, Tony Gonzalez, who took a very broken me and helped me believe in myself again. This book would not have happened if you had not caught me one fateful day as I was falling, seconds before my head hit concrete. It was a real catch and a metaphorical one as well. You grabbed me under my arms, lifted me up, held me tight, and have ever since.

Life hands you triumph and tragedies and if you can get to the finish line in one piece, then you have won at the game of life. I am working on it.

PROLOGUE AND DEDICATION

When I decided to clean up Human Resources after letting it languish for 25 years, I knew I needed help. As luck would have it, luck I have enjoyed over many ventures in my life, things fell into place and the person I knew I needed had recently moved literally down the road from me. Dr. Charles T. Brumfield, Jr. He was the one person I knew I could trust with the material.

Dr. Brumfield has been my lifelong mentor and best and most loyal friend of my lifetime. He saved me. From a devastating childhood with two severely damaged parents to two bad marriages where he pitched in to help me, he saved me. An educator deep into his soul, he is the person who built a foundation in me that was the launch pad for all that has followed in my successes in business. Due to his inspirations embedded in me, I climbed the corporate ladder in broadcasting and became the Corporate Director of Sales for a major market television group. Over the years I worked for the big broadcasters such as NBC, RKO, COX, Westinghouse, now CBS, and United Chris Craft, now CW. Human Resources contains an insider's view of broadcasting and pro sports as in my time as an executive I mingled with teams and sports stars exactly in the ways portrayed in the book. I know my world.

I met Dr. Brumfield in a graduate marketing class when I was 20. We were in Europe and the class was in Bremen, Germany. Dr. Brumfield has been an educator for many exceptional schools, including but not limited to University of Maryland that has worldwide campuses, University of South Carolina, University of Wisconsin, Cal Poly and California State Universities. I was a wild unformed girl and he was mature beyond his years in his love of learning. Because I was a provocative little sex pot at 20, I decided to run my bare foot up his leg as he lectured behind a podium and nine months later our son Chuck was born. Honorable to the core, we married. Best of my three husbands by far but I was too young, wild and wooly to grasp that learned men were not going also be party animals for their 20-year-old wife while writing their doctoral dissertations.

But in the chaos of graduate school and my own further education at University of South Carolina, after stints at University of Alabama and University of Maryland where I met Dr. Brumfield, he managed to make time for me to expand my thinking and reasoning and creative advancement. We would have the GREAT DEBATES. I got to pick my side of the debate and he would take the opposite even if he was on my side. For hours and hours, we would exhaust a subject. Politics, social issues, literature, current events, you name it, we covered it. I loved the GREAT DEBATES. No one had ever taught me what those debates taught me about using my brain. He also introduced me to all the greatest writers then and long before. Hemingway, Steinbeck, Pat Conroy, Dostoevsky, Tom Wolfe, to name a few. My gleam of interest grew in devouring literature the same way I loved to devour chocolate sundaes.

So, to you, Dr. Charles T. Brumfield Jr., I dedicate this book and much of my life. I thank you for being the most perfect dad to both my sons even though my second son was not your biological child.

Your devotion to both of them, your selfless gift of time of every free moment when you would take them on camping trips, read to them, tell them stories, take them on hikes, take them on educational trips, babysit them so I, the hedonistic lover of spas and vacations, and weekly business trips, could go without a care in the world because you would hold down the fort with the boys. The boys are both successful men and owe you as much as I do.

Charles, I could not have done this life without you. Nor would I have wanted to.

THE HOLLYWOOD REPORTER
MONDAY AUGUST 8, 1994

GEORGE CHRISTY'S THE GREAT LIFE
LA'S SILICONE PLAYPEN EJECTS EXECS!

"One of the most intriguing stories west of Hollywood and Vine is the big-time T.V. honcho and his news anchor who were permanently ejected Saturday night from Starlets on Sunset Blvd... (For those not in the know, Starlets is a very expensive, private boys' club where skin and sin are in!). Rumor has it that they had a little too much to drink at the honcho's private birthday bash, and the news anchor roughed up one of the cocktail girls... (which is a real NO! NO!). L.A.'s finest were called in to break up the ruckus and our favorite anchor was hauled in for questioning. Bet you won't hear about it on the 10 O'clock News!"

On my way into breakfast at Norm's Coffee Shop on La Cienega in Los Angeles, I picked up a copy of the *L.A. Times* and *The Hollywood Reporter*. As I scanned the front pages, my eyes caught the degrading headline. A familiar shame, a remnant of my weekend debacle, crawled over me.

Breakfast went down with great difficulty and in silence, while I avoided the greetings of my friends in the restaurant. An ever-increasing weight of humiliation seeped deep inside my being as my viscera churned the neon image of what went on that night. There was no place to hide from George Christy's article, read faithfully by the movers and shakers of the entertainment industry.

Christy's Starlets story would become a joke passed around at the water cooler and cocktail parties, a tidbit, an hors d'oeuvre of the well-heeled set. The only way to distract the gossip mongers from this juicy morsel would be when something juicier and more delicious came along. What I failed to realize then while reading the column over and over during my quickly souring breakfast, was that the disgraceful incident at *Starlets* turned out to be a prophetic marker of things to come.

Nothing like good intentions gone bad. I threw Brian Buchanon's 55th birthday party at *Starlets* to make him feel like it was old times again. He and I. Brian and Paddy. Best buddies. The *Starlets* party was planned out of sheer desperation, which was my attempt to revive our flagging ten-year friendship that was now at its all-time low. You see, Brian Buchanon and I have enjoyed a quite long and memorable history together. In fact, if you asked him, he would say I owed my entire career to him and, in many respects, he would be right.

Brian Buchanon is the President and General Manager of KKLA Television in Los Angeles, and my boss. In fact, he is the boss of over 200 of the most talented people in the business, the television business, the "Biz" as we insiders call it. He's the undisputed king of local television in the L.A. market. I'm the prince, anointed, appointed by him, owing him everything. We go back a long way. Brian hired me, Patrick McGurk (more commonly known by the esteemed citizens and television viewers of Los Angeles as "Paddy"), to anchor the late news on WWNY Television in New York City. That was many years ago, but it was the beginning of our long, and now tumultuous, relationship.

Our relationship is rooted in my lifelong fascination and devotion to television. I grew up on a farm in rural Ohio with one brother and sister, a live-in uncle, and two hard working parents. My father was very wise and made us earn our time in front of the magic picture box. Like most parents dispense sweets, my father used television as the treat that came after all our chores were done, baths were taken, and homework was finished. Each night, we would gather around the television set to watch the programs of the day. We sat spellbound with our mouths drooped open through the "Twilight Zone", "Perry Mason", the "Ed Sullivan Show", "I Dream of Jeannie", and "The Andy Griffith Show". We treasured every corny minute. But what I remember most was the family gathering around the T.V. set to watch Chet Huntley and David Brinkley on the evening news.

When I was in my early teen years, during the peak years of the Vietnam war, our family dinners were spent glued to the tube, with no one talking and hanging on every heart-wrenching word of the brave reporters who risked their lives on a daily basis to bring us the triumphs and tragedies of faraway conflict. My mother would cry silently beside me sitting at the table each night as pictures of exploding bombs, grenades, helicopters, sounds of gunfire, and images of war-ravaged bodies being rushed on stretchers filled the room. There was a reverential solemnness in our home during that era of television, no matter what entertainment followed the news broadcasts; the night was always overshadowed by those haunting images and countless losses. It was then when I was a juiced up, testosterone fueled teen-aged boy, that I realized that I wanted to be a television journalist. The ongoing drama pulled me in each night and, afterward, I would lie in my bed and dream of faraway places, dangerous assignments, finding the truths, and righting wrongs. After the war ended, my passion for news grew inside me like a well-tended garden.

It was during the Watergate trials that I became the editor for the high school paper. This included going on to win awards in high school journalism competitions, where I became known for my ability to compose thought provoking articles. Even though I had a gift for the written word, my heart was in television. I loved the whole evocative feeling made possible by combining the written word with the visual images, making the words come to life before your eyes. Television offered me the opportunity to write to the story, the ability to use my words to enhance the images unfolding on the screen. The combination of both was so much more mesmerizing, so much more compelling.

With the help of a partial scholarship, I worked my way through Notre Dame in four years. While there, I was fortunate enough to work as an intern at several television stations during my junior and senior years and became the "darling" of the news departments at each station. I loved everything about the news: the immediacy, the drama, the unpredictability. Each day was a new adventure. After graduating, my first real, or may I say paying, job was at WDAY in Dayton, Ohio. I started in the mail room for six months, moved to an assistant producer position on the Morning News, junior reporter on the Morning News, then feature reporter on the Five O'clock News, and finally investigative reporter on the Late News at eleven. I was the young phenom of Dayton, and all that exposure on the air was great for my social life, which made all those hometown girls yearn for my body. I was very spoiled, very fast; in other words, I was a big fish in a very little pond.

After two years of uncovering unsuspected vice in the heartland of America, I became the pride of WDAY's news department and was rewarded with the anchor position on the late news. Anchoring was not as challenging, or as much fun might I add, as investigative reporting; but the pay was definitely better. So, still young and impressed with such things, I convinced myself anchoring was the job for me. Besides, I finally got to sleep in. A bachelor's dream: big bucks and great hours.

By the time Brian Buchanon entered my life I was a "self-made man", or so I thought. Anchoring the late news in Dayton, at the comparatively youthful age of only twenty-nine, made me damn proud of myself. But even though I had a lot of success for so early on in my career, I was still totally in awe of Mr. Brian Buchanon. He was already a mythic figure in the world of broadcasting. He was bigger than life, bold and engaging, and was considered the greatest strategist in the broadcast business. The placid personalities populating Dayton, Ohio and WDAY seemed vanilla, white bread by comparison. Brian came to town and handpicked me that fateful week in early Fall of 1981, when he was visiting one of his old Michigan State fraternity brothers who owned a string of car dealerships in the Midwest. The evening prior to his leaving town, Brian watched me anchor the late news on WDAY. He liked what he saw and decided then and there that he wanted me to anchor his late news in New York. Like a bloodhound on a scent, he tracked me down early the next morning while he was at the Dayton Airport waiting for a flight out and asked me to come to New York for an interview. I was flattered and scared, but eagerly accepted the invitation. He proceeded to treat me like the big brother I had always longed for. He was a pro at creating the instant bond, his calling card and his way of getting and maintaining control. It was terribly seductive and, looking back, I was incredibly naive.

Brian and I had so much in common back then. We were Irish boys with black hair, blue eyes, white skin, what we call "Black Irish", and were from big Catholic families; the norm for our generation of Catholicism. We were both former athletes and loved sports of any kind but were especially obsessed with the mainstream sports of base-ball, basketball, football and the aging athlete's game of choice, golf. But our connection, more than anything else, was the fact that we were men in the classic sense of the word. We hit it off immediately.

Brian bought me a first-class ticket to "The Big Apple" and had me picked up at Kennedy Airport by a limo. The limo dropped me off at The Plaza Hotel and there was a bottle of chilled Dom "P" wait-ing in my suite that overlooked Central Park. I'd been to New York before, but not like this. The elegance of The Plaza, the excitement of New York, and the sophistication of its people were enticing. For the entire weekend, Brian romanced me like a college coach hosting a small-town rookie with a lot of raw talent. No expense was spared. The money he spent on me that weekend was more than my father made in a month. I was like a kid in a candy store. Brian played me like a fiddle, offering me a staggeringly generous contract, and I signed on the dotted line without a moment's hesitation. The de-cision made that weekend, to put my future in the hands of Brian Buchanon, was, I have since found, a far greater commitment than the terms of the original contract.

I moved from Ohio to New York during the garbage strike of '81. At that time, we should have been enjoying the Christmas season and all its beauty, instead the whole town reeked of rotting garbage. Everywhere you walked, the sidewalks were filled with bags of spoiling refuse that was spilling out into the streets. Everybody in New York was pissed. New Yorkers are an angry breed, and the garbage strike sent them over the top. The tirade in the daily headlines of the Times and the Post trashed the unions, exposing rampant corruption and screams for resolution. At any social or business gathering in the city, no con-versation would be complete without the airing of views on the strike. The politicians were running out of rhetoric.

The intensity of public outrage over the garbage strike was an opportunity for the television stations in the market to capitalize on their local news numbers because the viewers were glued to their tubes hoping for news of an end to the ever-growing trash and stench. WWNY was the "hind-tit" station in New York, an independent station viewed as a second-class citizen, so we had to make the most of this boon to local news. Historically, our late news pulled pitiful ratings and was truly an embarrassment. We were constantly in last place in the news ratings because the big affiliates controlled the news audience and we had to settle for the leftovers.

Brian, the most fiercely competitive General Manager in the market, was not willing to settle for being number four out of four for long and was determined to dominate local television in "The Big Apple" by creating a news operation at WWNY that changed the way New Yorkers watched local news. I now believe that's why Brian hired me. I was young, arrogant, behaved as though I knew it all, and had the kind of spirited personality that would fuel New Yorkers' anger. Brian cast me in the part that I was born to play. Me, the marionette, and him as the master.

One Friday night, a week into the garbage strike, Brian took me to a discreet place for dinner to share his secret strategy for exploiting the strike to our advantage. We took a limo and ended up at Peter Luger's in Brooklyn. It later became our favorite haunt for martinis, fat steaks, and Cuban cigars, *Cohibas, Monte Cristos, Romeo and Julietas.* Luger's was noisy and anonymous, filled with Mafia types and their wives with ratted hair and bright red three-inch nails, and noisy kids that got slapped. The perfect place to get away from the advertising types crawling all over Manhattan "Chi Chi" night spots. The patrons at Lugers were too busy inhaling their cholesterol count for the week, porterhouses as big as an oversized dinner plate that were liberally doused in their famous Luger steak sauce, butter, and sour cream laden potatoes, artery clogging creamed spinach, and beefsteak tomato salad with red onions and tons of blue cheese.

Brian leaned into me conspiratorially at the end of dinner and said, "Paddy, what have we got to lose? Let's give them something to talk about. There's no such thing as bad press. The only bad press is no press at all. And that's what we've got now." His idea was outrageous, unorthodox for news, and, frankly, it scared me. But in Brian Buchanon's world, there was no room for fear. I became a quick study.

Brian was my boss, my mentor, and, because of that unspoken obligation, I felt I had no choice but to go along with his schemes. With the bravura of the naive, I said "What the hell? Why not take the risk?" I was young and dumb enough, then, to eagerly accept being fed to the lions by my fearless leader. Besides, our news was going nowhere fast, and this outrageous plan could possibly turn the tide.

That weekend, we brought sacks of garbage into the studio and placed them around the news set. Monday night on the 10 O'clock News, I announced to our meager number of viewers that the WWNY news crew was going to do their jobs with the stench of garbage just like the rest of New York. "Garbage will adorn our news set until the strike ends", I proclaimed with authority. Well, you know New Yorkers! They loved it! So did the rest of the country.

Howard Stern declared us the KINGS OF THE CITY! He and Robin Quivers made a meal of our audacity and riffed daily on our pluck in the news wars literally until the strike was over. Then Rick Dees and Ellen K picked up on it in LA and continued the promo train to the west coast. The New York Times, New York Post, LA Times and Hollywood Reporter all covered our boldness. Heady stuff! We became celebrities of a sort and Brian lapped it up, crowing daily.

In one stroke of broadcast brilliance, we had become the "people's" station in a town of jaded viewers. The competition's lofty news perch, that appealed to the intellectuals and upper crust, was no longer favored by the proletariat viewers. We had secured the allegiance of the masses at WWNY and the ratings went sky high. Our news director was livid at management's lack of professional tactics, but Brian ignored him, as usual. The station's reputation grew, Brian's grew, and mine grew.

WWNY started a trend that continued through the ensuing years to push the edges of the envelope of news propriety and, no matter what attention-grabbing scheme we came up with, it seemed like we couldn't do anything wrong. We became golden and wrote a new chapter in broadcast history. Over the next four years, WWNY became the top station in New York. "Paddy McGurk's 10 O'clock News" was the envy of news departments across America, and our overwhelming success made me an even bigger believer in the potent powers of Brian Buchanon. Brian loved to set the standard, to lead the pack. The majority of the General Managers of major market television stations are attractive and gregarious male figureheads holding on to their big, fat paychecks through playing golf and slapping backs with the all the right people. They would never make "rock the boat" decisions that could upset their security apple cart, because they wouldn't want to risk losing the stock options that roll in year after year. Brian is different. In all the years I've known him, Brian has never been afraid of risk. He rolls up his sleeves and tosses the dice daily. He is truly fearless. The garbage strike strategy is only one of the many creative maneuvers made by Brian during his career. That's what set Brian apart. He read the public perfectly and then followed his gut which continually made him successful in business. Even when Brian's methods made me uneasy, I always followed his lead. No matter what his detractors would say about him, (and believe me there are plenty who have nothing nice to say), there's only one Brian Buchanon.

It came as no surprise when Brian left New York in 1987 and moved to the West coast to take over KKLA, which was a major L.A. station that was in trouble. Birmingham Steel Industries, (BSI), the corporate owners of KKLA, were big money people from the South. They made their money in steel and used broadcasting to provide a lucrative tax shelter for them and their many heirs. BSI came after Brian and offered him everything but the deed to Charleston to take over their mismanaged and floundering station. Thanks to BSI, Brian was rumored to make several million a year, plus perks. I was impressed by the money, but more impressed by his formidable power, his ability to hold all the cards and deal them the way he wanted.

Before Brian made his move to Los Angeles, I gave him our first of many "Viking Parties". They were deemed "Viking Parties" because on the way there, Brian insisted on buying Viking helmets with horns for the occasion ensuring our hard-drinking rowdy gathering would descend into a night of serious debauchery. So, my lavish going away party at Peter Luger's, with every major player in New York media in attendance, had everyone wearing our crazy horned helmets and it loosened up an already primed crowd into a wild and no holds barred event of epic proportions. Peter Lugers is still recovering from that party. The Vikings partied till dawn and paid our respects to the most feared and envied man in major market television. Although I knew my life in New York would never be the same after Brian left, I stayed in "The Big Apple", enjoying my celebrity. I must admit I was initially a little scared at losing Brian and his perennial backing. But, in a way, it was an important test for me to continue to succeed without his ever-vigilant support.

Despite the physical distance, Brian and I stayed tight over the years. Every chance we got, we'd get together to play golf and chase women on hell-raising trips to Scotland, Puerto Rico, Mexico, Hawaii, and so on. All on the company dime, of course. Brian found a way to set up a little "business" on each vacation. He'd invite along a big client to round out our golf foursome, one of the usual suspects, the big guys from the airlines or auto industry, preferably anyone with an Irish last name. It qualified as a "business trip" in Brian's book, and the BSI corporation turned a blind eye. He made money, so they let him spend it. We lived life large with premium booze and expensive women. When I look back on it now, our antics seem childish, decadent and also a little embarrassing, but then it was just downright fun.

Through the decade of the self-involved eighties, Brian and I both stayed bachelors by choice. Whether we took a week-long golf trip, or had a night on the town, we never bored each other. Because Brian and I have always been completely compatible socially, it's easy to say that over the years I came to love him. Although, even then, I knew he had a frightening dark side. I chose to ignore all the warning bells, sure they would never toll for me.

Although I am now pushing my fortieth birthday, I have never married. For many years now, I have enjoyed my life as a T.V. personality and the beautiful, willing women it drew to me. I'll confess that some of them I used for only one night, others were special, but all were too good to give up. The most magnificent women in New York had been available as my playthings, for my pleasure. My perspective got warped with the pick of Manhattan, and then L.A. at my beck and call, which made it very difficult to settle down. I didn't want to miss out on what might come along next. But when you've screwed around with spectacular women for as long as I have, you become jaded. I was no longer able to experience the precious and magical feeling of a budding romance. After each new conquest, I felt longing, a feeling of emptiness. I knew I was searching for someone special, for something beyond the physical. When I look back and feel guilty about how I was then, I have to remind myself that I had to live that life, to be that hedonistic clone of Brian, to experience how hollow it really was. The sinuous path to today was unfolding for me all along.

Brian, a hopeless womanizer, had been married at one time with an ex-wife and a family he had left in Chicago during one of his career stops. Because of a stringent court order, he faithfully sent a big alimony and child support check to Chicago, but only spent time with his three kids twice a year when he'd take them on fantasy vacations to exotic places. His "Ex" hated his guts, but she was happy to collect the alimony payments and live the life of a well-to-do Chicago matron.

It was a bitter divorce that was the gossip of the broadcast business for months on end. Brian had strayed with the live-in nanny, and the whole pre-divorce scenario was particularly vicious. His wife was from a well-known blue-blood family, and the very public negative press was extremely humiliating for her. The rumor mill had a field day with the persistently ripening details of the story. Apparently, the nanny became pregnant and pressured Brian to divorce his wife and marry her. He tried to get her to have an abortion, but she refused. When the nanny finally figured out that she wasn't going to be the next Mrs. Buchanon, she sought revenge by spilling her guts to Brian's wife. Eventually, she got the abortion but the damage to the marriage had already been done.

Brian's wife had always suspected that he screwed around but, wisely enough, she chose to ignore his indiscretions. She was involved in her charity work and women's clubs. Unfortunately, this time Brian had struck at home and was caught with his pants around his ankles. His enraged wife threw him out and nailed him to the wall. He deserved it and knew it. That's why, like clockwork, he wrote the big check every month. It was his penance. He absolved himself with the check. His wife didn't need the money, but she loved to extract it from him. The more he made, the more she took, and her vindictiveness drove him crazy. But it was the price he paid for his arrogance. Once Brian moved on, he never looked back and his current lifestyle, in the Southern California home of hard bodies, suited him to a "T".

Back in New York, my life without Brian went smoothly for several years. Then, late in 1991, the general manager of WWNY changed news directors during a big middle management shakeup. The new turkey put in charge of news was a real tight ass, a card-carrying, traditional journalist with a chest-beating, sacred attitude about how news should be presented. He wanted conservative news. Everything that Brian and I had built up, he began to tear down. Although I secretly agreed that news should be sacred, the trend had already begun to a more sensationalized news, so I was put into a straight jacket and hated being a pedantic talking head more than anything. The sanctimonious attitude of a traditional anchor took away the part of me that was best.

Just about the time I was ready to ring the bastard's neck, Brian called.

"Hey, you good for nothing asshole," he greeted me.

"Brian! You're here?" I asked, excited at the prospect of seeing him.

"Not yet. I'll be in town next Thursday to negotiate syndication at NAPTE and I'm staying the weekend."

"That's great!"

It was going to be great to see him. NAPTE is the National Association of Programming and Television Executives. Each year, they have a big convention in a major market to hawk the latest programs that are available for syndication. All the program directors and the general managers from television stations come to NAPTE to look over the "merchandise". Even though it's television and "showbiz", it's still the typical convention scenario with lots of boozing, broads, and bullshit.

"Peel us off a couple of weak lambs from the herd and let's tear up New York City!" He boomed back into my ear.

"You got it, boss!" I replied, ever the good soldier.

"Still breaking the hearts of Manhattan's loveliest?" he prodded.

"Not lately."

"Why? What's up?" He knew me like the back of his hand.

"I really need to see you," I said with a slight whine.

"What's the problem?"

"Get me out of this pest hole!" I begged.

Brian chuckled. "Old limp-dick finally getting to you, eh? I wondered how long it would take."

"Help me get a gig out West," I pleaded.

"We'll talk when I get there," he said as he hung up.

I was relieved! I knew he would rescue me, and he did. After we partied during NAPTE, Brian went back to California. He called a few weeks later with a lucrative contract for me to anchor KKLA's early news. I was elated! I was going to California to work for Brian Buchanon! I was on top of the world.

When I gave notice to the WWNY news director, he was irate and decided to play hard ball with me and hold me to my contract which had another year to go. My news director's reaction caught me off guard and I panicked. When I called Brian, he calmed me down and told me to sit tight. He used his influence at the highest levels, calling in markers from his old drinking buddies in the corporate structure of WWNY's parent company, who were many management layers above the news director. He spent endless hours hammering out an agreement that would mollify them and made the deal.

Within a couple of months, I was on Brian's payroll. It actually was a step down to move from late news to early news, but it didn't bother me. I'd proven myself in New York and knew I'd get my shot again at late news. In television, news anchors aspire to the late newscast because late news gets the biggest local news ratings and ratings are the litmus test for T.V. Late news is the "big show." Early local news has to compete with network news out of New York. Viewers like to watch network news in the early evening and local news after prime time before they go to bed. In spite of all that "king of the mountain" bullshit, I gratefully anchored KKLA's early news for a couple of years. My ego handled it. Besides, I liked being off work by 7 PM. It helped me get to know my new home, L.A.

L.A. was a town of contrasts. I loved the crisp, cool mornings with the orange and pink sunrises. Being a hopeless creature of habit stemming from a childhood on a farm, I'd get up early every morning, with the chickens as they say, and drive my newly purchased black with tan interior BMW convertible, top down, straight to my favorite coffee shop, *Norm's* on La Cienega, for breakfast.

My condo was near the beach in the Pacific Palisades, a "smog free zone" cleansed by ocean breezes that blew pollution inland from the Pacific to the less fortunate in East L.A. On my way to Norm's Coffee Shop, I'd inhale the fresh ocean cleansed morning air and take the surface streets through the boutique towns, never taking a freeway if I could help it. There was so much to explore in West LA. Such as Sunset Blvd., which ran from the Palisades to the heart of L.A. which was several miles east of Sepulveda. There is a saying in LA: "There is no life east of Sepulveda". Sunset was sanitized and pristine, otherwise known as the boulevard of the stars. There was never so much as a piece of trash or a word of graffiti anywhere to be seen. After New York, I marveled daily at the clean streets and polished lawns of Beverly Hills, Bel Air, and Brentwood.

There were many other seductions along my daily trek. Everywhere I looked, there were stars. I'd pull up to a light on Sunset, and there would be Jack Nicholson in his BMW on one side of me and Lew Wasserman, the dean of the movie studios, in his Rolls on the other. Jogging down the median of Sunset, in shaggy sweats, would be Steven Spielberg. For a kid from Ohio, it was the validation that I had arrived, that I was in the big time. I was part of the Hollywood scene.

Once I left the residential part of Sunset, up on the Strip a whole other reality hit. My tranquil morning ride was assaulted by the gargantuan billboard face-off promoting every new movie and album. Fresh faces with toned and tanned leather clad bodies adorned each billboard message. The hype for each movie or album was short lived, up and down in a couple of weeks, to make room for the next "latest and greatest" to take over. Hollywood was synonymous with "Hype-land", whatever was new was best. Youth mania gripped this town. Plastic surgeons had a two-year waiting list. Whatever was old was death.

Below the billboards of fantasyland were the hookers out plying their trade. On my way to work in the mornings, the dregs were on the sidewalks. The stores weren't open yet, but the cleaning people were out washing the sidewalks and the hookers that still needed a "john" were trying to get an offer. They always hollered at me as I drove by and began to recognize me after a while, and I'd wave. Some were females, some were males, and some were males dressed like females, but most were friendly in a carnival atmosphere kind of way.

I genuinely loved my enduring routine each morning. At Norm's, I'd buy the *L.A. Times* and *The Hollywood Reporter*. It made me feel particularly comforted and cozy that Norm's wasn't a "hip" or "trendy" breakfast place, but, instead, an old-time coffee shop that catered to the neighborhood. Mostly retirees and geezers on a fixed income held down the tables. As they got to know me, I became an equal member of the regulars. I knew their life stories and latest ailments. They treated me like an ordinary guy, which is what I wanted. The hostess, Verna, always kept the same booth for me and made sure I was happy. I spent at least an hour a day at Norm's, from 8AM to 9AM every morning, as it became my company cafeteria with KKLA conveniently located just a few blocks away at La Cienega and Melrose.

Norm's was one of my first, and greatest, discoveries in L.A. I stumbled into it when I was ravenous on my way to catch a plane. As I shot down La Cienega toward LAX, I saw the big, tacky, 1950's Norm's sign and pulled in on two wheels to grab a sandwich. It was love at first sight. Living in the fast lane of L.A. I needed something to ground me and Norm's became my morning mecca, my home away from home, my connection with the real world. It reminded me of some of the coffee shops I went to in Ohio. Just a warm, friendly place with no pretense, something that wasn't easy to find in "La La Land".

After I spent a couple of years on the early news, Brian decided he wanted me on the late news. The early news numbers had shot up when I took over, so he wanted a repeat of my perceived magic at 10 O'clock. Brian said my success was because L.A. loved a pretty face but, though I would take the compliment, I hoped it was more than looks that increased my ratings. Brian saw me as the white knight that would lure the young professional woman to our late news audience, and he became increasingly obsessed with seeing if I could jump start the ratings plateau that existed at that time.

Joe Jackson, the late news male anchor, was getting a little "long in the tooth", and Brian wanted him out. Jackson was in contract negotiations. Brian made him a low-ball offer and Joe quit in a snit. Joe believed his own press releases and sincerely believed the late news couldn't function without him. Joe should have shut up, signed his contract, and continued to live his life in fat city. He got played for a sucker and never knew what hit him. But for safety sake, Brian kept his much beloved, female co-anchor, Lani Green, in place. I thought

Lani was a pain in the ass, but I had no option. I had to put up with her. Brian put me in Joe's late news slot co-anchoring with Lani and, at long last, Brian and I were back in the driver's seat with the late news franchise. It was just like old times.

In spite of the fact that he was considered a "has been", Joe Jackson had a following. After Jackson left, there was a momentary blip in the ratings which sent Brian to the drawing board. He was determined to create some excitement in the KKLA newsroom. One night in March of 1993, Brian took me out on a drinking binge. I'd only been anchoring the late news for about three months when he decided the time was right to make our move. As we sat in Tom Bergen's Irish Bar just south of Wilshire on Fairfax, Entertainment Tonight came on the big screen T.V. Leeza Gibbons was interviewing the stars who were up for Oscars for best actor, best actress, and supporting actor and actress. As we watched the screen, Brian cooked up an unbelievable plan.

On April first, a few nights after the Oscar's worldwide telecast, my lead story on the 10 O'clock News alerted our viewers that the Academy Awards Ceremony was a sham! Statues had been presented to the wrong actors, directors, screenwriters, and songwriters because a computer hacker had broken into the tabulated voting files and altered the results. For the first time in the history of the Academy Awards, all the statues were being recalled and Hollywood would have to redo the entire awards ceremony! What a scoop!

As I broke the news that evening, pandemonium broke out. We had calls from all over the country during the newscast. Everyone from movie studio execs to airline stewardesses were talking of nothing else. Viewers and competitors jammed our phone lines. We galloped through the rest of that night's news like a bunch of old pros. War, starvation, and politics got no reaction from our public, but everyone wanted more on the Academy Awards story, so we had a news frenzy on our hands. At the end of the hour-long newscast the cameramen did a close-up shot of my face. I smiled benevolently into the camera and ended the broadcast with this sign off. "April Fools!"

The next morning, our April Fool's joke made the front page of the *L.A. Times* and *The Hollywood Reporter*.

The L.A. Times headline read:

KKLA MAKES A FOOL OUT OF HOLLYWOOD!

The Hollywood Reporter screamed:

THE OSCAR GOES TO KKLA!

KTLA Morning News' venerable entertainment reporter Sam Rubin commandeered the broadcast to at once admonish us but also praised us for our pluck, guile and creativity to pull a fast one on the big shots of Hollywood. We created better fiction than a best picture script. It also made the second and third pages in most of the nation's papers.

Rick Dees and Ellen K, radio's number one morning drive team, had the rubberneckers transfixed during their miserable commute on the 405, the 5 and the Ventura Freeway. They could talk of nothing else.

Howard Stern said to Robin Quivers, "Why did we let this potent duo leave NY? It hasn't been as much fun since!"

The FCC was not amused and slapped our wrists. They also fined us $25,000., a pittance compared to the notoriety that cost us nothing. The rest of the media community called us "irresponsible journalists" and "scumbags", but L.A., the city that lives and breathes the movies, loved us. They loved our balls, our drama, our intrigue, our imagination. In a town beyond titillation, we had jerked everyone's chain. I became the darling of the Hollywood party circuit for my fifteen seconds of fame. Our ratings shot through the roof. Brian had won again.

From that point on we sailed along like a first-class racing vessel with an America's Cup crew, leaving the rest of the jaundiced L.A. media crowd in our wake. It was a glorious run! Brian had the Midas touch, and he once again allowed the glow of his good fortune and instincts to rub off on me and my career. My unspoken debt to him grew accordingly.

I have to admit there were times over the last ten years that I felt wormy and sincerely questioned the ways and means to our many successes, but the rewards were seductive and continued to compromise and erode my principles. I remember an evening when I had the courage to question Brian as to why we didn't play it straight and fight our battles with superior news. He looked at me, shamelessly, saying, "But this is so much easier," as he laughed, and laughed at my fleeting integrity.

Some months later, on a balmy night in Fall of '93, I met Brian for a couple of drinks after my newscast. When I got to the bar, he was fuming.

"What's eating you?" I asked.

"Those damn bastards! You wouldn't believe it if I told you," he said.

"Try me."

"Greg Mead called and asked me one of his big goddamned favors." (Greg Mead was the "Big cheese" in the front office of the L.A. Dodgers and Brian was trying desperately to hold onto the broadcast rights for Dodgers games. Brian and Greg were in the middle of very intense negotiations.)

"Jesus! Whatever he wants, give it to him," I urged him.

"It's not that easy. Listen to this crap. You won't believe it!" he said, disgusted.

"What?" He had my attention.

"Greg's trying to sign Ahmed Brooks from the San Francisco Giants for the '94 Dodgers season." Ahmed was a legend, the top center fielder in the country with a batting average of 335.

"Wow! What's so bad about that?" I was a big fan of Ahmed Brooks and I knew Brian was too.

"That's the good news. Here's the bad. Ahmed's girlfriend is a small town T.V. reporter at KCRA up in Sacramento. It's been easy for the two of them to get together with him based out of San Francisco. He won't take the deal with the Dodgers unless he gets this broad a gig on a local L.A. station. Greg wants me to put her on KKLA, so that Ahmed won't have to fly north for some pussy. Can you believe it? I'm supposed to hire some star-fucking whore from Sacramento so Ahmed can get a regular piece of ass. Do I look like a pimp or what? What the fuck are you laughing at?" Brian's eyes were bulging out of his head.

I was howling with laughter. This was just the kind of thing that Brian did himself, extracting outrageous favors from other members of the "Boys' club". It was certainly nothing new for television people. Brian was a good ol' boy, so Greg Mead, a good ol' boy himself, would naturally feel comfortable asking Brian for this type of favor.

"Well, he's got you by the balls. What are you going to do?" I asked, still unable to mask my amusement.

"I'm flying the broad down here. What the hell else am I going to do? I'm sure ol' Ahmed didn't dream this up on his own. She put him up to it. I can hear her now. 'Oh Ahmed!' Brian imitated in a high pitched, whiny voice, 'I'm gonna give you the best blow job you ever had if you get me a gig on a big-time T.V. station in L.A.'"

"What's her name?" I asked, sure I would hear it again as a four-letter word.

"Georgia Conroy. The next 10 O'clock News anchor if ol' Ahmed has his way," Brian spit out furiously.

"Is she white?"

"How should I know? Probably. You know those black athlete's all have big assed white girlfriends. To cap it off, she's probably blond. I'm screwed. I'm totally screwed."

"Brian, you haven't even met her. Maybe she's decent."

"Yeah, right!"

"Stick her on the morning news as a field reporter. When old Ahmed finally gets enough, you can unload her."

"Damn straight! You know how much I hate this bullshit?" He spat.

I tried to empathize, though secretly amused. "I've got a pretty good idea."

He had his butt in a crack. He was going to have to hire Georgia Conroy and there was no way out of it. Ahmed Brooks was forcing him to give in to a woman's demands. I knew that's what bugged him the most. I have to admit I was anxious to meet Miss Georgia Conroy. It takes a real smooth operator to get control of any situation with Brian Buchanon. Ahmed Brooks was obviously under her thumb as well. My hat was off to this mystery vixen.

In the years that I've known Brian, I have never seen a woman get under his skin. He is a man's man. Women are merely a reflection of his success trip. Brian always said, "I may not have a big dick, but I've got a big title and the bucks to go with it." He had a new woman every time I saw him. He liked them young, and very dumb. As we aged, they became younger and dumber. I'd started teasing him, saying he would have to learn how to change diapers if he kept it up.

I had my share of pretty women even before I was on camera. Brian envied that about me. It helped that I'm more than ten years younger than he so I was always more like a younger brother than a peer. The age difference gave him a justification he could live with for my successes with the fairer sex. Brian was losing his looks, which made it extra important for him to be seen with beautiful women. He has always said that he got the brains and I got the looks. Brian was right. He had a big title and it worked because he got more tail than a toilet seat.

Women carp that men like Brian are jerks but look at women! They drop their drawers for any man who looks successful. That's another reason I never married. I've screwed so many "star fuckers" that it's hard to know which ones are genuine. I don't want to be a woman's meal-ticket or her identity and, because of my cynicism, I began from time to time to lose hope that I would ever truly fall in love. Brian is the opposite and knows he never wants to fall in love or to remarry. Commitment is not a word in his vocabulary when it comes to women. He uses women, then throws them away like tissue paper.

Brian has gotten his tail in a wringer on more than one occasion because of his escapades. It's still the one area where he definitely had a blind spot. Even the embarrassing circumstances of his divorce didn't slow him down.

One of the worst times was when he broke off an affair with a young girl in the production department and she screamed harassment to the corporate headquarters causing a big stink.

Then, less than six months later, he started having an affair with Lorraine Mackey, the traffic manager. She was ambitious and thought he was her ticket to the top. Brian led her on. When he finished with her, he built a case that her work didn't pass muster and she was fired, but it came back to haunt him. She filed a complaint with the EEOC. Lawyers came and went in droves. Brian just never learned.

One afternoon, at the height of his problems with her attorneys, he called me into his office.

"What's up, boss?" I said, as I plopped in a chair in front of his desk.

He looked exhausted. "I need you to do me a favor." The way he looked at me I knew what was coming. A bolt of fear shot up my back.

"What's that?" I asked, knowing I wouldn't like the answer.

"I need you to swear under deposition that you slept with Lorraine. I want you to say that she had it in for me and planned to ruin me." He never took his eyes off me.

"Jesus, Brian! I can't do that!"

"Sure, you can! I'd do it for you." I believed he would. He had pinned me, hard.

"Look, before I perjure myself, what are your chances of winning this case without me lying in a deposition?"

"Decent, but I need extra insurance. Besides, I want to bury the bitch," he said with venom.

"Brian, if I lie and they start asking questions, dates, times, I could get caught and then it would be worse for you than it already is. You need to stick to the truth, or you really will get your butt in a sling."

He rubbed his forehead and looked out the window. He was quiet for a while. Then he turned to me and said in a whisper mostly to himself. "I should chop my goddamn dick off. All it brings me is grief." It was a fleeting, but profound insight.

I scrambled to try to cheer him up. "Look, Brian, you'll win this one. Lorraine made a play for you at the Fourth of July picnic in front of the entire station. She wasn't coerced. You're getting paranoid, that's all."

"Maybe you're right." He laughed a joyless laugh and said. "Thanks, buddy, I knew I could count on you for a reality check. Forget what I asked. I'm getting squirrely with all these goddamn corporate lawyers around here."

I breathed a heavy sigh of relief as I narrowly escaped Brian's shocking request but, with a chill, realized that I was no longer permitted to only be a spectator in his epic dramas with women. The good times with Brian were very, very good, so, it would stand to reason the bad times would be very bad. It was a necessity that I accept that aspect of our relationship. Through sheer determination to be his friend I stood by him through extraordinary tests while he gave my commitment little thought. In this particular instance I was grateful I didn't have to perjure myself to demonstrate my loyalty.

In the end, it was proven that Lorraine went into the affair willingly. Brian built an iron clad case about her poor job performance using his cronies to corroborate his side of the story. He barely squeaked out of that self-inflicted mess by the skin of his teeth.

Later that same year, when a former Junior Miss applied for a summer internship at the station, Brian propositioned her during her initial interview. Normally interns did not interview with Brian, but he saw her in the lobby and called her into his office. One thing led to another and he got caught, once again, with his dick in his zipper.

Birmingham Steel Industries had spent a lot of money buying off all of the claims against Brian, but they felt it was a price they had to pay. BSI would never give up as brilliant a broadcaster as Brian Buchanon. Those buy-offs were chump change in comparison to the bottom line that he delivered to them each year. After Lorraine's suit and the Junior Miss incident, for a way to make things look better, BSI insisted we create a Human Resources Department. Prior to that, we had a "personnel director". She was a paper pusher who was not equipped to do anything more skillful than filling out forms and filing. Human Resources was to be set up to protect employees and allow them to air their grievances without fear of retribution.

Brian, of course, outfoxed corporate and named one of his best buddies, Red Kelly, an aging sportscaster, to head Human Resources. Red was the consummate "good ol' boy". We joked that Red wrote the book on "good ol' boyism" and Brian wrote the introduction. Red had been a sports anchor back in his heyday. His star fell, and the younger guys took his place about the time that Brian was forced to come up with a head for Human Resources. Red was the obvious choice for Brian's purposes. It was a big comedown, but Red needed the work. He could have gone to a small market and done sports, but his family was in L.A. and he was a big celebrity to all the locals. So, he stayed and accepted the position, gratefully. Brian overpaid him but that was Brian's way. He took care of his friends and they, in return, took care of him.

Red had one kid in college, and one in grad school and a few more starting out their own families. All of them counted on Red. He was a widower and, literally, lived for his kids. His wife Mary had been a pillar of the community. She was very involved in Catholic charities and did a lot of fund raising. Right after Red took over his new position Mary had a long bout with ovarian cancer and lost. The company supported Red through all of his trials during her illness. For over a year, he was rarely at work because he insisted on keeping Mary at home. He hired a full-time nurse, but many evenings he took care of her and was wasted by morning. Brian covered for Red and made him stay home and rest in the mornings. Red couldn't afford to take disability leave because of the cut in income, so Brian let him work half days and let them count for full days while everyone just looked the other way. When Mary passed on, Red as much as canonized her as the whole station went into mourning.

After Red came back full time, he attacked his position with a new vigor. Human Resources was a cushy job that gave Red lots of time to "kibbutz" with his cronies. His assistant did most of the paperwork, but Red took his job seriously and it gave his life purpose, plus Brian thought up projects for Red to give him more significance in the running of the station. He appointed a Steering Committee to set station policies for the employees and put Red in charge of it which expanded his powers.

Red was loyal to Brian because Brian had saved him from the aging talent refuse pile that struck most television talent "out" after the age of fifty. Red's allegiance to Brian was a powerful bond. That's why anything that was said to Red about Brian ran the risk of being repeated, and due to their close relationship, there was no trust or confidentiality in Human Resources. No woman dared complain about Brian again at KKLA. Brian had survived all previous accusations, and Red became his future insurance.

In late November of 1993, we got word through the rumor mill that our late news franchise was being threatened. Soon after, this pernicious buzz was confirmed by George Christy in *The Hollywood Reporter*. One of our biggest competitors, KHLY, was formulating a master plan to move their 11PM newscast to 10PM in February of 1994, during the same two weeks that they would be broadcasting the Winter Olympics. KKLA was the only late news that aired at 10PM in the L.A. market which gave us a tremendous competitive advantage. We captured every available news viewer in that time period. In L.A., where morning commutes can take at minimum of forty-five minutes because of huge traffic snarls on the freeway, the bulk of the population wanted to be asleep by eleven to be up by seven. We had enjoyed our exclusive prime news positioning for years and sure as to hell didn't want to share our coveted domain with KHLY during that precious 10-11PM time period.

Our late news was our primary meal ticket. Advertising dollars allocated to news were the bread and butter of local television programming and each news rating point in the L.A. market was worth millions, so we battled fiercely for every tenth of a rating point. Our profitability would shrink if the audience was splintered between two newscasts at 10 O'clock. Plus, the late news on KABC and KNBC at 11PM would receive ratings boosts when KHLY changed to 10PM because there would be less competition in their 11PM time period. Our rank in the news ratings would be weakened from all fronts.

It was a calculated move on KHLY's part to use the Winter Olympics in February '94 to introduce their 10PM News to the L.A. market. The much-hyped Olympics would provide the perfect lead-in vehicle to give KHLY's fledgling 10 O'clock News a big boost in ratings.

Brian took the assault very personally. He would not tolerate losing audience to a competitor. This was the most serious attack on KKLA that had ever been launched in his tenure at the station. We only had a couple of months to prepare our defensive strategy and, as the pressure mounted, Brian's moods became unpredictable and hostile as he fueled himself for battle each day by chewing up the scenery. Whoever was in his path would feel the force of his fury. Word of his moods spread through the building like wildfire. If he was in a foul humor, people would literally hide in the bathrooms until he left their departments.

Even I was not exempt. One day he caught me in the hall. "You're gaining weight." He pointed his finger in my face.

"What?" I asked, incredulous.

"You're getting fat. I want you to go on a diet and stop drinking beer. Your face looks fat on-air," Brian retorted, steamed.

"That's ridiculous! I'm within ten pounds of where I always have been," I defended.

"See! You admit it! You are fat, goddamn it! Ten pounds show on camera. You know that. Pull your fat ass away from the food trough and get your shit together. Lose that ten pounds in the next two weeks," he commanded as he turned on his heels.

"Brian, you're letting this news thing make you crazy."

I tried one last time to reason with him. Brian whipped around with his finger aimed at my face and said, "You're damn right I'm crazy. I'm the only one who gives a damn around here. We're in the fight of our lives and you're busy stuffing your fat face. What do you think this is...a Carnival cruise? Your career depends on your looks. Get those ten pounds off! Now!" He stomped away, head down for battle. That hideous moment of chagrin witnessed by several of my peers, evoked feelings deep inside me as I stood in stunned silence tasting the first stirrings of war.

2

DECEMBER 1993

The Los Angeles news wars would begin in earnest with the February 12, '94 Winter Olympics in Lillehammer. Like a military offensive being set out against our bitterest of enemies, our news department worked like slaves through the Christmas holidays to gear up and get ready. No one in news dared take a long holiday vacation. A focused and dedicated effort was demanded from each-and-every one of us. World leaders, mass murderers, and movie stars stayed at home like everyday people to watch television during the Olympics. The Olympics were sacrosanct. KHLY's brilliantly calculated maneuver having the television ratings Titan, the Olympics, introduce the entire L.A. marketplace to their news at 10 PM made our blood run cold. The Winter Olympics would lead the viewer to KHLY's late news for two weeks straight like sheep being led to the slaughter. The other big ratings bonus for KHLY came from the Nancy Kerrigan and Tonya Harding skating battle. The world was holding its breath to see whether the Luke Skywalker or Darth Vader of skating was going to win the gold in Lillehammer. Their rivalry was an additional ratings bonanza just waiting to happen.

KHLY had created a shrewd master plan that would work like a charm. The viewers were lazy by nature. The chance of the Olympics audience changing to KKLA's news after watching the games all night on KHLY was remote, at best. This well thought out KHLY strategy was a nightmare for KKLA. We needed, and prayed for, a miracle.

Brian commanded us to come up with stories that would compete with the Olympics which was a tall, almost impossible, order. I didn't think we had a chance in hell of beating KHLY during the Olympics, but Brian would not accept defeat. He threw a news related tantrum almost every day. Herb Rudnick, the news director, was riding us hard. We knew it came directly from the top. Although there was plenty to cover in a local news market as volatile as L.A., I knew we would need a lot more than the latest race riot or movie star drug scandal to top the Olympics.

Integrity, thoughtfulness, the common good in broadcast journalism, all got mislaid somewhere during times like these. Ratings became the sole focus of our daily existence in the news department and something precious, even profound about reporting the news without hype, sensationalism, and insensitivity, was lost.

Just as I was about to throw in the towel and surrender to the cunning of KHLY, I stumbled onto a hot story near Belize at the northern tip of Honduras. One of the sales execs had just come back from a scuba vacation in Belize. He told a grizzly story to me in the lunchroom one afternoon when I was scrounging up a Snickers from the vending machine. The essence of the story was that there was a big profit in supplying lobsters to fill the American appetite. American chain restaurants featured lobster as a loss leader and staple of their promotional efforts to bring in customers. To meet the ever-increasing demand, fishing companies in Honduras hired local Miskito Indians and sent them into deep ocean waters to catch the lobsters. The fishing companies were exploiting the destitute Indians by letting them dive to extraordinary depths with inadequate instruction and made them use primitive equipment. Many of the Indians were dying or were coming back from the deep paralyzed and brain damaged from the bends. The bends are horrifyingly painful and caused when tiny air bubbles get into a diver's blood stream because of either faulty equipment, improper diving techniques, or lack of proper training for the diver. The bends are extremely dangerous, and often deadly.

I needed a budget to fly to Belize with a crew and get the story. When I went to Rudnick for the money, he said he didn't have a penny left that hadn't already been allocated for news operation expenses. He liked the story idea, but Rudnick was such a wimp that I knew he wouldn't pressure Brian for the extra backing to finance my plan. I had to get the cash myself. Brian, a tightfisted miser when it came to going over budget, might just give it to me because of his never-say-die obsession with thwarting KHLY's assault on our news.

While racing down the hall from the newsroom to Brian's office I spotted a big black Mercedes S 500, with smoked windows, rolling slowly up to the front of the station. I stopped for a second, out of curiosity, to see who would get out. The sight of stars and politicians, who arrived by limo, was nothing new at KKLA, but after all these years, I still loved this part of being in show biz. When the driver's side of the Mercedes opened, I immediately recognized Ahmed Brooks, the best center fielder in baseball. It was such a thrill to see him that the little kid in me rattled off his stats in my head. Ahmed was a shoo-in for the Hall of Fame. At 34, he was out playing the young "phenoms" of the game. Ahmed Brooks was already a legend but hadn't slowed down one bit to rest on his laurels. He was uncommonly handsome and in perfect shape, even in the off-season. Ahmed languidly stretched his legs as he got out of the car, then stood, took a long moment to look around and straightened his suit jacket. He was tall and sleek like a panther and dressed impeccably. Hanging from Ahmed's ear was a small platinum ring with a miniature, platinum encased, ivory carving of the continent of Africa suspended from it.

After a few seconds, Ahmed walked with long lean strides to the passenger door. When he opened the door, he blocked my view. Predatory, he stood directly in front of the door and faced the passenger. In mesmerized silence I watched, feeling like a voyeur. All I could see was an arm here, a leg there. As I caught a flash of long flaxen hair, I saw Ahmed reach down and scoop up the blond female into a hot embrace. They stood there clutching like a couple of teenagers in broad daylight. My mouth went dry and I felt rather foolish observing this intimate scene, but I couldn't look away. As they turned to enter the building, she took his hand, that famous hand that could field any ball, as he tenderly brushed an errant wisp of golden hair from her face.

I lost my breath. She was exquisite. From the top of her head to the tip of her toes, she was a vision. I have savored the most beautiful women in the world, but this woman exuded beauty that comes from far more than the physical. It was eerie how soft she looked, how fragile. Delicate. Pink. Light. Luminous. Like an angel. Her features were perfect. She had full, sensuous lips, light eyes and eyebrows, and porcelain skin. Her body was lean, and yet female. Very female. Her hair was a thick, shoulder length mass of soft, golden curls. She had on a business suit, but it was not your standard navy or black interview uniform. It was a pale pink knit with soft grey accents. This was not a girl. This was a woman, in the richest sense of the word. I was dumbstruck. I followed Ahmed and the provocative female with my greedy eyes until they entered the building.

I found myself behaving rather juvenile. My heart raced as I ran over to the elevator and took it to the second floor. When I got off, I peered over the second-floor balcony that looked down on the reception area. In honor of our southern owners, KKLA was designed like an old southern mansion with a sweeping staircase. The mezzanine at the top of the stairs gave me a bird's-eye view of the lobby. Ahmed Brooks and Georgia Conroy were signing in. I felt like a schoolboy gawking at them. As I rushed into Brian's office his assistant, Judy, called in to him. "Ahmed Brooks is here with Miss Conroy," she said.

"Oh, for Christ's sake! She had to bring him with her?" Brian boomed.

He spotted me. "Paddy, get in here."

"She's gorgeous!" I said, breathless. I realized that my enthusiasm was showing, but I was helpless to stop myself.

"You saw her?" Brian asked, eyes wide.

"Coming into the lobby."

"Is she white?" He asked, without a trace of irony.

"Peaches and cream," I said, dreamily. I hoped he couldn't see my mounting excitement over this miraculous woman.

"But can she read and write?" Brian asked under his breath.

Ahmed Brooks filled the doorway, smiled a knowing smile, and said, "She's Phi Beta Kappa from Wellesley with a master's from USC. If there aren't any more preliminary questions, I'd like to introduce Georgia Conroy."

Georgia peered around Ahmed's looming frame and gave us a shy smile and a wave. I think that's when I fell in love with her. She could have been a real ball-buster, but she was as insecure as any other person on a job interview.

Brian was struck dumb for a split second. No one else in the room noticed because they didn't know his normal response time, but I saw it, and knew what he was feeling. He regained control and shook hands vigorously with Ahmed. "Hey, I haven't seen you since last year's All-Star game. Great to see you again, Ahmed."

Ahmed turned and gestured to Georgia. Georgia walked over, held out her hand, and with a sweet smile said, "I really appreciate you taking time out of your day to see me, Mr. Buchanon."

Brian boomed, "Brian. Call me Brian. Come in. Sit down and make yourself comfortable. Judy! Come see if anyone needs coffee or a soft drink. We are always on the look-out for new talent, Georgia. When Greg Mead said you were moving to Los Angeles with Ahmed, I told him how anxious we were to meet you. Right, Paddy?"

I was glad to finally be included. "I'm Paddy McGurk. The anchor for the late news here at KKLA," I chimed in as I extended my hand.

Ahmed's million-dollar hand reached over to pump mine. "It's great to meet you, Paddy. We're both familiar with your work. Georgia and I always watch your 10 o'clock news when we're in town," Ahmed said. He had the smile of a contented man who got to watch the 10 o'clock news because he wasn't out on the prowl late at night like the rest of us.

"How long have you been in news, Georgia?" I asked.

"I've been a news writer-producer for ten years, ever since I got my masters. But I recently got my first shot at on-air reporting in Sacramento last January. It's been a long haul, and that's why I've been reluctant to give it up to move to L.A." she answered, as I stood mute, and hoped no drool was showing at the corners of my mouth.

I recovered and responded reassuringly. "I don't think you'll have to give up anything. What Brian is saying is true. We are always on the lookout for new talent. Did you bring any of your tapes from Sacramento?" I asked, trying to meet her yellow-green cat's eyes.

"Yes, I brought them along. Would you like to see them now?" she said, reaching into her bag. Brian cut in to guide the focus back to himself. He had to have control.

"No, not now. Let me take you on a tour of the station, Georgia. Not to worry. I'm sure we can find a place for you on our morning show."

"Oh, good!" Thank you, Brian" she answered him with a radiant smile. As we filed out of Brian's office, Judy offered everyone refreshments, but I was the only one who took a Lemon Calistoga. My mouth was parched dry from the emotional stimulation and I wanted to freshen my breath.

"Ahmed, we'll take good care of Georgia at KKLA. We're like family here," Brian said, congenially, as he gestured to Georgia and Ahmed and headed to the stairs. "Come on. Let me show you around."

With that, Brian was off to present his dominion to Ahmed and Georgia. I felt awkward in the little entourage, but I was determined to hang in there for as long as I could.

Once we hit the newsroom, I excused myself and pretended to have a lot of work to do. Georgia turned and stopped to watch me as I started my retreat, "Paddy, it was very nice meeting you," she said through a sly smile.

"Likewise. Good luck."

"Thanks. I'll need it," she responded with charming humility.

"Don't worry. Brian is a man of his word. You're a shoo-in. I look forward to working with you, Georgia," I said, quite formally, as I extended my hand. She took it, shook it ever so gently then held it for a split second longer than warranted.

"I want to become a pro like you, Paddy," she spoke with sincerity. Feel free to critique me when the time comes, it won't hurt my feelings. After ten long years of churning and burning stories in Sacramento, I've still got plenty to learn. Promise me you'll take some time to help me learn the ropes." She looked at me with that green gaze again.

"Absolutely," was all I could manage before I turned away. It was too difficult to look directly into her eyes for an extended time. It was overpowering. They were vulnerable, and yet inviting.

Brian boomed through the newsroom like a king in his fiefdom. Everyone avoided his glare and put their heads down. Brian Buchanon was not popular here. He was regarded as a loudmouth who didn't understand the intricacies or intellect of a news operation. Brian was tolerated for one reason only. He held the purse strings. I was considered a spy and a traitor because we were friends. But, because I had been in the same political bullshit before at other stations, I just didn't give a damn.

I always said only the call letters change. When you work twelve to fourteen hours a day at a T.V. station with the same 200 people, you have to expect fights, jealousies, and pettiness. Every person jockeys for position and would stab you in the back to elevate their own stature. The bottom line on all of it was, you couldn't trust anybody. Nobody was your best friend. It was the law of the jungle. It was a job, and when you left, everyone said in unison, "Next." I felt sorry for the people who misunderstood this and believed that they were making lifelong friends in the workplace. In most instances, not all, but most, it was out-of-sight, out-of-mind. That's what made it all the more special that Brian and I had remained such close friends. He always was there for me, and me for him. We even joked that when we were retired old farts, we'd be sitting together in the old folk's home, reliving the good old days of television and trying to squeeze the titties of the candy stripers.

While I watched my friend and mentor, undetected, from my cubicle, Brian introduced Georgia and Ahmed to Lani Green and the other key players in the newsroom. Lani dripped saccharine to the assembled males while giving Georgia a cool once over. In that instant, I knew that Lani would be Georgia's enemy. Lani would, without question, be extremely threatened by someone with Georgia's physical and intellectual attributes.

Red Kelly, the head of Human Resources, rounded the corner from the morning news set. Brian called him over.

"Red, get over here and earn your keep. This is Georgia Conroy and this man needs no introduction," Brian roared, gesturing to Ahmed.

Red beamed and shook hands and slapped backs all around. Because of his sports anchor background, Red was in rare form with a sports celebrity in the station, especially one the caliber of Ahmed Brooks. He rattled off Ahmed's stats for the past ten years and regaled everyone with amusing trivia about America's All-Star center fielder. Ahmed seemed embarrassed but played along with Red. He was having such a good time it would have been cruel to throw a wet blanket on him once he was on a roll. Everyone was laughing and jovial as Red finished his sports commentary.

After more cursory formalities and chitchat, Brian, Red, Georgia, and Ahmed left the newsroom and headed upstairs. I felt a gut-wrenching ache. I wanted to study Georgia Conroy a while longer, but she was gone. I went back to work and didn't have the good fortune to run into Georgia again that morning.

After a late night prepping the next day's news, I headed home to my lonely condo and made a simple dinner of salad and steak on the grill. As I sipped my merlot from Robert Mondavi, I relived in minute detail my first meeting of the dazzling Georgia Conroy. I felt myself get hard as a rock. Although the real thing would have been so much more to my liking, I needed relief from my growing sexual need to devour this woman from head to toe. Somehow carousing the usual haunts of LA just would not do to satisfy my growing desire. I lay in my bed and stroked myself to a massive orgasm with just the picture of her face in my mind's eye to bring me there. Although slightly ashamed of my sophomoric response to meeting the peaches and cream femme fatale, I often think of that night and how powerful my feelings were at that early juncture. I was not alone. Georgia Conroy was the apex of every man's sexual fantasy. But she was more to me already. She exuded something so enticing, unforgettable, that I had never experienced in any of my many conquests.

A month later, in early January 1994, the weather had turned cold in L.A. I was looking forward to my sun filled trip to Belize. Brian wanted a full five-part series of special reports on the abuse, and sanctioned homicide, of the Miskito Indians. He demanded that we make this story into an Emmy caliber investigative piece to help thwart the Olympic challenge in the February sweeps. In a week, I was leaving with my favorite shooter and producer. Sitting that morning at my desk I fantasized about golden, sun scorched beaches, crystal clear azure waters, when in walked the vision of a golden goddess, Georgia.

"Surprise! It looks like we'll be working together sooner than I thought!" Georgia said with a big smile.

"Georgia! You've started?" I grinned widely with pure joy at the sight of her. She was in a pale-yellow turtleneck sweater and straight skirt, that hung discreetly over her knees. Her long mass of blond curls was pulled back and tamed in a gold ribbon at the base of her neck.

"Yes, this morning," she said in a half giggle.

"Well...welcome. I'm happy for you. You've found a place to stay?" I said, as I tried to calm down my escalating enthusiasm.

"I'm staying with Ahmed till I can find an apartment. I'm looking in Santa Monica."

"That's close to me."

"Really? Where is your place?" she asked.

"Pacific Palisades."

"Oh, I looked there as well. Too pricey for me."

"So, what's your first assignment?" I was trying to keep our conversation going.

"I don't know yet. The assignment editor asked if I spoke Spanish. Something in the barrio, I'm guessing" she answered.

"Do you?" My mind started to work overtime.

"Do I what?"

"Speak Spanish?" I asked a little too anxiously.

"Fluently. I lived with a family in Seville, Spain during the summer before my senior year of high school. Plus, languages were my minor at Wellesley," she said with some pride.

"Comes in handy in L.A., the third world country of the U.S.A."

"So, I understand."

"I sure could use you on my next big story. None of our crew speaks Spanish and we're going to an undeveloped part of the world." My wheels kept turning.

"Where?"

"Belize."

"Lucky you! I love Belize. The scuba is heavenly there," she said with passion.

"You've been?"

"That's Ahmed's favorite vacation spot. No one recognizes him in Belize and we both love to dive. It's the perfect hide-a-way, but it's primitive! Hot and humid with lots of mosquitoes and no air-conditioning at the dive spots, only in the city."

"I wish you could go with us. We need a guide." With that statement, my spinning head formulated a plan. For many reasons, not the least of which was I had respect for Ahmed, I was forcing myself not to entertain the idea of seducing Georgia. But I wanted desperately to be around her. Her very presence filled my senses like no other women had. I knew, from the first time that I saw her, that I would settle for whatever form our relationship would take. For now, it would be as colleagues in the newsroom. I wanted her on that trip to Belize, and I needed to get Brian to buy off on it.

Later that day, I was going over my travel plans with Herb, the news director. "I'm a little shaky about our assignment. None of the crew speaks Spanish and the area is quite primitive. In Belize City they speak English, but out in the fishing villages near Honduras, they speak a Spanish dialect." I gave him a legitimate barrier.

"Take someone who speaks the language down with you," Herb said, falling neatly into my trap.

"Who can you spare?" I said, keeping my fingers crossed.

He thought a minute... "You know, Georgia Conroy said she speaks fluent Spanish. She's not up-to-speed to do any on-air just yet, but her tapes look like she's a fantastic writer and producer. Maybe we should send her down to produce instead of Larry."

Herb fell right into my trap. Larry was the best producer in the newsroom, and I hated to lose him on the story, but I wanted Georgia. She was a gift from the gods in many more ways than her bilingual ability. I let Herb give her the assignment news. I acted surprised when she told me.

"Georgia, that's great!" I said, a little too heartily.

"I hope you don't mind. I'm not as experienced as Larry, but I have produced other five-part news features, and Larry said he'd help with the edit when we get back." She was modest, but so excited about the turn of events.

"I'm sure you'll be great. Besides, you have the advantage of the language."

"I don't want to disappoint you," she said.

"Stop worrying. You won't. We're a team. We'll all support you." I reassured her.

The next night I went to a late dinner with Brian. "What's this I hear about you and Georgia going on a little tryst to Belize on the company's nickel?"

"Herb made the call," I said, too defensively. "I need someone who speaks Spanish to get through all the red tape."

"My ass. Are you after some of that?" Brian countered, testing me.

"She's not my type," I lied.

"Yeah. Too pretty and too smart," he said, sarcastically.

"Fuck you, Brian. Give me a break."

"Keep your dick out of those panties if you know what's good for you," he said in all seriousness.

"Do I look stupid to you? I wouldn't compromise the station like that." I lied again, but at that moment I thought I was sincere.

"You're a "schmuck"! I would, if I could get in her pants." He toyed with me.

"You would?" I acted surprised.

"Shit, yeah. That's a choice piece of ass. I'd throw her legs behind her ears like a grocery store chicken. Even if it was sloppy seconds."

"You're rank!" I said.

"I've never denied it," he said, enjoying the banter.

"Only because your reputation precedes you." I stuck my neck out further.

"Fuck you!" he said, laughing.

We both laughed and changed the subject, but his message was clear. He wasn't going to score with Georgia, and I'd better not.

Within days, we were on our way. In news, you can't hold onto a story idea for too long. I don't care how secretive you are with a concept. If the idea is out there in the ether, before you know it, the whole world is doing your story.

When we met at LAX, Georgia was with Ahmed. He wasn't happy about losing her for a week. "Ahmed, how's it going?" I extended my hand for a long handshake.

"Georgia's making me miserable, as usual," he answered.

I laughed.

"Aren't you?" Ahmed said as he turned to her playfully, but with a tone of seriousness.

Georgia rolled her eyes and looked at me for support. "Ahmed is puffing around because I won't let him go with me. He said he'd be our second grip," she said, with an edge.

"Hell, Ahmed, we don't even have a first grip. This is news, not the movies," I explained.

"See baby. I told you I could be of some use. It's off-season. I've got time on my hands," Ahmed continued to plead his case. "Paddy, would you let this woman out of your sight if she were yours?"

"Don't put me in the middle. That's a loaded question" I answered with mock caution.

"Ahmed, let's get one thing straight, I'm not 'yours'," Georgia fumed indignantly.

"Now, don't get all women's lib on me, Georgia," Ahmed countered.

"Ahmed, it's not professional to have your boyfriend on an assignment. We've gone over this territory. That's the end of the discussion," Georgia said as she kissed him quickly. Loaded with carry-on bags, she stomped up to the gate in her hiking boots and chinos.

"Looks like you struck out that inning, Ahmed," I said.

Ahmed looked at me. "Paddy, can I trust you?"

"What do you mean?" My stomach churned in response to his question.

"I think you know," Ahmed said as he looked further into me. "Just keep your eye on Georgia. She's impulsive and headstrong. I don't want her starting a revolution or something. Women are subordinate in that area of the world, and Georgia does what she wants."

I over justified as I responded. "Frankly, Ahmed, I normally wouldn't take a woman on a rough assignment like this. But we really need her Spanish. I'm sure none of the fishermen in Honduras speak English. But with Georgia asking the questions, I hope they will at least be cooperative."

"I'm sure she'll do a great job but..."

I looked at the gate closing and interrupted him. "Don't worry. I'll make sure she stays out of trouble."

As I trotted away, I heard him say quite clearly, "Just make sure you're not the trouble."

We boarded the aircraft with the usual fanfare. Every eye was on us. T.V people, and sports celebs, are always the center of attention in airports and on airplanes. People want to know all about you. Being a celebrity was usually a lot of fun, but the truth was I was only a minor celebrity. Because I'd worked in two major markets, New York and Los Angeles, there was usually someone that recognized me on each flight I took so I usually got more than my share of attention. It's a great ice breaker if you're in the mood to chat.

But instead of enjoying the prying questions and eyes of the stewardesses and passengers, I was anxious to settle in next to Georgia. For the first time in my life, I didn't want to be noticed. As I took my seat next to her, she gave me a warm, welcoming smile. All I wanted in that moment, more than anything else in the world, was to be anonymous.

3

JANUARY 8, 1994

The big *Mexicana* jet lifted off loaded down with humanity. We were changing planes in Mexico City and then flying on to Belize City. The marathon journey threatened to be an entire day devoted to the discomfort of air transport but, despite the cramped conditions and lousy food, I was elated as it would give me time to get to know Georgia. It is a universally accepted quirk of human nature that whatever secrets one had spilled out in the intimacy of an endless airplane ride. That turned out to be the case with Georgia and me on that long trip to Belize.

At first, we were a little shy sitting arm to arm. It was, physically, the closest we had ever been to each other. Georgia had worked up a sweat hauling her bags onto the aircraft and had a faint mist of perspiration covering her face and body. The proximity made my every cell alive and tingling as I quietly inhaled her alluring and sensual musky scent. The rosy damp glow on her face gave me a preview of what it would be like to look at her after making love.

"I hope I didn't forget anything important." She started.

"Typical travel anxiety!" I laughed.

"I know I forgot something." She rifled her handbag.

"As long as you have your passport, we can buy whatever else you might need in Belize City." I reassured her.

That seemed to help her settle in.

"This is so much fun." She said finally.

"What is?"

"Going on an adventure."

"It sounds like you and Ahmed have lots of adventures." I probed gently.

"I guess that's true, to a degree, but Ahmed leaves nothing to chance."

"Not the adventurous type, eh?"

"Hardly! He meticulously plans every detail of our trips. He wants everything to be perfect for me."

"So, you like perfection?" I asked. This conversation was headed where I wanted it to go.

Georgia thought a moment before answering. "Not entirely. It takes away some of the joy of discovery and fanciful accidents of travel." She said wistfully.

"Why is Ahmed such a planner?" I thanked God he had a flaw. He was overwhelming competition.

"Baseball is total chance. Anything can happen. When Ahmed is on vacation, he wants predictable occurrences. That way he can relax. So, he's become a bit of a control freak in his private life."

"Sounds like you don't like that part of him," I ventured further.

"I didn't say that. I have never been so well cared for."

"Why is it, in the decade of the woman, most women I meet want to be taken care of?" I asked, honestly wanting to know.

"I can't speak for most women, but I was not very well taken care of as a child, so I guess that's why I need to be with a man that fills that role for me."

"Sounds grim." I was curious.

"It was. My parents were children emotionally. Oh, I had nice clothes to wear and food to eat, and a roof over my head, but other than that, I was on my own. It was not a warm or nurturing environment by a long shot," she answered with a trace of bitterness."

"I see. Not the Donna Reed Show then, I take it?" I was startled by her candor.

"No, not even close."

"Where are you from?" I wanted to know everything about Georgia Conroy.

"I was raised in the South, in Alabama, by my mother and stepfather."

"So that's where that slight twang comes from." I teased.

"Is it still noticeable?" She seemed embarrassed.

"A little."

"I've tried so hard to lose it." She showed her disappointment.

"Stop trying. I like it." I really did.

"Ahmed doesn't."

"Because it's southern?"

"Exactly."

"How does your family feel about Ahmed?" I knew the answer to the question before I asked it. Pretty blond girls from the south did not date blacks, not even successful ones.

"It's not up for discussion." She answered crisply.

"That bad?" A little illumination for me.

"They are not a part of my life anymore," she said with unwavering resolve.

"You sound bitter," I said carefully.

"I am. And I should be. But at least I don't have to deal with them."

"Alabama's a far cry from Wellesley."

"I had an aunt that gave me some money for my education. I used that and scholarship money to get the hell out of the south and away from my family. It was the smartest thing I ever did."

"Your parents didn't help you?"

"My mother wanted me to go to Auburn, so I would be close to home. When I decided to leave the south, they cut me off. They're real rednecks to be frank."

"Then how did you escape being a redneck too?"

"My aunt I suppose. I even took her name, Conroy, for T.V. Mine would never have worked on air anyway."

"What is it?"

"Goldfarb." She said with chagrin.

I laughed. "I think you made a good decision. Are you Jewish?"

"Half Jewish, half Irish. My brains are from the Jews and my looks from the Irish."

"Good combo. We Irish have never been known as brain trusts." We both laughed.

"What was your major at Wellesley?"

"Liberal Arts."

"And your Masters?" I felt like an undereducated clod with my paltry BA in this very 90's conversation. This was certainly not the kind of conversation I had with my usual collection of women.

"Broadcast journalism at USC." She was proud as she answered. Smart and beautiful. Too good for broadcasting, I thought.

"I'm surprised you didn't land a reporter gig in L.A. when you finished your Masters."

"I tried. Believe me, I tried," she said, ruefully.

"What happened?" I continued to marvel at the stupidity of my industry as I looked at the magnificent creature sitting next to me. How could anyone turn this woman down?

"Every news director I met was looking for the girl next door, someone pretty and pert. They felt I was too beautiful, that I would alienate the female viewer. That line of bull." She was clearly hurt by the rejection of my peers but covered it with anger.

"It's quite a curse to be beautiful in news but at least you're getting your shot now at KKLA!" I chimed in, putting a positive spin to what I knew to be true.

"Yeah, ten years too late. I'm thirty-four. It took getting wrinkles and cellulite to be taken seriously."

"I don't see any wrinkles." Taking the opportunity to study her amazingly voluptuous face more closely.

She looked to the heavens and said with sincerity, "Thank you, Kiehls!"

"So, you went to Sacramento after graduate school?"

"No, I didn't give up on being in a major market that easily. I went to New York and stayed with some of my old Wellesley pals and looked there as well."

"New York is one of my old stomping grounds" I interjected.

"Yes, I know! In fact, I remember when you were first on WWNY anchoring the news." She smiled as she let out this little secret.

"You're kidding?" I said, thrilled.

"It was so impressive to see you in the number one market when you were so young! I was busy pounding the pavement, being rejected on a daily basis. It was very disheartening. But there you were, big as life. I thought you were such a hunk. My friends did too. We all had a serious crush on you." She laughed like it was long ago. I was blown away. She was turned on by me. I don't know why it surprised me so much, I had many female fans in those days, but Georgia was different. It was hard to imagine the evocative definition of woman as a groupie or a silly young coed for that matter.

"Great fucking timing. Why didn't I bump into you back when you thought I was a hunk!" I wanted more insight into her attraction to me, but she wasn't going to give it to me.

"I guess you have the luck of the Irish," she answered, amused by me.

"So how did you get to Sacramento?" I gave up and decided to change the subject from my fleeting image as a hunk.

"One of my friends from USC got a gig at KCRA in Sacramento and recommended me as a writer/producer for their news. KCRA has a first-class news operation that would rival any major market station. It was a fantastic training ground."

"I know. KCRA's the envy of news departments across the country. How did you meet Ahmed?" It was time to get down to the nitty gritty.

"I was producing a story on the top Giant's talent for KCRA. We carried the Giants and it was a pre-season hype kind of thing for the news. It was also a way for the sales department to stretch the revenue potential for the season. It certainly wasn't hard news. A soft feature sort of thing. Of course, Ahmed was essential to the story. I had already interviewed the other players and had my hands full. Those jocks are a bunch of chauvinistic, disrespectful assholes."

"Careful now!" I teased.

"They are. I'm not kidding!" She had her dander up.

"I'm just giving you a hard time. Women are an easy commodity with jocks. It's not that different with T.V. talent."

She looked at me with a little smirk. "I'm sure."

"So did Ahmed grab your thigh?"

She laughed. "That's certainly what I expected. I was dreading him the most. I guess that's why he fascinated me. He was the polar opposite of what I thought. He was kind, thoughtful, intelligent and respectful. He seemed to genuinely care about the job I was trying to do and did what he could to help me far beyond his own interview. He got his teammates to open up to me and to stop the macho bantering. It... he was amazing!"

"How did you get together, as a couple, I mean?" I wanted to know all. Knowledge was power. What was interesting was I consciously continued to deny to myself that I would cut in on Ahmed Brooks even if I had the chance, yet my subconscious must have been working overtime because I couldn't stop my subtle pursuit of Georgia. She continued openly, unaware of my veiled intentions.

"It was gradual. As fascinated as I was by his nature, because of my southern upbringing, I had little experience around black people in a social sense. I mean, the blacks outnumber the whites in the South. It's not like I hadn't been around them. However, even though there is legal integration, there certainly is no social integration. So, Ahmed was an exotic creature to me. I feared any intimacy with him, and I think he sensed that."

"What changed?" I persisted in encouraging her openness.

"Well...that's an interesting question...I'm not sure I have a succinct answer. We were thrown together after the initial interviews because Ahmed, the control freak, wanted to be in on the edits. He wanted to make sure what he contributed wasn't distorted in any way. So, there was a lot of togetherness in the edit suite till late at night, running for a bite to eat, the exhaustion, the intensity of the work, the giddiness when things come together. You know the drill. Working together can be very seductive."

"So, it all began in the ol' edit suite, eh?" I chuckled.

"You might say that. I was comfortable around him and began seeing him, and not his color. He still didn't make a move for a very long time."

"It is odd for a woman born and raised in the South to have a black boyfriend." I interjected.

"Yes, I guess it is." She answered as if this was not a new thought.

"What kept it going?"

"Well, he called me from time to time. He was pretty busy at the beginning of the season. And he was on the road a lot. We had the best phone conversations. He never asked me on a date. Maybe he was afraid of rejection. Then, in mid-season, he made a move, well, more of a gesture, really. He gave me tickets to the "All Star Game" to thank me for portraying him in such a positive light, or so he said. He put me up in a fabulous hotel and he took me to dinner. I have to admit I was anxious to see him again. It was then that it happened."

"You fell for him?" I hated saying those words.

"Actually, I fell for him long before that, after all those phone conversations. Maybe that was his plan all along. I couldn't see him on the phone, so, I'm guessing he felt I would get to know him without my always seeing black. He never has said this, and I have never asked. It might insult him. But Ahmed is quite sensitive and very intuitive. He is an amazing man, really."

"Perhaps you bring out the best in him. He fell in love?" I asked, again pained by the question.

"He fell in love. I fell in lust." She laughed heartily, and then giggled mischievously.

"So, the myth of the black man's sexual prowess is true?" Another pain in my chest.

"I shouldn't have said that." I could tell she wished she could take back her last statement because she blushed.

"You were honest. It makes this white boy feel inadequate though," I answered openly and honestly.

She brightened and chuckled again. "Sorry. I'm sure you do quite well with women, Paddy. I can't work up too much sympathy for you!" she teased.

"You're marrying him for lust?" I wanted a clear picture of the attraction.

"I'm marrying him for love. Oh, the lust is a big factor, for sure, but he makes me feel loved in a way that I never have before. His care of me, his consideration of me, has made me love him profoundly. You know, a lot of people probably see us as the typical white woman, black jock kind of scenario, but Ahmed didn't choose me because I am white any more than I chose him because he's black. He is a very intelligent man. Baseball is his means to an end, but he is not one dimensional by a long shot, and I am anything but a baseball groupie. Believe it or not, Ahmed never had a white girlfriend before me. We are together for all the right reasons." She answered with clarity.

"So, you're sure?" I asked, wanting at least a sliver of hope for me, and yet, I had no idea what I'd do with it.

"As sure as you can be. I can't imagine life without him. There is something very potent about being taken care of. The little girl's fantasy. I am an independent woman. I don't need his bank account or his superstar status. But I need that part of me filled that cries out for someone to take care of my emotional needs. Ahmed's both a parent and a lover. I guess that's the best way to explain it. You saw how he was at the airport. I become irritated sometimes when he's overprotective, and yet, at the same time, I cherish it. It's chivalrous. It's not that common these days in men."

"You don't make my species sound too appealing." I pleaded the cause for all us good ol' boys.

"Don't get me wrong. I like men. And men like me. But Ahmed is a cut above on many levels."

"Tough competition if someone wanted to cut in," I tested.

"Are you applying?" she teased.

I hated that she could see me. I'm sure I blushed. "I couldn't compete, I'm not that nice," I stammered quickly.

"Oh, I'm sure you have a few of your own charms," she toyed with me.

"I'm pushing forty, and no one has wanted me yet," I answered modestly.

"Perhaps they have, and you aren't available." She had my number.

"I would be for the right woman." I left a door open.

"What are you looking for?" Touché!

"I'm not sure." I answered honestly. "I've thought about it a lot, believe me. But I think if you try to define it then you are diminishing chance. I believe we all have a soulmate and if destiny is on our side, we eventually run into them." I felt quite the cerebral thinker and evolved spirit saying this and hoped she was impressed.

"Hmm, soulmate. An interesting concept." She was thoughtful.

"Why?" I got her going!

"I often think I have never met my soulmate."

"What about Ahmed?" I was making headway.

"We are perfect partners, and friends. But I wouldn't call us soulmates. I am a free spirit and he's not. He's many things to me, but not my soulmate."

Check!

"You sound pretty sure of that."

"I am." Mate!

We stopped talking then. I had opened up a dialog that led to dangerous territory for both of us and made further revelation far too risky. We settled into our books and started reading. It was hard for me to concentrate on my book. As my thoughts drifted back to our exchange, I found myself searching for any encouragement that all was not well between Ahmed and Georgia. But, based on her feelings for Ahmed, I had to conclude my mental machinations with meager expectations. I finally gave up on reading and took a fitful, dream-filled nap.

The trip was long, uncomfortable and exhausting. We negotiated the Mexico City transfer and landed in a rainstorm in Belize City. Belize was a growing third world mini metropolis. The waters near the city brought air caravans of divers to see the riches of the waters and reefs. It was tropical. Hot. Humid. Buggy. Jungle surrounded the city. Although the temperature was less intense than in summer months, there was no escape from the 100% humidity, even in January. The crew, Georgia and I all squeezed into a Jeep that had seen better days and headed south towards Honduras. The atmosphere was heavy from the recent rains which made the close proximity all the more unbearable. I felt as if I were gasping for oxygen. To make matters worse the air conditioning on the four- wheel drive sputtered out a clammy dew that left us dripping. After driving south for an hour, we checked into a minor resort that featured thatched huts over the water and fell into our mosquito netted beds, exhausted.

The next morning, we got an early start toward the area where the fishing boats set sail to open waters. The sound-and-lighting tech and the cameraman fussed with the equipment while I drove, and Georgia navigated. Most of the natives spoke some English till we reached the docks. The Indians that were hired by the fishing companies spoke a Spanish and Indian dialect.

We ended up hiring a guide that spoke the dialect and he translated to Georgia in Spanish. It was a complicated process. We recorded everything on a small hand-held recorder so that we could decipher it all later at our leisure. The cameraman shot a ton of "B" roll (background shots of the land, water and general scenery) and followed the goings on with attention to all aspects of the story we had come to record.

We were far from Belize City. It was an even hotter, steamy jungle in the tropics. The land was marsh and gave the mosquitoes a natural breeding ground. But the water was heavenly. As blue and clear as a blue white diamond. I could see why scuba and surfing were the big attraction here. It sure wasn't the shopping, night life and restaurants, or the culture for that matter.

We rented a small fishing boat to take us out to sea. The bigger boats of the fishing fleets, pulling the Indians canoes' behind them, made large waves in their wake which caused our ride to be particularly choppy. The trip was long because the big boats didn't move very fast and the water was rough the further we went out to sea. I began to feel queasy, and so did Georgia. At points in our journey dolphins followed our boat and, at times, led our boat. The cameraman was ever watchful and taped them at play as a contrast for the story at hand.

The fishing boats sailed far out in the ocean, at least 100 miles offshore. Because of the demand, lobsters were becoming more and more scarce and could only be found in abundance in the deepest waters. Once we reached the best location to catch the lobsters, the boats anchored. We had a few hours of daylight left so the crew fitted the Indians with tanks for their first dive. The Indians got into their canoes and paddled way out from the larger boats to do their dives. We all waited anxiously through each dive that transpired over an endless two hours.

Georgia sat at the back of the boat dangling her feet in the water. I went back to bring her a Coke.

"Hot?" I asked as I plopped beside her.

"Parched. Thanks." She said as she took a big swig of her Coke.

"Still queasy?"

"Yes. but not as much as before."

"This looks pretty tame. The divers actually look like they're having a good time to me." It was true that they were laughing and joking among themselves.

"Ignorance is bliss. Those tanks look like they were requisitioned from World War II." She snapped. The heat and nausea were making her cranky.

"Easy now." I got up and went back up with the crew.

The first day everything went along quite smoothly once we accepted the heat, nausea, inferior accommodations and bad food. There was a great harvest on the big boats, and everyone was in a jovial mood. At night, the natives jostled in fun and talked loudly and bravely to the Latin music that blared until after midnight.

We settled into the evening on our crowded cabin cruiser as best we could. Dinner was fresh fish and rice. I was hungry from the salty air, and the fish fit my taste. Georgia barely ate and went to bed early. The ride and the mission were getting to her. The interior cabin was small and not particularly clean but, because she was the only female on the board, Georgia took over the cabin for some measure of privacy. We guys all slept in sleeping bags out on the deck under the stars. There was a cool breeze across the bow of the boat that made me feel sensuous despite the hard wood deck attacking my joints. An exquisite black sky wrapped around the boat and was lit with a million stars for me to count to sleep but, until the noise settled down, there was no rest to be had. So, I spent my time searching the inky sky and dreaming of what I'd like to do with Georgia. Having her near me was far more stimulating than I had anticipated. I don't know why I burdened myself with this form of self-torture but couldn't help myself. I was under her spell.

The next morning, we all woke early and got to work. Georgia was exhausted from sleeping fitfully in the hot and stuffy cabin. I would have loved her sleeping with me under the stars, even platonically, but, unfortunately, I was not alone. The crew was right next to me, blowing farts and snoring.

The men on the big boats were up early as well. They were drinking and laughing above on the decks while the Indians dived below into waters far too deep to be safe. Once the Indians submerged, the watch started again. The tanks were only good for thirty minutes, so Georgia began timing the lengths of the dives. She started to yell at the men in the lead boats about a half an hour into each dive. She was tired and anxious and wanted them to bring the Indians back to the surface. But no one paid attention. With that, she became more agitated, and as they began to laugh and shout at her, she tried harder to scream above the sound of the wind and the waves. I tried to calm her down, but she wanted them to pay attention.

"Hey, times up! Bring them back," she shouted again and again at the boats. Her voice was lost in the wind.

"They can't hear you," I said.

"What are they waiting for?" Georgia asked.

"They're signaling for them." I tried to comfort her.

"They've been down too long," she said with fright.

"How much air was in those tanks?" I asked.

"Not a lot. They only had on one tank. About 30 minutes at best," she said.

Then, one by one, the Indians began to surface, and Georgia breathed a sigh of relief. They had large lobsters in their baskets. The Indians were poor, untrained and didn't adequately understand what incredible risk they were taking. This was a way for them to feed their families. That's what they understood. When we were on the docks preparing to leave on this journey there were Indians sitting in wheel-chairs that were clearly brain damaged and paralyzed from these dives. No one seemed to notice them. It was a way of life that had gone on for as long as anyone could remember. Like so many of the wrongs in life, we begin to accept them as a part of the human condition. This was accepted too. The Indians were anesthetized to the dangers.

After about ten more minutes most of the Indians had surfaced. Then it happened. A body, blood spurting from its nose and mouth, popped up into the air like a cork coming out of a champagne bottle. Georgia said, "Oh my God!" like a prayer of disbelief. The Indian's mask and tanks were off. They hoisted him onto the nearest boat. He was dead. He must have been struggling to the surface when his lungs exploded. All of it was recorded. Georgia slumped on the deck with her head in her hands. I squatted beside her and put my arm around her shoulders. We were still and reverent, respecting the moment of a life ending. A few more Indians surfaced. The crew brought them on board, retied the canoes and hastily headed home. We followed at a distance. Our fateful voyage was over. We got the guts of our story and Brian would be pleased. But I felt sick. I simply wanted to go back to civilization.

"I can't believe they can get away with this. I want us to nail those bastards." Georgia fumed as we neared the docks.

"We'll get them. We've got our story" I said.

"The story? The story! What about that man, and his family?" Georgia was indignant.

"Georgia, I don't want to sound callous, but we can't take on the problems of the world. We just report them."

"What?" She was incredulous. "We need to crucify those bastards. This is not a fishing trip gone awry, Paddy. It's genocide. Those fishermen know exactly what they are doing to the Indians. You saw it. What's the matter with you?" she fumed.

We rode back in silence. She was upset and I knew she was right, but I also knew, realistically, there was nothing we could do but report the story. There was no point in arguing with her. Ahmed was right. She could start a revolution.

When we docked, I wanted a drink and so did the crew. Georgia was quiet and withdrawn but went along because she had no other options. We had the vehicle. We found a small outdoor bar and ordered beers and drank out of the bottles. No one talked much, the heat and futility made us listless. The shooter (cameraman) said he had all he needed from the boats. He was going to get more "B" roll the next morning when the light was better. Georgia and I would line up some interviews with the boat captains and try to corner a few government types. We needed to find out why this was being allowed to go on. But we'd bitten off all we could handle for one day.

We went back to the huts, exhausted, to rest. At about eight I wanted to get dinner and went to find Georgia. She wasn't in her hut. I heard some splashing and went to the edge of the sand, took off my sandals and walked through the shallow water to find her. She was like a little kid playing in the surf, splashing around a few yards out.

"Sharks feed at night, you know." I said as I looked at her bathed in moonlight.

"The only danger around here comes from the flesh eaters on land," she replied.

"Maybe you're right."

"Your pants are wet," she said, amused.

"They'll dry soon enough in this heat. Enjoying yourself?" She looked happy.

"I couldn't stand my steamy hut one minute longer. Besides, I needed to wash the day away," she answered as she treaded water in front of me.

"You knew what you were going to see when you came down here," I reminded her.

"Spoken like a true hardened news hound," Georgia said, splashing.

"I've seen worse," I spoke truthfully.

"That doesn't diminish what's happening here." She was firm.

"No." I agreed. "I'm sorry that you had to experience it, but stories like this happen every day. I've learned over time to distance myself from my feelings, so I won't go crazy."

"I know. I'm not angry with you, I'm just angry, period."

"Still friends?"

"Yes, we are, Paddy. You're half wet. Put on your suit and jump in here with me." With that she turned and lay down to float in the waves. The moonlight made her appear like an apparition, all light and shadows. Her eyes were closed and her body slack with the gentle waves holding and caressing her. I looked at her for a long time and knew if I got in the water with her, I would do something I might regret later. She was vulnerable and a long way from home. I ached to take advantage of the situation, but something stopped me. Perhaps it was my fear of rejection, but I wanted to think it was my integrity. I turned, walked back through the shallows to the sand, and sat down to wait for her to finish her solitary reverie.

The next couple of days were a blur of interviews with Indian families and government officials. No one would open-up to us in this primitive land. The hierarchy turned a blind eye to all types of questionable commerce regardless of how illegal or exploitative. The good old U.S. of A. began to look rather tame and certainly good by comparison. Whatever our faults, our system had a semblance of order and control that had been set up to protect our citizens. We were in a time warp here in Central America, a culture where anything goes. Their motto was, "Make money, ask questions later."

We were at our last interview at the central police headquarters. Georgia had managed to corner the police captain and one of his officers. I was busy helping the shooter and tech load some gear into our jeep for our journey to the airport.

"You mean to tell me that no one can do anything about the atrocities the fishing companies commit here in your country on a daily basis?" She asked the captain, indignantly.

"My dear lady, you do not understand our country very well." The captain was being solicitous. "This is a poor country. We all do things here that are a risk to our lives." The captain patronized. "I must risk my life every day to feed my family."

"I doubt that," Georgia retorted, condescendingly.

"Are you calling me a liar?" His eyes flared at her. Latin men did not take kindly to an aggressive female, no matter how beautiful they are.

"I'm saying that you have a big, cushy job in the government. I doubt your life is ever on the line." Georgia said, challenging him. Her emotions were showing again. Now it was clear to me why she had not made it into reporting earlier in her career.

"What do you know about me? You come down to our country and try to make big trouble. Take your people and get out of here." He gestured with a wave of his hand for us to scram.

"I'm not leaving until you answer my question. Why aren't you protecting the Indians from exploitation?" Georgia was insistent, pushing too hard for a woman in this male dominated country. The police captain turned to walk away from Georgia and said something to his officer. Georgia reached for the captain's arm and he jerked around. She had gone too far. You never touch the person you are interviewing. You keep a professional distance. The officer grabbed her and gripped her tightly. He started dragging her towards the jeep. She looked like a doll flailing about in his firm grasp as she shouted at him in Spanish and kicked him as hard as she could. I ran over, pushed him to a halt and said to let her go. She continued to yell in Spanish at him and at the captain. The captain had turned back and was watching as the officer let Georgia go. The officer took a swing at me. The cameraman recorded us as we scuffled. The officer was on top of me, punching me in the face. Georgia jumped on his back and started to hit him as hard as she could with her fists. We heard a gun go off. Georgia jumped up and so did the officer. I was still lying on the ground and afraid I had been shot but felt no pain. The captain was holding up his smoking pistol that had fired the warning shot. It was clear the next shot would be for real.

"Get up and get out of my country. Pack your things and leave now," the captain commanded.

The officer started to grab us again. Then the captain said to let us go. The officer backed up and walked away. Georgia put her arms around me and led me to the jeep. She was full of adrenaline and so was I.

"Those bastards. Look what they did to you." She tenderly touched a small cut above my eye as I brushed myself off.

I was shaking from the fear of what could have happened. Her tenderness made me want to take her in my arms and hold her, but I knew I couldn't. It was the wrong time and circumstance. Instead, I firmly removed both her hands away from my face. "What the hell did you think you were doing back there?" I had to make an impression on her. Her impulsive behavior scared me.

"I wanted a straight answer" she defiantly replied.

"You grabbed him, remember? Professional distance. Hands off!" I reprimanded her.

"But he wouldn't give me a straight answer," she said, stung by my rebuff.

"So, you pick a fight with them?" I continued to chastise her.

"They were treating me like what I was asking was unimportant. Those Indians are giving up their lives for the price of a goddamn lobster."

"You lost your professional demeanor over there and could have cost us our lives."

"You coldhearted bastard!" She looked at me through tears with such disappointment in her face. She was clearly hurt by my rebuff.

"I've heard enough. You endangered the safety of this whole crew, yourself included, by indulging your emotions."

"Do we have to be detached observers? Is it enough to only report this story?" She was sorrowful, but angry.

"You know I'm right." I remained firm while she looked defeated.

"As a professional, yes. As a human being, no," she said, partially conceding.

"You're here as a part of a news team, Georgia. You report the *news*. You don't become part of it. This isn't 'Fun in the sun with Ahmed'." The minute I said it I knew I'd gone too far. It just slipped out.

"You jerk! What a low blow!" She glared at me. She was really steamed now. My inner conflict over her relationship with Ahmed slipped out where it didn't belong.

She hopped in the jeep and we headed for the airport. No one spoke of anything but the basics.

When we boarded the plane and sat down, Georgia turned to me and apologized. I accepted, and returned an apology, gratefully. I knew I had let her down by not fighting harder to effect some change in the antiquated system, become a vigilante of justice, in our brief stay in Central America. Georgia wanted a hero, a savior, and I couldn't be that for her or the Miskito Indians. We were so completely drained from the work, the heat, the futility as we settled in for our flight back that we were silenced from exhaustion. The minute the plane took off, and the air-conditioning started, we both fell sound asleep.

We would run the story of the Miskito Indians, and America would be appalled. Then they would forget. Life would go on here as it had before we came and made our fuss.

JANUARY 13TH, 1994

A few hours past midnight Georgia arrived home from the airport by cab to her small apartment in Santa Monica. Ahmed was out of town at a meeting with his agent and for that gift of timing, she was quite grateful. She would see him tomorrow for dinner and much more, but was glad she had this time alone to relax and unpack. Tomorrow would be hellish at work getting caught up and looking at all the tapes, trying to pull together a story.

After getting her clothes unpacked and organized Georgia undressed and relished in a long, hot soak in her massive claw foot tub that was gratefully spared during the *de rigueur* renovations to the Santa Monica neighborhoods preceding her arrival in LA. Despite the comforts of home, as she stretched her weary frame in the bubbles, she couldn't stop herself from fantasizing about Paddy and that was beginning to annoy her. He got under her skin on the trip to Belize. In fact, she admonished herself, she had given him far too much of her psychic energy from the moment that his black Irish eyes first burnt into her skin. It wasn't his looks, his wit, his celebrity that attracted her to him. It was far deeper than that. She felt as if he belonged to her, that they had known each other always. When they were together, there were many words that were spoken aloud to one another, but underneath a non-verbal dialog was being punched out. Each word of the hidden dialog hit her stomach like a hammering, breath sucking blow. She was reeling and exhausted from the intense and unrelenting contact with him. And because of the intensity of their contact, she felt like the pressure of it all made her behave foolishly and out of character. She was aware of a giddiness and girlishness, an almost hysterical quality to her actions. That shamed her, that he could see her that way. She blushed with humiliation thinking of how badly she had conducted herself on the trip. She had always been the consummate professional, but her demeanor and judgment was impaired with Paddy around. Because of her over stimulation she became irresponsible, said and did things that she was now regretting.

Georgia resolved in the soothing scented waters of her tub to pull back from Paddy. He represented a danger she could ill afford and certainly did not understand. She had the perfect, storybook life. Ahmed adored her. She had the perfect job, the one she always wanted. Life was finally the way she had longed for it to be. Paddy McGurk represented a threat. Besides, he now probably thought she was a lightweight, a bubblehead. She was busy convincing herself he couldn't possibly find her in the least attractive at this point when the phone rang. She lay still in the water and listened. She wasn't about to get up from the comfort of the tub when she felt so nauseatingly vulnerable and stupid.

Her message rang out from the bedroom and then the beep followed by Paddy's voice booming into her few moments of solace.

"Hey, Miss Conroy, defender of the weak, the downtrodden, just wanted to call and make sure you got home OK. Give me a buzz so I can stop worrying about you and can go to sleep."

Hearing his voice and his tormenting of her, making light of her, Georgia slid deeper into the comfort of the tub and groaned. Later, after she dried off and gathered her wits about her, she called him while lying on her bed naked, flushed pink from the steam of her bath. It made her secretly glad and incredibly sensual to be exposing what she knew he would like to see.

He picked up on the first ring.

"Georgia!" He answered, knowing it was her.

"You are getting as bad as Ahmed! The last thing I need is two micro managers!"

"Don't say that, for Christ sake!" He spat. "I just wanted to make sure you got home, that's all. It is three AM and we do live in LA."

"My cab driver was very accommodating, and even brought my bags up the stairs for me."

"Good. Well I'll see you in the morning then."

"Yes." She couldn't think of a thing more to say, and yet, she wanted to keep the conversation going.

"Goodnight, Miz Georgia," He ended with a southern twang just to aggravate her further. The dial tone greeted her before she could say another word.

Oh, he made her blood boil. Now she would never get to sleep. So damn formal. So stilted. The concerned and responsible co-worker, the "friend".

In the weeks and months that followed, Georgia burned with inward fury when she listened in on her peers at the morning coffee klatches in the lunchroom where, each day, Brian and Paddy's latest escapades were hashed and rehashed. She felt sick at heart whenever there was mention of a new conquest for Paddy or a sighting of him with a new companion. He was hers in some deep and primitive way. But her hand was dealt, and she knew that she could never act on her feelings. Far too much was at stake. It was the kiss of death in business to get involved in an office romance, and even more disastrous to get involved with someone you worked with in the same department on a daily basis.

Also important in her decision was the undeniable love she had for Ahmed. He was a fantastic lover, loyal friend and all she had ever thought she wanted in a relationship. So, after much heart-wrenching, she deepened her resolve to ignore all that she heard and strive for the most professional of relationships with Paddy. Intimate contact of any kind with Paddy McGurk was simply out of the question.

4
JANUARY 14TH, 1994

Brian Buchanon felt heat on his face, a beam of sunlight making his eyes flutter open. Friday morning was in full swing and he needed to get moving. As he stretched in his bed his arm brushed against something that was not familiar. His eyes opened fully as he turned to look at the woman lying next to him in the bed. He groaned with recognition as he surveyed his damage to the blond still sleeping with her back to him. Pissed with himself that he had fallen asleep before ushering her out the night before, he reached over a little too roughly to shake her awake.

"Get up," he commanded.

"What! Oh, good morning," she said cozily, smiling as she wiped the sleep from her face.

She was an attractive, long legged actress/waitress with big breasts, silicone, but big, nonetheless. She personified his favorite array of body parts. But in the light of day, she looked a little worn; the bloom off the rose, and he wanted no part of her.

"I said get up," Brian repeated.

"Jesus. What's the matter?" she stared at him, hurt.

"You have to leave. I need to get to work." He hated mornings after.

"Go ahead. I'll take a shower after you leave," she said as she snuggled back into her pillow.

"No. Get up and get your crap out of my bedroom and leave. I'll call a cab while you get dressed."

She got the message and got up in a huff. "Bastard," she tossed at him as she grabbed her things and went into the bathroom to pee. Brian made a quick call for her ride and flicked on the T.V. to watch the morning news on KKLA. A good-looking young chef was hawking his latest cookbook. That would keep the broads in the audience paying attention, he smugly thought to himself.

As soon as the chef finished up Georgia came on to do a live shot from a school where a kid got killed by one of his classmates. The gang wars in L.A. were getting worse. However, they were good for the ratings. Georgia looked beautiful, tan and relaxed from her trip to Belize. He'd like to fuck her, he fantasized to himself, and wipe that cheery smile off her face. Brian made a mental note to get Red to ask around about that little trip Georgia took with Paddy. He needed to make sure Paddy didn't score, or even try to score, with Georgia. That broad was trouble. He could smell it a mile away.

Brian got out of bed and rapped on the door to the bathroom. The door opened and his one-night stand pushed him out of the way and left. He didn't give a shit, he thought, sour. She was a whole lot of nothing. He went in and started getting ready.

When Brian got to the station, he called Red to his office.

"Hey, you sure left the bar early last night...it must have been that chick giving you the ear swab. She sure was hot for you," Red said through a laugh as he rolled in the door. Since Mary passed away, Red lived vicariously through Brian's sexual exploits. Brian figured old Red couldn't get it up anymore and this was his way of having a little fun, so he went along with it.

"Yeah, she balled my brains out last night and again this morning. I'm pooped." O.K. so he lied a little about this morning. Red needed the entertainment he rationalized.

"Whew! She sure was a looker. Good eh?" Red's mind devoured the thought salaciously.

"Damn good!" Brian played along.

"Damn! You lucky dog you! So, what do you need coach?" Red called all middle age big cheeses "coach". A hangover from his announcer days.

"Heard anything about Paddy and Georgia's trip to Belize?"

"Not a word." Red would tell him if he has heard a whisper. He loved to be in the know about such things.

"Ask around, would you? Find out if he porked her."

"Sure, no problem. But I doubt they'd share that tasty tidbit with me."

"Ask the shooter, casual, you know. No big deal." Brian tried to act casual himself. He tried to give Red the impression that it was mild curiosity.

"Gotcha!" Red said with a wave goodbye.

After Brian finished with Red, he called Lani. She wasn't in yet. Probably busy putting spackle on her face he chuckled to himself. Brian could only take Lani in small doses, but she was "Ms. L.A.", so he patronized her. She might even prove useful in keeping tabs on Paddy and Georgia. He left a message for her to come to his office as soon as she decided to grace the station with her presence.

One thing Brian Buchanon hated, more than anything else, was not knowing what was going on in his station. That's why he came in at odd times, sometimes in the middle of the night, on the weekends, his surprise attacks he called them, so he could see what was going on when his employees thought they could get away with something. He wanted them to fear him, he wanted them to know who was running the show. When he caught someone doing something they shouldn't, he put them through the ringer because he needed to set the tone for the rest of his troops. No infraction could be tolerated no matter how small. It wasn't good for the morale. He set the rules and they needed to be followed, the alternative was anarchy. His duty as a Marine in Vietnam had served him well in his ensuing career in broadcasting.

It was time to go to his staff meeting. Brian silently vowed to blast the news department. Brian was pissed that Herb Rudnick didn't have a solid plan to beat KHLY during the Winter Olympics news change-over. That guy was making 200 grand a year, he grumbled to himself, and could be replaced and would be if he fucked this up. Herb was planning on Paddy's story from Belize to do the trick, but Brian had no faith that there was sufficient interest in a few brain-dead Indians from Central America to pull in the ratings needed to kick the butt of those fucks at KHLY. His mood darkened further as he entered the conference room.

All the department heads were assembled, seated and holding notes in front of them for show and tell. They wanted to brag about what their department had done in the last week to justify their existence. Each week he tolerated their bullshit, but he wasn't in the mood this morning. He had a headache from too much booze and too little sleep. That broad had kept him up half the night trying to impress him with what a sex queen she was. His dick was still sore from her gnawing on it. Late last night he was just drunk enough to play along with her, but now he was too damn tired to deal with this meeting.

He looked out at the sea of eager, ass-kissing faces looking at him as he took his seat. He had nothing prepared so he would wing it. He started.

"We are facing a crisis of epic proportions. For the last month, I have warned all of you that we had to do 150% every day, weekends, nights, whatever it takes to crush those bastards at KHLY. Those low rent pukes think they can steal my news viewers with a couple of weeks of Olympics to help them. And what are you doing about it? Nothing. I am sick and tired of coming to these meetings every week and hearing the same old whining crap about what you can't do, how you need more money, how you need more personnel. You people are *spoiled*. You have the best facility, the best equipment, the best personnel, the best support in the west, in the country even, and all I ever get is bitching. You have two more weeks, two more short weeks, and all you are doing when you come in here is cover your asses. Well, I've got news for you. This is you and your asses' last hurrah." He heard some audible gasps which made him rev up further. He started to get into what he was saying, "If those no talent bastards at KHLY beat us two weeks from now, they're going to get a letter in the mail from me. That letter will have a note of congratulations and in that note will be a job offer to take your place. Stop staring at me with those dumbfounded mugs. Let me make this clear for you. I will only have the *best* working for me. There is only one way to define the best. The best always comes out on top. So, you have a choice ladies and gentlemen. Be number one, or, be replaced by those who are. That's all I've got to say. I, for one, have got a lot of work to do!"

Brian got up and left the room. As he walked down the hall to his office, he chortled to himself. He loved watching those shocked faces as he got up and walked out on them. That little lecture would send them scurrying back to their offices. He congratulated himself for such a stirring, impromptu sermon. When he came into his office Lani was sitting on his sofa smoking a cigarette.

"You know I hate that shit," Brian said through a sneer, "Put it out."

"You weren't in here, sorry," she said, crushing the butt in an ashtray.

"This is my office. You'll stink up my furniture. So how come you're in before ten?"

"I called in and my assistant said you needed to talk to me."

He hated having to cozy up to old Lani, but he needed to keep tabs on Paddy and Georgia. She sat only a few feet away from them and he knew she would see all. She'd make a point of it.

"What's going on downstairs?" He started a little clumsily, not wanting to tip his hand too soon.

"What exactly do you mean, 'going on'?" She would be coy, not giving an inch.

"How's Georgia working out?"

"Fine, I guess. She's a favorite with the men anyway. I can't see it myself. She a pretty thing, but so common, sleeping with a black and all," she said in her cattiest confidentiality.

"What about Paddy?"

"What about him?" Lani answered, playing it close.

"Is she *his* favorite too?"

"Most definitely. He never takes his eyes off her. Why do you care, Brian?" She knew exactly why, but she continued to play cat and mouse with him. He decided to get to the fucking point.

"I want you to do me a personal favor. I need to know whatever you see going on between those two. I can't have my relationship with the Dodgers compromised because Paddy gets an itch in his pants, and Georgia decides to scratch it. Get what I mean?"

"Clear as crystal. I'll be happy to keep you posted. But I don't understand why you don't unload her and save me the trouble, Brian," she chimed happily, glad to be in on this little intrigue. He hated her more but was stuck with her.

The best defense was a good offense. He would have the last word. "It's not important that you understand, Lani. I'm the general manager. I make the decisions. Just get back to me if you see something." He finished with her and was glad she got up and left with his dismissive statement. She wasn't so dumb that she would stick around after she got what she wanted. He knew Lani would love this assignment. It gave her power. He hoped he wouldn't rue the day he gave it to her.

5

THE NORTHRIDGE QUAKE
4:31AM JANUARY 16, 1994

A few days after we arrived back home from Belize I was sleeping soundly, dreaming of white sands lapped by azure seas, when I, literally, was tossed out of my bed. I woke up fast, frightened to the core. The severe jerking sensation of my condo felt as if the earth had jolted loose from its axis! My mind was spinning, convinced that the world had come to an end. Completely disoriented, I jumped up from the floor as fast as I could and groped for my robe in the winter darkness. The room continued to vibrate as I tried to think of what to do next. I knew it was an earthquake, a very big earthquake. The L.A. natives say that earthquakes are not a big deal, a little quiver in the Earth if anything, but this earthquake was a very big deal. I feared for my life. As dishes were hitting the floor and the T.V. that I had failed to turn off the night before broadcasting pure static, I ran toward the screaming outside my living room and headed into the unstable dawn through my front door.

Everyone in my condo complex was doing the same. We were breaking all the earthquake preparedness rules, but were too panicked to stop and think. Someone had the presence of mind to shout that we needed to shut off the gas. We all scrambled to find a wrench. It was pandemonium at its worst. The women could not stop screaming. All of us were in our nightclothes or less. Some of the men were in their boxer shorts and some of the women were in nighties, but no one was self-conscious. We were too busy trying to stay alive. As dawn finally broke, the aftershocks were rumbling through the Palisades like waves at the beach. I kept wondering if California was finally breaking off and falling, inch by inch, into the sea. We had no way of knowing how bad it was or the epicenter's location.

As the aftershocks continued to roll, I went back into my condo and tried to call the station, to see if they had any information on the damage, the fatalities, and, being honest with myself, to find out if anyone had heard from Georgia, but the phone lines were dead. I agonized for a short while longer then made an impulsive decision to strike out into the unknown and try to find her apartment. Georgia lived two blocks north of Wilshire on Eighth Street and, although I wasn't sure of the exact address, I'd heard her describe her apartment as a duplex with lots of Cup of Gold Vines growing on the stucco. That was all the information I needed to head out. I got dressed and jumped in my car even though I knew better. I drove like a madman, taking only surface streets. An eerie quiet, a stillness, enveloped the neighborhoods that I passed through, pierced only by the cry of an occasional siren. No one was leaving home. When I got to Eighth Street I drove to Georgia's block. There were apartment buildings on each side but they each had multiple units. Feeling frustrated and disoriented, fueled by pure adrenaline, I was about to enter a new block when on the corner I found, hidden by a much larger apartment complex, covered in a tangle of plants, a funky two-story duplex. I parked and hopped out of my car and ran to the front door to ring the bell. The door opened immediately.

"Oh!" A woman in gray sweats said, as she brushed her hair from her face.

"Does Georgia Conroy live here?" I asked, knowing I frightened her.

"I thought you were my boyfriend," she said, looking confused.

"I'm sorry. Are you O.K.?"

"Just shook up. That's all" she laughed nervously. "I made a pun. Leave it to me."

"Is Georgia here?" I asked again.

"She lives upstairs but her boyfriend, the ballplayer, picked her up about five minutes ago."

"She wasn't hurt?"

"Not that I could tell. Who are you?"

"A friend. Sorry to bother you. Do you need anything?"

"No. But thanks for asking."

"Well, then, goodbye. Thanks for your help." I turned to walk down to my car.

"Who should I tell her came by?"

I turned and smiled. "Her secret admirer."

The Los Angeles earthquake of 1994 became the lead story on KKLA news, and all local and national news, for the next two weeks. The news reports flowed nonstop as L.A struggled to cope with the downed freeways, crushed buildings and devastated lives. Our news-room cranked round the clock to keep up with the stories pouring in about the quake and its victims. I saw Georgia at her worst each day, with greasy hair and dirty clothes, as we all lived at the station and fought exhaustion to keep up with what needed to be told. I hadn't had a shower or change of clothes in days, and I looked it on air. But our strung-out presentation added to the drama of the situation.

When things finally began to calm down about the earthquake, the Olympics began as scheduled. We barely had time to catch our breaths.

The Olympics became a media circus. The pageantry, the history, the lifelong work and single-minded dedication of the athletes, the mystique of the "gods of sport" that fascinates the average man about the Olympics, became blurred, for the first time in the history of the games, because of the Nancy Kerrigan and Tonya Harding showdown. It hurt to see the way that something once so pure and good in the evolution of man and sport was turned into a trumped-up contest between good and evil. It played to the lowest common denominator in all of us. The '94 Winter Olympics became a bad "made for T.V." movie.

The week of Nancy and Tonya was the week that Brian decided to run our Belize story. To have the story seen by as many viewers as possible I convinced him to repeat the segments on our morning newscasts. I didn't have confidence that our story could rival the on-going Olympic saga, but I was wrong. The public was sick and tired of the circus atmosphere.

Our morning show numbers, during the half hour we aired the Miskito Indian story, were the highest since Desert Storm. Then, later each morning, when the overnight ratings came in from our late newscast, we were amazed to find that the viewer who was watching Olympics all day and into the early evening turned to KKLA when our late newscast began at 10 PM. It was remarkable! The ratings were staggering, even for the Olympics. Every night the shares of audience watching the Olympics were in the high twenties and the ratings were in the high teens. But, miraculously, at ten, the couch potatoes would channel surf over to our news to watch our special series on the lobster-diving Indians of Central America. KHLY, the network owned and operated station carrying the Olympics, couldn't hold onto the Olympic lead-in numbers they needed to boost their new ten o'clock newscast. To rub salt in their wounds, the *L.A. Times* followed with their own flattering wrap-up of our Indian series, as well. The Times called our story "A thought provoking and intelligent alternative to the Olympic debacle". Our newsroom was jubilant.

Brian took Georgia and me to dinner to celebrate the "coup" on our story. Ahmed came along. We went to the Palm, the old standby for all the "see and be seen" crowd. The Palm was Brian's kind of place. No "nouvelle cuisine" for him. Big, fat lobsters and thick, marbled steaks were their specialty, plus waiters that were hired to cater to the well-heeled set. The irony of the choice of a lobster restaurant was lost on Brian. It amazed me how the help could remember everyone's name that came through the place, but this was no ordinary waiter gig. These guys were pros and made big bucks.

It caused quite a stir when Ahmed strode into the room with Georgia on his arm. Robert Wagner was there with one of his daughters, Heather Locklear was with her latest heavy metal boyfriend, and O.J. Simpson was powering down rib-eyes with his buddy Al Cowlings, but none got the looks like Ahmed and Georgia. Ahmed was hard, glossed ebony next to Georgia's soft, shimmering pastels. They lit up the room. I felt downright dowdy next to them, but Brian rose to the occasion. We drank magnum after magnum of Dom "P" and ate like Vikings. Georgia and I avoided the lobster and stuck with swordfish, but we made up for our discretion with champagne. Ahmed was getting ready for spring training, so he behaved himself and looked after the rest of us.

Brian was in rare form, telling jokes, acting out the parts, and playing host to the hilt. He loved center stage, the perfect raconteur, and this was his moment to gloat. "King of the Hill" was the part he played best. No one begrudged him his braggadocio, even though it was our work, our success and achievement that had gotten him so jacked up.

Brian went from table to table glad-handing everyone he knew like a southern senator seeking re-election. He loved the spotlight and made sure it was on him that night. Ahmed, Georgia and I exchanged looks and laughs as we watched him parade around. He wanted to impress us and everyone within earshot. He told the waiters, the maître 'd, and anyone who would listen about the way we kicked ass over the KHLY. It always amazed me how people indulged him, but it was hard to resist the big Irish kid in him. Brian always said that he hired the Irish for jobs that needed people skills and the Jews for jobs that needed money skills. The general sales manager, business manager, program manager, executive producer and news director were all Jews. The on-air talent, human resources manager and Brian, were mostly Irish.

When he believed something, even if it was a gross generalization, he lived by it. In many ways he was simple. Black and white. No shades of grey.

We were laughing and talking when he finally came back to the table.

"We sure showed those bastards!" he chortled.

"Yeah, you hit a grand slam, Brian. What does that mean to you other than it feels good to kick ass?" Ahmed asked.

"It means we hold onto our news rating in one of the most important books of the year. We live with that fucking February book all year long. One or two rating points in my late news means millions of dollars lost or gained over the year. Those damn agency time buyers would love an excuse to fuck me. They love to screw the independents. I have to fight for every cent I get. Now I can shove this Olympic season down their fucking throats. Those bitches haven't got a clue. They are at the bottom rung of an ad agency. But they act like they rule the world. They would argue that KHLY's Olympic lead-in ratings for their new late news are real. No fucking way! With that kind of lead-in, the late news could be hosted by Bozo the Clown and do a rating. It's total bullshit. But I got them this time. KHLY's late news sucks wind even with the Olympics to help their launch. I've got those bitches right where I want them. You kids did a great job, an outstanding job."

That was one of Brian's favorite battle cries. He hated time buyers. The "queens" of the business. Time buyers were usually women (or gay men), that lived their social lives through their jobs. They were wined and dined by the account executives at television and radio stations. The time buyers had their little empires and their subjects were the account people. They made television account executives lives miserable. The bright and/or attractive time buyers moved on to bigger and better things in the media and account departments, and that left the pathologically sadistic and power hungry as the career buyers. There were exceptions to this stereotype to be sure but more than not, you were going to suffer. If you called on a middle-aged career time buyer, watch out. That was a sign your life would be misery. But account people were paid to be miserable. They were the highest paid in the station next to talent. They all pulled down over a hundred and fifty grand. That was the minimum in L.A. They spent their whole existence sucking up to the time buyers. I had heard many an account person referred to their task as "whoring". And from my vantage point, they weren't far off base.

Brian shouted "Hey, Buddy. More Dom P all around."

Brian had pet names for waiters in his favorite restaurants. "Guido" in Italian restaurants, "Pierre" in French, "Jose" in Mexican, "Seanie" in the Irish pubs and "Buddy" for All American eats. It was his way of being familiar without having to remember anyone's name. But no one took offense, at least not outwardly, because he left such big tips in all his favorite haunts. No matter how many times he came back, he always requested the same table and waiter and called them by his pet name.

"Georgia, you're a lucky girl to be working with pro's like Paddy and the KKLA crew in the second largest market in the country. Here's to a job well done, Georgia. You lived up to our expectations. You've become part of our team," Brian toasted again.

"Thank you, Brian. I am lucky," she answered generously. Georgia was an excellent writer and producer. We were lucky to have her, but Brian wanted to keep her indebted. He was good at that. I always felt I owed him my entire career. I would still be in Ohio without him. He never said so, but the balance of power in our relationship left me in the subordinate position. That was O.K. with me. I did owe him a lot. He deserved my loyalty.

"So, you going to give me a pennant to sell in '95, Ahmed?" Brian asked.

"I'll do my best. The competition will be tough, and I won't have Barry Bonds and Matt Williams on my team anymore. But you know the Dodgers. Anything can happen with Lasorda running things."

"How many more years are you going to play?" Brian quizzed.

"I'm 34 now. I only have a couple of good years left and I want them to count. I need to set a couple more records and this is my season to do it. That's why I'm training now, even though spring training doesn't start for another couple of weeks. I need the edge," Ahmed explained to Brian.

"Between my job and his training schedule, we never see each other," Georgia moaned.

"At my age you have to keep in shape year-round. If I slack off, I'll never achieve my goals. Believe me, there are a lot of things I'd rather be doing on these sunny Southern California days than sweating in a gym for four hours," Ahmed answered candidly.

"Where do you go?" Brian asked.

"Gold's in Venice. Then after that, I run for five miles on the bike trail from Santa Monica to Marina del Rey," Ahmed continued.

"Well it's working. You look great. Not an ounce of fat on you. I wish my anchor had your discipline." Brian said this just as I was popping another wad of fried onion rings in my mouth. He smiled benevolently at me. I blanched and swallowed hard. Everyone looked at me and laughed. I laughed too. The timing was uncanny.

"Why do you always do that to me when it's time to order dessert?" I retorted, genuinely embarrassed.

"That's why I do it. You aren't having dessert. Ahmed won't eat dessert. And Georgia should be dessert." Brian chortled at his own humor and we all laughed heartily.

Things revved up more with each glass of champagne.

"Paddy, why do you put up with him?" Georgia said with a look.

"At least I don't have to sleep with him" I said.

"That'll be in your next contract." Brian hooted. "Now let's get out of here. There's a new R&B band over at the House of Blues that I want to hear."

"You're a R&B fan, Brian?" Ahmed asked, amused.

"A true product of the sixties. Vietnam Vet. Marine. The whole damn scene."

"Which bands are your favorites?" Georgia asked.

"I like rock that has a blues flavor. The Stones, Eric Clapton, Rod Stewart, Lynard Skynard, the old guard. But this new band is like that. Sort of a Black Crows, ZZ Top, Spin Doctors and Blues Traveler rolled into one. I feel like dancin'. Dancing keeps me young. Besides that's where all the "sweet young thangs" hang out. That's why Paddy and I go there. Right, Paddy?"

Georgia looked at me with raised eyebrows. I had to answer. "It does attract the young girls."

"Hell yes! The younger the better. I want them while they're still naive enough to think because I run a T.V. station I can make them a star," Brian admitted.

"You are morally bankrupt human being, Brian," Georgia teased.

"At my age, you bet your ass I am. What choice do I have? Young beauties like you that have brains, won't go out with me. I have to settle for young beauties with no brains," Brian defended.

"What about beauties that are your age and have brains?" she countered, neatly.

"I'm damn near fifty-five, for Christ's sake. Women my age are too set in their ways. They would never put up with me." He spoke the truth.

Georgia laughed heartily. "I get your point! You'd be a test of any woman's patience, that's for sure." We all laughed. Brian laughed loudest because he liked Georgia's teasing.

Brian signaled for our waiter.

"Hey, buddy, what's the damage?" Our waiter gave us the check. While Brian looked it over Red Kelly walked in the door with one of his sons. He spotted us and gave a hearty wave as he headed for our table.

"What are you desperadoes doing here? Christ, I can't get away from you." Red said in greeting.

"Red, you good for nothing bastard. I pay you too much if you can bring your kids to this place, for Christ's sake."

Everybody was laughing. "You remember Chuckie don't you Brian?" Red said as he hugged his red-headed son around the neck. "He's my baby boy."

Chuck looked embarrassed but stuck out his hand to Brian. "Doesn't look like a baby to me. Good to see you again, son." Brian said as he shook his hand vigorously.

Introductions were made all around. Chuck Kelly was a senior at UCLA. He had moved back home with Red after Mary died. He looked like a younger version of his Dad, red hair and all. Red just had a few sprigs of red hair left and young Chuck's hairline was already beginning to recede.

"Chuckie did great on his finals, so I'm bringing him out to his favorite restaurant. He loves the lobsters. I do too, but it's too rich for these old veins. Got to keep the ticker pumpin' til I get this one out of college and off the dole," Red said as he banged his chest with his fist.

"What's your major, little Red?" Brian asked Chuck.

"Broadcasting, what else?" Red answered for him.

"Following in the old footsteps, eh kid?" Brian asked.

"I want to do hard news, not sports like Dad. But, yeah, in the footsteps, I guess."

Red looked askance. "What do you mean "not sports"? You're driving that new red Jeep Wrangler off those sports dollars, and you don't seem to mind tooling around in that."

"You know what I mean, Dad."

Red hugged him again. "I love this kid. I tease him cause' I love him so much."

"How's the coed crop this year at UCLA?" Brian asked with a twinkle. "I'm hard up for dates."

"Oh, brother. Not again. He's relentless!" Georgia chuckled.

Red laughed a big belly laugh. "This kid has the girls lined up. They see all that red hair and just melt. Like they did for his old man, right son?"

Chuck blushed. "I wouldn't know, Dad. You seem to be the only one that remembers your exceptional luck with the ladies. All I can vouch for is you scored with Mom six times."

We all howled with laughter at Red's charming kid. The Dom "P" had made us giddy.

"My kind of kid!" Brian chuckled. "Have you worked in a station yet, kid?"

"Not yet. I need to get an internship this summer. Dad won't give me a job at KKLA, though," Chuck said regretfully.

"Why the hell not? We need good talent." Brian boomed.

"Dad says it's against the rules for family to get those jobs so I'll have to beat the streets pretty soon." Chuck answered.

"That's bullshit. Jesus, Red, I'll make an exception for your kid." Brian turned to Red.

"You mean it?"` Chuck asked excitedly.

"I never joke about jobs, kid. They're too hard to come by," Brian said very seriously.

Red looked worried. "I don't know if that's a good idea to make an exception and all, Brian."

"Hell, rules are made to be broken, Red. Especially if I'm doing it. I'm Brian Buchanon. I can do whatever I want in my television station. This kid is in!" He slapped a beaming Chuck on the back.

"I hope I don't get a bunch of grief about it." Red was still worrying.

"Fill out the paperwork on Monday and if anyone gives you grief, say I insisted on it. They can take it up with me. That'll shut them up."

Filled with self-importance, Brian handed the waiter the check with flourish and strode though the restaurant while saying over his shoulder, "See you this summer, kid." Chuck watched our exit with mouth open, eyes wide.

Red put his arm around his son's shoulder and said: "Isn't that Brian Buchanon the best, the fucking best. He always takes care of his people, son, and don't you forget it."

Georgia, Ahmed and I followed behind exchanging knowing glances. You never knew whether to be amused or offended by Brian. His grandiosity defied all rules of appropriate behavior.

We tumbled into our waiting stretch limo and were whisked off to the House of Blues.

The band was in full tilt when we arrived. They were an unkempt looking group of four young bucks called "Daddy Dog". We groped in the dark for a table and ordered drinks. The music was just as Brian had described. Heavy blues rhythm with a rock spin. The lyrics were sexy, and the sound got your body parts moving. The party atmosphere was contagious. It always amazed me how music was the common denominator that connected the many generations that loved rock 'n roll. Whether you are fifteen or fifty, you have to love the Stones. They kicked ass once again with the Voodoo Lounge Tour. The old guard held on and were revered by the younger upstarts like "Daddy Dog".

With the coming of the Rap generation, the feeling was that rock was dead. But the prognosticators were wrong. Rock would live on just as classical music had. It would always have its place in society as long as people loved to dance with no inhibition. Rock, especially R&B based rock, was the music that brought out sexiness. And that night, we were all aroused by it.

Brian asked every sweet young thing he could corner to dance. Ahmed and Georgia hit the dance floor as soon as the drinks arrived. I sat, holding the table down, until a young, dark beauty asked me to dance. We all shook our asses shamelessly. Georgia was a vision on the dance floor and Ahmed looked at her like he wanted to inhale her. His eyes burned into her. I envied him with every fiber of my body.

When we had all worked up a generous sweat, we drifted back to the table. I had just joined Ahmed and Georgia at the table when Brian came to sit down.

"Whew! Where's my drink? I'm too old for this shit. Just don't tell that long, lean blond leaning against the bar. She's next," Brian said.

"How do you keep it up?" Georgia said.

"You should see me in the sack." Brian blundered.

"What the fuck is that supposed to mean?" Ahmed spat, incensed.

"Ahmed, you're not the jealous type, are you?" Brian baited him.

"Georgia is not up for grabs Brian, for you or any of your buddies for that matter!" Ahmed took me into the equation with a sweep of his eyes.

"Ahmed, stop!" Georgia said.

"Yeah, buddy, lighten up. We're here to have a good time. I'm just horsing around." Brian said giving Ahmed's arm a little punch. "I'm harmless, right Paddy?" Brian, again, got me to bail him out.

"Not harmless, hopeless. Trust me Ahmed, don't worry about Georgia, or anyone else with good taste or breeding, falling for Brian," I retorted. Everyone laughed, and the situation was diffused.

Brian was grateful to be taken out of the awkward situation, but I could tell I had offended him by what I had said.

"Come on, Paddy. You owe me a dance." Georgia said as she stood up.

"Sure," I said, getting up and following her to the dance floor.

It was a slow song. A slow, sexy rock ballad I hadn't heard before called "Streetlight". Georgia was stiff and angry. "He makes me so damn mad when he does that," she said through a clenched jaw.

"Brian is a bull in the china closet. He doesn't mean anything." I said.

"Not Brian. Ahmed. Brian is just a typical drunk Irishman making a fool of himself. Ahmed treats me like I'm property. That diminishes me. I can take care of myself in these situations. I hate for him to act possessive in public" she said emphatically.

"I thought you liked him taking care of you?" I repeated his virtues.

"With kindness and care. Not this macho bullshit. I'm a big girl."

"I'll say," I said dreamily.

"Don't you start now." She threatened and then smiled with a suppressed giggle. My teasing her broke her mood, and she relaxed in my arms. She felt good. Soft and warm. Her scent, the sweat mixed with her musky perfume, filled my senses. I wanted to remember how this felt when I had to let her go. Her body fit mine perfectly. I wasn't tall like Ahmed. Our parts were in the right place for each other. The slow, plodding rhythm of the music began to have a soothing effect on both of us. For a few moments we both forgot where we were and were in perfect rhythm, body and soul. When the song suddenly ended, we came apart and felt embarrassed. We ambled back to the table separately, not touching and avoided eye contact for the next few moments. Brian had left the table to chase another skirt, and Ahmed was just leaving the table to go to the rest room.

"Ahmed, would you get me an Evian on the way back. I am so dehydrated," Georgia said as he left the table.

Ahmed was contrite. He was very willing to do anything to get back in her good graces. They had been a couple long enough to have their own silent language. He knew very clearly that she was furious with him. When she had asked me to dance, she sent a clear message that he was in the doghouse.

We both stared at the dance floor. After a few minutes she said. "You're a good dancer."

"Thanks. All those Catholic school dances. Heavily chaperoned, of course. Sort of like tonight."

She looked at me and smiled mischievously, "Let's ditch them."

"You don't mean that." I said.

"No. Maybe not. But it's a delicious thought, isn't it?" She smiled provocatively.

"Yes, I would say delicious is the appropriate adjective."

Ahmed walked up with her water and poured it into a glass.

"Here you go. Still mad at me?"

"Who said I was mad at you? You did your caveman routine in front of the people I work with every day of my life, that's all. What's to be mad about?" She turned bitchy. I was glad not to be in his shoes tonight.

"Come on now, Georgia. Sorry. Really." Ahmed said sincerely. He was such a good guy. And so obviously loved Georgia. I felt guilty even though I'd done nothing.

"I'm tired. Let's go," she said, abruptly.

"Not a minute too soon for me." Ahmed said.

"I'll get Brian so we can take the limo," I said as I headed across the dance floor.

He saw me coming. "Hey, I saw you on the dance floor with Georgia. After a little of that, are we?"

"She asked me." I answered defensively and then wanted to kick myself for being obvious.

"So, I saw. Didn't sit well with old Ahmed." Brian said with hostility.

"Yeah. You're not at the top of his list either."

"Fuck him if he can't take a joke!" Brian spat.

"They're tired and want to go home." I replied.

"Good riddance. Let 'em take the limo and you and I can stay here and party without the happy little couple."

"I'm pretty pooped, too. I think I'll go with them." I said knowing he would put up a fuss.

"Jesus, are you going soft on me?" He looked me over.

"I'm worn out. I won't be any fun," I pleaded.

"Suit yourself." He turned away.

Brian had a short attention span. He'd be over being pissed at me by tomorrow if he even remembered tonight. Georgia, Ahmed and I rode in the limo through Beverly Hills. The red carpets were rolled up at that hour, and the streets were empty.

"Hey, Paddy, sorry, man. I didn't mean to lump you in with Brian. He just pissed me off, that's all. Is Brian always like that?" Ahmed tried to make an apology to me more to appease Georgia than for my benefit.

"You mean a wild-assed, sex crazed, party animal with no regard for anything but himself...Yes!" I answered. Ahmed laughed and Georgia joined in.

"I think he's pretty harmless." Georgia said.

"We have a few like him in baseball. But not so much in management. He is an odd bird for a corporate executive. I'm surprised he survives in that buttoned up world," Ahmed said.

"He's good. You can't argue with success. He's had his hand slapped a few times, but in the end, he performs, and that's all that counts. Not that different from baseball, I'd say." I answered.

"You're exactly right. I can't believe what some of those ballplayers get away with. Ahmed is dedicated, but he has teammates that live on the edge. But as long as they show up and do the job everyone turns a blind eye." Georgia added.

"L.A. is the mecca for the self-absorbed. And here we all are." Ahmed said with a great deal of cynicism.

"I'm just a good old boy from the mid-west. The L.A. scene continues to be a revelation." I said.

"You can't be serious!" Georgia said with raised eyebrows.

I laughed, "You have to stay one step ahead of this one."

"Tell me about it. She knows my shit. Don't you, baby?" Ahmed said

"Yes, I do, and I'm not your baby" she said firmly.

The limo pulled up to some elegant condos in Bel Air.

"Uh oh. Here's my stop." Ahmed gave Georgia a look, "Want to stay here tonight?"

"Not tonight. I have to get up at six tomorrow. I'll call you in the morning," she demurred.

"Paddy, check her apartment for her. I don't want her walking in there alone." Ahmed made intense eye contact with me for affirmation and reassurance.

"Ahmed!" Georgia cautioned sternly.

"This isn't Sacramento, baby. It's dangerous here." He was pleading again.

Georgia looked exasperated. "Stop treating me like a baby, big dad-dy," she said sarcastically. Ahmed deflated again.

"I'll get her locked in tight. Don't worry" I said reassuringly. If she were my lover, I would feel the same way. Ahmed got out.

"Georgia." He started.

She smiled at him and said "I love you, Ahmed" with such purity that he glowed. The limo pulled away with Ahmed standing at the curb like a love-sick dog. I felt sorry for him and envied him at the same time. I understood.

"I love the night...the late night. There's something magical about the stillness," Georgia said as we settled in for the rest of the ride. With that she stood up through the moon roof and let the ocean breezes blow through her hair. I sat, looking up at her, and wondered what made her tick. Something was elusive about her. Ahmed felt it as well, I am sure. That's why he was over-protective, possessive. Georgia was a free spirit. Each time I thought I had a sense of her, she would surprise me. Like tonight.

"Paddy, join me. I have to get the cigarette smoke out of my hair and lungs."

"That bar was thick with smoke, that's for sure."

"It feels so great up here," she smiled down at me.

"Is this the way you conduct yourself every time you ride in a limo, young lady?"

"Just tonight. I needed some fresh air," she said.

She turned and leaned against the side of the opening and looked down at me.

"Happy?" I asked.

"For the moment, yes!" she answered emphatically.

"Me too."

"I wish I could feel this way all the time."

"You're beautiful, you have a great career, a famous boyfriend, what more do you want?"

"You always want what you can't have. I guess I'm just another fucked up female."

"I prefer you a little more complicated, if you want to know the truth."

"Thanks. I find most well-adjusted people such crushing bores."

"Those well-adjusted types are boring, aren't they?" I teased.

"I know. My roommate, my freshman year at Wellesley, was one of those terminally cheery people, from one big happy family, types. It was nauseating. She never had an original thought or interesting observation about anything. Little Mary Sunshine, I used to call her. Her name actually was Mary."

"Did you stay in touch?"

"Hardly!" she said archly. "What about you, Paddy? What's your story?"

"I'm a mid-west farm boy who dreamed of being an actor but ended up as a newsman."

"That sounds like a press release. Now the truth."

"You want my life story while you ride through Santa Monica with your head stuck out of this damn limo."

"Precisely." The limo driver pulled up to Georgia's apartment.

"Here I am. You're saved, for now, Paddy McGurk, but I intend to hear your story."

We got out of the limo and went upstairs to her apartment. It was in the old section of Santa Monica. Santa Monica had been a small beach town at the oceans edge of Los Angeles. Now the beach front was high-rises, hotels and condos. Georgia's place on Eighth Street was a two-story home that had been made into a duplex. It was stucco and wood, and the yard was filled with bougainvillea and cup of gold vines winding over everything. The day of the earthquake I was too panicked to pay attention but tonight I soaked it in. It looked like Georgia. I could understand why Ahmed worried. There was no security anywhere.

She had left the porch light on. We walked up the stairs to the second floor to her porch.

"Well, good night, Paddy," she said as she peered into my soul.

"I better go in and look around," I said.

"Oh, God. You aren't serious, are you? I hope I flushed my pee."

"Yes! I agree with Ahmed. No place is safe these days." I was firm.

"I give up, go ahead." She opened the door but waited for me on the porch. I walked through her apartment feeling a little silly. I even looked inside the closets and the shower. No one was there, of course. She smiled as I came back to the porch. "Happy?"

"Looks safe to me," I saluted and clicked my heels, and then felt foolish.

"Good. Well thanks, really. I'll see you tomorrow, Paddy."

She leaned over and gave me a chaste kiss on the cheek and a big hug, went inside, gave one last smile and a wink and closed the door. I stood on the porch a second, smiling, then slowly walked back to the limo.

6

MARCH 1, 1994

Spring Training. The time of year that all red-blooded American males become kids in the sandlot again. If you believed press releases, all teams were going to win a pennant! The series! Each team was in first place and none admitted weakness.

Brian had the sales force out selling a pennant even though the Dodgers were coming off a shit year. It was spring, and there was no looking back, only forward. Optimism permeated the station. No matter how bad the Dodgers played in '93, we pinned our hopes and dreams on the new crop of ball players.

I doubted the Dodgers would ever again achieve the magic of the old infield with Steve Garvey on first, Davey Lopes on second, Bill Russell at short and Ron Cey on third, but Tommy Lasorda just kept on trying. Why Tommy wouldn't retire and rest on his laurels, I couldn't answer, but he'd lost weight again, felt rejuvenated and looked like a million. You'd have to get a crowbar to get him out of Dodger blue. Tommy Lasorda is an institution. A player's coach. They love him like a father, not just the players, but the fans as well. The outfield crop for 1994 was vastly strengthened by the addition of Ahmed Brooks in center field. Ahmed was the missing link that could put the Dodgers on top again. They desperately needed his big bat in their line-up, plus were depending on Ahmed to control the action in the outfield.

At KKLA, we had to bill fourteen million dollars with our baseball commercial inventory to break even on our Dodgers broadcast contract. Brian had the sales department in super-hype going into spring training. We were taking a bunch of high rolling clients and their ad agencies to Vero Beach, Florida to spend a long weekend watching the Dodgers. The clients wanted to see first-hand what the team had going into the '94 season before they cut loose with the cash for a big sponsorship. These spring training trips were a sales gimmick. The best way to get those big money sponsorships was to let the clients meet and greet the players and coaches in an informal setting. Once they were on a first name basis with the starting lineup, played golf with a few of them, had a few pops with them, the client was putty in our hands.

I played host right along with Brian and our sports director. I was the big-name talent at the station along with my co-anchor, Lani Mead, but Lani didn't come to Spring Training. Thank God! She was afraid she'd break a nail. Lani stayed back at the ranch and held down the late news.

Lani Mead was a card reader. She got into news when women were first breaking into the business, and she became an institution in L.A. Trailblazers have a way of doing that...becoming institutions. Not necessarily because they're good but because they're first. Brian couldn't stand Lani, but the audience loved her. She was so L.A. A real society matron. Betsy Bloomingdale haircut, long red nails, Armani and Chanel suits. She was separated from her fourth husband, a real estate broker, and had no kids. There was no room in Lani's life for kids. Lani needed to be the center of attention. She was not a news hound like I was, but just a talking head. Regardless of her lack of talent, she was what the viewer wanted, and Brian was not foolish enough to get rid of her for personal reasons. All our qualitative showed that old Lani attracted an affluent audience, the audience that would buy a BMW or Mercedes, and that's what you wanted from news. That's where the big ad bucks came from in news. Upscale cars.

Lani resented me big time. I was the first wave of the new order. Losing her longtime sidekick, Joe Jackson, who I replaced, was a blow. It sent her a message that she had an expiration date.

Lani liked it when I went out on an assignment, like spring train-ing, because she got to have the spotlight and anchor desk to herself. I was a threat. If I looked good, it might mean that a younger woman might also. But I wasn't out to do Lani in. What she didn't realize was she was my job security. She made me look good because she was so bad. No one took her seriously in the newsroom. She was, after all these years, still a dilettante. She never wrote her own copy, covered a story, thought of any series ideas. Her main concern was how she *looked* on camera. Many a make-up artist had been released from their duties at KKLA because old sawhorse Lani didn't like her looks on camera.

The rites of spring began with a chartered flight filled with sales types, clients, ad agency execs and station middle management, pro-motion people and talent. We turned the plane into a cocktail par-ty at thirty thousand feet. By the time we touched down in Miami we were all feeling no pain. Brian had glad handed every single client and agency type before we landed. So had I. That's why I was invited. Featured entertainment. It felt cheap somehow. The blatant tackiness of the schmooze, set up strictly to impress, was the T.V. business at its most basic. Television is the instrument of sales. T.V. lives and dies by the sales department. Sales is the lifeblood of television. I never forgot it. Brian never let me. There were a lot of news directors that forgot over the years, and Brian brought them back to reality. Sales ran the station. If it made a lot of money, we did it. It was rare, indeed, when integrity got in the way of a buck.

So here we were in Florida, on a bus filled with booze, motoring to the Boca Raton Hotel and Beach Club. It was away from Dodger Town, but it was definitely more elegant and worth the bus ride. The Boca was a wonder of the world. Every man's fantasy fulfilled. Fantastic golf, tennis, meals, entertainment and grounds with long-legged nymphets lounging by the many pools and beach. The service was impeccable. We were going to have a good time or die trying. We piled out of the bus when we got to the Boca and went to our rooms to change for dinner.

When I checked into my room, I took a shower and got dressed. I decided to give Ahmed a call and see how spring training was going. I liked Ahmed. Being friendly with him assuaged my guilt.

"Hey, Ahmed. It's Paddy. I thought I'd missed you. Practice over?"

"Yea. I just walked in. You guys got here early."

"Yeah, you know Buchanon. He had us at LAX at 6:45 AM."

"Great way to start your trip. I'm sure your clients were thrilled with that itinerary."

"They were four sheets to the wind thirty minutes after take-off. They've forgotten all about it. I sure am looking forward to the game tomorrow. How do you guys look?" I asked, looking for fresh cocktail banter to use tonight with the clients.

"Rusty. Plus, the heat is killing us. Don't get your hopes up." Ahmed said honestly.

"You better win, or Buchanon will have a coronary. He's lied so much about the team to the clients, he believes his own bullshit."

"I don't play ball to facilitate Brian Buchanon's sales effort," was Ahmed's chilly response.

"Yeah, I'm sure you don't." I tried harder.

"How's Georgia?" Ahmed, ever protective.

"Last I saw she was working away at her desk on that story about Johnny Depp's Viper Room."

"Yea, she loves that investigative shit, doesn't she?" He was proud of her.

"That's because she's so damn good at it, Ahmed."

"She is good, isn't she?" He asked earnestly.

"So, you got any free time over the weekend?" I asked. I actually wanted to get to know him better to see why Georgia was so hooked on him.

"Tomorrow's good, if you can get me out of your client party and all the autograph sessions."

"Ahmed, I hate to break this news to ya'... you gotta schmooze those clients for Brian. But we can duck out early and go grab a drink... or in your case a Coke." I teased.

Ahmed laughed. He was loosening up.

"I'll see you at the party tomorrow then. Just get me out as soon as you can. I can only take so much beer breath from the L.A. Ford Dealers," Ahmed laughed at himself.

"I'm with you, man. I'll do my best." I promised. We hung up, and I left for dinner.

Ahmed was so right. I went downstairs to the cocktail reception and was surrounded by clients all wanting to have a ninety second meaningful exchange with me so that they could drop my name like we were close and personal friends. After a few drinks we were herded out to big tents and served a southern barbecue with my favorite Key Lime Pie for dessert. The food was great, and I ate heartily avoiding Brian with every bite. He was at another table but made an effort and turned to shout things at me from time to time. These were the times that he shined most. He could get up and make an impromptu speech and keep them laughing in the aisles. Everyone would leave this trip saying what a great guy Brian Buchanon was. And that impression was useful and valuable. Brian would cash in on all these "friendships" when he was unhappy with a share on a buy the station got or when he needed a personal favor. He was shameless about asking for favors. He got everything at a discount or free. He used his contacts to get first class airline tickets at tourist rates, new cars for used car prices, the best seats in restaurants and have the meal "comped". Everything else that he did that required money he found a way to charge the company for it. It was amazing. It became a creative game for him. It gave him great delight in screwing the company. But he got away with it. So "more power to him" I always said when I heard negative remarks around the station.

After dinner Brian got up and introduced us all and said a few blatant untruths about the upcoming season. Everyone ate it up and cheered loudly. After dinner the promotion people brought out boxes of baseballs and hats for the clients. They gave the players felt tip pens to sign all the balls. A photographer recorded the whole scene for posterity. Another perk for the client. The pictures would be developed by tomorrow night's dinner and the client could get the picture autographed. There was no end in sight to the schmooze.

After drinking myself into a haze, I slipped out and headed for my room and a good night's sleep.

Vero Beach

The next morning, we were all up bright and early for a buffet breakfast and a bus ride to the ballpark. The morning air was crisp and clear, and you could see for miles. Florida was heaven on earth if you hit the weather right. The teams were warming up when we got there. It was a Reds/Dodgers preseason showdown and a party atmosphere prevailed. The athletes strutted their stuff, and the rookies flexed their muscles at every opportunity. All the women "ooo'd an ahhh'd". They argued furiously about who had the best buns on the team. Brian stood up and threatened to moon the women and show them the best buns there. They all dared him to do it and, of course, he dropped his shorts in a hot second. Everyone roared and a photographer took a picture. Brian leapt from the stands, grabbed the camera, ripped out the film, exposed it and stomped it into the sand. The crowd went wild. It was completely out of control, and that's what made it memorable.

We had the best seats in the stadium. The respective crowds were cheering for their team. I spotted Ahmed right away. He looked strange in a blue and white Dodgers uniform, but he still looked good. I'm sure all his jockstrap testosterone was a turn-on for Georgia. I felt slightly ill for a second watching him during the game. Oblivious to my discomfort, the show went on and the Reds won with many boos from our contingency. Brian got up and said loudly, "Stop making a liar out of me, you bums!" and got a big laugh. After many hot dogs, popcorn, peanuts and beers, we stumbled back on the bus and headed back to the Boca.

The sun and booze made me drowsy. I headed for my room as soon as we hit the hotel. I lay down and fell fast asleep. The phone woke me with a start.

"Hi! How's the good life?" I heard Georgia on the other end.

"Georgia! I must have fallen asleep," I said, as I wiped the sleep from my eyes.

"Sounds like it. You're slurring your words, Mister. Maybe it's all the wine, women and song."

"Could be. What's up?" I asked.

"Ahmed called me and he mentioned you were going out for a drink tonight."

"Yeah, if we can break away from the groupies!" I teased.

"Very funny! I'd love to have a groupie."

"You've got me and Ahmed. Isn't that enough?" I flirted, recklessly.

"Are you my groupie, Paddy?" Georgia retorted neatly.

"What do you think?" I gave right back to her.

She was silent for a long second. "Paddy, please do me a favor?"

"What's that?"

"Ahmed is all whipped up over something Greg Mead told us at dinner the other night. If he brings it up, please reassure him for me."

"You're speaking in code. What exactly did Greg say."

"Well, you know Greg. He gets a few drinks in him and if it's good for a few laughs out it comes! The other night, before Ahmed left for Vero Beach, we all went out for dinner and Greg started going on and on about what an operator Brian is and how rumor has it that he uses the women at the station like one-stop sex shopping."

"What?" Not real bright on Greg's part. Loose lips sink ships.

"He said that for years Brian had put a lot of pressure on young and attractive interns and secretaries to go out with him. Corporate got wind of it about six months ago, a few months before I started, and put a stop to it. Greg said Brian has a terrible reputation for his blatant womanizing. Is that true?"

"In essence, yes, I guess it is. But the interns and secretaries wanted to go out with Brian. One of them got disgruntled when her career didn't take off like a rocket, after giving Brian a little nookie, and decided to make a stink. Of course, all the women's libbers jumped on it and had a field day. But it wasn't that big a deal. Corporate gave Brian a hard time, that's all. Greg Mead should have kept his mouth shut."

"Jesus, you men are thick as thieves. Just listen to you defend him. I heard it was more than one incident and much more serious than that." She was indignant about the situation.

"Alright. He's a cad. Happy now? So, what's this got to do with Ahmed?" I didn't want to talk about this with Georgia.

"Greg Mead thought the whole story of Brian's womanizing was hilarious but, of course, Ahmed went ballistic. He said he never trusted Brian in the first place. Now he has validation for his instincts. I'm sure he'll grill you for details."

"Oh! So that's what's going on. When I mentioned Brian's name to Ahmed yesterday, I wondered why there was a distinct animosity."

"He's obsessed with the notion Brian is going to try to hit on me." Georgia said genuinely concerned about Ahmed's overreaction.

"Georgia, Brian's too smart for that. He wouldn't risk pissing off Greg Mead at the Dodgers."

"Convince Ahmed. I don't want him interfering with my career. We are doing battle on this one."

"Georgia, I don't belong in the middle of this." I really didn't.

"Please, Paddy. Ahmed won't listen to me. I need your help."

"I'll do my best." I could never turn her down.

We chatted for a few more minutes about work. Evidently, Lani was behaving badly. She loved to play the star bitch around the newsroom, especially with Brian and me not there to cramp her style, and Georgia couldn't tolerate it. So, after catching up on the latest gossip, we said good-bye.

When we hung up, I thought about the irony of my reassuring Ahmed that Brian won't hit on Georgia. Ahmed should be watching me. I was still unsure why I had not made a move on Georgia myself. It was not like me to have this kind of self-control.

Ahmed met me in the lobby of the Boca, and we headed for the dreaded dinner and video presentation. I felt uncomfortable having conspired secretly with Georgia only moments before. I was already doing things behind his back. One further step over the line, and it would seal my fate.

"Hey, big night on the town," Ahmed said in greeting.

"You only have to do your duty for one evening. I have to put up with this shit three days straight," I reminded him.

Brian blasted up behind us, "Ahmed, you good for nothing bastard. You whiffed on all three ups today. What gives?"

Ahmed replied with a chill, "Would you like to try out for my spot on the roster?"

Brian put his arm around Ahmed's shoulders, "Just giving you a hard time, Ahmed. Man, these clients are eating this up, aren't they Paddy?"

"It's not too hard to have a good time with the setup here." I gestured around me.

"We've got 'em by the balls now. Ahmed, you guys have to win tomorrow before we head back to L.A. and we will clinch a lot of deals on the plane ride back. What do you say? Can you do it?"

"We'll do our best," Ahmed replied with an edge. Brian was so pumped up he didn't take note of Ahmed's sour attitude. Brian sped off as fast as he came. He was headed for the big white tents on the sprawling lawns of the Boca to do more schmoozing. Ahmed stopped just short of the door that led out to the tents.

"How do you tolerate that man?" Ahmed asked, full of venom.

"I ignore the bad and focus on the good. We've been friends for a long time because of it." I answered honestly.

"Better you than me. Let's grab a drink before we get sucked into the angry horde," he pleaded.

"Sounds good to me." And it did.

We made a sharp right turn and headed for the bar. Ahmed ordered a beer and took a long swig.

"Thirsty?"

"No, not really. I need to anesthetize myself for these kinds of things," he said with a grimace.

"Yeah, I feel ya'."

"I feel ya'?" he repeated with a smile.

"I'm trying out some street slang I heard on the radio the other day." I was trying to be cool with some ethnic slang.

Ahmed laughed, "You're pretty cool without that jive, Paddy."

"Thanks."

"Georgia certainly speaks of you with reverence, Paddy. She says you help her more than anyone else in the newsroom." He said this like he was testing me, sizing me up.

"That's surprising. Georgia is the one that's gifted. I'm benefiting from her talent. It's in my best interest to help her any way I can." I tried to cover my guilt by justifying my attentions to Georgia.

"Well, you definitely have a mutual admiration going. That's one of the reasons I wanted us to get together. Frankly, I'm worried about Georgia."

"Why?" I responded innocently.

"In a word...Brian."

"Brian Buchanon?" I acted surprised.

"He's an unscrupulous character, according to Greg Mead, and a few others I've talked to recently. I don't trust him. He's a womanizing pig. I don't want him trying anything with Georgia," Ahmed said earnestly.

"You have nothing to worry about, Ahmed."

"How can you say that when he has the reputation of a snake?" Ahmed wasn't buying it.

"First, and most importantly, Georgia is not interested and second, Brian's not stupid, Ahmed. His relationship with the Dodgers organization is too important. He is, first and foremost, a good businessman. Georgia is off limits for him."

"I'd like to believe you, but I don't trust that prick with Georgia at all."

"It's difficult for me to be in this conversation, Ahmed, because Brian is my best friend," I answered honestly.

"You two are so different. It's hard for me to fathom," Ahmed said sincerely.

"We're not as different as you think. We both chase women, love to party, are confirmed bachelors and live for our careers. We have a lot in common."

"Well, let me put it this way. You haven't left a trail of bitter and battered women in your wake. The buzz on Buchanon is fairly sordid," he said with obvious distaste.

"Ahmed, you've been listening to Greg Mead too much. Greg has room to talk. He has a tendency to blow things out of proportion for a few laughs. I'm not saying Brian's innocent, though. He's definitely gotten his hands slapped by the company from time to time. Brian has a tendency to throw caution to the wind. His ass has been in a crack on more than one occasion, but he really isn't all that bad."

"If he ever hassles Georgia, he'll regret he ever knew me," Ahmed said through clenched teeth.

"I don't think you have anything to worry about." I reassured him again.

"I better not. She's all I've got in the world that means anything to me except for baseball."

"What about your family?" I grabbed at the chance to change the subject.

"They're gone."

"Gone?"

"My mother passed away last year, and my father was killed in the Sudan five years ago."

"The Sudan?"

"My father was a general in the Sudanese army," he revealed.

"I'd never heard that."

"My mother met him when he was a student at New York University. They met on the subway. They fell in love. Unfortunately, shortly after meeting, my father graduated and went back to the Sudan. He was going to send for my mother, but his family objected. They had a wife picked for him there. I was the result of their brief union."

"Did your mother ever marry?"

"No, she carried a torch for my father till the day she died. And he for her, I believe." Ahmed said a little sadly.

"Did she ever see him again?" It was a great story and I genuinely wanted to know more.

"Yes, many times. After I grew up and got into baseball, he would come to America in the summers to see me play. They would sit together at the games and hold hands. It was a bittersweet love from beginning to end."

"So, you knew him growing up?" I was fascinated.

"Not really until I was twelve. I resented him something fierce for leaving us in America. My mother had to work like a slave for the rich people on Park Avenue while we lived in the South Bronx," he said this with a trace of bitterness.

"How did you finally meet him?"

"My mother insisted. She wanted me to see how different, how proud a race, the black man was from the Sudan. So, when I was old enough to travel that long distance, my father sent for me to come visit him in the summers, one month every year."

"That must have been a culture shock!"

"Here I was, this kid who grew up in a cramped two room apartment with my mother and played stick ball and basketball on the street. I go to a lush paradise where my father and his wife and kids live in luxury in a big, beautiful white house with servants, animals and land. He worked hard to help me through my resentment for all that I didn't get, that they had. But it was the pride of my father, and the other black men that were his friends, that made me believe that I, too, could have these things. And, of course, now I do. My mother knew exactly what she was doing. It was a gift, you see, to see the other side. The desire to achieve burned in my belly from then on."

"A smart woman." I said.

"Yes. I miss her every day," he said with a great deal of emotion.

We paid our check and moved to the party which was in full force when we arrived. Ahmed leaned over to me as we entered the tent and said softly, "Can you believe I have to demean myself with this shit?" And with that he strode into his sea of fans. Ahmed played his role to a tee. He posed for pictures, shook hands, slapped backs, and signed balls, gloves, pictures and tee shirts. He never stopped smiling. No one could tell that he hated being there. He was the consummate gentleman, an all-around good guy. I was impressed by Ahmed. It was definitely the main reason I hadn't gone after Georgia. He trusted me. I didn't want to betray him as much as I wanted her. I was in the emotional tug of war of my life.

Georgia was my fantasy woman. She was who, and what, I wanted. Every time we were together, I was pulled to her with every fiber in my being. But it was Ahmed that held me back. I could never give her as much, I wasn't as good a being, as kind or thoughtful. But the longing remained; it was an ache in my gut that was killing me.

The next day was filled with too much sun, too much booze, and too much frivolity. After the game, which the Dodgers lost, we all headed home on a late afternoon flight. I sat next to Brian and he was not a happy camper.

"I can't believe we lost again. Jesus, I'm charging an arm and a leg for those damn Dodger packages and they play like a bunch of Little Leaguers," Brian moaned in his beer.

"No one pays any attention to the preseason. Don't worry about it."

"What do you know? The sports writers are having a field day with the Dodgers lousy pre-season. Your 'best buddy', Ahmed, isn't living up to his advance billing either," he said with hostility.

"What's that supposed to mean?" I asked.

"You two are thick as thieves. I saw you hanging out together all weekend."

He said this like the accusation of a jealous lover.

"We had a couple of pops together, that's all. Why make a big deal out of it?" I could never reason with him when he got a hair up his ass.

"He hangs with you and treats me like I've cut loose with some bad gas." He sensed Ahmed's distaste for him.

"So, you're not his cup of tea. What do you care?"

"I don't. It frosts me that I gave his piece of ass a job at my television station, that's all."

"Georgia is worth her weight in gold. He did us the favor if you ask me." I hated him for a second for attacking Georgia's worth just to take a shot at Ahmed.

"I'm not asking you. I'm telling you that I don't like Ahmed Brooks. I didn't like him the minute I saw him with a white woman. Who does he think he is? He's got that God given, jungle sports ability, that's all. So, he has to have the requisite white woman to go with it?"

"You're crude!" He was baiting me, but I couldn't stop myself from falling into his trap.

"I speak for all us *white* boys. I don't like to see a beautiful, blond woman on the arm of some spook. I don't care how much money he makes."

"You are a sick bigot. Georgia is not with Ahmed for the money," I said heatedly.

"Maybe she's into his big black weapon!" he said with a snort.

"Your dick runs your life, Brian. Georgia and Ahmed are not anything like you." I was furious with him and couldn't stop myself.

"Getting a little hot under the collar, are we?" he said sarcastically.

"You're an asshole!" I took off my seatbelt and stalked down the aisle. He laughed as I stormed off.

Brian loved to test our friendship. This wasn't the first time. He knew he had the upper hand. I hated him for using it. I sat in the back of the plane talking to the stewardesses. I couldn't go back up front. I was fuming inside at him for his pettiness toward Ahmed and Georgia. Usually, when he behaved badly, I would humor him and go along. It was only on rare occasions that we were at odds with each other. But every time it happened, he would act like it was all a big joke. And that's exactly what happened this time. I was coming out of the lavatory at the back of the plane and there he was. He put his arm around my neck and said, "I really got you going that time, eh, buddy?"

"You piss me off," I said. I wasn't going to let him patronize me this time.

"You know what they say...better to be pissed off, than pissed on. You've gone soft on me, Paddy. Georgia's got you so hot and bothered you've even teamed up with her black dugout boy. What about me? I'm the one that signs your paychecks. Or have you forgotten?"

"That's just fucking great. You're pulling rank on me. You'll do anything to win, won't you?" I didn't realize at the time how prophetic my words were. I stomped back to my seat, while Brian goosed the stewardesses in the rear of the plane. I closed my eyes and went into a deep, troubled sleep. When we landed at LAX, Brian woke me up.

"Too much party time, eh?" he asked, convivially.

"I guess so," I answered groggily.

"Go home and get your beauty rest. We need to win back the ratings I'm sure we lost with the old battle-ax, Lani, holding down the anchor desk." He chuckled, and I chuckled too.

This was his way of making up with me. Taking a shot at Lani. He knew I couldn't stand her. It made us conspirators again.

7

THE MOMENT OF TRUTH

The baseball season was in full swing, our newsroom was humming, and all was right with the world. In spite of the lackluster performance of the Dodgers at spring training, Brian convinced himself that we were going to have a fantastic May rating book. It was late April. Brian spent his days and nights planning a big advertising campaign on radio for the May book that would blitz the L.A. market and bring our competitors to their knees.

I was happy because Lani was gone for a week on vacation to Aspen for some spring skiing. I couldn't, for the life of me, imagine her skiing, but the glitz and showbiz crowd drew her there year after year.

Georgia was engrossed in a follow up story on the L.A. and San Francisco earthquakes. It looked like L.A. was far better at recovery than San Francisco and that made for a good local story. L.A. had its share of bad press and disillusionment, but the quake brought us all together and the rebuilding gave us a sense of purpose again.

A few days before the May book started our news director, Herb, came storming out of his office.

"Shit, shit, shit. Goddamn it to hell. That dumb broad!" Herb shouted.

"Jesus, Herb, what's the problem?" I looked up from my desk and asked.

"Lani. She had a skiing accident. She can't ski for shit, and yet she insists on going. Now I'm fucked."

"Is it serious?" I feigned with concern.

"She is in excruciating pain. She severed her ACL and shredded her medial collateral. She will be in rehab for a year but first she has to have a goddamn operation."

"You're kidding! What about the news? What about the May book?" I was serious about the book. You need everything in its proper place during a ratings survey. As big of a pain as Lani was, it would be a catastrophe for her to be out during a "sweeps" month.

"We're fucked! She won't be back for at least three weeks. Brian's going to have a hemorrhage!" Herb was beyond hysterical at this point, running around in circles rubbing his bald spot.

"No shit! You better go tell him." Brian was not going to be a happy camper about this little piece of news.

Predictably, Brian was in a rage. He blamed anyone who came in his path, but mostly he blamed Lani for being irresponsible right before the May sweeps. He stormed around the building like General Patton. Two days before the sweeps began Brian called me and asked me to run out for a quick lunch with him. I gladly accepted. We went to Tommy Tangs and I ordered sushi and he ordered Tempura. He was tearing into his fried shrimp, talking with his mouth full, about his predicament and calling Lani every name in the book when I said, "Why don't you give Georgia a shot?"

"No way. You're just looking for a quick ticket into those crotchless panties."

"Brian, that's bullshit. I want a big score in the ratings as much as you do. She'd get big ratings. Every man in town will be watching."

"That's for damn sure. Do you think she can do it?" He looked like a lightbulb had come on in his head.

"Jesus Christ! We stake our lives on that bimbo Lani every night of the week. Georgia can only be an improvement."

"You've got a point." We both chuckled. "Besides, I'll take credit for using her. It'll give me leverage to get in that fine ass since you are too goddamn loyal to your butt buddy, Ahmed, to do it."

He pissed me off, but I bit my tongue for Georgia's sake. I wanted her to get this opportunity.

Brian announced that Georgia would replace Lani on the 10 O'clock News during the May sweeps. The announcement caused an uproar with the other female reporters, as well as, the other female anchors of the morning and noon newscasts. But Brian had spoken, and he didn't give a damn what anyone thought about it.

Georgia was terrified. She had not asked for the chance and felt unprepared, but grateful for the opportunity.

"So, it looks like it's up to you and me, Kid!" I teased her. She looked embarrassed.

"Thanks, that's comforting. I'm nervous enough, thank you very much."

"Brian wouldn't have named you if he didn't think you could pull it off." I tried to reassure her.

"Did you have something to do with it, the decision, I mean."

"Nope. It was Brian's idea. He thinks you'll be great." I denied any part in the decision because I didn't want Georgia telling Ahmed that I engineered this break for her. It would make him suspicious of me. He was obsessive enough already about Georgia.

"I hope I don't disappoint him. I've never anchored before."

"Don't worry, it's a cakewalk. We'll be fine." I wasn't worried a bit. It was my dream come true.

The newsroom was abuzz with gossip about Georgia's new-found status. There was speculation that she was sleeping with Brian, and that's why she leap-frogged ahead of the rest of the fray. Jealousy was running rampant apparently.

This was typical female behavior and I tried to ignore it. Whenever a beautiful woman gets a break, all of the less attractive women go on the attack, but girls will be girls. We guys recognized it for what it was and had more than one chuckle at the expense of our female peers.

Brian, of course, claimed my idea as his own and sighted this maneuver as another stroke of his broadcast brilliance. He boasted that KKLA would have the anchors with the most sex appeal. He said our anchor desk would have star appeal. That didn't go over with the hardened news types, but he never worried about what they thought anyway. He wanted big ratings, and he would get them one way or another.

I have to admit, when I'm feeling melancholy and put the tapes from those few glorious weeks on my VCR, I look at the newscasts and feel incredibly proud of Georgia. We did look pretty awesome sitting side by side at the anchor desk. She with her platinum hair, green eyes and porcelain skin and me with my coal black hair and dark eyes. We looked good together.

One night, Georgia was late for make-up. She came in looking pretty worn out. I was already done, and on my way out of the green room. She gave me a quick wave and ducked into the ladies' room before I could say anything. She arrived on the set a little late, as well. The floor director rushed to get her lit correctly and check her sound. We were all rushing, and I didn't take time to ask her what was going on. When the newscast started, she seemed a little off. As things progressed, she stumbled over a few words and lost her train of thought. When we broke for a commercial, I reached under the anchor desk and gave her hand a little squeeze.

"You O.K?" I asked.

She started to reply, when Brian came bursting on the set.

"Georgia, don't you know how to read?" he boomed through clenched teeth.

She blushed deep red, "I'm sorry. It won't happen again."

"Make sure it doesn't. Pretty girls who can't read are a dime a dozen in this town. Don't fuck up again, or you'll be joining them in the unemployment line." Brian threatened as he turned on his heels and left.

She was devastated. But before she could take a breath the cameras started rolling again and we were back live. Luckily there was a five-minute piece on about Hispanic health problems in the barrios of East L.A. Georgia looked at me and couldn't speak.

"You'll make it through. Just take your time and focus. Whatever else is going on behind those eyes, will wait till later." I wanted so badly to comfort her.

She smiled weakly. She was visibly shaken. But she made it through till the bitter end.

Georgia and I had a new pattern of going out for drinks after the news each night so I could critique her. That was her idea. She always wanted me to help her get better and felt we should go over her work right after she got off the air while it was still fresh in our minds. This night was to be no exception.

After she took a sip of her grapefruit juice and vodka I asked, "Feeling better?"

"Much. I sure blew it, didn't I?" She was so humiliated, and it showed right through her.

"You did seem preoccupied tonight." I answered honestly.

"Was it that obvious?"

"Is something wrong?" I probed.

"Nothing and everything. Brian was right to get after me, though. I should leave my problems at home. He gave me a shot, and I disappointed him. But what he said really hurt." She teared up.

"Brian's delivery leaves a lot to be desired. What's bothering you so much that it comes into the newsroom with you?" I continued to help her open up.

"It's Ahmed."

"What the problem?"

"He's miserable. I think that's what's really going on. But what he says is he's lonely because he never sees *me* anymore."

"He's on his way to setting a new record in RBI's for a regular season and he's got the most beautiful girl in L.A. in his bed. What's to be miserable about?"

She smiled at me, "Your flattery will get you everywhere. Seriously, Paddy, Ahmed feels that a baseball strike is imminent. The players are pissed because the owners want to impose a salary cap. If the strike happens, Ahmed is screwed. He was only going to play for two more seasons. This will ruin his plans. Plus, he's having an amazing season. It's just not fair. And then I get this new assignment and I'm busy all the time. I'm not complaining, believe me. It's the chance of a lifetime, but I haven't seen Ahmed for more than a couple of hours in two weeks. I just don't have time for him right now, and he takes it very personally. But I'm not going to give up this opportunity just to nursemaid Ahmed's feelings. When he's on a road trip I'm supposed to sit tight. Now the worm has turned. Maybe when Lani comes back things will get better between us."

"I'm sorry things aren't going well on the home front. I heard they may strike in late July or August. If they strike, the going will get rougher." I hated seeing her like this, but this little bit of inside information gave me hope that all was not well between Ahmed and Georgia. Ahmed should kiss the ground in thanks every day for Georgia, but Ahmed wanted it *all*. He could lose her if he held on too tight. I would be happy to be there to pick up the pieces. I felt guilty but glad.

"No kidding. Am I wrong to resent it? My career is important too. I want to enjoy this moment and not have to be all down because of Ahmed's problems. Sometimes I get so damn tired of baseball. But when I feel that way, I end up being a bitch and that gets me nowhere."

"Sounds like you need another drink." I signaled for the cocktail waitress.

I started telling Georgia funny stories and the latest jokes making the rounds. I wanted to cheer her up. She began to laugh at my ridiculous humor and forgot for a moment her troubles with Ahmed. I felt like we were on a date. I watched her lips as she talked and fantasized about kissing them. I became erect under the table. I wanted to lick the inside of her mouth. I wanted to lick the inside of her. I ordered more drinks. We began to really have a good time. She was more than a little high and became giddy.

"It's so nice and warm out tonight. Let's go for a drive." I recklessly suggested. She offered no resistance.

We paid the check and jumped in my BMW. I put the top down and we drove up to Mulholland Drive and looked out over the San Fernando Valley. The lights of the Valley were shimmering below us. The air was clear and crisp. By the time we parked, Georgia's hair was blown in twenty directions. She pulled down the car mirror and tried to pull it together.

"Here, let me help." I took some strands and untangled them to the sides of her face.

"Thanks...I love it up here on top of the world." She looked radiant.

"It's the only peaceful spot left in L.A." I said, breathing in the clean spring air.

"Thanks for bringing me." She opened the door of the car and got out and walked to the edge of the cliff. I got out and followed her.

"I wish I knew what would make me happy." She said that like a wish, and to no one in particular.

"I know what would make me happy." I was getting ready to step over that line and couldn't stop.

She turned and looked me full in the face. "You do? What would make you happy, Paddy?"

She sincerely wanted to know, and I had to answer truthfully.

"You. You would make me happy." Now I had revealed too much.

She smiled and then looked at me for a long moment. She took a step toward me, then was in my arms. Our first kiss was long and thirsty. I couldn't get enough of her mouth, her lips, her tongue. I wanted to let that kiss go on forever. Her body was mashed against me. I felt my groin ache as we moved against each other. I was starved with my longing for her. I backed her up against the hood of my car. The hood was warm and held her hot body up to me. I pulled up her blouse and squeezed her nipples and filled my mouth with her breasts. She moaned as I sucked her like a baby. As I sucked her breasts, I reached my hand under her skirt and pulled it up above her hips.

My fingers pushed aside the crotch of her panties and found her throbbing warmth and while I probed her, she came. She pulled at my pants and belt. I helped her undo my zipper. She took my hot cock in her hand and hungrily shoved it inside her. We rocked together against the hood of the car until she came again. Then I came with such a force of need that I felt as if my heart would stop. Afterwards, I sucked her lips and caressed her face until we both caught our breath. I wanted her again immediately.

"Get in the car." I said roughly.

"Where are we going?"

"To my place."

She didn't argue. We drove in silence. When we reached the bottom of Mulholland, she lay her head in my lap. In moments, my pants were unzipped, and she had me in her mouth. I was in exquisite agony trying to drive while feeling her mouth and tongue torturing me, teasing me. I came hard again. I was out of control. All that I had fantasized was happening. It was more than I could comprehend, more than I could handle. I was intoxicated with feeling. Georgia began to doze from too much alcohol, as I made my way through the surface streets of West L.A. to my apartment in the Palisades. I tried to think of what to do. I thought about how to handle this new and very scary situation. But all I did was come back to my insatiable need to have Georgia in my arms. All other considerations became meaningless.

When we pulled into my garage, I gently woke her, and we went up the elevator to my condo. When we got inside, I led her to my bedroom. I wanted to make love to her again. But this time I wanted to see all of her, to undress her and lay her on my bed. I stood over her and looked at her body. She glowed like the finest pearl. The skin of her body was luminous like the skin on her face. It took all my control to slow down. She was squirming beneath me with passion. Her hips were thrusting and driving me wild, but I held back and let her orgasm for a long time and then I pulled out. I put my cock between her breasts. As I pushed back and forth thrusting into her breasts she licked and sucked the tip of me. I was wild with urge. I dropped back down and put myself back into her and we came violently together. We were exhausted and wet with sweat and sex. We didn't speak and fell asleep in a tangle of sheets.

A bright spring sun woke us early the next morning. I had forgotten to close the curtains in my frenzy. Georgia looked like a little girl as she woke up, all pink and fuzzy. I loved her. There was no turning back. I kissed her awake and made love to her again. Afterwards she got in the shower and I ran out to the market and bought a carton of eggs, orange juice, milk, coffee, and English muffins. I was making her breakfast when she came into the kitchen in my baby blue bathrobe. Her hair was still wet and curly around her face. I stopped myself from taking her again. She leaned against the door to the kitchen.

"Hungry?" I asked cheerily.

"Is this how you entertain all the girls the morning after?" She looked at me with genuine inquisitiveness.

"No, just this one," I reassured her. I was happy.

"I bet. I drank too much last night," she said as I looked at her longingly.

"Not me!" I was still being cheery.

"You didn't use any protection. I hope you're clean."

"I don't have AIDS, if that's what you're driving at. Come here." I said hoarsely.

She walked towards me, and I tugged the belt of the robe and it fell open. My hand went inside, and I caressed her breasts while I made breakfast with my other hand.

When I scooped the eggs on a plate, I pulled her over to the dining room table and made her sit down and eat. I stood behind her and let my hands pinch her nipples and touch her parts while she ate. Then I sat down and wolfed my breakfast. I didn't realize how hungry I was.

"I shouldn't be here." Georgia said as I finished my coffee.

"What?" I hadn't expected her remorse.

"What about Ahmed?"

"He doesn't have to know, not now anyway."

"He trusts me and you."

"I know."

"I feel guilty, Paddy. I love Ahmed, and now we've both betrayed him." She was getting upset.

"Georgia, we haven't done anything wrong. You aren't married and neither am I. We are free to do what we want. Ahmed doesn't need to know."

"I'm confused. I need time to think."

I felt sick. "What do you mean confused? What just happened between us?"

"I need time to sort out my feelings," she said genuinely distraught.

"I'm in love with you, Georgia." I was pleading, scared.

She looked at me sadly for a long moment and said, "You better take me back to my car so I can go home and get ready for work."

I was enraged, "That's it! You want to go get ready for work, just like that. Georgia, we made love like we were connected. I thought last night was the beginning of something incredible."

"We both drank too much and ended up in bed together, Paddy. Let's not make it into a mystical experience."

"Well it felt goddamn mystical to me."

"I'm not denying I enjoyed you sexually, maybe more than anyone I've ever been with, but that doesn't mean we are meant to be partners. There's more to it than that."

I was really steamed now. "More to it...like that big multimillion-dollar contract of Ahmed's?" I said nastily. I regretted it the minute I said it. I knew that it wasn't about the money, but I wanted to hurt her.

She got up from the table and threw down her napkin. She stormed out of the dining room and went into the bedroom. I went in the living room to cool down and turned on the stereo, put on some soft jazz, while I was thinking.

She was right. I was being an ass. I would have a hard time facing Ahmed myself. Even with him not knowing. Georgia must be suffering. I went into the bedroom and she was almost dressed.

"I'm sorry. I'm an ass." I was trying.

"I've called a cab," she said.

"Why?"

"I want to go home."

"I was going to take you as soon as I took a shower."

"I'm going now. I'll see you at the station, Paddy."

"You're mad at me?" I said, stating the obvious.

"Yes. I'm mad that you think so little of me. That you think I make my life decisions based on money. And I'm mad at myself. I could easily fall in love with you, Paddy. Maybe I already do love you. But I love Ahmed too. I've betrayed him. It feels shitty. Please understand that." She walked out of the room and I heard the front door close softly.

I sat down on the bed and began to howl like a trapped animal. This one I couldn't win. There was no solution, no way out. I lay back on my pillow and stared at the ceiling. I pulled her pillow over to my nose and smelled her. I wanted Georgia with every bit of my being, but I felt this sick feeling of loss. All morning I stayed in my underwear and my blue robe she had tossed on the bed. It was sort of like playing hooky from school on a cold rainy day. I wanted to stay under the covers and hide. But, ironically, at noon, Brian called, like he had a sixth sense, and asked who I was shacking up with that kept me from getting to work on time. He said there was a big story breaking at city hall and to pull my dick out and get moving. There was no further chance to feel sorry for myself that day, or in the days that followed.

The next few weeks were a blur of activity. The May sweeps kept everyone moving at full tilt. Georgia and I didn't go out after the newscasts. She went straight home and left me wondering if I had imagined that we had been lovers after all. I wanted to leave the next move up to her. I knew if I rushed her, she would bolt on me. And the truth was I didn't know how to deal with the whole thing either. It happened and there was no turning back but how to move forward was not clear. We exchanged a lot of looks those few weeks but were strictly hands off.

When I look back on it now, I wish I'd just grabbed her and run out of the building and headed for a remote island. We were in a situation far more precarious than either of us knew at the time.

Lani came back to work with a vengeance, on crutches, the first week in June. She was in a foul mood and looked like hell, but she wasn't going to let Georgia have her spot on the 10 O'clock News one minute longer. Sitting in her sick bed, watching Georgia upstage her, had humiliated Lani. There would be hell to pay. All her saccharine sweetness was gone. She was operating like an army drill sergeant. We all cleared a wide berth around her. Georgia was especially sensitive to Lani and left the newsroom for home as soon as Lani showed up the first week that Lani was back. But that wasn't good enough for Lani. She started a hate campaign directed at Georgia and enlisted all the old-timers who had been around since she was hired.

It was the old guard against the squatters. It became an infantile attempt of Lani's to smokescreen her inadequacies as a news anchor. But, for a while, it worked like a charm because there are always the types who love to hate management in any big organization and KKLA was no exception. Lani made a big stink that Brian hadn't used one of the more senior reporters or anchors from our other newscasts to replace her. She tried to turn the talent against management. She left me out of it because she knew better.

About two weeks after Lani got back, she discovered her very expensive mobile work phone, some cash, and make-up missing from her desk. She made a big deal out of it and said someone was trying to sabotage her. Taking her make-up truly was sabotage. She looked scary without it. Security came and checked the area. Red Kelly sent out a memo offering a reward to the person that gave any information leading to the discovery of who was pilfering Lani's desk. I thought that was the end of it. Then a few more things disappeared. Someone made off with a Beta tape machine worth $9,000.00. The shit hit the fan. Memos came from Brian saying when the thief was caught, they would be fired immediately, without notice, and prosecuted to the full extent of the law.

Georgia came over to me holding the memo and said, "Some things of mine were taken too."

"Like what?" I asked, happy to have her talk to me. She had avoided me like the plague since our encounter. But to make myself feel better I reminded myself that Ahmed had also been at home the last two weeks. He was going on the road in two days.

"What was taken?" The thief was getting to be a little too brazen.

"A few pictures of me and Ahmed. And my Sony hand-held recording machine."

"You're kidding! Who would take something personal like that?"

"A fan. They could sell the pictures to a tabloid."

"Yeah, I guess. I miss seeing you, Georgia," I ventured.

"Not here, Paddy."

"Where, then?" I said, looking at her like a lovesick dog.

"I'll call you at home in a few days. I promise." She smiled secretively at me and turned and went back to her cubicle.

It was early June and Red Kelley's son Chuck started as my summer intern. He was great. Always upbeat and worked like a dog. His enthusiasm was infectious. He helped me remember why I got into news in the first place. His energy revved me up, and I began to focus on my job again instead of my gloom over the situation with Georgia.

Summer was almost here and every day at noon, Chuck and I would go out to the parking lot and shoot hoops at an old, rusty basketball net hanging near the motor pool. We'd both get sweaty and work our asses off. He was an all-around better athlete than I was, and a hell of a lot younger, but I had a hook shot that drove him crazy. One day, he caught me off guard and asked about Georgia.

"So, what's with you and that hot piece, Georgia?" he asked with twinkle in his eyes.

"What do you mean?" I asked defensively.

"You know what I mean. Every time you look at her you do the twenty-one- gun salute with your power drill."

"Get out of here," I laughed.

"You fuck her?" He got right to the point.

"She's engaged to Ahmed Brooks."

"That doesn't answer my question." This kid wouldn't give up.

"If I ever did fuck her, you'd be the last person I'd tell."

He laughed heartily. "If you fucked her, you'd be shouting hallelujah! So, you're still at the wet dream stage aren't you, white boy?" He teased.

"What got you going on Georgia Conroy?" I was intrigued by him and his chutzpah.

"She likes me. I can tell. And before the summer's over, I'm gonna fuck her, Ahmed or no Ahmed."

"What makes you so sure?" I asked, amused.

"Goddesses like her get their kicks breaking in the young bucks like me. I'll just act all virginal and golly, gee whiz and those crotchless panties will drop."

"Think so, huh?" He was so cocky.

"I told you, she wants me. I'll make my move in a few weeks."

"Keep me posted." I chuckled.

"Yeah, so you can go home at night and pound your hog thinking about it, right, old man." He laughed mischievously as he grabbed the ball from me and swished a beautiful shot.

That night I went home exhausted. I wasn't sleeping well. I needed the relief of sex, but my group of regulars just didn't appeal to me anymore. I sat down with a beer and thought about Georgia for the millionth time. Maybe the kid was right. I'm an old man, and she already has a younger man with lots of money. How can I ask her to give all that up for me? After my third beer and an hour of feeling sorry for myself, the phone rang.

"Need company?" Georgia said with a smidge of humor.

"Where are you?" My heart jumped.

"At home."

"I'll be there in fifteen minutes."

"No. I'll come to your place. Bye." She said as she hung up.

I was elated. My hormones started to pump. All my senses were alive and working overtime. Each of the fifteen minutes seemed like an hour. I paced. I brushed my teeth. Then I took a fast shower as an afterthought. I put my blue robe on. My lucky robe. The one I hadn't washed since Georgia was with me the last time. My dick stood erect no matter what I did or thought about to calm it down. I was like a fifteen-year-old kid. I felt ridiculous, glorious.

When she knocked softly on my front door, I bolted towards it. But just before I yanked it open, I stopped myself. I realized she might be coming over to talk, to end what had barely begun. That thought sent a shock through me. I took a deep breath and opened the door. She stood there under the light looking like an angel. She had on a long, white silk dressing gown. I could see the outline of her breasts and hips through the fabric. She was barefoot. Her hair was wild and curly. With the glow of the backlight it looked like a halo surrounded her head. I was speechless for a second.

"Can I come in?" she said with a tiny smile.

"Sure." I took her hand and led her in the door.

"Are you surprised to see me?" she asked.

"Yes and no. I thought I would hear from you when Ahmed left town. But I didn't know it would be like this. I've been afraid that you would tell me that what happened between us was a mistake."

"It was. But I need to be with you. Whatever it costs me in the long run." She said with a touch of sadness.

I couldn't wait any longer. I kissed her and her body became fluid with mine. My hunger took over. I undid the front of my robe and sat back on the couch. I pulled her down on top of me. My hands went under her gown and pulled it up to her waist. She straddled my body as I entered her slowly. As she moved with me, I pinched her breasts through the thin silk and kissed her. I was in ecstasy. I came quickly and so did she. But we didn't stop. My erection never left me entirely. We continued to sway together until I was hard again. The second time lasted much longer. I pulled out, took her gown off and turned her over. I entered her from the rear. I wanted to claim every part of her. This was not my usual style in bed, but Georgia brought out a possessiveness in me that made me want to own her, dominate her. I shocked even myself. She yelped slightly as I thrust into her, but I couldn't stop myself. I had to have all of her.

When we were finished, she turned and looked at me.

"That was a little rough," she said as a statement without judgment.

"You liked it, didn't you?"

"Yes," she said in a whisper.

8

JUNE 14, 1994

June 14th was the day the world stopped. The white Ford Bronco carrying O.J. Simpson and Al Cowlings cruised the freeways of L.A. in the melodrama of the century. Never before in the history of television has one man's tragic fall been so trivialized by proselytizing anchors and reporters. A seminal moment in news. Looking back at this time in our collective history, I realize this sad story became the door opening to the sensationalized news that we have today. The dignity of my heroes, Chet Huntley and David Brinkley, has been eradicated from today's tabloid journalism. O.J.'s saga made the Olympics look like child's play. I couldn't believe it. It made me ashamed to be in news. It made me ashamed to be a part of the whole spectacle. It defied good taste and responsible journalism. While the drama unfolded around us, we scrambled to keep up with it. It was a ratings bonanza. Brian took full advantage of it and integrity be damned.

But there was another drama unfolding inside the newsroom of epic proportions for those concerned. On June 12th, a number of pieces of small, but expensive recording equipment and more mobile phones were found missing from the newsroom. All personnel that were not working in news were barred from the newsroom unless they got a written pass from their manager. Brian was not going to tolerate one more piece of equipment walking out of the building. We felt like an armed camp and everyone became tense and testy as a result. The O.J. spectacle keeping us working overtime, combined with this latest internal scandal, had created a seething bedlam.

Georgia was working late on the O.J. story. I passed her in the alcove leading to the restrooms. She looked haggard.

"Are you alright?" I asked.

"I'm not sleeping well. Ahmed is hovering over me like a vulture."

"Do you think he suspects?"

"I think he can tell that I'm upset, but I'm blaming it on work. I don't know how much longer I can hold up. This is tearing me apart," she answered with her voice breaking.

I took her by the neck, shoved her against the wall and pulled her face up to mine. I took her hands and pushed them against the wall and pinned her. I kissed her lips roughly. She fought me and tried to pull away. She was afraid of being seen. But I needed to have my body parts next to hers. We had never been physically close before in the newsroom. It felt dangerous, hot, exciting. I hadn't seen her for a few days and wanted her desperately.

"When is he leaving again?" I growled in her ear.

"Tomorrow night after the game," she answered, breathless.

I put my fingers in her mouth and she sucked them. I was rock hard when she pulled away. She had brightened a little. She gave me a quick naughty look and ducked into the ladies' room. I went in the men's room to calm down. We had been playing a waiting game. Ahmed was going through a lot with the looming baseball strike.

Georgia wanted to protect him from any distractions during the season. She was extremely loyal to Ahmed. I still was not sure which way she would turn in the end. But I was captive and would wait an eternity to find out. I wanted to push her along, but I knew better. Also, I felt like a bastard for going after Ahmed's woman. Sure, I justified it to myself, but deep down I felt lousy about it. I just couldn't stop myself.

Georgia and I got together whenever we could over the next few weeks while Ahmed was on the road. Georgia was frustrated. Ahmed was becoming more and more suspicious and she was beginning to freak. He didn't suspect me at all. He was focused on Brian. For that I was grateful, but he was making Georgia's life miserable and that kept my time with her fragile. I felt like I was stepping on eggshells. Ahmed was in a terrible funk because his baseball season, and his career aspirations, looked like they were going to be a big bust. He was very depressed. He began to lean even more on Georgia because that was all he had left to control. She was ready to bolt from both of us. It was my worst nightmare. I did everything I could to hold her together, but the stakes kept going up.

After the O.J. story got slightly less immediate, towards the end of June, I was sitting at my desk reading the *L.A. Times* looking for a new angle or spark for his story. It had been hashed and rehashed. I was already sick of it and the circus was only beginning. My phone rang. It was Brian.

"Where have you been hiding?" he asked with accusation.

"What do you mean?" I asked, knowing what he meant. I had not gone out for a drink with him in over six weeks. That was completely unheard of in our relationship.

"I haven't seen your ass in weeks except on the fucking 10 O'clock news. You got a new piece to hammer on every night or what?"

I laughed to cover my fear. "I wish that was my excuse. I've been so damn busy covering this O.J. thing that I'm too beat to party." That was, in fact, a partial truth.

"Yeah. I bet. Come up here to my office. I need to talk to you about a little detail disturbing my days and nights."

"Be right up, boss." I said as casually as I could. A chill ran through me. I had nothing to worry about. No one knew about me and Georgia, but I felt guilty all the same. I had to protect her, at all costs. When I got to Brian's office my worst fears were realized.

"Sit down!" Brian ordered.

He walked over and closed the door.

"Paddy, we've been friends for a long time," he continued.

"Since you had hair." I tried to joke.

"Yeah. Well, I've got a problem. More serious than my hair loss. Ahmed Brooks thinks I'm fucking his girlfriend."

I tried to laugh but it came out like a nervous squeak. "So, he thinks everybody's trying to fuck her." I tried to cajole.

"There's a difference. He doesn't think I'm trying. He thinks I *am*. He said he calls her when he's on the road, a couple of hours after he already has talked to her, to see if she is still at home in the middle of the night, and she never is. He thinks she's with me. Do you know where she might be at 2AM in the morning when Ahmed's on the road?"

"Maybe she turns her phone off to get some sleep. Sounds like there's no sleeping with ol' Ahmed doing bed check all night." I said trying to make light of Ahmed's obsessive behavior.

"That's not all. He talked to one of the neighbors and they said she leaves every night at midnight. Where do you think she's going?" Brian's eyes bored into mine.

"Why are you asking me? Maybe she's Cinderella. How the hell should I know?"

"You'd tell me if you were fucking her, wouldn't you, Paddy?" His eyes were still on me. I tried not to squirm in my seat like a kid caught cheating on a midterm.

"Brian, they are a normal couple with a little jealous crap going on. Look at fucking O.J. This is kid's stuff. Ahmed gets horny on the road and decides to cook up something to worry about. You know the guy. He's obsessed with Georgia. I don't blame him. She's a beautiful woman and if she were mine, I'd be worried to. Georgia is my friend. This is not the first time I've heard about Ahmed's paranoia. This is his shtick with her. We should stay out of it." I hoped I'd covered my increasing panic with this line of reasoning.

"Yeah. You're probably right. I need to get him off my back." Brian looked relieved.

"Christ, tell him the truth. Georgia's too old for you. You're a goddamn pedophile!"

"Good idea!" he chortled. His mood shifted.

He laughed, and I laughed. The tension was broken for the moment.

"Let's go get a drink. I'm sick of worrying about keeping Ahmed Brooks happy." Brian said as he grabbed his jacket.

I chose not to tell Georgia about my encounter with Brian. I knew I should, but she would get paranoid, and curtail her time with me. I didn't realize then what a selfish and dangerous breach of trust that was. We both needed to know that the stakes were getting higher. But, my lust for her made me keep it to myself. I needed every second I could get with her. She was skittish enough.

A few days later, I was amusing myself watching Chuck coming on to Georgia. She was working on a project for the 10 O'clock News. Chuck was leaning over the side of her cubicle hanging on her every word.

"I have extra time on my hands today. Why don't I help you put that together?" He offered.

"Great. If Paddy doesn't need you, I sure could use some help. Try to get in touch with every one of O.J.'s old football buddies and set up a time for me to interview them over the phone." She said to the salivating Chuck.

"Why would they give us an interview? I bet all the networks are trying to talk to them," Chuck reasoned accurately.

"You're right! I know...Tell them Ahmed Brook's girlfriend wants to talk to them. That'll do it," Georgia said triumphantly.

Chuck was impressed, and I was amused. Georgia was a true newshound and would use whatever trick she could to get the story. Lani Green looked over her cubicle and scowled at Georgia.

"How disgusting! I can't believe you'd get your story invoking your lovers name. That's unprofessional," Lani said with a sneer.

"Go back to buffing your nails, Lani. I've got work to do," Georgia snapped.

"Your days are numbered here, Georgia. As soon as your lover boy dumps you, so will Brian Buchanon. So, don't get uppity with me" Lani shot back as she sat down. Lani hated Georgia, and the feeling was becoming mutual. Georgia had a low tolerance for bullshit. She was all business in the newsroom, and Lani was the antithesis. She came to work to gossip and get attention. Georgia got up and went to the ladies room. I could tell she was upset.

When Georgia left her seat, Chuck went inside her cubicle, picked up her chair, and took a long, noisy sniff all over the seat of her chair. Then he imitated a dog and chattered his teeth together like he'd smelled something extremely stimulating. The women in the newsroom went nuts and started screaming and throwing pens and wadded up paper at him.

Chuck came over and whispered in my ear. "Very tasty! Don't you just love those cat fights. It gets my pecker all hard. See, I told you Georgia wants me. Now we're working on this project together. Next we'll be going out to dinner and next..." Chuck giggled with sinister delight. "I told you. I am going to fuck her. She wants my young, fresh meat. Eat your heart out, asshole. I'll call you and give you a blow by blow," he chortled as he skipped away.

Thank God for Chuck. No matter how tense my summer was, he kept me laughing. That youthful enthusiasm, anything is possible attitude, was hard to resist. I even liked it that he had the hots for Georgia. I liked watching his pursuit. It amused me and reminded me of when my life was less complicated. All I used to care about was my next meal, next lay and next paycheck. Being in love made life too painful.

Lani came over to my desk. She looked at me with a smirk. "You sure are chummy with little miss got rocks over there. She has her nerve talking to me that way."

Lani and all the women in the newsroom that were her allies were furious that Georgia had gotten a diamond necklace from Ahmed for her birthday. They constantly made nasty remarks about her "rocks".

"Lani, your claws are showing," I said with a sneer.

"You're seduced by her looks just like that moonstruck kid of Red's. I got where I am through hard work. I never had the luxury of a black sugar daddy to pave the way for me."

"That was a low blow, Lani, even for you. Georgia is one of the best producers and reporters in the newsroom, Lani, and you know it. You are still sore that she took your place on the news. That's what this Georgia bashing around here is all about. I, for one, am sick of it." I turned back to my work for emphasis. But she wasn't through.

"Her days are numbered."

"You think so?"

"I know so."

"What makes you so sure?" I asked, trying not to act too involved, no matter how she answered.

"Just mark my words. Her days are numbered. You can take that to the bank." She turned on her heel and marched back to her desk triumphantly.

What a bitch. I felt really sorry that Georgia was surrounded by such petty, spiteful women in this newsroom. I wondered what Lani meant about Georgia's days being numbered. Probably some insane fantasy cooked up in her demented brain. Not much else is happening up there. Georgia ignored them all. She was too busy using her brain to give Lani's drivel her energy.

I knew that I would see Georgia tonight. I lived for those moments that we were together. When I left the newsroom after the late newscast, she was still working away. As I passed her desk on the way out, I stopped.

"All work and no play, as they say..." I ventured.

"I want to finish this up. I'll leave in a few minutes. I promise."

Her flaxen hair brushed the desk as she worked with single-minded concentration. I took my hand and cupped her face and whispered "Hurry." She smiled at me and went back to her work.

As I was exiting the building, Brian came rushing down the hallway headed to the newsroom.

"Hey, boss. Where are you going?" I called out.

"Maybe I should be asking you that question. I'm sure you're the one with the big evening planned," he said venomously.

"What?" I asked, shocked, but he turned and kept moving.

He was getting stranger by the day. My encounters with him were more and more unpredictable.

When I got to my car, Chuck was pulling in.

"What are you doing here at this late hour?" I asked.

"I came back to help Georgia. I had a date, but I blew her off early because I felt guilty. So here I am back at work. This shit is addictive. Well I guess I'll go in and get frisked?" Chuck said glibly.

"Frisked?"

"Just making a joke. Those missing recorders and phones have my dad whipped into a frenzy. But he told me they have a foolproof way of catching the thief. I asked him if they were going to frisk everybody because if they were, I'd like to volunteer to frisk Georgia, but he won't tell me what they are doing," Chuck said matter of fact.

"I hope they get them, whatever they have up their sleeve. I'm sick of all the tension. It takes the fun out of coming to work."

"Not for me. As long as I get to sniff Georgia's chair every time she goes to the ladies room, I'll be happy. She keeps me going, or is it coming?" he laughed his sinister laugh.

"Go earn your keep." I said as I jumped in my car.

It was another clear summer night in L.A. All the stars were out, and the winds had blown the smog inland earlier in the day. As I went through the neighborhoods my thoughts were jumbled. I wanted to think only of Georgia and what I would do with her tonight. But something kept pulling me away from that and back to the way Brian was behaving. He had a real hard on for me tonight. I could feel it. He must suspect something, but I know I've covered my tracks. What was he so angry about when he saw me? He acted like I was his enemy or worse. His distaste for me was right out there for me to see. I wanted to confront him, but I was afraid to get him going. I was afraid of what he might know. I knew he didn't have facts, but he had a sixth sense. I felt vulnerable. Brian was ruthless. If he found out that I was lying to him he would bury me. He expected complete loyalty from me. And he deserved it. Throughout our relationship he had it.

But, this was different. I couldn't come clean with him because of Georgia. I had to protect her at all costs, even if I lost my relationship with Brian. Georgia was the first woman I had ever loved, really loved. I had cared for other women from my past and when I was young, I'd had the usual puppy loves. But this was the real thing and it was killing me on every level. A lot of the time I didn't like or know myself. I was a mess and there was no end in sight. I felt afraid for Georgia and for me. Fear was never a part of my vocabulary before. I hated it and me for feeling it.

I stopped at an all-night market and bought some chilled Rodney Strong Chardonnay, grapes, apples, and a big, ripe slab of Brie. I snagged the last sesame ring, my favorite bread, from the Pioneer bakery on Main Street in Santa Monica. I picked out some Greek olives to round out our midnight snack and drove the rest of the way home.

When I got in the apartment my message machine light was blinking. The first message was from Georgia.

"Paddy, something's happened. I'm afraid to come over. Call me at home in about thirty minutes. It's eleven forty-five now."

The next message was from Brian.

"Hope you're having a good time tonight, big guy." He slammed the phone down.

I froze. What the hell happened? I looked at my watch. It was twelve ten. It was early to call Georgia, but I tried anyway. My hands were shaking as I dialed her number. She picked up on the third ring. She was breathless.

"What the hell is going on?" I shouted into the phone.

She started to cry. When she started to speak her voice broke and she cried harder.

"Georgia," I started again more softly, "What happened after I left tonight?"

She heaved a few more times and blew her nose. "I'm scared, Paddy. Brian came down to the newsroom just seconds after you left."

"I know. I saw him in the hall on the way out."

"He made a beeline for my desk. As soon as he got there he asked if I had plans for tonight. I answered honestly, that yes, I did. He asked with who. I said a friend. Why? I thought maybe he wanted me to stay and work on something. He said just checking. I said checking what. He laughed and said Ahmed wanted to know... and had I told Ahmed that I was going out tonight. I said I didn't have to tell Ahmed my every move and asked what business it was of his anyway. Then he leaned down and put his face into mine and said if you're screwing around with one of the employees here and your boyfriend Ahmed thinks it's me then it might as well be me. Why don't you change your plans for tonight and meet me in the parking lot in fifteen minutes? Then he turned and stormed out." When she finished, she let out a long sigh.

"Jesus!" That's all I could muster.

"I know!"

"What did you do?" My heart was pounding.

"I grabbed my coat and keys and ran for the door. Chuck came running after me to see what was wrong, and I'm afraid I told him too much because I was hysterical."

"You told him about us?" I felt nauseous.

"No. Do you think I'm crazy? I told him what Brian said. He said he'd cover for me when Brian came looking for me...I love that kid. He was so protective. He said his dad had told him that Brian was a big womanizer and not to take it seriously, but he doesn't know the whole story. He doesn't know about us. Brian acts like he knows something, Paddy."

"I think he's guessing," I said this fearing I was wrong.

"He's acting awfully aggressive if it's just a hunch. I think he knows something. Do you think he's followed me?"

"Georgia, you're getting paranoid. Brian trusts his instincts and risks everything on a hunch. That's his style. That's his M.O. If he acts like he knows something you're more likely to break down. You have to come back at him. You shouldn't have run away scared. You should have told him to go to hell. You are acting guilty." I was frustrated.

"Thanks for the support, asshole. I am guilty. Guilty as hell, and so are you. Easy for you to say stand up to him. He terrifies me." She wailed into the phone.

"You're right. I'm sorry. He acted strange when he saw me, too. He even called here and said to have a good time tonight. Here, listen." I played his message to Georgia through the phone.

"Oh, God!" She was afraid.

"Jesus Christ. Maybe he does know something. I just don't know how he could know for sure." I couldn't trust my feelings on this at all.

"What are we going to do?"

"Act as if nothing is happening. When you go in tomorrow, if he says anything about tonight, act like you thought it was a big joke. You left when you finished work and went home. Act like he couldn't have been serious. My guess is he won't even confront you. He'll be too embarrassed after he thinks about it."

"I hope you're right. I can't take much more."

"I want to see you."

"Are you out of your mind?" she snapped, incredulous.

"Georgia, all we've got is each other. We need to be together. I want to hold you. Come over here. It will make us both feel better."

She let out a long breath filled with anxiety. "You're right. Let me call Ahmed and I'll be over in about thirty minutes."

When I hung up the phone, I poured myself a Stoli. I needed to calm down. My heart was racing. I almost never drank hard liquor at home, but this was one time it was a necessity. My hands were shaking as I held the glass. What was happening? I needed to keep my wits about me and figure it all out.

I was sure there was a logical explanation. For the life of me I didn't know what it was. It was clear that Brian was very agitated. He knew, or at least suspected, something. My mind raced over the possibilities.

Maybe someone had seen us and told him. But we'd been so careful. We never went out in public. We only met at my apartment. Never at Georgia's, with her nosy neighbors. Georgia lived in Santa Monica, which was a retirement community of sorts. Those people had too much time on their hands and had active imaginations. My neighbors were too busy earning a buck, trying to keep up with the Jones's, to stay up till midnight spying on me. I'm sure none of my neighbors had seen anything. It was lights out at about ten for this neighborhood, but what kept nagging at me was Brian and how he zeroed in on us tonight. Something about the timing...

There was a soft knock on the door. I opened it and Georgia walked in. Her eyes were swollen almost shut from crying and lack of sleep. I'd never seen her look worse, but she was still the most beautiful creature on earth to me. I took her in my arms and led her to the couch. She laid down and put her head in my lap. She was in a long, pink bathrobe and a white nightgown. She smelled of soap. Her hair was still damp from shampooing and there wasn't a drop of make-up on her face. She looked like a child to me tonight. I stroked her head and she fell fast asleep. We didn't exchange a word. I think her brain shut off out of self-preservation. She couldn't handle one more moment of stress.

All my life I'd been a good ol' boy. Now I didn't qualify. I'd broken the unwritten code. The good ol' boys club code of honor was threatened. I'd stolen another man's girl. The girl everyone wanted. Now the good ol' boys were after me. My behavior would not be tolerated. I understood that mentality. But how did they find out? My mind worked over all the details that I knew. Then it began to play tricks on me, paranoid tricks. I fantasized that Brian and Ahmed had hired detectives. But that didn't wash because Ahmed suspected Brian. At least that's what Brian said. Maybe they were in it together to trap us and Brian was just saying that to throw us off guard. No. That was too farfetched. They didn't even like each other. They had both made that clear back when neither of them treated me strangely. There was a missing link and I didn't know what it was. Georgia stirred. I got up to pour another drink and put a pillow under her head and she went back into a deep sleep. I had to find out what was going on.

After I finished my drink, it was almost 2 AM. I needed to get some sleep if I wanted to stay ahead of them. I lifted Georgia up and carried her to the bedroom. She barely woke before going back to sleep. I got undressed and took a long shower. I was tired to the bone from all the stress, and my body was tense. My muscles ached like I'd been in a fight. After I dried off, I slipped between the sheets as quietly as possible and lay looking at the light from the streetlamp outside my window. It was going to be a long night.

I tossed restlessly for six hours, waking every hour or so and looked at the clock. At 8AM I gave up. I got up and put on my robe. The house was quiet. My mind kept going over the facts as I knew them. Brian knew something, but what and how I didn't know. It was driving me crazy. Georgia got up and wandered into the living room.

"Have a nice rest, sleeping beauty?" I smiled and tried to be cheerful.

"I'm sorry. I couldn't stay awake. I didn't realize how tired I was. The stress! It's killing me!" She answered.

I put my arms around her. We held each other for a moment. "What do you think is happening? Do you think he knows, Brian, I mean?" Georgia asked.

"I've spent the entire night trying to answer that question and I still don't know for sure. I don't know how he could, but he sure is a great actor if he's bluffing. Never underestimate Brian Buchanon. I've learned that the hard way."

"I hate him." She was getting emotional again and that was dangerous. You make mistakes when you get emotional.

"He's not my favorite right now either, but I've betrayed his friendship and loyalty, so I'm not a saint either."

"That's bullshit. He's not your friend, Paddy. He *uses* you. Don't you see? You're a toy for him. A playmate. What is between you and me, is none of his goddamn business. You don't owe him an explanation. He's just convinced you that you do," she answered vehemently.

"We need a plan." I got back at the task at hand. My relationship with Brian was a topic for later discussion.

"No kidding. We should have had one a long time ago. It's my fault that all this is happening. I shouldn't have gotten involved with you until I broke up with Ahmed. None of this would have happened if I'd had integrity in my relationship. But that's spilt milk. Maybe I should find another job."

"No. You've worked your ass off. Why should you walk away from your investment? I'll go." I was being chivalrous, if not practical.

"Well let's just take out an ad in the *L.A. Times* that we're having an affair and save you the trouble! You are a high-profile person in this town, Paddy. You can't quit without a lot of attention being given to why. I'm new, and work way down the food chain. I'm the one that should leave. Ahmed would be relieved. I could tell him I didn't like working for Brian. He'd love hearing that."

"Let's not get hasty. We're panicking. If either of us makes a move, we will confirm their suspicions. Maybe Brian really doesn't know anything and is just guessing. You don't blow up your entire career because your boss is having an acid flash. We need to keep our cool and not overreact."

"So, what do we do?" Georgia finally relented.

"Let's just go in and play it cool," I said with more conviction than I felt.

"I don't feel very cool," she said as she went to get dressed and leave for work.

When we went into the station later that morning, we avoided each other like the plague. Lucky for both of us, Brian wasn't in. The receptionist told me he had been in early and left for the airport at about nine. I was so relieved to have time to regroup, I felt joyous. During the day I kept busy, but occasionally I would get an anxiety attack. When I looked over at Georgia, she had her head down and looked completely engrossed in her work, but I knew she was avoiding any contact with me or anyone else. We both were in hostile territory. We both had our nerves rubbed raw from the last few days. Even contact with each other required too much energy. I hated myself for putting Georgia in this position. She blamed herself, but the truth was I had created our relationship. I had willed it to be from the first time I laid eyes on her. It wasn't always a conscious effort on my part, but it was always in my subconscious. I was like a beacon pumping out that needy energy. I needed her to breathe life into me. Until we began, I never had felt love, vulnerable love. And now I know why, love is not fun. Once love enters your life, the chance to feel pain and to suffer loss, begins.

The days wore on. In a way, things began to return to normal. We were all so busy with O.J., and his latest drama, that the newsroom was humming at a high pitch. Brian was gone for the entire week. While he was gone, Ahmed came back to town from the road. Georgia returned to her familiar routine with Ahmed. We both were lulled into a false sense of security. I called her a few times at her desk and at home, but I kept it to a minimum. She was uncomfortable talking to me. It hurt, but I understood. She was in a whirlwind and was trying to stay under control.

It was good to take a step back and not blow this thing way out of proportion. What could Brian know for sure. Nothing. As each day passed, I became more convinced that it was all a bluff. Ahmed got Brian going. Brian became suspicious. Brian concocted a plan to smoke us out. It was vintage Buchanon. As long as we kept our cool, he would not have the ammunition he was looking for. The worst thing to do would be to act any differently than before. We needed to lay low and wait it out. Brian had a very short attention span.

Chuck and I were out playing basketball in the parking lot before lunch. We had worked up a good sweat and stopped to take a drink of water from our bottles. "What's the matter with Georgia lately?" He asked.

"Nothing that I know of." I lied.

"She sure seems uptight. She's no fun anymore. I'm bummed."

"Maybe it's all the intrigue because of the stealing going on. That has everyone on edge." I lied.

"Yeah, no shit. I hope they catch the thief soon. My dad says they're close now. Maybe when all that settles down, I can start my pussy campaign again. The vibe isn't right with Georgia so uptight. I need to make my move when she's in a better mood."

"Still holding out hope, eh?" I loved this kid.

"I told you I'll score on that. But I need the choice moment to make my move." He tried out more bravura.

"Have you found out the station's strategy to catch the thief?" I asked.

"My dad and Fred fixed up something that Mr. Buchanon said would do the trick. But I'm not sure what they've got up their sleeve. It's all very hush hush. You know Fred. He thinks he's 007. He and Dad get together and have these big pow wows," he said as he gestured like he was jerking off.

We both laughed. Chuck continued "You know how Fred is. He's such a nerd. He and my dad love all this cops and robbers stuff. Fred has been chief engineer since my dad started in sports. They've been buds for years, and this gives them a chance to work together. Big do-ings in river city, if you get my drift."

Fred Frank was a nerd. Chuck was right. He was the best at what he did, though. Anything electronic in the station ran without a hitch. We had the best engineering staff in L.A. Fred and Red were long time buddies whose wives had been best friends as well. The stealing at the station fell under both their jurisdictions. Red was over personnel and Fred was over engineering. They both would look bad if they didn't crack the case soon.

"Maybe they really are putting up metal detection devices in the doorways to see what people take out of here." I ventured.

"I don't think so. Whatever they are doing is already done and we'd have noticed that."

"What do you think they are doing?" I asked.

"I'm not sure. I'll try to find out if you really want to know. Fred's such a "goober" and gets so excited talking to my dad that I'm sure I could listen in and he'd never notice."

"Great. See what you can find out. Now you've got me curious," I said casually with my heart pounding.

Brian came back on Friday. I was knee deep into Nicole Simpson's family. We were uncovering a lot about Nicole's big sis who was a recovering alcoholic. There was speculation that O.J. was the cash machine for the whole family, and they kept quiet about what O.J. dished out to Nicole. If true, it would be no wonder the guy had a lot of anger. It sure would send a message to America that the almighty dollar is worth more than your own child or sister. But when I looked down my nose at the elements of the case, I saw a reflection of myself. I was the manipulator in the quadrangle I'd created. No one had created this but me. I was putting the one and only woman I ever loved in great jeopardy because of my own selfishness. Was I any better than

O.J. or Nicole's family? Probably not. I was a selfish and dishonest bastard with no integrity or regard for my friends. My self-loathing was growing. The O.J. drama made me look at my motivations on a daily basis. O.J. wanted to control his world. How was I any different? I was tormented but there was no stopping me. I had to have Georgia at all costs. I wanted her to tell Ahmed, so we could move on in our lives. We could go to New York and start over. I could get a great job there and so could she. We could be far away from all of the prying eyes. We'd be a tabloid item for a while, but we'd survive.

I made a resolve to go to New York and start sniffing around for a job. I could keep it quiet if I talked to only my friends. Once I scored, I could move, and Georgia could come with me. A new start. That's what we needed. If I could make that happen soon, we would be safe. I made mental plans to take a vacation in two weeks.

First, I had to go to the All-Star game with Georgia. Being with them for a weekend would be like going through a mine field for me. Georgia insisted that I had to go because Ahmed had invited me and trusted me, but I was afraid to be around them together. It would be too painful. But I was going to do it for Georgia, and for Ahmed. She wanted to maintain this charade as long as she could to protect Ahmed's season. I should have never become his friend. Georgia said this was the price I had to pay for getting too close to Ahmed when I had the hots for her. She was right, of course. It would destroy his season if he found out about us. It would be all over for him. I resented having to go. I was Ahmed's rival, but I felt guilty. So, I was going to play along.

Georgia's "friend". Ahmed's big buddy. What a fucking worm I'd become.

9

JULY 12, 1994

THE ALL STAR GAME

Brian was giving me the cold shoulder. Georgia was afraid to be with me. My life was turning to shit. The All-Star Game was tomorrow at Camden Yards in Baltimore and I was obligated to go with Georgia. I was feeling very sorry for myself, like the victim in a Fellini movie.

Due to my commitment to Ahmed, I'd go to the game. Fans can get out of hand, and Ahmed wanted Georgia protected. I understood my role. At the time he asked me, it seemed like a reasonable request and fun besides. I had enthusiastically accepted his invitation. If I tried to get out of it now, he would be suspicious. Georgia didn't want me there. She knew I had to go, but she made me feel like it was my fault that I was going. Her big argument was that had I never become good friends with Ahmed in the first place, she wouldn't be put in this duplicitous situation. And she was right.

The bottom line was that my whole world was turning upside down and I was powerless to stop it. I was being swept along with the tide.

I was beginning to doubt that Georgia and I would ever be together. Up until now, I had felt that somehow, someway, things would work out for us. You know, the whole true love prevails. That fantasy, but Georgia was less responsive to me lately. She was less comfortable with me, more on guard, since the whole incident with Brian.

As I got packed to go to the airport, I had a sense of foreboding. My imagination was working overtime. How could I spend 48 hours with Georgia and Ahmed and not slip up? Was I insane? I thought of every possible excuse I could give Ahmed, but none rang true. I was doomed. I was going to the guillotine and I knew it. Somehow it seemed a fitting end for a guy who'd betrayed his boss, his friend and, in all honesty, the woman he loved. Georgia was my victim too. I had withheld critical information from her. Plus, I made my calculated move on her when she was at her most vulnerable. I knew I was going to pay dearly for my sins.

When I boarded the plane, Georgia was already in her seat. I was late. She looked up at me and stared.

"Hey! Thought I'd chickened out, didn't you?" I started, lightheartedly.

"I knew you'd be here. Responsible Catholic Boy. Live up to your commitments at all costs. Right?" She was being a bitch. I was not in for a peaceful flight.

"Georgia. Stop."

"Stop what?" She was being a coy bitch now.

"Stop taking your frustration out on me. We're in this together, remember. I love you. We can make it through two days. It's no big deal," I lied.

"Excuse me? Are we not starring in the same movie? I thought we were the couple that was fucking around behind Ahmed Brooks' back and now were going to go watch him play in the All-Star Game and make like it never happened!" She said caustically.

"Jesus, Georgia. You don't have to announce it to the whole plane."
I looked around me to make sure no one we knew was in earshot.

"I can't stand this any longer." She spat out.

"I know." I sat down next to her and gave her a short kiss. She
didn't return it at all. It was like kissing a statue.

"Paddy, is sex all you can think about?"

"I gave you a kiss, I didn't rape you, for Christ's sake. Lighten up!"
I snapped.

That did it. She picked up her book and buried her nose in it and
ignored me. A part of me wanted to keep at her but then we would
land, and Ahmed might pick up the tension, so I let it drop.

I sat looking at my magazine and seeing nothing. I spent the time
fantasizing. Why couldn't I have walked into Norm's one morning and
bumped into Georgia buying a bagel? We could have struck up a conversation and taken it from there. Why did I have to meet her at work?
Why was there an Ahmed to contend with? Why couldn't I have what
I wanted without all this garbage in the way? Why?

When I look back on it all, it was on that flight, that I faced reality.
I knew, then, I would never have Georgia. The price was too high. Even
if we made it through all the hurdles, we would be so trashed, would
have hurt and betrayed so many people, the joy would be lost from our
union. But even though I knew those things intellectually, I kept the
wheels in motion for longer than I should have. I couldn't bring myself
to walk away. I wanted so badly for things to be different. I wanted a
miracle. Some of the things you want most in the world you are not
destined to have. Maybe there's a reason. But I still can't see what that
reason was. Georgia and I belonged together, and we would be together
today if fate had been kinder. But it wasn't. Fate was going to be cruel.
Relentless and cruel.

About mid-flight I decided to try to talk to Georgia again.

"I'm sorry this is happening. This isn't easy for me either, you know," I said sincerely.

She softened. "We just have to go through with it. That's all. We have no choice. I'm so stressed. Forgive me?" She looked like an angel.

"Kiss me, and I will," I teased.

She leaned over and gave me a soft, long, tender kiss. It made me feel so sad. I never would have her. I knew it deep inside me. I wanted to weep. We held hands the rest of the way there. I rode with a lump in my throat and a pain in my belly. I was dying. I wanted to die. Only then would my pain go away.

When we landed Ahmed was waiting at the gate. Everyone was watching Ahmed. When he spotted Georgia, he loped over and grabbed her up into a big hug. He held her a long minute. It was painful for me to watch them together. He loved her. She was safe with him. I was the outsider. The interloper.

Then he reached around and shook my hand vigorously.

"Hey, Paddy! Great to see you again, man!" He said, enthused.

"Yeah! Wouldn't have missed this for anything. Thanks for the great tickets." I hated myself.

"How was the flight? You guys hungry?" Ahmed asked before we could answer.

"I'm starved," Georgia said.

"Yeah, me too. I hate airplane gruel." I tried to be funny.

"Great. I made reservations at a super place that's right on the way to the hotel. Is this all your luggage?" he asked.

"Yeah. Let's get out of here." I said. The gawking crowd was getting to me. I wasn't in a tolerant mood.

We all headed out of the airport and into the privacy of the waiting limo. We were whisked to dinner, and then we all went to the hotel to get a good night's sleep before the big game. We made idle chit chat the entire evening about work and gossiped about the baseball strike. Ahmed was in his glory. He was the "star" of the All-Star Game. Everywhere we went the buzz was Ahmed. Georgia and I basked in his glow. The guy deserved it. He was cool. He was kind to everyone. He radiated black chic.

The next morning, I hid in my room. There was nothing I needed to see in Baltimore. I ordered room service and read all the papers. At around noon, I took a shower. When I was getting out the phone rang. It was Georgia.

"You about ready to go?"

"Georgia? What time are we leaving?" I said as I toweled off my hair.

"The limo will pick us up in thirty minutes. Ahmed left two hours ago. Why didn't you call me?"

"I didn't want to interrupt anything." I knew I was being an ass, but I couldn't help myself.

"Fuck You!"

"You can't tell me you didn't give him a special little greeting last night, probably this morning too." I was really pushing it.

"I can't believe you're stooping to this."

"Sorry" I said sarcastically.

"Yeah, bullshit!"

"Hey, this is your little game, Georgia. You're making all the rules. If it were up to me, I would have told Ahmed long ago so we could have a normal relationship. Not all this sneaking around shit." I lied. I wanted to hurt her because I was hurting. I wouldn't have had the guts to tell Ahmed either.

"This is going to be a lovely fucking day!" She was hostile.

"Fine. I won't go then."

"The limo leaves in twenty minutes. You better be in the lobby." The phone slammed down.

I was taking all my frustration out on her. There was no way out that was easy. I finished shaving and got dressed. I went to the lobby, and she was waiting. She had on a pale pink linen pantsuit and a pink ribbon in her hair. She looked like a little girl all pink and scrubbed. I wanted her so bad it hurt, but she was scowling at me.

"I'm an asshole. I'm sorry. Really," I offered.

"I'm so mad at you I could spit nails. How dare you treat me this way!"

"I'm sorry." I really was.

"What is the matter with you?" Steam was coming out of her she was so pissed.

"I hate all this."

"Then you shouldn't have come" she said emphatically.

"It's a little late for you to give me that option."

We left for the game, and the traffic was a mess. When we finally got there, the game had already started. Ahmed was in center field, and he saw Georgia come to her seat. He tipped his hat. I guess he had been looking for her. Now he could focus on the game. The guy loved her. There was no doubting that. He would do anything for the woman he loved. Could I say that?

The game was long. No one scored for the first five innings. Baseball is slow anyway, but scoreless innings can put you to sleep. We were sitting with all the wives of the other players on the field. Georgia made idle chit chat with the wives and mothers, and I sat there feeling morose. I decided to fly home after the game. I would plead exhaustion and get myself out of this before any damage was done. I shouldn't have come, but I could still make a fast getaway. I turned to Georgia.

"I'm catching the next plane out after the game." I announced in her ear.

She looked at me with disgust. "Fine." She snapped.

"That's all you're going to say?"

"What else do you want me to say?"

"That you wish you could go with me would be nice" I whined.

"You're being petulant, and you want me to play along. Sorry. I'm not going to get sucked in. I'm here to support Ahmed, and I'm not going to let you manipulate me with your 'poor me' routine."She answered coldly.

"Are you staying?" I asked in a whine.

"Yes. I'm staying."

"Are you sleeping with Ahmed?" I was such a worm that I hated myself.

"I'm going to pretend you didn't ask that."

We both turned back to the game. Ahmed was in center field looking, much to my chagrin, cool as shit. The bases were loaded. The American League was smelling a victory. There were two outs, and the clean-up batter was at the plate. He hit a fly ball deep into center field. Ahmed hustled back to the fence and made a spectacular catch by jumping high into the air, reaching back and catching the ball after it cleared the fence. The crowd jumped to their feet and screamed. Georgia was jumping up and down and cheering. I stood there and smiled. He was magnificent. There was no way I could do anything but admire his ability. Camera shutters clicked in our faces. The press wanted to capture the thrill of the moment from our perspective. Watching Ahmed was a thrill. He was a virtuoso. His body was his instrument. He looked like a prima ballerina leaping for that ball. Only Ahmed could have pulled off that move. There were very few that could match his grace, now or ever. I was overwhelmed with emotion. I felt myself well up with tears. My throat got so tight I could hardly breathe. I stepped into the isle and began to walk up the stairs. Georgia came running up after me.

"Where are you going?"

"Home."

"But the game isn't over. What am I going to tell Ahmed?"

"Tell him I got sick. I have to go, Georgia."

She looked at me. I think it registered with her what was happening to me. She understood. She reached over and squeezed my hand. I turned and left. I caught a cab back to the hotel, packed, called the airlines and got on a flight. I went to the mini-bar and made myself a drink. This whole thing was turning into a nightmare. I think I saw it more clearly than Georgia. She was still deciding what she wanted to do. But I knew what she should do, and I had to help her do it. She had to give me up. She needed to be with Ahmed. I wanted to help her make that decision herself. I wouldn't, couldn't, reject her. I wanted her to reject me. I didn't want her to experience the feeling of rejection. I would shoulder that for her. I loved her. It was the least I could do for her. Ahmed would take care of her, love her, give her a good life. If she went with me, we would suffer so much from the tabloids, the gossip, that we wouldn't make it. All that we were together would be trivialized. Georgia deserved better than that. I wouldn't tolerate her being humiliated, the subject of tabloid journalism.

I spent Sunday morning puttering around Westwood. Having brunch at the Westwood Marquis. Looking in shop windows. I needed time to myself. I stopped at a newsstand and picked up a copy of the *L.A. Times*. When I looked down at the front page a shudder ran through me. The front page had two full color pictures. One was of Ahmed Brooks making his amazing play. The big, bold headline read *"Ahmed Brooks Miracle Catch Saves the Day for The National League."* The other picture was of Georgia and me cheering. I froze. It was the first time I had ever seen us in a photograph together. She looked so beautiful. Happy. Even I looked happy. I knew I would keep that picture always. I wanted to remember her happy. I wanted to remember that I had been a part of her life for a brief while. Someday, when she and I were old, we could get together and remember when we were once in love. Tears began to cascade down my cheeks, but I wasn't crying out loud. The tears fell silently. I couldn't stop them. I got in my car and headed home.

The front page and the sports section were filled with Ahmed. He was a hero. America loved heroes. Especially heroes that were nice guys and good role models for kids. Ahmed fit the bill. Sponsors loved him as much as the public. He would have his pick of all the product endorsements, those big deals from the likes of Nike. Georgia would be taken care of. I wanted her to have the best of everything. Ahmed would provide it. I would provide her freedom from a shameful life. It was the best gift I could give her.

I sat around my apartment and mulled over all the things that had been happening in the last couple of months. It was the best and the worst time of my life. I was so in love with Georgia that it was intoxicating. There was a natural joy, a high in that feeling. But always looming just at the edges of that wondrous feeling was the grim realization that our love was fraught with danger, discovery and loss. I couldn't enjoy it for what it was. Not like any other relationship would be. Free to grow and flourish.

Brian was on to us. There was no question about it. He almost never spoke to me. I didn't have the courage to confront him on it. Mainly because I was so guilty. I guess someone saw us, one of Georgia's neighbors perhaps, or he had a detective follow us. But it didn't really matter how he knew. He knew. I could deal with Brian. It was what Georgia had to go through that was painful to watch. All the women in the newsroom ostracized Georgia. She was left out of their little lunchtime "get togethers", and gossip sessions. She said she didn't give a damn, but I knew that it hurt to be so blatantly ignored. Chuck and I gave her lots of attention as did a few of the male editors, shooters and producers. All the men liked her and not just because she was beautiful, but because she was smart and fun and creative to work with. When Brian came in the newsroom, of late, he would chit chat with everyone there, pointedly ignoring Georgia and me. He would even come over to Chuck and make a lot of jock talk and laugh and giggle and then walk away without so much as a glance at either of us. Everyone noticed. Lani even cackled that I wasn't the fair-haired boy anymore. She seemed to fully enjoy our discomfort. Work had become "work". My love of news was completely diminished by what was happening. I dreaded going in.

No one ever found out who was doing all the stealing, but it stopped. They stole enough to get the station in complete turmoil, transformed into an armed camp, and create a general paranoia. Then they went elsewhere. It was probably a part-time worker. But what was sad was the texture of the newsroom was permanently altered by all of these goings on. Newsrooms are like fraternities. Yes, there are always the petty jealousies and the egos, but what had happened at KKLA was different. That special energy had been tampered with. That zeal and frenetic style was muddied and replaced with a convoluted internal drama. We began to look over each other's shoulders. There was no trust. No team. It was the kiss of death.

Our ratings began to suffer. Because my relationship with Brian was on the skids, I knew he would blame me. I thought I should find another job, but I was paralyzed for the moment. I needed to see through my relationship with Georgia. I couldn't leave her there to deal with Brian alone, or fend off Lani and company either. Even though Georgia was smart and tough in many ways, there was also a vulnerable part of her that made me want to protect her. Ahmed responded to her in the same way. He felt it too. That's why he could never be my enemy, my rival. We both loved her. We both wanted the best for her. We both felt compelled to protect her whether she wanted us to or not. Ahmed and I were kindred spirits when it came to Georgia. That's why I felt so wormy about betraying him. I couldn't find fault with him. He was a consummate good guy. A much better guy than I was if you were counting positive attributes. He would never cheat with a buddy's girlfriend. He had ethics. Integrity. A code of honor. I was blatantly void of those virtues.

I knew Georgia would be flying back that evening, but I kept myself from calling her. I had nothing to say. I wanted her. Desperately. But I couldn't see her. She had been with Ahmed. I was still in second position. I knew I would stay in second position for the rest of the season, maybe longer. I needed to get out before she made her move. If she made her move. I was flattering myself. She might decide to stay with Ahmed all on her own. In fact, it was likely she would, even though she outwardly never made me think she had reached a decision. But I knew Ahmed was right for her. Right for her and for me. I just couldn't go through with it. I couldn't put her through it. We had to give each other up. It wasn't the "Hollywood Way," the right thing to do.

At about eight I went out to grab a bite to eat. I drove out to Main Street in Santa Monica and went to the Bay Cities Italian Deli and had a big fat Godmother on sesame bread. It was comfort food and made me feel better. I needed to feel nurtured and the homemade sloppy sandwich made me feel good. It also made me feel good that I had a plan. I just needed to think it through a little more. I was resolved to help Georgia make the decision to stay with Ahmed. I needed to figure out how without hurting her or making her feel I didn't want her. I needed to act fast because every day it was becoming more stressful for both of us. We needed to move on. We should both leave KKLA and start our lives over at new stations. Georgia had to stay in L.A. because of Ahmed, but I could leave the market. As soon as I could, I vowed to begin a serious job search. I would miss L.A. I would miss Georgia more. But it was the price I had to pay to extricate the woman I would always love. I had created her dilemma and I would willingly pay the price to relieve her of it. Every time I thought of her, I ached. The ache grew greater, deeper every minute of the day. When I got back to my apartment there was a long, rambling message on my machine from Georgia.

"Hi, Paddy. I'm back. Are you alright? I'm really worried about you. I'm sorry I've been so bitchy. The stress is overwhelming me. I wish you were here with me. Holding me. I know it's hard on you. Me being with Ahmed and all. But I have to do it. I love Ahmed too. He's the best friend I've ever had. I can't let him down right now. I have to support him like he has always supported me. It's bad enough that I've screwed around behind his back. Oh, I don't mean it like that sounds. You're not just a screw. I fell for you. But I still feel guilty. Like I have betrayed my best friend. I've asked so much from you. To put up with this charade is not easy. I know that. No one else would have indulged me this way. I love you even more because of it. Maybe I'm not doing the right thing. I don't know. I am suffering so much trying to figure all this out. I guess you're out and about, but I just wanted to talk to you. I'll see you at work tomorrow if I don't talk to you tonight. I'm sorry. Forgive me? I love you. Good night."

I went in the kitchen and got a beer. I went to the couch and sat down and played the message again. There was fatigue in her voice. She was wearing down. I could have gone over to see her, but I kept my resolve. It wouldn't be fair to her to allow any more bond to grow between us. Making love once more would make the break that much more painful. I had to think of Georgia now and not my own selfish needs.

Having reached that conclusion, a wonderful calm came over me. For once, I was thinking with my heart and not my dick. It felt good. After I finished my drink, I took a hot shower and went to bed. I slept like a baby. It was the first good night's sleep I'd had in months.

When I headed for work the next morning I stopped at Norm's for breakfast. All the regulars were there. They had the picture of me from the paper and they all wanted to talk about the All-Star Game. I played along. I was their local celebrity. If they knew how miserable I had been at the game, they wouldn't be so envious. But it looked glamorous to them.

After a hearty breakfast I drove to the station. Georgia's car was in the lot. I knew she would be hurt that I hadn't returned her call, but I needed to create a distance to go through with my plan. As I walked down the long hall towards the newsroom, I saw a flash of Georgia running into the green room, the room where we kept the guests for our morning news interviews. It was odd for her to be doing that. There was no reason to run to the green room unless a guest was late for the morning show, but the morning show was long over. When I got to the green room Georgia was barricaded in the ladies dressing room.

I knocked on the door.

"Georgia, are you alright in there?"

"No."

"What's the matter?"

"Go see for yourself."

"See what?"

"The bulletin board," she said in a choked whisper through the closed door.

I walked into the newsroom. Everyone avoided looking at me. No one greeted me. It was an eerie feeling. My stomach started to churn as I approached the bulletin board near the assignment desk. From about fifteen feet away, I saw the front page of the L.A Times tacked on the middle of the bulletin board. As I got closer, I reread the headline, "Ahmed Brooks Miracle Catch Saves The Day For The National League." Scrawled in bold, black magic marker directly beneath the headline was, "While Paddy McGurk Scored At Home". To make the message even clearer, there was a black heart drawn around the picture of Georgia and me.

I tore the paper off the board. I was in a blind fury. I headed back to the green room to Georgia. On the way, Chuck, just coming to work, rounded the corner and came towards me.

"Hey, how was the All-Star Game?" he asked, oblivious to my anguish.

"Not now Chuck." I brushed past him.

"You O.K.?" he called after me.

"No!" I answered as I headed into the green room.

"Georgia?" I said through the closed door.

"I have to get out of here," she said, firmly.

"I know."

"They won't stop till I'm gone."

"What do you want me to do?" I wanted to help her.

"Get my handbag for me. I'm leaving."

"Right now?"

"I'm not going back in there."

"Let me in." I begged. I wanted to comfort her.

"No. I don't want you to see me right now. I'm humiliated, Paddy. Just do as I ask. Please." She pleaded.

I didn't want to leave the green room. I went to the phone and dialed Chuck's extension.

"News. Chuck Kelly," he answered.

"Chuck. It's Paddy."

"What's going on? Everybody's acting fucking weird, man."

"Bring me Georgia's purse. I'm in the green room."

"Is something wrong? Is Georgia O.K." He was genuinely concerned.

"No, I'll explain later. Just bring me her bag. O.K." I tried to sound calm, but I was trembling.

"You got it."

Within thirty seconds Chuck was in the green room with Georgia's bag.

"Where's Georgia?" He asked, still in the dark.

"She's in there." I pointed to the door to the dressing room.

"Is she sick?"

"Yes." It was not a lie.

"Should we get her to a doctor?"

"I'm going to take care of her. You go back to work."

"O.K. Call me if you need me."

"I will, Thanks."

I knocked gently on the door after Chuck left. "Georgia, I have your bag."

She opened the door. Her eyes were swollen almost shut. She took the bag without a word. She pulled out her sunglasses. She put them on. Then she walked out.

"Where are you going?" I asked, already knowing the answer.

"Home."

"Are you coming back?"

"Never."

With that she was gone. I went down the hall and headed upstairs for Brian's office. He was in on this. I was sure of it. When I got there, I walked in without being announced. Judy didn't try to stop me. Brian was hunched over his desk working on a document. He looked up when I stormed in and motioned for me to sit down. I didn't.

"What the fuck is this?" I slapped the newspaper front page on his desk.

"Jesus!" He looked shocked.

"Is this your idea of a sick joke?" I was fuming.

"I don't know what the fuck you're talking about. I had nothing to do with this. Get the fuck out of here. I'm busy. I don't have time for yours or Georgia's personal bullshit. I've got a station to run," he scowled at me, shoved the paper back at me, and went back to his work.

I wasn't going to let him dismiss me. "Who did it then?" I demanded.

"I have no idea. Where did you find it?" He was calm, so calm. Patronizing.

I was taken aback. I knew him so well I could tell he wasn't lying.

"It was on the bulletin board in the newsroom when I came in this morning." I spit out.

"Who saw it?" It was a mere curiosity to him.

"Everyone down there. How could they miss it?"

"It's true, isn't it?" He measured me.

"Not anymore."

"Good. Things can get back to normal around here."

"That's all you've got to say."

"You take your chance and you pay your price, Paddy. What else is there to say?"

"Georgia left. For good."

"No loss. She didn't belong here in the first place."

"You are a cold-blooded bastard." I snarled at him.

"That's what they say." With that Brian went back to his work and left me standing there. I picked up the newspaper and left. I left the station. I drove to Georgia's apartment. When I knocked on her door, she shouted. "Just a minute!" A few seconds later she opened the door.

"Paddy! What are you doing here?" She was barefoot in jeans and a white tee shirt.

"I wanted to make sure you were alright."

"Come in." She gestured to come inside.

I went into her apartment. There were boxes scattered everywhere.

"What are all these boxes doing in here?"

"I'm moving."

"Why?"

"After what happened this morning, you have to ask? I'm sick of these nosy neighbors reporting my every move to that bastard, Brian Buchanon." She was back to her old self. She had her fight back. I was glad.

"Brian didn't do it."

"Don't be naive." She said with reproach.

"He didn't. I asked him."

She sat down. She looked tired and worn out. "What did he say?"

"It doesn't matter what he said but how he said it. I could tell he didn't do it."

"Then who did?" She wanted to understand so she could leave it behind.

"That cunt, Lani, is my guess."

"Ugh. I hate that word. But in her case, it fits perfectly."

"What should we do?"

"I don't know about you but I'm going to do what I should have done a long time ago." She was not referring to us as a twosome. The distancing was in motion.

"What's that?"

"I'm finding another job, moving to a new apartment, and marrying Ahmed on Christmas Eve." The bomb was dropped. I crumpled beneath it. My legs folded to the floor. It was what I knew should be. It was what I wanted her to do. But hearing it, the finality of it, took every ounce of life left in me away.

"When did you decide to marry Ahmed?"

"This morning in the green room." She looked at me levelly.

"When did he ask?" I needed to torture myself further with intimate details.

"He's asked many times. I've always demurred. After the All-Star Game, he asked again. He said he wanted something to look forward to since there would be no baseball season in a few weeks. He thought Christmas Eve would be a good wedding date. He said it would be easy to remember our anniversaries. He was teasing me."

"You said yes." I was chilled to my bones. My heart was thumping in my chest like it was beating in drying glue.

"I said I'd think about it."

"Would you have said yes if this morning hadn't happened?"

"I don't know. This morning did happen. So, speculating is a waste of time." She got up now and went in the kitchen. I followed her. She was making tea. She offered me a cup. I took it gratefully.

"What are you going to tell Ahmed about leaving KKLA?"

"I set the stage for that a long time ago. I've been telling him about what a bitch Lani is and also how I can't stand Buchanon. I've been saying I want to leave. It won't surprise him if I tell him I walked out in disgust."

"What if someone tells him about us?"

"He travels in a different world than we do. The chance of him ever having contact with any of those people is slim. If he does, I'll handle it then. I'm not worried." She was sure of herself.

"What about us?"

She looked at me a long moment. Tears welled up in her eyes. Her bravado was gone. She touched my face. "I'm so sorry, Paddy. I have loved you so much. I just don't know what else to do. It's for the best. You may not see it now, but you will."

I broke down. The reality of it all fell hard on me. I took her in my arms and kissed her hair and face. I kept saying over and over again "I love you." I couldn't let her go. She took me by the hand and led me to her bed. She tenderly laid me down on the pink comforter. She took off my shoes, then my shirt and pants. She took off her clothes and laid down beside me. I smothered my face in her hair and breathed in her scent. I wanted to remember her scent forever. We held each other for a long time, our legs and arms entangled. I kept kissing her face and drinking her in. My hands moved across her features trying to memorize her. Letting her go was the hardest thing I would ever have to endure. Nothing in my life, before or since, ever matched these sorrowful last moments.

I got the strength to prop up on my elbow and look down at her. She was so beautiful, lit by the noontime sun, streaming through her bedroom windows. She was looking into my eyes with those green cats eyes all soft and warm with half closed lids. She was weary. I lifted her face to me. We kissed as my hand traced the outline of her breasts. I kissed her neck, her chest, her breasts. I took her breasts in my mouth and sucked them gently. Gone was the anger, the frenzy, of our love-making in the past. My mouth sought out her warm mound of love and my tongue and lips hungrily drank in her juices. I wanted to take all of her with me. Inside me. She moaned in pleasure and in sorrow. She cried softly as she came with a violent jerk against my mouth. I then climbed on top of her and slowly and gently entered her until we came together. Her face was hot and pink from the passion. I loved to look at her face after we made love. I stayed on top of her and left myself inside her. We kissed and clung to each other for the longest time. She fell asleep. I covered her with a pink knitted throw. I got dressed and stood over the bed watching her sleep. She was my angel. My golden girl. I got my coat and I quietly let myself out the door.

10

A NIGHT TO REMEMBER AT STARLETS

When I went back to work, I avoided everyone. I hated that bitch Lani. In fact, I hated them all. They could all go fuck themselves. They had taken something very precious and turned it into the office joke. It would be a cold day in hell before I would be civil to them again. Chuck was acting strange towards me as well. I guess he'd heard. I made a pledge to talk to him but today was not going to be the day. I was too sorrowful. I wanted to get through the newscast at ten and go home.

I called my travel agent and booked a flight to New York the week prior to the Labor Day weekend. I would stay the full nine days and look for a job. I had to leave KKLA, but I was going to leave on my terms. I had lost Georgia. My career was all I had left. I had to fight for it in any way that I could. It was a poor substitute for a life with Georgia, but it was the only substitute that appealed to me. There would never be another woman in my life. Not a serious one. I wasn't going to become a monk, but Georgia would always be the undisputed love of my life. As I made my plans, I began to feel a little better. I would keep myself busy and motivated by looking for an escape route to New York.

In the meantime, I would try to mend fences with Brian. He had been an asshole to me for the last couple of months. But how could I fault him? He believed we were best friends, and I had betrayed our friendship. Sure, he was a manipulative S.O.B., but our relationship had been founded on that premise. He never claimed to be otherwise. The rules had always been clear. As long as I maintained unflagging loyalty to Brian, he would take care of me. I was the one who had breached our implicit understanding. That understanding had served me well for many years. I made a conscious choice to change the rules of the relationship, and I was paying for it. I was never naive enough to think I wouldn't pay if he found out about Georgia and me.

August 6th was Brian's 55th birthday. We had talked many times about celebrating it together. I decided that I would plan a surprise party for him with all his cronies in attendance. I didn't want to burn a bridge with Brian. We needed to do a little male bonding. A Viking night to eat, drink and pillage like Norwegian ship captains! His birthday party would be the way to get us back on track with each other. We had been friends too long to hold onto this grudge between us. Sure, I was still angry with him, but I owed it to him to be the first one to extend the olive branch. His birthday was the perfect setting to let bygones be bygones. I made a resolution to start putting the plans together tomorrow. I could get Red to help me. He loved to organize things. I would come up with the concept and let Red do all the details.

After I finished the news, I headed out to my car for a fast getaway. Just as I was getting in, Chuck came jogging up to my open door and scowled down at me as I sat down in the seat. My top was down. He held the door open and wedged his body between the door and me.

"Hey, asshole! Why didn't you tell me?" He was shaking with anger.

"Tell you what?" I knew what he was referring to, but I wasn't in the mood for true confessions.

"You let me make a fool out of myself, throwing myself at Georgia, while you were fucking her and probably both laughing your asses off at me!" Chuck was a macho guy and now he felt foolish.

"It wasn't the way you think it was. And neither of us ever laughed at you." It was the truth.

"I bet my ass. You just strung me along, playing me like I was some stupid naive kid. I should have known you were screwing her. She screwed a black guy, why wouldn't she screw an old has been like you." He was lashing out like a kid in the sandbox, with whatever ammunition he could find.

"That's enough. She wasn't a fuck for me, Chuck. I loved her, not that it's any of your goddamn business." I pushed him out of the way of my door and slammed it shut. I hit the accelerator and shot out of the parking lot. I saw him in my rearview mirror standing there, hurting. I had hurt him too.

My sins. What price would I pay for my sins? I had lost Georgia. Would that be enough? My Catholic conscience measured everything by purity and reward, guilt and penance. I was guilty as hell, and I would pay. But I had no one to ask the extent of my penance. When would I be absolved of my sins? What pain endured, what loss, would finally release me from my obligation to suffer?

I drove home and had a miserable night. Every few minutes my hand would reach for the phone to call Georgia. I'd dial her number, getting through a few digits, or all but the last, and then hang up. I wanted to hear her voice, but if I let her answer and hung up, she would know it was me. So, I played my game with myself. Just dialing the digits made me feel closer to her. I knew I would go on to live my life without the pain, but I also knew it would be a long time coming.

I accepted this as part of my punishment. After far too much beer and much tossing and turning I fell into a fitful sleep. I dreamed I parachuted behind enemy lines and there were soldiers looking for me. I hid behind a rock and they passed right by me. But just when I thought I was safe, they turned around and came back toward the rock. As I was about to be discovered I woke up in a sweat.

I got up and walked around the apartment in my boxer shorts to cool down. It was only 5AM. I was beat. I turned on CNN and the first face I saw was O.J. I murmured to myself "things could be worse." That poor bastard had really fucked up. I'm sure it was the drugs. But to cold bloodedly kill the mother of his children. It was more than I could fathom. Those two kids would pay for his insanity for the rest of their lives.

I drank some juice out of the carton and lay on the couch. Today I would plan Brian's party. I picked up the telephone pad and began to make a guest list. Red, Brian and I were at the top. I added a few of the department heads that weren't stiffs. Then I included a few clients that were hell raisers, some of the Dodgers front office and our sports anchors. That should do it. Then I wrote down a list of possible locations to hold it. BB Kings, House of Blues, Tom Bergen's, and then it hit me. For a true Viking night, we needed women. But we didn't want women guests. That would throw a wet blanket on our shenanigans. I got a brainstorm! Starlets! Starlets was a new, upscale strip club with fantastic looking girls dancing and waiting tables. Starlets had a four-star chef and a four-star clientele. All the big-name male stars got their kicks at Starlets. It was a private club that cost $5000.00 to join. Luckily, Brian had a membership, but I didn't want him to know what I was doing. The party would be a surprise. I could work out the details with the manager. The more plans I made the better I felt. It would be fun. Lots of laughs and bad behavior. It had been a long time since

I'd misbehaved. I'd spent the last seven months pining over Georgia. Maybe this party would help get her out of my system.

When I got to work, I went straight to Red's office. He was a little strange at first, but once he found out that I wasn't coming to make a scene about what happened to Georgia he settled down. He was completely turned on by my birthday plan. His getting excited got me more excited. We spent the rest of the week planning the party.

All that week Chuck gave me the cold shoulder. I decided to ask him to Brian's party. Maybe that would help heal his wounds as well.

A few days before the birthday party Red was going over the final details with me at my desk. Chuck came over to shove some copy at me, and I made my move.

"Chuck, come back a minute." I said as he turned to stride away quickly.

"Whaddaya need?" He responded sullenly.

"I'm sure you've heard your dad and me planning Brian's birthday. I'd like for you to come."

"I'll think about it." He said as he turned away.

"Chuck!" Red admonished, embarrassed by his son's rude behavior.

I turned to Red. "Do you feel O.K. about me corrupting your son for one night, Red?"

"His mother would never forgive me, but he's 21. He makes his own decisions. Do you want to come, son?" Chuck had turned back towards us and was listening in.

When you're twenty-one a good time always overrules honor.

"You're going to that stripper club, right? Yeah. I guess I'll go!" He responded indifferently, trying to hide his excitement.

"Good. It'll be great to have you there. You know how Brian loves to initiate the young and innocent into the art of being a Viking." I smiled up at him. He begrudgingly smiled back. It was good to see his goofy grin again.

Although Georgia was never far from my thoughts the party breathed new life into me. I went to Brian's office one afternoon to ask him to go out to dinner on his birthday, which was only days away.

"Hey, boss, still pissed at me?" I asked with my head stuck in his door.

"I have better things to do with my time." He answered curtly.

"You're turning the big five-five Saturday!"

"Is that the latest news flash. No wonder the ratings are slipping." He was beginning to joke. It was a good sign.

"How about going out to dinner with me over at Starlets on Saturday. We could have a night out on the town, just the two of us."

"Hard up for a date?"

"Yeah. She left me for the better man."

"That's for damn sure!" It hurt when he said that, but I had set him up for the comeback.

"Come on. Let's do something fun together. It's been a long time."

He put his pen down and looked at me fully. It was a long and very pregnant pause. "O.K. We'll see how it goes. Get a limo. I don't feel like driving."

"Done!" I scampered away, thrilled that he would go. The chasm was closing.

Red would get everyone assembled at Starlets, and I would get Brian there at the appointed time. The surprise party would go off without a hitch.

Saturday morning, the day of the party, I went out to find Brian the perfect gift. I went from store to store on Rodeo Drive and all the surrounding streets. At around 1PM I was still searching. It was a hot

August day and I was running out of patience. I sought refuge from the scorching sun at the bar in the Beverly Wilshire Hotel.

"Whew! It's a hot one." I said to no one in particular.

The bartender looked at me and understood.

"Need a cold one?"

"You read my mind." I answered gratefully. There's nothing so seductive as a sensitive bartender. He handed me a frozen mug of draft.

"You're my hero for the day." I continued. "I'm looking for a gift for my boss's 55th birthday. Got any ideas?" I made more chit chat.

"Your boss? Something expensive...like that jacket over there." He pointed behind me to a small men's boutique in the foyer of the hotel. In the window was an incredible cream-colored jacket.

"Wow! It's perfect. Thanks!" I chugged down the rest of my beer, slapped a ten on the bar and hurried over to the shop.

"Can I see that jacket in a 42 long please." I pointed to the display.

"Sir, a 42 long would not fit you properly." A perfectly groomed gray-haired gay man answered.

"I know. It's a gift." I answered impatiently.

"Quite a special gift for your friend, 100% cashmere. The finest fabric money can buy." He held it out for me to touch the fabric. It was like butter. Brian would love it, the extravagance of it.

"It's for my boss." I didn't want him to think it was for my lover. He might get ideas.

"A wise investment in your future."

"You might say that. How much?" I asked, already knowing I would pay it. Penance.

"$2,500.00."

"That's quite an investment! I'll take it. Could you gift wrap it for me?"

"Certainly. Will that be cash or charge?"

"Charge. Might as well get a few free miles. Besides, I rarely have that much pocket change."

He sniffed at my joke and walked away. He didn't like me, and I didn't care. He could join the club.

After I paid my bill, I headed home to take a short nap and get ready. It would be a late one and I needed a little rest to make it through a night of hellraising.

At about 5:30PM I was relaxing after my nap, reading the rest of the morning paper when the phone rang.

"Paddy, it's Georgia."

I lost my breath. "Georgia...how are you?"

"I'm fine. I just wanted to give you my new phone number."

"You've moved already."

"A few days ago. I love my new apartment."

"Tell me about it." I wanted to stretch the conversation as long as I could.

"It's in the Hollywood Hills. It's an older, 1950's garden apartment. I have the most beautiful mature roses on the patio outside my bedroom. I sit out there and read after work. But best of all, I have a fireplace. Not one of the dinky modern ones like most apartment fireplaces post code restrictions, instead, a great big deep one."

"Too hot for a fire right now."

"No kidding. But I'm having fun with it anyway. I found a fabulous pair of French andirons for it. They have a big "Fleur de Lis" at the front. I'm going to put a basket of azaleas on them during the summer months."

"I'd love to see it sometime. You've already landed a job?"

"Well, not a job exactly, but a freelance producer gig for PBS. They want me to do a full hour on the Miskito Indians, can you believe it?"

"Wow. Good for you!"

"I know. I never felt the story dug deep enough into the American involvement in the exploitation, and now I have a chance to find the dirt. In fact, I'm going to try to use some of KKLA's footage, so I don't have to go out on that damn boat again. I hope Herb will let me use it."

That was a tiny shot at me, but it was O.K. because I was getting to hear her voice. She could have been shouting obscenities at me, and I would have been all ears.

"I'm sure. He has no use for it now. Besides, it's PBS. How are the wedding plans going?"

"I haven't given it much thought. Maybe it's a Freudian omission."

"I won't touch that...How's Ahmed handling the strike?"

"Not well, I must say. He's been very cranky. He's so involved with his own trials and tribulations that he barely acknowledged what happened with me at KKLA. The gift of timing saved me from having to make too many explanations."

"Good."

"How are you doing, Paddy?" she asked softly.

"Miserable. Lonely. Suicidal!" I said only half joking.

"Stop!"

"I'm surviving, Georgia. In fact, tonight I'm going to Brian's birthday party."

"So, you two have made up?"

"That's stretching it. We've called a truce. I'll see how it goes at the party."

"He has no reason to be mad at you. What happened is none of his business," she said righteously.

"He doesn't see it that way." I answered honestly.

"We never have agreed on the subject of Brian Buchanon. Well, I guess I'd better get going. Got a pencil handy?"

"Sure."

"Here's my new number, 393-8068. Call me whenever you want."
She offered.

"Thanks. I'll try not to be a pest."

"Do you miss me?" She asked tentatively.

"Every minute of every day. In fact, I'm going to New York in a
couple of weeks to look for a job. I need to make a new life for myself."

"I wish I could go with you."

"You can."

"I've made my bed. I'll have to lie in it. Talk to you soon, Paddy."
She sounded down. Resigned.

"Good-bye, Georgia."

As I hung up the phone, I realized my dick was harder than super-
man's elbow. It had been a long time without Georgia. Without anyone. I jumped in the shower and fantasized about Georgia. My body
exploded with pleasure. I felt like a teenager I came so quickly. My sex
life was becoming very one dimensional, I mused, and chuckled at my
own humor. While I dried off and shaved, I went over our conversation
in my head. She didn't sound terribly happy with Ahmed but, strangely, that didn't make me feel any better. I wanted her to be happy with
him. I wanted her to be happy, period.

The limo was picking me up at 7:30PM and then on to Brian's at
8. Just as I was splashing on some after shave, I heard a rap at my door.
The driver was waiting outside. I finished getting dressed, grabbed the
gift for Brian, or should I say "bribe" for Brian, and headed out the
door.

It was still daylight, and the L.A. traffic was thick. Everybody was
out for a Saturday night on the town. As we cruised through the west-
side we came to Brian's palm tree lined street in the heart of Beverly
Hills. He loved being in the neighborhood of the stars. His home was
designed by Frank Lloyd Wright. It was all glass, stone and brass that had

turned green with age and weather. It honestly fit Brian to a tee. Lots of open space and minimal furniture. He has a vast modern art collection that he treasures more than his own kids. Lining the walls leading to his bedroom are pictures of him with his arms around big-name celebrities. There were hundreds of photos. The framed photos surround huge framed jerseys from the NBA, MLB, NHL, and Pro Football plus a few college teams as well. All were autographed. It was his vanity wall. I'm sure it impressed the young girls as he leads them to his lair. He is a Leo, August 8. He's proud of that; the king of the jungle.

Brian was in the shower when I rang the bell. I stood outside and looked up into the sky. The sun was beaming gold as it sank in the west and the sky was turning pink. I took a deep breath and waited. He came to the door wrapped in a towel and growled.

"You're early!"

"Take your time. I'll wait."

"There's everything you need in the bar. Help yourself." With that he was off. I was hot and thirsty. August in L.A. is always hot and smoggy. No breeze to blow the junk inland. I made my way to the bar and found beer in the small refrigerator that was designed to hold wine. But Brian was not a wine kind of guy. So, it was fully stocked with beer, mixers and, of course, expensive champagne for his female guests. The beer felt good going down. I walked around looking at all his memorabilia. He saved and displayed everything that made a statement about who he was and what he'd done. Articles, photos, letters, awards all had an assigned place in his home. It was a shrine.

He came bounding out of the master bedroom and poured himself a Scotch on the rocks.

"One for the road." He said as he tossed it down.

We hopped into the limo and headed for Starlets. I dreaded the long ride with Brian in a confined space.

"Another year older!" I started.

"Yeah, and I feel every bit of it too."

"Doesn't seem like it." I tried to flatter.

"The strike is killing me. The way things are going I won't hit my bonuses with corporate because of the lost revenue."

"How about putting on some college games?"

"No one is going to pay top dollar for college ball. I can make more with the regular programming. We'll need a hell-of-a fourth quarter to hit the budget."

"Then there's hope."

"Yeah. If everyone keeps their eye on the ball. Now that you've pulled your nose, dick and every other part of you out of Georgia's snatch maybe the news can get some ratings." He said, looking at me squarely. I knew it was coming but it still hit me between the eyes.

"How did you find out?" I asked as I recovered.

"I hear things. I know what goes on in my television station. Make sure you remember that next time you get any bright ideas."

"Hey, it's your birthday. Let's let bygones be bygones. O.K. Boss?" I tried to turn the conversation.

He looked at me a moment, "We've been friend's a long time. You let me down, Paddy. I don't get over things easily."

"It just happened."

"You could have told me. Ahmed Brooks could queer our deal with the Dodgers. I needed to know for the security of the station."

"Jesus, Brian. 'Hanky panky' runs rampant at that station. It's never been a big deal."

"You were fuckin' warned to keep your dick out of that broad. If anyone in the goddamn place was going to get a piece of that it should have been me. But I didn't. You did. She didn't like me anyway. Fuck her."

"Well, Ahmed has her now. So, let's drop it." I was seething. But there was no way out. Luckily, we pulled up to Starlets, and I jumped out like a man on fire.

I loved the decor of Starlets. Everything from the breast like chandeliers to the bulbous booths were shaped like parts of a woman. Full, round, rosy, sensual. The light cast a glow on all who entered and especially flattered the scantily clad cocktail girls. When we arrived, there was a beautiful Asian woman doing a slow strip tease as she walked among the tables and booths. We turned our heads to watch as we were led to the back room where a full-blown party was already in progress. Although everyone yelled "Surprise!" I don't think Brian was surprised. He smiled broadly and laughed out loud. Never at a loss for words he said. "Hey, what the fuck is this? A convention of the Dead Peckers Club!" The evening was finally off to the right start.

Everyone that was invited showed up. It was one of those parties that you didn't dare miss. You wanted to brag that you'd been there almost as much as you wanted to go through the experience. Chuck stuck close to his dad and acknowledged me with a slight nod of his head. He was still mad at me. I missed him. Someday I would make it up to him. Maybe after I moved to New York, I'd invite him to come stay with me for a while. We could have a few laughs and get through the discomfort that had come between us.

We all stood around laughing, talking, joking and drinking for over an hour. Because we were a private party, we got our own cocktail waitress. She was a tall Nordic blond with high cheekbones, long sun-tanned legs, and a round high-water butt covered with a tight white cotton micro skirt. You could see the outline of her string panties through the sheer white cotton. She had perky breasts that were braless under a formfitting sheer white tank top. She was wearing gold leather roman sandals that wrapped around her well-toned calves to just under the knee. The sandals had thick soles that elevated her lean frame to at least six feet tall. Every time she entered the room, the men eyed her hungrily as they continued their jock talk. She was pleasant but distant to all of us. No flirting at all. Friendly without a come-on. She did her job. Nothing more, nothing less. Brian tried to engage her more than once with personal comments, but she never took the bait. She was a pro at handling him and every man in the room.

It was clear that she was not on the make. My guess was that she was a wannabe actress or student working here to pay her rent. Her name was Tiffany. It didn't suit her. She needed a bigger, stronger name. Helena, Katherine or Margaret. Perhaps Tiffany was her "stage" name. Tiffany was for bimbos, and this girl didn't fall in that category.

Brian was holding court in one corner of the room. Red had him laughing uproariously at all his bad jokes. As I stood on the periphery of the group and nursed my third vodka tonic, I could hear Red loud and clear.

"And here's one for your 55th birthday, Brian. A nurse came up to the doctor and said, 'Excuse me doctor but why is that old man sticking out his tongue and holding up his middle finger?' Red looked at the faces around him for a split second. 'Simple, nurse,' answered the doctor, 'I asked him to show me his sexual organs'." Everyone broke up not so much at the joke itself but at Red's glee at telling it. Red was like everyone's favorite uncle. He was Brian's "Chia Pet".

"Here's another one," Red was one a roll, "How do you know when you're getting old?" Another pregnant pause, "When your wife gives up sex for Lent and you don't find out till Easter." Another round of guffaws!

"I've got one for you, Red." Brian started. 'What's the difference between a pussy and a cunt?"

Red's face was lit up with too much booze as he tried to figure out the punch line. Brian continued. "A pussy is soft, warm, inviting...and a cunt is the person who owns it." As they all laughed Brian turned to me and said so everyone could hear. "Paddy can appreciate that one, right, buddy?" Before I could answer he turned back to the group. I flushed with anger. It was a direct shot at Georgia and at me. I'm not sure everyone caught the inference. But a few did. There was a brief, uncomfortable silence till Red jumped in to rescue the moment.

"Hey, birthday boy, I've got one to top that. What's the ultimate in embarrassment for a career woman?" Pause. "When her Ben-Wa balls set off the metal detector at the airport." Red said through a nervous laugh. They all cracked up. The moment was diffused for everyone but me. The party atmosphere was regained.

Tiffany came in and brought our latest round of drinks and asked if we wanted to start our dinner. We all ambled over to the massive rectangular table set with liar's dice between each place setting. Later, there would be all-night poker. It was going to be a true Viking night. But now we got to sink our teeth into our Viking dinner.

Brian took his place at the head of the table and announced, "All hogs to the trough," as we settled into our seats. He signaled for me to sit next to him. I saw that as a sign. Not of forgiveness but control. He was still in charge.

The dinner started with a sumptuous caprese salad fit for Vikings,, followed by enormous porterhouse steaks and twice baked cheese potatoes. The steaks were smothered in onions, garlic and mushrooms. There were massive baskets of garlic bread and cheese bread placed down the middle of the table like centerpieces. Brian picked up the wine list and ordered six bottles of 1984 Far Niente Cabernet. Those bottles were over $100.00 apiece. I blanched inwardly. Penance. He was going to make me pay through the nose. With the jacket and the party, my tab for his birthday would be over ten grand. I was leaving soon, but at least I could leave on an up note, I rationalized. No more extortion. No more anything. I would leave my mentor and begin my new life in New York out of his shadow. With this thought a small jolt of fear went up my spine. I didn't know if it was fear of not getting a job in New York or of leaving the protection of a mentor like Brian. I would soon find out.

Everyone grew silent as the eating frenzy began. It was late. Almost ten. We were all full of booze and needed to get some real food in our bellies. There was lots of grunting, pointing and passing of the various platters, baskets and wine. Tiffany tried to keep up with our demands, and I could tell she was running out of patience. Brian kept trying to pat her ass as she rounded the table. It was clear that she didn't like him one bit. Besides, the rules at Starlets prohibited touching the merchandise, but he was the birthday boy, so she was cutting him some slack for his lack of manners. Brian started telling a string of black jokes.

"What do you call a white man surrounded by three blacks? Victim."

"What do you call a white man surrounded by five blacks? Coach."

"What do you call a white man surrounded by ten blacks? Quarterback."

"What do you call a white man surrounded by three hundred blacks? Warden."

Racial sensitivity was never part of Brain's repertoire, and we didn't have the guts or integrity to intervene. Everyone was laughing with their mouths open, food flying everywhere. It was gross and disgusting, but that's what a Viking night had to be. Miss Manners was nowhere in sight, and political correctness was checked at the door. Brian was having a great time and that was the point.

I was busy savoring my steak and wasn't paying too much attention to the reverie when Brian gave me an extra hard smack on the back and said, "Here's one Paddy can relate to from first-hand experience." I looked at him and felt sick. I knew something unpleasant was coming.

He continued, fully aware of my chagrin. "Why was a black man acquitted of rape on the grounds of temporary insanity? Because when he got an erection his dick got so big there was no blood left to flow to his brain." He laughed at his own joke till tears came in his eyes.

When he finished laughing, I couldn't stop myself from asking "What the fuck is that supposed to mean?"

He grabbed me playfully around the neck. "Now don't get your bowels in an uproar. You know us Irish boys are long on personality and short on peckers. Georgia may have liked you Paddy, but when it got right down to it there was no way you could bang the "G" spot like her African stud."

"Fuck you. Georgia Conroy was not about that and you know it."

Tiffany was pouring more wine and asked, "Are you talking about Georgia Conroy, the news reporter?"

Brian answered, "Yeah, honey. She a friend of yours?" and then laughed uproariously.

"No. I watch her on television. She is one of my favorites."

"How nice that Georgia has a fan. See this guy here. She's one of his favorites too."

"You're drunk." I said as I threw down my napkin. "I need to take a leak." As I brushed past Tiffany on the way to the men's room Brian called out after me.

"Hey, buddy, don't run away mad. You're among friends. Now that it's all over, give us the inside scoop. Was she a good fuck?" Out of embarrassment or allegiance everyone broke up laughing.

I went in the men's room and took a leak. As I washed my hands, I looked in the mirror. What was I doing here? I knew better. Brian wasn't going to let me off the hook just because I threw him a party.

I wanted to walk out of the men's room and out the front door, but I couldn't. Something, some need to be punished, to atone, forced me back into that room. It was like an out of body experience from that point on.

Tiffany was carrying in the birthday cake as I came back in. It was a massive cheesecake with fifty-five flaming candles. Everyone started singing. I stood behind my seat to give Tiffany room to set it down. I liked having the time to recover out of sight of Brian. I was feeling so sour I didn't want to join in. Before Brian blew out the candles he said, "Where's Paddy?" and turned around to look at me. I obediently sat down in my seat and he blew out the candles to much cheering and laughter.

The cheesecake was flown in from the Carnegie Deli in New York. There was much grunting of approval from all the troops over that little detail. I dove into my massive piece and tried to bury my feelings by feeding my face. Brian started opening his gifts. Red and Chuck bought him a pair of rollerblades and all the gear that goes with it. He got tickets to concerts, a weekend in the Napa Valley, dinner with Tommy Lasorda. Everyone guffawed at that one. Brian said, "Christ, my worst nightmare. I guess we'll be having Slim Fast or he'll eat the food right off my plate!" Then, at the bottom of the pile of presents was my large gold box. As he reached for it, I cringed. It was so obviously a peace offering that I felt embarrassed that I'd done something quite so transparent, especially to be unveiled in these circumstances. It had seemed like a good idea at the time.

When Brian opened the box and pulled out the luxurious jacket a quiet fell over the room. He turned to me. "Jesus, this is magnificent. Who picked it out?" Everyone laughed.

"I did."

"Do I pay you enough to buy this?"

"Visa." More laughs.

"I love it." He stood up and took off his jacket and tried the creamy cashmere on. "Perfect fit." Everybody clapped and cheered as he turned around to model it. He touched the fabric lovingly. "This feels good enough to eat. Very sexy. I might get laid in this. Hey, Tiffany, what do you think. Can I get laid in this jacket?"

"Maybe on Hollywood Boulevard." She retorted smartly as she poured more red wine in my glass. Brian sat down and as he did, he smacked her on the ass and said simultaneously, "Smart mouth for a two-bit cocktail waitress." With that she turned from pouring my wine and proceeded to leave the turned down bottle to run red wine down the front of the jacket. Brian let out a yell like a wounded animal. I jumped up and gave Tiffany a shove away from Brian and the ruined jacket that was so hard it knocked her down on her ass. Brian was on his feet screaming at the top of his lungs.

"You cunt. You mother fucking cunt. Look what you did. Jesus Christ. I'm going to kill you, you stupid goddamn bitch." Red grabbed Brian on one side and I grabbed him on the other. He was foaming with profanities. His eyes were popping out of his head. He looked like a rabid dog. I think in an instant he would have killed her if we hadn't grabbed him. He was drunk. We all were. Once Tiffany got her composure she started screaming. She pointed her finger at me and started shouting "You hit me, you bastard," over and over. The manager ran into the room.

"What's going on in here?" He looked at Tiffany on the floor and the soiled jacket, put two and two together and figured out that there was big trouble before anyone had time to answer. Tiffany was still pointing at me and screaming over and over, "You hit me."

The manager told another of his girls to call the police. Pandemonium broke out. Everyone was talking at once. The manager and Chuck helped Tiffany to her feet and out of the room. Brian was still spewing obscenities as he took off the stained jacket and handed it to me. He asked like a small kid whose toy has been broken. "Do you think they can fix this?"

"Maybe. Maybe they can replace the front panel if they can find some of the fabric. I'll take care of it." I knew that's what he was asking me to do it anyway. To fix it.

Within a few minutes the cops showed up. They asked us a lot of questions and took some statements. Evidently, Tiffany accused me of assault and battery. She was in the other room. I didn't hear her statement, but it was damaging enough for them to tell me I had to come to the police station. The manager made Brian turn in his membership card and kicked the entire party out on the street. Brian started screaming threats at the manager for all the world to hear.

"You better enjoy your last night on the job, asshole, because when I'm done with you, you'll have to leave town. I'm going to sue your puny little ass. I'm Brian Buchanon. KKLA is going to bury you and this low rent club. You'll be out of business in two weeks. Tune in to the Ten O'clock News tomorrow night, buddy. You'll be the laughing-stock of L.A."

The cops herded us away from the entrance to the club. Brian was still cursing and screaming.

As I was being put in the squad car, I heard Brian say to Chuck:

"Hey, kid, follow them to the police station so Paddy has a ride home."

Chuck hesitated and looked at his dad. Chuck didn't want to be in close quarters with me. He was still angry. Red touched his shoulder ever so slightly and said, "Go on, son." Chuck dutifully hopped in his jeep, and Red got in the limo with Brian.

Nice touch! Everyone got to go home and sleep it off while I went to the L.A.P.D. I felt resentful and angry. I had gone out of my way to plan a special evening, and this was my reward.

The ride to the police station was long, quiet and miserable. This was the first time in my life that I had been taken into custody by the police. If my mother and father could see me now. At least I wasn't handcuffed. The streets were lit up like a carnival. The sidewalks of Hollywood were alive with hookers, drug dealers, and kids out for a Saturday night on the town. Everyone was having a good time but me.

When we pulled up to the police station the dregs of society were on the sidewalk. An officer ushered me in. The glare of the florescent lights was unbearable. The noise level, the screaming of the hookers, cops yelling at drug dealers, gangs cursing and spitting, phones ringing in all parts of the building was unbearable as well. I had a splitting headache that got worse every minute I waited. They signed me in and had me fill out a lot of paperwork. I was fingerprinted and photographed. It was humiliating. I saw Chuck watching me through the glass. I couldn't hide my embarrassment from him. I thought I saw pity in his eyes. That was the worst part of all of it.

After I was through with the routine procedures, they took me into a room to make a written statement. They read me my Miranda rights and asked me what happened. I told them the truth. I didn't mean to push Tiffany down on the floor. The wine was spilling on the jacket and I pushed her in a spontaneous reaction trying to get her and the cascading wine away from Brian and the jacket. I meant to shove her away, not hurt her. And even though she fell I was sure she was only stunned and pissed, not hurt. The officers were cordial and acted like this was just a routine that had to be followed. No one was rude or aggressive. Bored and tired was more like it. They joked among themselves and sometimes with me. But when I was unresponsive, they interacted exclusively with each other and ignored me. After about two hours I was released on my own recognizance. The police were not sure if Tiffany was going to press charges, but they thought her case was pretty weak. They had done their part. Time would tell on the wrath of Tiffany. They advised me to consult an attorney just in case.

Chuck and I left the station in silence. I still had Brian's cashmere jacket draped over my arm. A reminder of the failed night. When we got in the jeep, Chuck spoke.

"Rough night, eh?"

"Doesn't get much worse. That party cost me over ten grand, and now this."

"Yeah. Tough break."

He was making small talk. Gone was our camaraderie. I felt so defeated I wanted to cry, but I had humiliated myself enough for one evening. We both grew silent. I needed to call Brian. We needed to do damage control and make sure what happened tonight didn't make it into the papers. Brian had a trouble shooter on the take at the *L.A. Times* that he paid to control our press. We needed to get him on the lookout in case there were any overzealous reporters hanging around the police station or Starlets tonight.

Chuck drove like a bat out of hell through L.A. We hit the freeway going eighty miles per hour.

"You better slow down. You've been drinking. You might get stopped." I cautioned.

"You've got a lot of room to talk! Am I confused or did I just haul your ass out of the LAPD?" He responded defiantly.

"I just don't want you to get a DUI. You could lose your license."

"Don't talk to me like you're my dad. I didn't drink much. That's why I drove. I knew my dad would want to tie one on. I needed to stay sober to drive him home."

"Sorry you didn't get to." I apologized.

"I bet you are. That waitress is going to fry your ass if she can."

"She won't have much of a case. She wasn't injured. No damage. She'll be over it by tomorrow. She got her revenge having the cops take me in. I'm more worried about the bad press."

"Since when do you care about bad press? You sure didn't give a shit when you were fucking around with Georgia."

"What's that supposed to mean?"

"Did you really think no one would find out about you and Georgia when you two had your picture plastered on the front page of the *L.A. Times*?"

"We went to the All-Star Game together. Big Deal."

"Yeah, fucking right under Ahmed's nose. Boy, with a friend like you who needs enemies?"

"You're never going to forgive me, are you?"

"There's nothing to forgive. I will never trust you again. I don't have friends I don't trust. *Comprende*'?"

"I was your friend, Chuck, and I am your friend. I fell in love with Georgia and I had to respect her need to keep our relationship under wraps. It wasn't about you; it was about her. Someday when you fall in love you'll understand."

"Don't patronize me."

"Sorry, but I want you to know that I would never hurt you intentionally. It was just a very awkward situation for me."

"Yeah, well it made me feel like an asshole."

"I'm sorry."

"Let's just drop it," he said, unconvinced.

It hurt that Chuck was still so angry with me. The loss of our relationship was now a reminder of my many failings. Chuck dropped me off at 2AM. The streets in my neighborhood were deserted. I thanked him for the ride and went inside. I turned on the lights and immediately called Brian. He picked up on the second ring.

"It must be Paddy." He answered.

"Yeah. I wanted to make sure this didn't make the Times."

"Don't worry. Red and I have got you covered. How did it go at the LAPD?"

"They asked me a few questions, made me fill out some forms, took my picture, finger-printed me, and got a statement. Nothing too serious."

"Good. Don't worry. I'll handle everything. Get some sleep and I'll see you on Monday."

"O.K. Sorry about your jacket."

11

BACK TO NEW YORK

I slept late on Sunday morning and woke up with a splitting headache. It was probably a continuation of the one from the birthday fiasco. I turned on the tube and slobbed around in my robe till almost three. When I couldn't stand my own company any longer, I took a shower and drove out to Zuma Beach to lie in the sun for a few hours. It was a hot August weekend and the whole world had the same idea. The beach was crowded with weekend warriors, but I found a patch of sand and spread out a towel. I lay down in the hot sand and feel fast asleep. I had that same haunting dream again. But this time I saw my plane. It was on fire. I pushed the eject button just as the plane exploded. I parachuted to safety, but I was behind enemy lines. It was dark. I was scared. I could hear voices and feel movement all around me. I was looking for a safe place to hide. My heart was pounding like the waves hitting the rocks in front of me. I broke into a cold sweat. I could feel the sweat dripping on my body as I worked my way through the thick forest to find a hiding place. I hid behind the familiar boulder from my last dream. I felt safe and hidden from the soldiers that moved past me.

But just when I thought they had missed me completely, they came back again, closer, louder. They grabbed me. They were shaking me. I woke up and there was a man kneeling next to me with his hand on my shoulder.

"Hey, buddy, you O.K?" He was looking at me, concerned.

"What?" I looked at him, trying to focus, confused. He was still gripping me.

"You were moaning like you were in trouble. Is everything all right?" He was worried.

"Bad dream. Must be the heat. Thanks." I got up, embarrassed, ran over the hot sand and jumped in the cold Pacific. The water jolted my body awake. The dream was still floating around in my head. It needed clarification. I was under too much stress. My mind was playing tricks on me. I relaxed in the waves. My body felt relieved to be held up by the water. Brian's party was the last straw. My days in L.A. were numbered. I was sure glad I had a job hunt planned at the end of August. Just a couple of weeks and I could begin to reconstruct my life. What I had left here in L.A. could be put in a few suitcases.

After my swim I picked up my towel and headed back to the Palisades. On the way I stopped at Spruzzo's and had a light dinner of shrimp scampi, salad and mineral water. I needed to lose a few pounds to look good for interviewing. Maybe Brian was right. My looks were my meal ticket. After dinner I headed home for a good night's sleep. When I got to my apartment my message light was blinking. It was Georgia.

"Hi, Paddy, it's me. I just wanted to see how you're doing. I'm lonely and bored. It was so great talking to you yesterday. I realized how much I miss you. Well, since you're out I guess you're not as lonely as I am. Talk to you soon." She hung up. I rewound the message and played it again. It wasn't intentional, but she was torturing me. I was too raw with feeling for Georgia to be her buddy. But I was going to suffer through it because some of her was better than none of her. I couldn't just be smart and let go.

It was late and I didn't know if she would be asleep. I dialed her number. She picked up with a drowsy hello.

"Georgia, sorry. Go back to sleep."

"No. It feels good to hear your voice when I'm in bed. That was one of the best parts of us. Remember?"

"Do you have to ask?"

"I wish you were here."

"I wish I were too. Things not going well between you and Ahmed?"

"Not really. First of all, he's gone all the time. He's gone more for the strike than he was when he was on the road during the season. Instead of taking this time to be with me, he had to get himself embroiled in the negotiations. He's in New York constantly. I'm alone a lot."

"The strike will be over soon. Things will get better then."

"Maybe, but that's not all of it. I feel like I got pushed into making a commitment to Ahmed because of what happened at KKLA."

"You don't have to do anything you don't want to do." I said as my heart soared. Maybe my luck was turning around.

"When are you leaving for New York, exactly?"

"Two weeks from yesterday."

"I leave for Belize one week after you get back. On that Sunday. Maybe we can get together before then."

"If you think it's a good idea. You know I'd crawl over broken glass to get a glimpse of you but you and I together in the same room is like having a match meet gasoline."

"Umm. Sounds hot, very hot."

"Stop. Don't tease me when you mean so much to me. It's not a game for me."

"I'm sorry. It's not for me either. I hate being in the middle of all this. No matter what I do, someone gets hurt."

"That's true. I can't help you there, unfortunately. It's just a part of life."

"I better get some sleep. I have to pick Ahmed up at the crack of dawn. He's coming in on a night flight."

"Georgia, before you hang up, I want to be clear with you that I can't go through too much more Sturm und Drang". I need for you to make a decision once and for all."

"I understand. Good night, Paddy." She said sadly.

I was back in dangerous waters. I was breaking my vow to let Georgia go. But my life without her was no life at all. Maybe I was being selfish but if she wanted me, I would be there for her. My life in L.A. was becoming intolerable. I needed to get the hell out of Dodge. If there was any hope for Georgia and me it had to be far away from this town. She might decide to go with me, and I needed a place to go. I had to keep my options open and look in other markets besides New York. It would be a mistake to put all my eggs in one basket. I resolved to call my old college roommate, Bix, in San Francisco, and go see him as soon as I could. Bix owned a restaurant in the heart of the financial district that was the "in" spot for the movers and shakers of that very hip town. Bix, endearingly self-absorbed and snobbish, named his restaurant "Bix" after himself and a distant cousin, Bix Biederbeck, the horn player. Bix knew me better than almost anyone. He would give me sound advice that had no hidden agenda. While in San Francisco I could sniff around for jobs. I had been drifting for the last few weeks. My plan felt good. I took a shower and went to sleep. For the first time in a month I slept like a log.

When I got to Norm's the next morning, I picked up my newspapers and headed inside. As Verna got me settled, I unfolded The

Hollywood Reporter and there it was, big as life, smack dab in the middle of the front page...

"LA's Silicone Playpen Ejects Execs!"

I read the article. I felt sick to my stomach. Embarrassed and humiliated. I was in deep shit now. After I wallowed a while in my shame, I got up from my booth and went to the phone and called Brian.

"Yo," he answered.

"Have you seen *The Hollywood Reporter*?"

"No."

"Listen to this," I said, as I began to read the article. He said a few choice curse words as I read aloud to him.

"BSI is going to be pissed if they find out about Saturday night. Goddamn it to hell. I'm going to call that dilettante' social butterfly, George Christy, and threaten to sue his ass right off this planet." Brian shouted into the phone.

"On what grounds? Everything he said is true."

"Haven't you learned anything from me? The best defense is a good offense. I'm going to scare the shit out of that asshole!" He growled.

I felt better. Brian could play better hard ball than anyone I've ever known. He couldn't tolerate any more embarrassing scandals in the harassment department. Brian would find a way to scrape the whole mess under the rug.

When I got to work, I was ignored by everyone in the newsroom. The article was stuck up on the bulletin board. Written across the article was "Lover boy strikes again!" With Georgia gone I could act out my rage without hurting her. I yanked down the paper and stomped over to Lani's desk. She had her head down pretending not to notice me.

"Lani, what the fuck is this?" I jammed the paper in her face.

"I don't know what you're talking about," she lied.

"Don't give me that bullshit. I don't appreciate your bitchy innuendoes. Why don't you get yourself laid and stop sticking your shitty discount nose job in my business."

"You fuck around with that slut and have the audacity to tell me to mind my own business. Who are you to be challenging me?"

I lost it. I grabbed her arm more tightly than I should have. All eyes were on us. "Georgia has more substance in her thumbnail than you've gathered in a lifetime. Don't you ever speak of her again. Do you understand?"

"Let go of me, you fuck-wad!" With that she wrenched her arm away and got up and left the newsroom. I figured out that she was going to tattle to Brian that I had manhandled her. He would be pissed but I knew he wouldn't nail me. He couldn't stand her and secretly wished he could do the same. Every man in the place at one time or another had wanted to smack Lani. Until today we'd controlled ourselves. I couldn't control myself any longer. I hated her.

About ten minutes later, Brian called and summoned me to his office. When I got there Lani was perched on the side of his desk in an overly familiar way. Brian spoke first. "O.K. I want you two to kiss and make up. We've got our news department to protect. I can't have my anchors squabbling like a couple of kids in the school yard."

"I want an apology," Lani demanded.

"So do I. One for me and one for Georgia."

"Not her again! Jesus, when will you give that broad up, Paddy?" Brian spat.

"Whether I have a relationship with Georgia or not, I won't have this bitch dragging her name through the mud."

"You're confused, Paddy. I'm not the bitch in heat. Georgia's the one screwing a black man and a white man at the same time." Lani crowed!

"O.K., that's enough!" Brian slammed his fist on his desk and got up. "Lani, go back to the newsroom. I want this shit to stop or I'll throw you both out on your boney asses, contract or no contract."

Lani got up and walked out. I turned to Brian. "Thanks," I said.

"She's a cunt, but you gave her the ammo. You fucked up getting involved with Georgia. You've lost credibility with your peers."

"I don't give a shit about them." I was truthful on that point.

"Then you should leave." He said without emotion.

"I'm going to as soon as my contract's up."

"Good. That will solve a lot of problems."

"I guess our friendship is over?" I asked.

"I demand loyalty, Paddy."

"I understand." As I turned to leave, I felt a flood of relief. Everything was out in the open. I could look for a job and plan my future without having to sneak around. I'd done enough sneaking in the past months to last a lifetime. I was sick of it.

I went through the next week like a sleepwalker. I did what I need-ed to do at work and spent as little time there as possible. Georgia and I chatted a few times, but I told her nothing. I would tell her when the time was right. My number one priority was to find a good job in a top five market.

I left for New York on a night flight after my Friday newscast. I slept most of the way. When we landed at Kennedy the heat and humidity hit me in the face like a warm, damp towel. I'd gotten spoiled by the arid west coast. San Francisco was looking better by the minute. I took a limo to the Righa Royal. It was a fairly new all-suites hotel on 54th be-tween 6th and 7th. I'd heard about it from the national sales manager at KKLA. The prices were reasonable, and I wasn't traveling on an expense account. Plus, it was in a prime location. I checked in, ordered breakfast and went back to sleep. I got up at about three New York time. I took a shower and hit the streets. I walked up to 5th Avenue and visited all my favorite shops. I even went in the jewelry stores, Tiffany, Graff, Cartier, and looked at engagement rings. I lied to the salesclerks and told them I was getting married and needed to look at rings. It felt good. I wanted to be with Georgia, and this was my way of being with her.

The streets were packed and after a few hours the heat got to me. I stopped at Bice' on my way back to the Righa and had a few ice-cold beers. I had them bring me a couple of their dinner appetizers and ate like a contented cow. As it began to turn dark, I headed back to the hotel and settled in for the night. I rented a movie and fell asleep in the middle of it. I was exhausted. The emotional upheaval of my life was wearing me out. I vowed to take better care of myself when I woke up in the morning. It was Sunday so I got up and walked a few blocks to St. Patrick's and went to Mass. The singing of the choir was so moving tears began to stream down my face. I prayed for resolution to my disheveled life. I felt vulnerable and needy in the cathedral. When I left the sun was beating down and the humidity made me wet with sweat in seconds. I caught a cab over to the Metropolitan Museum. It was cool inside, and I felt cared for in its endless rooms and corridors. I needed this. Time to amble. Time to get away.

I ate lunch in the museum restaurant and left at about three in the afternoon. I stopped at a few of the shops on Madison Avenue on my way back to the Righa. When I got back to the room, I peeled off my sticky clothing and sat in my boxers, air conditioning blasting, and watched the local weekend news. God, it was bad. This town needed me. I just hoped they knew it. I made an 8PM reservation around the corner from the Righa at the Trattoria Del Arte. I thought about calling some of my friends from the old days and asking them to join me, but they were friends I had made with Brian. Somehow it didn't seem appropriate. This would be a solitary trip.

I arrived at Trattoria Del Arte right on time. The place was jumping. I was seated right away and ordered from their antipasto bar, the best in the city. I ordered a crisp chardonnay, Burgess '91, and settled in for a food fest. After I finished the antipasto platter, I powered down some garlicky lamb chops. For dessert I ordered a baked peach cobbler with vanilla bean gelato. It was almost as good as sex, something I was short on lately. Stuffed, I waddled back to the Righa to sleep it off.

Monday through Friday I pounded the pavement looking for a job. When I stopped by each station, I tried to be casual. I'm in town on vacation, miss the vibe, would like to come back someday...that bullshit. I didn't want to seem desperate. I wanted them to come after me. Brian had taught me a few things about negotiation. Never let them see you sweat!

The best opportunity was at WWOR. They'd had a number of changes in ownership and needed to beef up their sagging late news. The news director and I hit it off. We vowed to keep the dialog going. I felt elated that there was potential. I spent the weekend doing more of the same, eating, drinking, sleeping. When I left for L.A. I was rested but had put on a couple of pounds from overeating. It was my response to the stress and upheaval. Overeating. My personal nemesis.

Landing at LAX was refreshing. It was a cool and crisp August evening with a breeze off the Pacific that was heavenly. It furthered my resolve to go to San Francisco to job hunt. When I got home, I had a stack of messages. I realized I hadn't retrieved any on my trip. I guess I really needed to escape. There was one from Georgia. "Paddy, I know you're in New York, but I'd like for you to come over for dinner at my new apartment next Saturday and I wanted to ask you before you made any other plans. I leave for Belize on Sunday and I want to see you before I leave. Don't worry. The coast will be clear. We need time to talk. Call me when you get home. I still love you. Bye."

All the emotions ran through me. Love, lust, excitement, followed by fear and vulnerability. Georgia had no idea how much pain I was going through, and I didn't want her to know. I would allow this to play itself out.

I went back to work with the same attitude that I had when I left. I just didn't give a damn anymore. I would give Brian notice the minute I found something, and we could both move on. I felt sad that our relationship was beyond repair. But I'd do it all over again for my time with Georgia. It certainly wasn't the first time a female came between best friends, and it wouldn't be the last. I still didn't know how he found out about us, but it didn't matter. What was done was done. You can't turn back the clock. I was going to have to live out the rest of my career without the boost from Brian.

I called Georgia when I got home on Monday night, and we made a date for an early dinner at her place on Saturday. She said Ahmed would be leaving for New York Saturday afternoon at about three. Georgia's flight to Belize was early Sunday morning so she needed to get to bed early. That worked out fine for me because I could catch a late flight to San Francisco after dinner. I wanted to begin my search in the Bay Area. The humidity of New York was a great motivator.

All week I fantasized about dinner with Georgia. I would take it slow with her. It had been a long time since we had been together. She and I had not seen each other in over a month. I wanted her to be comfortable with me, and then I would make love to her, slowly, agonizingly slow. Talking on the phone every week or so was stilted at best. I needed to look in her eyes to tell if she still cared for me. I had no doubts about my own feelings. I didn't even feel guilty about Ahmed. I was over that. The guy had his priorities mixed up. Georgia should be number one. She was with me. If he lost her at this point, he had no one to blame but himself.

On Saturday morning I woke up from a dream about Georgia with an enormous erection. I masturbated, justifying myself with the logic that if I made love to Georgia that evening I would come too soon unless I relieved my raging hormones. It sounded good at the time. Even after I finished, I still felt aroused. I made myself soft boiled eggs for breakfast. They felt erotic on my tongue. That got me going all over again. I had to calm down. I decided to do my laundry. I went in my bedroom and gathered up the piles of debris left on the floor from my trip to New York. Everything smelled of moldy sweat. That killed off my burning desire for about thirty minutes. Once I loaded it all in the machine, I looked around for another diversion. My weights! I couldn't remember how many months it had been since I picked one of those puppies up. I began to press in front of the full-length mirror in my bedroom. As my arms began to pump up so did my penis. Watching myself made my mind work overtime. I thought about being over Georgia, lifting myself up and down as I entered her hard. I was losing it. I had to get out of the apartment. I looked at my watch. It was only 11AM. I had a long wait. The clothes were finished in the washer. I dumped them in the dryer, hopped in the shower and got ready to go out. I needed some company. I was a danger to myself. When I got out of the shower, I impulsively called Georgia. Ahmed picked up the phone. I hung up quickly.

Georgia told me he was leaving in the mid-afternoon. What an idiot! I could have blown it. I didn't want to make him suspicious. He was paranoid enough without help from me hanging up in his face. I got dressed and headed for the Third Street Promenade in Santa Monica. I would look for a bottle of wine for dinner. Georgia liked Chardonnay. Her favorite was Cakebread. It cost a pretty penny but was worth it.

When I got to the mall it was teeming with Saturday shoppers. I drifted through the stores and stopped for a coke when my feet got tired. I bought a large bunch of tulips for Georgia. They were lavender beauties. When I got to the liquor store, I picked up a bottle of the Cakebread Chardonnay and also a magnum of Schramsberg Brut for insurance. All women, even Georgia, were susceptible to a glass of the bubbly. I felt like I had to court her all over again. But I didn't mind. I was looking forward to it. I never felt as if I knew her, possessed her. That was her allure. She was never mine. She would never be mine. That was Ahmed's fatal mistake. She said yes to the engagement, and now he was taking her for granted. I would never be that foolish. Georgia couldn't be left alone for long stretches. She was high maintenance and needed a lot of stimulation, sexual and otherwise.

After I covered the entire mall, I stopped by Wells Fargo to get cash for my trip to San Francisco. It would be late when I left Georgia's, and I needed to get as much done as possible before I left for her apartment. When I got home, I packed an interview suit and a pair of shorts and a tee shirt. Bix had said something about a bike ride along the Embarcadero on Sunday morning. My flight left LAX at 9:30PM. It was the last flight from LAX on Saturday night. I wanted as much time with Georgia as possible. I could leave her place by 7:00PM and have plenty of time to make it to the airport. Bix was picking me up and had made a reservation for me for the two nights. He was a pal.

It was 4:15. I called Georgia. She picked up with a breezy "Hello."

"Is the coast clear?"

Georgia laughed out loud when she heard my voice. "I'm so happy that you're coming over. It's going to be such fun. When can you get here?"

"How about in 15 minutes?"

She laughed again. "My, you really do miss me!"

"Stop torturing me. Can I come over now?"

"Hurry," was all she said. We both slammed down the receivers and I grabbed my stuff and headed for the door.

I drove like a bat out of hell. I'm amazed I didn't get a ticket. Georgia lived on a tree lined street in the Hollywood Hills. The well-manicured lawns of her neighborhood were filled with flowers. Georgia lived in a small complex of apartments that were straight out of the thirties. I screeched to a halt in front of her building. I jumped out with flowers, wine and champagne in my hands and trotted to her door. I rang the bell and waited what seemed like an eternity. She came to the door with a white towel wrapped around her head and a white terry cloth robe on.

"My God! That was fast. I didn't have enough time to finish my shower."

The sight of her wrapped in white took away all my resolve to take it slow. I reached for her and hungrily pulled her to me. I still had my hands full, but my arms held her against me. A lump formed in my throat. I loved her so.

"Paddy, are you all right?" She said tenderly.

There were tears in my eyes. I finally let go of her to set down the wine and flowers. Then, I took her face in my hands and kissed her eyes, nose, lips, hair and cheeks. I couldn't get enough of her. I wanted to pull her into me. "I love you, Georgia," was all I could manage through gasps of emotion. She closed the door to the rest of the world and led me to the sofa. I pulled the towel off her hair and the robe off her body. I began to devour her. I couldn't stop myself. I was like a starving man. I needed her sustenance to bring me back to life. Every inch of her body provided me with pleasure. I sucked, licked and kissed every part of her. I couldn't get enough. I was in a frenzy of emotion, trying to get all I wanted of something that couldn't fill me up. It was a futile exercise. No matter how hard I tried I would never get my fill of Georgia Conroy. But I knew I would try again and again. I pushed her to the floor and mounted her. We were fucking like two wild animals, screaming, gnawing, biting. The juices of our bodies mingled with our sweat as I plunged deeper into her depths in the lock of passion. We were drenched with sweat and exhausted when we came together like only the most familiar of lovers. Georgia giggled with joy.

"Thank you, God...I've missed that," she whispered.

"That or me?" My insecurity was showing.

"Both."

"Why are you thanking God?" I quizzed.

"That sex can be like that for me, for us. Not everyone is so lucky."

"I know. It always has been magic between you and me. You know, Georgia, I've tried to live without you, and I can't. I don't give a damn about Ahmed or anything else. I want you with me and I'm not giving up till we're together."

"Paddy..." she started. I quickly put my finger to her lips.

"Not now. We don't have to talk about it now. Let's just be together."

We lay in silence on the floor, her head resting on my bare chest. I was in heaven. I wanted to savor it. If I died in this moment, I knew I had loved, wholly and fully. This moment was enough to fill a lifetime of longing. Georgia was all I needed. Brian be damned, Ahmed be damned, she was all I wanted, and I would fight to the death to have her.

We dozed on and off for about thirty minutes. Then Georgia got up and announced, "You haven't even looked around my new apartment. Get up, lazy bones."

I was as content as a cow but to please her I got up and followed her around.

"This is my bedroom, and this is my garden," she gestured with pride. The French doors in the bedroom led out to a large stone patio with a border of rose bushes and climbing rose vines that draped over the wooden fence. It was exquisitely beautiful and very private. The fragrance was intoxicating. It filled her entire bedroom with a luxurious perfume. She beamed, standing naked in front of me, as she stood on the gray stone.

"It's perfect, beautiful, like you," I said as I walked out to join her.

"Do you like roses?" She asked as she took my hand.

"Yes. I'll buy us a cottage with a yard full of roses if you'll run away with me."

"Promise?" She looked at me like a little girl getting a firm commitment for something she wants.

"Promise."

"Why don't you sit out here and enjoy yourself while I make dinner."

"I'll help you." I offered, not wanting her to leave me.

"No. You'll make me nervous and I'm not that sure of myself in the kitchen. But it won't be long. I'm almost done. Here, sit," she said as she placed me in a lounge chair.

I had to admit that the roses were seductive. They made me relax. I daydreamed that Georgia and I were married, in that cottage. That she was pregnant with one of our babies. That we were happy. It felt so good to have her with me, to complete me. I never knew how alone I was until I experienced being connected to her. I heard a pop of the cork from the champagne. Georgia walked out, dressed in a thin pink silk shift, with a flute of the chilled champagne that I brought. I looked at her and said, "You should have let me do that for you." She smiled and kissed my forehead as she set it on the small wrought iron table next to me. Life could not get any better than this. After about ten minutes I got up and wandered into her kitchen.

"Perfect timing! I think it's all ready. Could you open the wine for me?" she asked as she handed it to me.

She was putting the tulips into a small vase and setting them on the table. The tablecloth was floral pastels and her china was cream colored with a thin gold band. She had candles lit even though it was still daylight. We sat down to a salad of fresh heirloom tomatoes, buffalo mozzarella, fresh basil leaves and capers with an olive oil and balsamic vinegar dressing. The taste of the ingredients and the wine made the sensation in my mouth go wild. My taste was heightened because of being in Georgia's presence. It was the best salad I had ever tasted.

Georgia followed up the salad with a penne pasta filled with chunks of smoked ham, fresh asparagus, and sun-dried tomatoes. During the second course we polished off the bottle of wine. We were both tipsy and glowing.

"I'm impressed!" I said, sincerely.

"That I can cook or that it's good."

"Both. It's not fair for the women of America to have to compete with the likes of you."

"Stop!"

"You were fishing, and you know it, so don't play modest with me," I teased.

"You know me too well. Wait till you see this!" She hopped up and carried the plates into the kitchen. In seconds she came back holding two creme caramel laced in orange burnt sugar sauce with a dollop of real whipped cream on top.

"If you cook like this for me all the time, we'll both get fat." I continued to tease.

"So? We'll be fat and happy as the saying goes." I loved her even more with that statement!

"I'll be fat and happy; you'll be fat and sassy!"

"True." As she said this, she winked at me and took a big bite of the custard and licked her lips suggestively as she swallowed.

This was turning out to be the happiest time we had ever spent together. All the burdens we carried throughout our brief relationship were not present this evening. We were playful, loose. That is the way it would be every day for the rest of my life, I vowed. I would create a world of happiness for Georgia and me. I would make a new life for us far away from L.A., Brian Buchanon and Ahmed Brooks.

After dinner we sat in the living room and drank coffee. It was strong and tasted good on my tongue. Georgia loved to sit on her couch and look at her fireplace. It was beautiful. It was made of rock, Arizona Sunburst. The antique andirons looked magnificent inside the majestic fireplace.

"I was so lucky to find an apartment with this much character," she said out loud.

"It is special."

"Do you like the andirons?"

"They're perfect!"

"I bought them on a day that I was feeling blue. I was missing you. So, I did what any self-respecting girl would do...I spent money on an extravagant gift for myself."

"Sounds reasonable."

"I can't wait for winter to have a roaring fire in the fireplace."

"Maybe we'll be in San Francisco or New York for winter."

"Maybe. Wherever I live from here on out has to have a big fireplace."

"Your wish is my command." And I meant it.

I turned her face toward me and kissed her for the longest time. I had missed kissing her more than anything. We kept kissing for at least ten minutes, and then I unzipped her dress and it fell off her shoulders to reveal her round bare breasts and pink nipples. I sucked her nipples as she moaned in pleasure. I made every part of our lovemaking last as long as I could stand it. She began to push my head down her belly. She lifted her buttocks up, and I slid the dress the rest of the way down her body. She had on a pair of lacy white bikini panties. My fingers probed and pushed the crotch of the panties aside. She groaned in pleasure as I stuck my fingers deep inside her. As I stroked her with one hand, I pinched her nipples with the other. She came while I continued to kiss her. She pulled my pants off and put my penis in her mouth. I was in exquisite agony. She knew exactly how to drive me wild. I came in her mouth sooner than I wanted, but I couldn't hold back any longer. We continued to kiss, the taste of me mingled with her on our tongues. I was aroused again and pulled her into my lap. She straddled me and I held her buttocks in my hands, sucked her breast, and worked her up and down in my lap. We were kissing hard as we came in a violent rush of passion.

At the end of our lovemaking there was nothing left. We were like a couple of drenched dishrags. Georgia got up and went into the bathroom. I heard the shower running. I couldn't move. Our passion was so fierce it felt as if this was our last chance. We wanted it all now. When I gathered some strength, I pulled myself up from the couch and got a cold glass of water from the refrigerator. The wine, dinner and sex had made me thirsty. After I drank a couple of glasses I went into the shower with Georgia. Her hair was wet again and hung in ringlets down her flawless face.

"I had to do this. I was sticky all over." She apologized.

"Me too." I soaped her all over and then soaped myself. The water felt good. My body was satisfied and so was my soul.

When we got out the doorbell was ringing insistently.

"Who's that?" I asked, on guard.

"I have no idea!" She said as she grabbed her robe and headed for the living room. I heard her say through the closed door, "Tony! I forgot you were coming. Could you hold on a minute? I'm not dressed. I just got out of the shower."

His replied, "Take your time."

Georgia came running into the bedroom. "Oh, god. I forgot all about Tony!"

"Who's Tony?" I asked, instantly jealous.

"Remember that freelance shooter/editor that we brought in when we were booked up and needed some outside help, you know, the one with the big nose and receding hair line."

That made me feel better and I did sort of remember him. "What about him?"

"He's going to Belize with me. He's brought me my tickets and itinerary. I have to ask him in. I'm so sorry. I forgot and now..."

I interrupted her. "I'll go. I'm planning a life with you. I won't be stingy tonight. Have a great trip, Georgia. Think about you and me when you're down there. I'll see you when I get back and we'll take it from there. We will be together, you know that, don't you?"

"Yes," she said as she pulled my face to hers and kissed me full on the lips. With that she was back in her pink shift and out to open the door. I finished dressing to the sound of their voices as she offered him a glass of champagne. I let myself out the gate of the patio and walked to my car on the happiest night of my life. It was only 7:30. It was still light out. I decided to ride out to the beach and take a walk along the boardwalk and watch the sunset. I wanted to remember this day. I wanted to savor every part.

When I got to Santa Monica the sun was on the horizon. I walked along the beach for a while then found a park bench and sat looking at the sunset. My life was going to change. I would finally have what I wanted. I felt bad about Brian. He had done a lot for me. But Brian needed absolute and unwavering control over my life for our relationship to stay strong. With Georgia in the picture that was not possible. I had been a good little soldier all these years, but now I was AWOL. I would never come back. I looked at my watch and realized an hour had passed. It was 8:30PM. I needed to head for LAX if I wanted to catch my 9:30 flight.

I got to LAX with ten minutes to spare. I stopped to grab a bottle of mineral water and boarded last. It was a short flight, and the wine made me doze on and off. Bix was at the airport to greet me looking like an ad out of GQ. Christ, he was just too perfect!

12

A DATE WITH DESTINY
IN SAN FRANCISCO

Bix took me straight to his restaurant. It was located in Gold Alley in San Francisco. "Bix", the restaurant, had been an assay house back at the turn of the century. The revamped decor reminded me of a supper club straight out of the thirties. It was sophisticated, like Bix. As we entered the restaurant, there was a small quartet with a black torch singer entertaining the well-heeled diners. I felt underdressed, but Bix put me at ease with a martini that was pure perfection. We sat, smoked cigars, ate, drank and talked till one in the morning. I told him about Georgia. Bix was a confirmed bachelor but earnestly tried to comprehend my devotion to her. He felt I was doing the right thing, getting out of L.A. as quickly as possible. He spent most of the evening selling me on the wisdom of coming to San Francisco. The drive in from the airport was quite convincing. San Francisco gleamed like the emerald city from the Wizard of Oz. I was already sold.

I had managed to set up an interview for late on Sunday afternoon. The news director and GM of KPIX, the Westinghouse Station, agreed to meet me at "Bix" for a drink at six. I was going to pitch them hard for a gig. I could already envision Georgia and me moving to San Francisco.

After we closed down the restaurant on Saturday night, Bix took me over to my hotel. It was a bed and breakfast called "1818 California". An exquisite Victorian had been converted into a multi-roomed bed and breakfast. Bix gave me the tour and the inside scoop on the place. Evidently, Robin Williams had lived at "1818" when he was first making it big. Lots of major Hollywood stars stayed at "1818" if they wanted to enjoy the delights of San Francisco without being in the eye of the general public. My room was decorated in French antiques complete with a canopy bed and a bathroom with a deep and comforting claw foot tub. As I settled in, all I could think about was how I would make love with Georgia in this room when we came to live in San Francisco. "1818" is where we would stay till we found our own Victorian cottage. She would love it.

I slept like a newborn, content with my plans. In the morning, I went down to a breakfast of fresh squeezed orange juice, rich coffee and the most sumptuous croissants and homemade jams I had ever eaten. As you might expect, I overate but justified it by saying that this was a celebration of my newfound home. I went out into the rose garden and finished reading the Sunday morning San Francisco Chronicle. Herb Caen was in his heyday, and I wanted to devour his insider point of view. The garden air was crisp and clean, filled with the scent of the roses and ocean breeze.

After about an hour I wandered back into my room and got dressed for a morning of hiking with Bix. He showed up at eleven. We drove over the Golden Gate Bridge to the Golden Gate Recreation Area. The National Park Service had preserved the best real estate by the Bay for hiking, mountain biking and horseback riding. Bix hiked looking like something straight out of the Eddie Bauer catalog, and I looked like a sweat hog. We made our way up the trails grunting and groaning like two guys who needed to do exactly what we were doing. Bix had thought about my predicament overnight and began with an insight. "You know, the tabloids will follow you here. This is Ahmed Brooks' old stomping grounds. He is still a hero to the Bay Area baseball fans."

"Yeah. That's crossed my mind. But the novelty of Georgia and I should wear off pretty quickly, don't you think?"

"You'll both be in high profile jobs."

"That's true. I can't let that stop me from coming here, though."

"Do you think Ahmed will give her up without a fight?"

"No. But leaving L.A. will help. My name will be mud when people find out, but I can deal with it. I feel bad about Ahmed, but relationships don't fail unless there is an underlying problem with them. You can't break up a solid relationship. Ahmed tries to control Georgia, and she resents it. Plus, with him, baseball comes first. He is crazy about her, loves her dearly. That's clear. But he is obsessed with his career, and she gets left alone a lot."

"And, of course, you took full advantage of that little detail," Bix chuckled.

"Well, you might say that. But, Ahmed made it easy for me."

"If she leaves him, what makes you think she won't leave you?"

"I will devote my life to her. I already have. For me to sever ties to Brian Buchanon was a big step. I thought he and I would be a team throughout my career. He has been my mentor for over ten years. It's been a very hard bond to give up. But I had no choice."

"Why couldn't you continue your friendship with Brian?"

"You'd have to know him. It's too complicated and hard to explain to an outsider. In fact, it would sound trite trying to. But let's just say that I defied his wishes and tried to conceal something that he thought was his business. I don't agree with him, that it was his business. We don't see eye to eye on that point and that's the crux of it."

"It sounds like something that could be worked out. It's a shame to end a friendship that has spanned so many years of your life over one disagreement, especially one about a woman."

"That would be true of most relationships, but Brian is different from most people. The rational rules don't apply in his case. Brian wants to own your ass if he's going to mentor you. He demands absolute loyalty and when I got involved with Georgia against his wishes I stepped over a very clear boundary. We're at odds now, and there is no resolving it. He feels that I've betrayed him and wants the relationship over."

"Whew! Sounds pretty autocratic if you ask me!"

"You don't know the half of it."

"Well, you can move to San Francisco and start over. No man should have that kind of hold over another man's life. You're better off. Trust me!"

"You're right. However odd as it may seem to you, I will miss him. We had a lot of great times together. And he took care of me. My career was as important to him as it was to me. I'm sure I'll never have that again in any business relationship."

"Paddy, don't be so naive. It sounds like pure manipulation."

"You're right, of course. But until now there were no unpleasant consequences. It felt good being used!" We both chuckled.

When we reached the top of the bluff, the view of the Bay was spectacular. The air was so clean and oxygen rich I felt lightheaded. This was paradise, and I was in it. To hell with New York. San Francisco was heaven on earth. Georgia and I would make our life here, raise our children here, and grow old here. This would be our home. I couldn't wait to tell her how much I loved it. I wished I could reach her in Belize, but I knew better. The phone system would never allow it. I'd have to wait till she came back.

Bix had a backpack filled with a gourmet feast prepared by the chef at his restaurant. He spread it out on a blanket on the bluff and served me like the needy friend that I was. We feasted on chilled prawns with pesto dipping sauce, feta and walnut stuffed cherry tomatoes, fresh corn off the cob mixed with a tart salsa, and a crisp Robert Sinsky Sauvignon Blanc. I was filled with sensation, of the view, the air, the food. But my heart and mind were filled with images of Georgia. I wanted to be with Georgia on this bluff. Not that Bix wasn't good company and a great friend to pamper me so well, but this was a day for lovers. After looking at the view and resting a little, Bix gave me a fresh pear tart with vanilla custard to top off his culinary surprises.

"Great meal. I'm going to look like Babe fuckin` Ruth for my interview tonight. Georgia stuffed me last night and now this. I hope I can squeeze into my interview suit."

Bix chuckled. "Don't wear a suit. You're meeting them on a Sunday night. You don't have to be in navy, you know. You could come in a pair of khaki's and a plaid shirt and blazer."

"You can get away with that. I'm not sure about my ability to pull it off."

"Sure, you can. It's much more in vogue than you think."

"This job is too important."

"That's why you have to appear secure. Not overdressing is one way to demonstrate that you feel confident that you're in control and not desperate. They're going to want to know why you're leaving KKLA."

"That will be tricky. I happen to know Harry Fuller, KPIX's GM, is a former news director, so I'm going to appeal to his sense of ethics. The entire industry knows Brian Buchanon would prostitute his mother for a buck, so the integrity of the news is not his number one priority. He constantly lets sales sell editorial. I can let Harry know how much that offends me. I'm sure it would offend him too. Then he will understand my need to move on."

"But what if he knows about your close relationship with Brian?"

"Then my goose is cooked."

"Why can't you tell him the truth?"

"I'm not sure what the truth is anymore."

"Well, I'd tell him. It starts your slate clean. You won't have to look over your shoulder anymore."

"You're right, of course. But I'm not sure I have the courage. It won't sound too great that I got involved with Ahmed Brooks' girlfriend, a woman I worked with, and Brian found out and that ended our relationship."

"I didn't mean to go into graphic detail with Harry, for Christ's sake. I meant give him the truth without going into much detail...for example you could just say that Brian has a reputation for control, and you got to experience it firsthand. He got overly involved in your personal relationship with a woman and you couldn't tolerate his unbridled interference in your business any longer. That's the truth without revealing more than you want to."

"You're a genius!"

"So, I've been told."

"Thanks. I'm not thinking too clearly these days. I just want this miserable part of my life over with. I have to get this job."

"You will."

The next morning Bix was outside "1818" with two bikes. We rode down to the Embarcadero for a brisk ride along the bay. It cleaned out the cobwebs for my interview and helped work off my face stuffing of late.

Bix was right. My meeting Sunday evening went very well. KPIX wanted to beef up their hard news staff. Because of my investigative background, they were very interested in making me an offer. I wouldn't be an anchor for them initially but would instead produce and host special series and reports. I loved the investigative part of the news and would welcome a chance to do something more flexible than the nightly grind of late news. I would have my evenings free to be with Georgia. That was what appealed to me the most. I might go back to anchoring when Dave McElhatton retired, but for now this was perfect.

I slept great Sunday night and got up at 5AM to catch the 6AM Shuttle back to L.A. The flight was over in one minute because I slept the whole way. I was relaxed because I could finally see my way out. Georgia and I would have our Victorian cottage sooner than we had planned. I couldn't wait for her to get back from Belize so I could share it all with her. Once this was behind us, Georgia and I would live happily ever after. Just like in the fairy tales. As soon as I landed, I got my car and headed to Norm's. I was starved for breakfast and wanted to share my success in San Francisco with my buddies at Norm's. I was like People Magazine to them. Every morning I was the featured entertainment. It was 7:45AM when I got there. Verna waved to me from the glass window. I stopped long enough to grab the *L.A. Times*. I caught the word "murdered" on the front page as I pulled out the paper. When I lifted the paper to eye level, I turned it over to the bottom half of the front page. The headline screamed out at me.

GEORGIA CONROY FOUND MURDERED IN WEST HOLLYWOOD

I must have passed out. When I looked up, I saw Verna looking down at me as I lay in a ball on the asphalt. There was a sound coming out of me that sounded far away. A wail. An animal sound. I couldn't move. Every part of me was limp. I had no strength to get up or speak.

Verna was trying to say something to me, but it was hard to hear her over the screaming. It was my voice I heard, but I couldn't feel myself making any sound. It was like I was throwing my voice. Verna kept trying to reach me, shaking me gently.

"Paddy, it's O.K. baby. Tell Verna what's the matter. Paddy! Stop screaming and let me help you."

I felt strong arms under my shoulders. Two of the old guys that were in the coffee shop each morning were holding me under each arm and helping Verna pull me into the restaurant. Verna put an iced towel on my head and gave me coffee to drink. I remembered why I was wailing and looked down at the paper again and read with tears flooding the ink.

"Georgia Conroy, fiancée of baseball legend Ahmed Brooks, was found murdered late Sunday evening in her West Hollywood apartment. Ms. Conroy was a former reporter and producer for KKLA Television. She most recently was a freelance producer for PBS. Ms. Conroy was on her way to Central America on an assignment for PBS. When Ms. Conroy failed to show up for a flight to Belize on Sunday morning, her production crew tried unsuccessfully to reach her by phone. The crew continued to try to reach her from their stopover in Mexico City. When they arrived in Belize, they alerted the LAPD that Ms. Conroy had not left any messages for them and had failed to meet them or, according to Mexicana Airlines, begin her journey to Belize. Sources close to the investigation revealed her time of death to be sometime Saturday evening.

Ahmed Brooks, the premier player on the L.A. Dodgers roster and one of America's most beloved center fielders, could not be reached for comment. He was in New York at the time of the murder. Mr. Brooks is one of the key players in the continuing negotiations of the baseball strike. Team members for both the Dodgers' and Giants' organizations said that Mr. Brooks is devastated and blames himself because he was away from Ms. Conroy when the murder occurred..."

I wanted to leave Norm's but couldn't find the energy to move. I was trapped inside an unwilling body. I was in shock. Verna was fluttering around me like a mother hen. I sipped coffee and stared ahead of me. So many thoughts and feelings flooded my mind that it was blank from the overload. I had stopped functioning.

After about thirty minutes, I stumbled out to the car. I drove through a surreal L.A. back to my apartment. My stomach was churning as I walked in the door. I rushed to the bathroom and began to vomit. I collapsed over the toilet and heaved until there was no more. I lay in the fetal position for about an hour. I knew I needed to talk to someone and find out what happened, but there was no one to turn to. I couldn't go to work. I had no friends, no comfort, there. I had no energy to deal with them anyway. Keeping breathing was all I could manage.

I crawled out and lay down on my couch and listened to the messages on my machine. The first was from Georgia. I froze when I heard her voice. She was hysterical. "Paddy, my God, I have to talk to you. You just left. I wish you had stayed. You forgot to tell me where you were staying in San Francisco. Please call me if you get this message. Something unspeakable has happened to us. I need to talk to you. I need to see you. I leave for Belize at 7am tomorrow. Please, please call. Damn! Where are you?" The hair on my body stood straight up. She was in trouble. The call came in at 7:45PM Saturday evening, just minutes after I left her apartment. I was on my way to Santa Monica when she called.

The second call was from Ahmed. It came in at 5:30AM this morning when I was still in San Francisco. Ahmed's voice was breaking. "Paddy, It's Ahmed. I... Oh God, Georgia! Jesus, what am I going to do?" He cried into the phone. "Paddy, you have to help me. Oh, God. It's my fault. I never should have left her...Sorry, I... I'm flying back to L.A. this morning. They called me too late last night to get a flight." Then his broken voice changed to rage. "I'm going to kill the fucking bastard who did this to her. I need you to help me, Paddy. Find out all you can from the L.A.P.D. They told me nothing, those worthless goddamn pricks, just that she had been killed in her apartment. I need to know how she died. Was there a struggle? Did she suffer?" As he said the word suffer, he began to sob uncontrollably but continued miserably. "I have to know. I have to know..." He cried harder. He managed to choke out, "I'll call you when I get in."

I knew I had to call the police. I had been with Georgia the night she was killed. Plus, I knew she had a visitor after me. Ahmed would find out that I had seen her. But I had a good reason for being in her apartment Saturday. Georgia and I were close friends and former co-workers and had worked together on the Belize story. It was logical that we would have dinner together the night before she left on the trip back to Belize. I had to protect Ahmed from the truth. He would go through enough pain without knowing that Georgia and I were lovers. It was a moot point now anyway. I had to do this for Georgia. She would want it this way. She loved Ahmed and had gone to great lengths to keep from hurting him. I could keep this final secret for her.

I called the police station and asked for homicide. They treated me like an annoyance. A detective came on the line. "Homicide. Detective Wagner."

"Detective, this is Paddy McGurk. I'm a friend of Georgia Conroy."

"Mr. McGurk, I'm glad you called. We need to talk to you."

"That's fine, but first I need to find out what happened to Georgia. How did she die?"

"Have you read the paper?"

"Yes, but..."

"That's all we can reveal at this point. If you wouldn't mind coming in, we can talk about this further. You may have information that could help us."

"Perhaps. Georgia called me the night she died. I saw her that evening as well."

"You saw her?"

"Yes."

"What time?"

"We had an early dinner together."

"That doesn't answer my question."

"I guess I got there at about 4:30, and we ate at about six and I left around 7:00 ish."

"Would you mind coming in this morning?"

"No. I'll be there shortly."

"Good. I'll see you in the next hour then?"

"Yes."

I was covered with dirt from lying on the asphalt outside of Norm's and puke from the bathroom. I took a quick shower and changed clothes. I called into the station and told them I was not coming in. I talked to Herb. He understood. I asked him what he knew, and he knew very little. The police were not talking. He said they had already questioned Brian and him and asked them if Georgia had any known enemies. They both, of course, said no. I could think of a few, that bitch, Lani, for one. But as much as I hated her, she wasn't a murderer.

The sadness that enveloped me made all my movements and thoughts slow. I literally dragged myself out to the car. I drove through L.A. and cried. How could this happen? Was this my penance? Had I caused this? This was way too big a price to pay for my sins. I banged my hands on the steering wheel and wailed. I cursed God. Why didn't he take me? I was the one. I was the one who should be punished. Georgia. Georgia. Georgia. What did she suffer in those last minutes? Why did I leave her that night? I could have saved her. I was in a state of near hysteria as I pulled into the L.A.P.D. visitors parking.

I went back into the same hell hole I had left the night of Brian's party. The same lowlifes, the same smell, the same noise. I found the homicide department without any trouble and asked for Officer Wagner. They called him, and he came out of his office and greeted me. Officer Wagner was not at all what I expected. He was tall and handsome with wavy dark hair and a late summer tan. I was surprised to see him dressed to the nines. As he extended his arm in greeting, I noticed hand-stitched monograms on his starched white shirt. Officer Wagner was a far cry from the vice cops that had picked me up from Starlets. He was slick as glass and all business.

As he led me to his office, I noticed a clock on the wall above the door. It was only 9AM. My whole life had passed by in a mere two hours. Officer Wagner gestured for me to sit down when we entered the office.

"So, Mr. McGurk," he started, "I appreciate your coming in on such short notice."

"I want to help you in any way that I can."

"Thank you. First of all, why don't you tell me what you know about Georgia Conroy and the night she was murdered." He turned on a tape recorder as I began to speak. As he began the recorder he gestured for my approval and I nodded yes.

"Georgia and I were very close friends."

"When did you first meet?"

"Well, I guess it was last December. She came to KKLA, the television station where I work, to find a job."

"That was when you first met Ms. Conroy?"

"Yes. She was the girlfriend of Ahmed Brooks, the center fielder for the Dodgers. I'm sure you know that. We were getting pressure from the Dodgers to help her break into television in L.A. We hired her of course."

"We? Did she work for you?"

"No. I'm using the universal "we" I guess. But we worked together on a lot of projects. I admired her ability and trusted her to work on my hard news projects."

"I see. How long did you work together?"

"All of '94 until about a month ago."

"Tell me about the night she was murdered. You said on the phone that she called you and she saw you that evening."

"Not in that order. I spent a few hours with her early that evening, and right after I left her apartment, she must have called me. I brought the tape of that call. In the message she left on my machine she seemed really upset."

"Do you have any idea why she was upset."

"No. She was quite happy when I left."

"Why were you with Ms. Conroy that evening?"

"She was on her way to Central America to do a series for PBS on the Miskito Indians. She and I had done a news series on the same topic at KKLA. She wanted me to come over for dinner before she left on her assignment so we could go over some of the things that we had discovered on the trip she and I had taken to Belize earlier this year."

"Did you notice anything or anyone unusual when you were with her?"

"No, although she had a visitor as I was leaving."

"Really?" I had piqued his interest. "Who was it?"

"I'm not sure. I didn't meet him."

"How do you know she had a visitor if you didn't meet him on your way out?" That question stopped me in my tracks. I hadn't thought this through before coming here.

"I was going out her backdoor and he was coming in her front door."

"Are you in the habit of exiting from the rear of people's homes that you are visiting?"

"I had used the bathroom and didn't want to interrupt her business meeting, so I let myself out the back patio. Is that a crime?"

"No. Odd. That's all. How do you know it was a business meeting?"

"She said she was expecting one of her crew to drop off her plane tickets."

"Do you know his name?"

"No. I'm sorry, I've forgotten. I think she said it, but it escapes me right now."

"Are you sure that's who was at the door?"

"Georgia looked out and saw him. She recognized him. That much I know for sure."

"When Mr. Buchanon from KKLA came down and identified the body he mentioned that you had been involved with Ms. Conroy at one time. Is that true?"

I was stunned again. Of course, Brian was called to identify Georgia's body. Ahmed was out of town. It made me sick to think of her lying there, cold, while he looked her over. And in a rush of sentiment he had to tell them of my affair with Georgia. "Yes. But I would prefer that not get out. It would hurt her fiancée`, Ahmed Brooks. He has enough to deal with right now."

"Unless it becomes pertinent to the case, there is no reason to share that information. Were you sexually involved with Ms. Conroy the night of the murder?"

"No. It was a business meeting."

"Is there anything else?"

"That's all I know about that evening. Now that I've given you what you want, could you tell me what you know about how she died? I need to know."

"She didn't suffer. That's all I can tell you. We need to keep the specifics quiet because they are unusual and only the murderer would know the details. You understand."

"Yes. Is that all?"

"Actually, Mr. McGurk, it would be helpful if you let us take your fingerprints and a blood sample while you're here. It's routine procedure and won't take much more of your time. Also, do you mind if I have a look at your hands?"

"No problem." I extended my hands and he turned them and looked them over thoroughly. "You already have my fingerprints on file. I was in an altercation at Starlets and was brought in for a few hours. They took a set of my prints at that time."

"That's right. That had slipped my mind. You were here a few weeks ago in vice. Mr. McGurk, you certainly have had your run-ins with women of late. First at 'Starlets' and then with Lani Green, your co-anchor. Well, we'll just need the blood sample then."

"No problem." I was numb with defeat. He had all the dirt on me from Brian. There was no point in arguing.

"I appreciate your co-operation, Mr. McGurk. I would ask that you don't leave town. You need to be available to speak with us again. We'll need to talk with you a few more times as we get more information from the lab."

"What are they doing to her?"

"A full autopsy."

"She needs to have a proper burial." I began to cry. My tears ran freely down my face as I thought of Georgia's body being probed by strangers looking for clues. She should be in my arms, protected. I would never hold her again. What had begun, I couldn't stop. She was no longer mine, to love, to cherish, except as a memory.

Once the tears started, they wouldn't stop. I think what got me was hearing about the autopsy. It made her death real to me. I went to the lab in the basement of the police station and had my blood sample taken as tears continued to stream down my face. But what kept the tears going throughout the rest of the day, even after I left the L.A.P.D., was the realization that this wasn't a dream, a nightmare, but a tragedy that would drag me to the depths of my misery. I wasn't going to wake up from this and everything be O.K. This was it for me. I would never recover. I thought when Georgia and I parted the first time, when she decided to marry Ahmed, that it was the most painful thing I would ever experience. But that pain was nothing. She had a secure life planned and I could imagine her in it. Even though she would be with Ahmed, her happiness gave me gratification. When we got back together on Saturday, I felt a joy and optimism about my future with her that was exhilarating. I was in heaven. But now she was gone forever. I would never hear her or see her or be with her again. I drove home and wailed in hopeless agony on my bed tossing from back to stomach and back again. I couldn't eat or sleep. My life was over. My life was over forever. I had nothing worth living for.

When I came home from the L.A.P.D., I had a message from Bix. I couldn't talk to him or anyone. I was too distraught. He had heard about Georgia, read it in the papers, heard it on the news. I would call him when I could, but now I couldn't.

No one from KKLA had called. An interesting omission. Brian had done me damage with the police, and I was sure it was intentional. He was a strategist. He knew exactly what he was doing when he let slip about my affair with Georgia and my run ins with Lani. This was his way of getting even with me. He had stooped to his lowest using the tragedy of Georgia's death to even the score. He had no soul, no inner morality or scruples. I had seen his ruthlessness dealt out over the years. I should have been smart enough to know that I might be on the receiving end of it someday. This latest maneuver signaled that he would stop at nothing to crush me.

I racked my brain all day trying to think if there were any clues as to who could have done this to Georgia. She had no real enemies. Lani, a few women at work, but they were not that interested in Georgia since she left KKLA. I had no idea. Ahmed might have a better idea. Maybe it was a racism thing. The O.J. trial had surfaced a number of suspected racist creeps like Mark Fuhrman who was accused of planting damaging evidence to implicate O.J. But that was far-fetched as well.

Around three in the afternoon I got a call from Ahmed.

"Paddy, I'm at my apartment. Have you found out anything?"

"No. The police aren't talking."

"You saw them."

"I went in and made a statement."

"Why did you have to make a statement?"

"I had dinner with Georgia the night she was killed."

There was a pained silence. Ahmed let out a long breath. "You had dinner with her? Why?" He was agitated.

"She was leaving for Belize. She wanted to go over some things about the trip."

"Wait a minute," he registered what I was saying, "you had dinner with her the night she was killed? Where?"

"At her apartment." More silence as he tried to comprehend what I was saying and what it meant.

"I was with her until three. She never mentioned it," he said mainly to himself.

"It was a spontaneous thing. She was panicked about her trip back to Belize and wanted a little reassurance and information, that's all." I lied.

"When did you get there?"

"4:30."

"I'd barely gone. When did you leave?"

"About 7:00."

"It must have been some dinner. Why did you stay so long?"

"She was lonely and missed having you with her. I cleaned up her kitchen and helped her get organized." I lied some more.

Ahmed was silent again as he measured the information. He was in shock and wanted to make sense of what I was telling him. "You were her mentor. She trusted you, Paddy," was all he could manage. He began to sob. He had held back until now, in that jock way, trying to be strong and in control. I cried silently along with him. We both needed resolution. We wanted answers.

"She was happy about her trip, up, very up. Thank God she didn't suffer." I tried to reassure him.

"How do you know?" he asked suspiciously.

"The police told me when I went in."

"How did she die, Paddy?" he asked through sobs.

"They won't give me a single detail, just that she didn't suffer. I'd like to get my hands on who did this to her."

"I'm going to kill the bastard with my bare hands," he vowed. "Did you see anything, anyone lurking around her apartment."

"One of the guys going on the trip with her brought over her tickets while I was there. That's all. The police are checking it out." I said.

"Georgia was so beautiful that any nut could have seen her and stalked her. I begged her to get in a security building. Damn. I should have made her do it. This is my fault. I shouldn't have been in New York. I should have gone on the trip with her. She wanted me to. I had a meeting on that goddamn strike. I should have blown it off and gone with her. Damn. Damn it all. Oh, God, what am I going to do without her, Paddy? She was all I had. I loved her so..." Ahmed softly wept.

Ahmed's voice was a torrent of emotion, tears, recrimination, regret. I understood it all so well. My face was covered with silent tears.

"Stop torturing yourself. You didn't know this would happen. It's not your fault." I tried to help.

"But I should have insisted she be in a safer place." He said.

"Georgia had a mind of her own. She would have fought you on that. You know how independent she was."

"I love her. Oh, God. This is just too hard, Paddy."

"I know." And I did know. "Ahmed, we need to get her remains from the coroner as soon as they finish the autopsy. We need to arrange some kind of a memorial, a funeral. Have you spoken with her family?"

"They don't want to deal with me. I'm sure they think I did it."

"Would you like for me to take care of that for you. Perhaps I can reason with them."

"I can't handle much more. I'd be grateful. I'm still shocked that you saw her right before she was killed. Was she worried about anything? Did she seem frightened? Had anything out of the ordinary happened?"

"I didn't notice anything unusual in her demeanor and she certainly didn't say anything to make me feel she was in danger. I never would have left her alone. You know that!" I reasoned.

"I know you cared about her. That was obvious." He made that remark with a trace of bitterness.

"Give me her family's number and I'll try to get something organized." I offered.

"Thanks, Paddy. I really appreciate it." He gave me the information and hung up.

I spent the rest of the afternoon trying to deal with angry, uncooperative parents and relatives of Georgia. They wanted the body flown back to the south and they didn't want Ahmed in attendance at her services. I decided to tell Ahmed that we should have a memorial here and let them have her remains. It was the only way not to have it become ugly for all concerned. Ahmed and I needed to concentrate on helping the L.A.P.D. find the bastard that killed her.

The next morning, I called in to the station to talk to Herb. I wanted to beg off another couple of days. He was in a meeting, but his assistant said Brian had left a message with her that he needed to talk to me when I came in. I had her transfer me.

"Buchanon here," he boomed into the receiver when he picked up.

"It's Paddy, what do you want?" I responded coldly.

"You in the building?"

"No. I'm not coming in today."

"I'm putting you on suspension. I'll pay you till the end of your contract, but I want you off the news and out of this station."

"Not that I give a shit but I'm curious under what grounds are you leveling this suspension?"

"You're a suspect in a murder, buddy. I'll do anything for big ratings but not have my main anchor a murder suspect."

"How nice to know you have some discretion. You love this, don't you, you sick, twisted fuck."

"Hey, I'm sorry that Georgia was murdered. I hope you didn't do it."

"You know damn well I didn't do it."

"Maybe. But I'm not coming to your rescue again."

"Nobody asked you to."

"Just stay away from here. I'll get Chuck to bring you the crap from your desk. Other than that, you'll get your big fat check till the end of the year. That should keep your attorney happy." He leveled me again.

"You cold blooded bastard. Fuck you!" I slammed down the phone. He had gotten to me. Naturally, I hadn't even thought of getting an attorney. He had to be the one to give me a reality check. I hated it that I would take one more piece of advice from him, but I found myself looking up the number of a few of the big names in the defense game. Wait till my parents got wind of this. I decided to call them. I needed a friend. My dad answered.

"Dad, I'm in trouble."

"Paddy? What's the matter, son?"

Hearing his voice, the comfort of it made me cry. "A close friend, Georgia, the girl I've been telling you and mom about, was murdered and the police think I could have done it."

"Jesus! Paddy."

"Dad, I loved her. I was going to marry her. I didn't kill her. But I was in her apartment the night she was killed. I look guilty as hell. I'm scared." Saying it was the first time I realized that fear was creeping into my grief. I was a suspect in a murder case. It was ridiculous, but I was the only one that thought so.

"What can I do to help you? Should we come out?"

"Not now. I just wanted to tell you before you read it in the paper."

"I must have missed it. Or our little paper didn't run the story. Are they accusing you?"

"Not yet. I guess it depends on what they find when they finish the autopsy and the rest of the investigation."

"How are you holding up?"

"Not great. Losing her is the worst thing that has ever happened in my life. And now to be a suspect is too cruel a joke to be played at a time like this. I don't know how to deal with it. My life is a mess."

"Can you come home for a while?"

"I'm sure the L.A.P.D. would not look kindly on my leaving town. Let me talk to mom."

"She's not here. Remember? The church bazaar is this weekend. She's in town helping the women's auxiliary get ready."

"The church bazaar," I repeated, comforted by something familiar from my childhood. Life goes on in small town America.

"She's going to want to come out." He said.

"No, I don't want you involved in this mess. I'll call you as things progress. I'm sure they'll find the real killer and this nightmare will be over. I'll come home then for some of mom's TLC."

"Keep calling us, son. You'll be in our prayers."

When I hung up it was only 11AM. I had a whole day ahead of me. I didn't know what to do next, but I knew I had to stay busy.

I called a number of churches in the west L.A. area. They were all available to hold a service for Georgia. I called Ahmed, and we settled on a chapel in Bel Air. It was small and secluded. We didn't want a media circus. I told Ahmed I would contact the people he wanted there. We made a list over the phone. Ahmed wanted a few people from the Dodgers' and Giants' organizations, Georgia's friends at KKLA, PBS and KCRA in Sacramento. He was so grateful that I was doing this for him. But it was me that I was doing this for. I needed to keep working on Georgia's behalf.

Georgia's family would not come out to the service, that was clear. I contacted everyone by phone, including Brian, and left voice mail messages that the service would be on Wednesday afternoon at 3PM.

It was Tuesday. Georgia had been dead for only 72 hours. My world without her was forming. I would be a friend to Ahmed. A mediator for her family. They liked me on the phone, and that pleased me. Even though Georgia was not close to her mother, I sensed that her mother loved her. We had that in common as a point of connection. I felt that her mother picked up, the way only mothers can do, that I had loved Georgia. She was quite tender with me on the phone. I knew I would meet her someday. I wanted to know more about Georgia. When all this was behind me, I would journey to the deep south and look at albums in a chintz filled southern living room with Georgia's mother. I wanted to know what Georgia looked like as a baby, a little girl, the foods she liked, the friends she had, the hobbies, the books she read, the room, the bed she slept in. I needed what was left of her to fill the growing emptiness that was expanding inside me.

That night, after I had a dinner of toasted tuna fish sandwiches and sucked down a half bottle of Stoli, I went to bed early. I was exhausted. I wanted to forget and dream of life with Georgia. I wanted to wake up and have this all go away. But I dreamed the dreams of the damned. I was lost, wandering in a thick forest. There were snakes, Hyenas and wolves peering at me from branches and behind the trees. Everywhere I moved, everywhere I looked, there was danger. I was in darkness filled with peril. And there was no way out. I woke at least six times and tried to alter my dreams, but each time I fell back into the troubled sleep. At six in the morning on Wednesday I gave up and got out of bed. I took a shower, got in my car and drove to the beach. The sand along the Pacific Coast Highway near my condo in Pacific Palisades was empty. There were a few lone surfers trying to ride anemic waves to the shore but, in essence, I had the beach to myself. I walked along the thin stretch of beach till I reached rocks where I could go no further. I picked a rock and sat down and cried. In all my life I had suffered no tragedies. My grandparents had died but it was their time. It was sad, but not tragic. Losing Georgia was tragic, for her, losing her life just as the bloom of her being was at its fullest and most beautiful, for me, losing the only woman I would ever love wholly and fully, holding nothing back, giving all I had to give. I wept watching the September sun flicker across the surf, lighting up the waves like translucent, glimmering glass. Georgia was missing this moment, and I was missing it as an experience with her. The richness of life would be lost to me forever without her to share it with. I think in that moment on the rock I came to understand fully what this loss would mean to me. For the rest of my life, all my experiences, my greatest joys and my greatest sorrows would be dulled without her as my partner. All my adult years, so many years, had been as a single man. I didn't think I would ever need a woman to complete my life. I was wrong. I didn't need a woman, but I needed Georgia. As I sat with the bright Indian summer sun warming my body, I knew my heart would forever, in this life, be cold with loss.

It was almost 10AM when I left the beach. I drove up the coast to a small French bakery across from the Malibu pier and had eggs, pastry and strong coffee. I headed back to my home, my dwelling was more like it, and got ready to go to the service for Georgia. As I entered my condo, I saw a fog rolling in over the cliffs that separated the Pacific Palisades from the coast. The weather was changing to fit the mood of the day, no longer bright and sunny pure California, but bleak, cold and isolating.

I dressed and drove to the chapel at 1:30. I wanted to be early to make sure everything was taken care of properly. Ahmed was already there. When he saw me, he came over and shook my hand and held it for a moment. He was filled with feelings, and the sight of me unleashed them. I felt sorry for him, sorry that I wasn't the friend he thought I was. The minister was an ecumenical sort and had a very meaningful talk prepared about the gift of life and the pain of loss. We all needed some comfort and he would try to provide it. Ahmed was going to say a few words and asked me to also, but I declined. I felt that it would be inappropriate under the circumstances. Brian would be in attendance. Ahmed had, against his own wishes, invited Brian in deference to the brass in the Dodgers' front office. I knew I would be uncomfortable with him there, but I had no choice in the matter.

The service started right on time at 3PM. I sat in the back and watched everyone be seated. I could have greeted the guests, but I just didn't have the energy. Chuck came in just at the service started and took a seat near the back. He didn't see me. I looked around for Red, but I didn't see him. I figured he had to take care of the station while Brian was doing his duty. Otherwise, I'm sure Red would have been there. He was at his best at these types of things with his fatherly manner and paternal looks and gestures. Chuck wept openly as the minister delivered the eulogy. He looked so young and tender it broke my heart. Chuck needed his dad today, that was obvious. I was sorry he wasn't there for Chuck. I was amazingly calm through the service. The morning on the beach had gutted my grief for that day and made it possible for me to maintain my composure.

As we filed out of the chapel to the front lawn, small groups assembled to chat and offer condolences to Ahmed. I stood on the steps away from the crowd and looked out at the somber day. It was misting now, one of those fine mists that comes from a summer fog. It fit the mood of the rest of my life. As the guests began to leave, a squad car pulled up and two officers got out, one was Detective Wagner. I thought it was particularly bad form for the LAPD to show their faces at this final gathering of Georgia's friends. The small groups that had assembled turned to watch the police as they walked across the lawn. I began to walk towards them to ask them to show a little discretion when I realized they were heading towards me as well. When we reached each other, they held out a piece of paper to me. I took it and looked around. The stragglers from the service had stopped and were looking at me as I read the document. It was a warrant for my arrest for the murder of Georgia Conroy. The judge had found probable cause from the evidence submitted, and I was the prime suspect in the murder. They were taking me in. It registered with me very slowly. Ahmed walked over.

"Paddy, what's going on?" he turned to the cops. "Couldn't you assholes have a little respect?" Ahmed was peeved that the officers had shown up.

One of the officers turned to Ahmed, "We're taking Mr. McGurk in and booking him for the murder of Georgia Conroy."

"What? Paddy, what's this about?" Ahmed's voice was rising.

"It's bullshit, Ahmed. I would never hurt her."

Ahmed's face contorted with torment. He grabbed me by my jacket. "My God, Paddy, did you kill her? Jesus. Paddy?" He looked me straight in the eye, searching for the truth. "Tell me. Tell me now."

One of the officers pulled Ahmed away from me as the other led me to the car. "I didn't kill Georgia. I loved her, Ahmed." I said as they pushed my head into the back of the vehicle. The mourners stood watching in mesmerized silence. Brian was at the edge of the group and out of the corner of my eye I saw him smirk as they closed the door on my freedom. As the squad car pulled away from the curb, Brian had made his way to Ahmed and told him something that made him turn towards me again and scream my name out loud. "Paddy!"

13

THE INTERROGATION

The ride was a long one. It took over an hour to make our way from Bel Aire chapel to the Hollywood branch of the L.A.P.D. It gave me some much-needed time to think. What exactly was my crime? I fell in love with a woman that was off limits, off limits because of work, off limits because she was the lover of a friend. My crime was a gross lack of integrity. That was it. But I couldn't help myself. I will readily admit that I knew what I was getting into when I began my relationship with Georgia. But in my wildest imaginings, I never once suspected it would end like this. Georgia dead. I was arrested for her murder. If I had even suspected that it would end like this, I would have found a way to resist her charms and the overpowering temptation of my own need. Not for my own skin but for hers. I would give up all that had transpired between us to have her alive and safe. The more I went over the details of the last week the more I felt the pieces didn't fit. Georgia was not stupid. She wouldn't have let anyone into her apartment that she didn't know. Whoever did this to her either knew her or forced their way in. The cops better come clean with me and let me know how

Georgia was murdered. I need their full disclosure of the facts of the case to help them find her killer.

I guess I should have been worried about my own skin but, other than my pervasive depression because of the loss of Georgia, more than anything else, I felt miserable about Ahmed. The one area where I was guilty as hell was in my betrayal of him. Sure, I could justify it, but I felt slimy just the same. He was basically a good guy and his love and devotion to Georgia were unquestionable. I should have been man enough to be candid with my feelings. While she was alive, I had to grant her wish to keep our relationship under wraps, but at the very least I could have come clean with him in the last couple of days. I just never found the right moment. He had so much to deal with, so many emotions unreleased. The pain of the betrayal would have been unbearable. Now Ahmed would find out the wrong way. It would be far worse.

If they had found the real killer all of this would be over. Ahmed could have been spared the gory details of my clandestine relationship with Georgia. But instead of finding the killer they found me, the easy target, thanks to Brian's big mouth and a few extenuating circumstances. My goose was cooked. And for this brief moment, this ride to the L.A.P.D., I didn't give much of a damn about my own hide. I had very little to live for except to vindicate Georgia. Remarkably, I wasn't afraid. I was calm and resigned in the back of the squad car. I knew I would go through a lot, but it would be child's play. Once Georgia was taken from me, I was so hollow with loss I felt I had nothing left to lose.

The Hollywood branch of the L.A.P.D. was becoming familiar territory to me. I was spending a lot of time there. When we arrived, I was whisked into a small green room with Formica tables and metal chairs, just like in the movies. There were two-way mirrors on either side of the room and a tape recorder in the middle of the table. The two cops that picked me up stayed in the room with me and filled out some papers. They offered me cigarettes which I declined and water which I accepted. It was a long while before Officer Wagner walked in. He was polite and to the point. First, he read me my Miranda Rights, asked if I wanted a lawyer present, which I declined because I didn't have a lawyer, and then we got down to business.

"Mr. McGurk, we have reason to believe that you murdered Georgia Conroy Saturday evening. Why don't you tell us what happened."

"I already told you when I voluntarily came in on Monday morning."

"Tell me again."

"I have nothing further to add."

"Did you have sex with Ms. Conroy?"

"Yes."

"You didn't volunteer that piece of information on Monday. What else have you left out?"

"Nothing."

"You didn't get into a fight with Ms. Conroy about her impending marriage to Ahmed Brooks?"

"No. She wasn't going to marry him."

"What makes you so sure?"

"Look, I didn't kill Georgia. Even if she was going to marry Ahmed, I wouldn't have killed her. Whatever she wanted is what I wanted. I loved her. I was never jealous of Ahmed if that's what you're driving at. I knew that in the end Georgia would follow her heart. All I wanted was for her to be happy, even if that meant losing her to Ahmed."

"Unusual attitude for a love triangle, wouldn't you say?"

"Maybe. But my love for Georgia wasn't usual."

"Oh! It was somehow superior, more rarefied than love for us ordinary folks?" He said with barely hidden contempt.

"Don't put words in my mouth! I wasn't the possessive type and never have been. It wouldn't have worked with Georgia anyway."

"You're not possessive, just violent?"

"That's bullshit!"

"Lani Green and Tiffany from your favorite hangout, Starlets, might not agree with you."

"I was pissed, but I didn't hurt either of them. I am not a violent person and certainly not abusive to women."

"That's interesting, Mr. McGurk. We have in our possession a tape of you roughing up Ms. Conroy when you both were employees at KKLA."

"What?"

"Do you remember the incident?"

"Where did you get a tape of me with Georgia?"

"Brian Buchanon."

"How did he get it?"

"He pulled a dub for me from his security cameras."

"Security cameras?"

"Mr. Buchanon had a few hidden cameras installed in the newsroom after some equipment was stolen. Over the doors to the bathrooms and exits."

"You've got to be kidding! That's a complete invasion of privacy."

"When you're a criminal you get your privacy invaded. That's how you get caught. You were pretty physical with Ms. Conroy when she tried to enter the lady's room."

"I don't know what you're talking about! I would never hurt Georgia."

"You don't remember shoving her against a wall and pulling her head back by yanking a hunk of her hair."

"No!"

"You don't remember then mashing your body against her and forcing her to kiss you while you continued to hold her by her hair?"

"What are you saying?"

"I'm saying that I've got a tape that shows you forcing yourself on Ms. Conroy while you were in the newsroom at KKLA."

"Let me see it!"

"Semen was found in Ms. Conroy's body. Did you force yourself on her the night she died?"

"No!"

"Did she resist your advances and then you raped her?"

"Rape her? No!"

"Did you struggle with her for the phone and strangle her with the phone cord as she tried to scream for help?"

"What?" The wind was knocked out of me with that revelation.

"Before Ms. Conroy died, she was in a violent struggle for the phone and was strangled with the phone cord. Were you a part of that struggle, Mr. McGurk?"

I put my face in my hands and was overcome with emotion. So that's how Georgia died, struggling for her life. I wanted to erase that picture from my mind, but I knew I never would. The pain of it was strangling me. I choked out, "I don't know what you're talking about?"

"I think you do."

I looked at him with venom in my eyes. "You're full of shit. Why aren't you out looking for the real murderer? What about the man who was at her door when I left?"

"We've already contacted Tony Fillipi. He said he dropped off her tickets and an itinerary to Belize shortly after 7:00PM. He was only there about ten minutes."

"And you believe him?"

"We have no reason not to. His wife was with him, waiting in the car. She was turning the car around while he ran inside. There was no time or motive for Mr. Fillipi to kill Ms. Conroy."

"I didn't kill her. Surely you must have some other suspects, some other fingerprints, something?"

"You didn't lay in wait until Mr. Fillipi left and force Ms. Conroy to have sex with you?"

"No. We made love. We were in love. Force was not used."

"The sides of Ms. Conroy's vaginal wall had small tears from excessive friction. You didn't cause that irritation?"

"We made love more than once. It was intense but not forced. I don't know. Maybe it tore her a little. But we always had that kind of sex. My God, do I have to give you a blow by blow description of our lovemaking, for Christ's sake?"

"Did anyone see you leave Ms. Conroy's apartment?"

"No."

"Where did you go after you left?"

"I told you on Monday, I went to Santa Monica to watch the sunset before I went to the airport."

"And no one saw you there of course."

"No."

"United Airlines said that you checked in right before the plane took off at 9:30PM. That gave you plenty of time after Mr. Fillipi left to rape and kill Ms. Conroy. Was the call on your message machine referring to a fight between you and Ms. Conroy?"

"Jesus! For the last time I didn't rape Georgia, and I didn't kill her. I loved her more than you can imagine. I'm telling you everything I know but I can't confess to a crime I didn't commit. This whole story is a figment of your imagination because you don't have the real killer."

"Mr. McGurk, we are booking you for the rape and murder of Georgia Conroy. You have a motive, you have no alibi, and the evidence is stacked against you. You better get a lawyer."

14

TWIN TOWERS CENTRAL JAIL

They led me to a phone, and I called Bix. I asked him to help me find an attorney, something I should have taken care of but was too caught up in my sorrow to face the reality of my precarious position. I had no other friends on the west coast that were not connected in some way with the station. Bix was happy to help in any way that he could. He said he'd take a few days off and fly down to support me. I needed to move fast. I was being arraigned in 48 hours. After I got the ball rolling with Bix, they took me to a cell and locked me up. In a few hours I would be transferred to the county jail.

Luckily, they did not put me in a cell with other prisoners. I wouldn't have survived for five minutes if that was the case, but the experience was chilling just the same. When the bars closed in around me, I panicked. Fear crawled all over me. I was being accused of murder, I had no alibi and, in the opinion of the homicide detectives, a strong motive and opportunity. I was in a dire predicament that had no simple resolution. My only hope was that they would find the real killer.

In a few hours the bus came to take me to the Twin Towers county jail. As I walked to the bus my fear for my life was accelerating. Twin Towers was the worst jail in the country. Every MS 13 gang member, every murderous drug dealer, and every contract killer is held at Twin Towers. I might not make it to my arraignment. It was not lost on me that I was accused of killing the girlfriend of a black icon, Ahmed Brooks, who had not only shown a greatness in sports but was considered the nicest guy in the game. An example for all black children wanting to change their lives and accept their opportunity for success. I was a dead man walking.

It was Wednesday evening. As the bus took me through the streets of L.A., I looked at the town I had grown to love and wondered if I would ever be a part of it or any town again. I could go to jail for Georgia's murder for the rest of my life. If they didn't find the murderer, my life would be over. I was fatigued, mentally and physically. I felt so depleted that I couldn't find the fight in me to go through what was coming up. I needed to fight for my life, and yet there was little left in my life worth fighting for. What kept coming up for me was a general apathy, inertia towards my situation. I was so beaten down by the events of the past month that nothing seemed to matter anymore, least of all me.

When I got to Twin Towers and the gates opened, I could barely breathe. My fear was racing through my cells, my brain spinning. As they searched me, they took my boxers and when I asked why they said so I wouldn't kill myself by using the elastic to hang myself. I had never thought of that, but without Georgia it was not a bad idea. They strip searched me. Fingers exploring my ass and my mouth. It was dehumanizing. Beyond the human indignities, the stench, the filth and the noises in the place were overwhelming.

My nerves were shot. But I had the presence of mind to ask for a phone call. They weren't happy about it, but they let me call Bix. I told him where I was, and he gasped.

"Bix, I'm not sure if I will make it out alive. But I just want you to know how much I appreciate you in my life. Please help my parents if this goes bad."

"We're going to get you out of there. Hold on buddy. Be strong. I found a great attorney. I'm calling him when I hang up."

As they led me to my cell the cat calls became a thunder of insults and threats because I was the guy who killed Ahmed Brooks' girlfriend. My days were numbered.

My cellmate was Hispanic. Chico is what he called himself. He had tats all over him, including on his face and shaved head. Once dumped in with him, the guards left, and I was on my own.

"You ain't gonna last here, motherfucker" Chico said with a sneer.

"At this point I just don't care. My life is over anyway."

"Yeah. That's what you think now. But when they get hold a you, you gonna cry for your mama."

"Look where I am. What the hell can I do about it?"

"I need to take a shit. It ain't gonna be pretty."

"It can't be any worse than the stink of this place."

"I ate a lot a beans for lunch with peppers. It's gonna make you sick."

I gestured to the open toilet.

"Be my guest."

Chico laughed at the absurdity of my invitation and plopped down and exploded. I felt a wretch come up my throat but tried hard to contain my weakness. After he flushed, he came over and looked down at me.

"You got money?"

"Some. I'm not wealthy if that's what you are asking."

"You know what this means?" he asked as he pulled up his shirt.

"MS-13. I'm in news. We know all about your gang."

"You gonna need us to protect you from the niggers."

"Why should I trust you?"

"You got anything else?"

"The law."

"Motherfucker, the law don't run this jail. We do. You pay us, you survive. You don't, you die."

"How much?"

"How bad do you want to live, motherfucker?"

"How much?"

"100 G's. For now."

"Done."

I wanted to see the bastard fry that did this to Georgia. I wouldn't have that pleasure if I killed myself or got killed. And if I got killed, case closed. I wanted to prove my innocence for my mom and dad. I lay down in my cot to the melody of farts and snores from Chico and went over all that had happened. I couldn't think of anyone that would have done it. No one hated Georgia that much. It must have been a random thing. Every time I thought of Georgia struggling for her life, fighting to breathe, I sobbed uncontrollably. Some low life must have been watching her. Although there were many parts of it that I loved, L.A. was becoming a cesspool. If I ever got out of jail I vowed to move to San Francisco, and get the hell out of L.A. I guess my job at KPIX is down the shitter, but even if I have to pump gas I'll be there. Hiking on the cliffs by the bay would help to heal my heart. San Francisco was the most beautiful place on earth. I needed to be there to remember Georgia. She belonged surrounded by that beauty. If I couldn't have her, I could have my fantasy of her there with me.

I fell asleep to the noise of the jail around me. I think I was so exhausted nothing could penetrate my consciousness. It was like I was in a deep dark coma. I woke up when they banged our cells to go to breakfast. Chico and I headed down. Where he sat, I sat. His gang members already seemed to know that I was their golden ticket. A cash cow. I got a lot of dark and evil looks from the black prisoners. I understood. I didn't blame them. They believed I did it, and they knew I fucked Ahmed's piece. And they hated this entitled white boy for his lack of honor of the guy code, especially with their hero.

They slapped some sad looking pancakes on my tray. Pancakes. I hadn't had those since I was a kid. Sunday morning pancakes with maple syrup. Dad always made them and served mom breakfast in bed. It kept their romance alive.

At 10AM Bix showed up with an attorney, Jack Pollack, one of the big names in celebrity defense. I knew when I heard his name that I better open up my wallet because he would get all that was there minus the 100 grand for the Chico agreement. They led me to the visitation room and left me alone to talk with Bix through a glass barrier. A guard stood discreetly toward the back of the room.

"How's it going, buddy?" Bix asked as if I had injured my leg and not my life.

"My goose is cooked. I didn't kill her, please believe that."

"I do. You're not a good enough actor to act the way you did this weekend and have just committed a murder. Besides, I know you too well. It's not in your character."

"Thanks. I'm sorry I've involved you."

"Say no more. I'm your friend. I brought you a bunch of books and magazines and some clothes, but they won't let me give them to you."

"No, I have my wardrobe provided by the state."

"Well, look at the bright side. Blue was always one of your best colors." We both chuckled hollowly over my blue jumpsuit.

"Thanks for getting me the attorney."

"He was the best available. Your jail mate, O.J., had the rest of the lawyers in town all tied up. This guy, Jack Pollack, has an impeccable reputation. He's not a sleazebag. You'll like him."

"Have you talked to my parents?"

"Yes. I told them you're innocent and that I would help you. I made them promise to stay in Ohio."

"Bix, thanks." I began to cry, "I don't know how I'll ever repay you."

Bix, ever glib, said, "I'll think of a few ways, but you have to get out first. I have to go now. I'll see you in a couple of days." He touched the glass that separated us with his hand, and I met it with mine. I could tell that seeing me in this situation was upsetting him. Jail was not his kind of place. He fled after staying an acceptable period of time. But his concern and support were genuine.

After Bix left, they brought me to a small room to meet my attorney. Once he shook my hand, he took out a note pad and asked me the same questions the police had asked. He took copious notes. He also had a tape recorder going. I asked him why he was writing while I was being recorded and he said because he was making notes to himself about what I was saying. He was an all business kind of guy. No bedside manner, no comfort. But he seemed genuinely interested in getting every fact, every detail, no matter how small or inconsequential I believed them to be. I tried my best to answer everything, racking my brain for any clues that could save my miserable hide.

When Jack left, they took me back to my cell. My arraignment was in only 48 hours, the longest and most expensive 48 hours of my life. I would have to face a judge for the murder of Georgia Conroy. It was more than I could fathom, but it was my reality. I could be convicted, and I was scared. Having Jack there trying to get an angle on my innocence made me realize just how close I was to guilt. I didn't do it, but everyone inside the judicial system believed I did. It's not true that you are innocent until proven guilty. I was in jail, suffering for a crime I didn't commit. Even if it was ultimately proven that I didn't kill Georgia, I would spend a great deal of time behind bars. Jack doubted if they would set a bail on this case. I would be held in custody through the trial. I was fucked no matter what the outcome. My career would be in shambles from all the adverse publicity. Not that I gave much of a shit anymore. All I cared about was that Georgia was gone. Even when and if I got out of this perilous situation, I had a dismal life awaiting me without her.

When I woke up on Friday morning, I got to take a shower and shave for court. A guard stood and watched me. I could tell it amused him that a T.V. type was here. First O.J. and now me. Big doings in the L.A. County Jail! But then he mysteriously disappeared once I was soaped up. And just like in the movies, in walked three big black thugs. It took my breath away and my knees buckled.

"Yeah. Bend over muthafucka."

"I didn't do it."

"Yeah, you fucked her. And you killed her because she wanted Ahmed. Not your white boy dick."

As they reached for me, Chico and his gang members rounded the corner.

"Leave, unless you want blood on this floor, bitch."

There was a stand-off. No one moved as I crumbled to the floor with fear. The blacks left with a parting shot.

"Don't sleep, cause we gonna shank you when you sleep. You too, Chico."

Chico came over and lifted me up. I rinsed off fast and got out of there. The guard never returned. Another guard showed up and escorted me to my cell. As I raged at the abandonment, the new guard just looked at me and said, "He has other things to do than babysit you. We're busy here." And that was it.

I sat in my cell until Jack came, and we walked together to the small courtroom on the first floor of the jail. As we entered the judge was handling a case of armed robbery. The courtroom had a number of prisoners, guards and attorneys waiting as each arraignment was handled. When it was my turn, I stepped forward and listened as the judge read the charges against me. Jack requested bail. The prosecutor argued that it was a capital offense and that I should not have bail. The judge ordered a hearing to decide on bail and set it for two weeks from today. That was the earliest they could accommodate me. Jack said we'd fight for bail. Although I felt hopeless, it was worth a shot. Getting out on bail was the only chance I had to uncover the real story. But I was not sure I could survive until then. Jack requested I be put in a special section of the jail for at risk prisoners using my shower ordeal as the justification. The judge had mercy on my soul and agreed. I got Jack to arrange a payment for Chico. I survived because of him. I was grateful. Humbled. I never saw Chico again. But his wife was delivered the money for her children and her. The code of honor unbroken. No contracts. No lawyers. Word as bond.

The wait was beginning. My trial would begin in a couple of months and so had only one hope. That I would get out on bail and find the killer or that they would stumble onto the killer. I knew the police thought they had their man in me. I'm sure they had stopped looking any further. I was their prime suspect. The case against me was mounting, and I had to defend myself.

On Saturday morning the guard came to my cell at about ten and announced that I had a visitor. I assumed that it was Jack with more questions. But when they took me to the room with the glass partition Ahmed Brooks was waiting for me. I took a deep breath when I saw him. I knew what was coming.

When I sat down Ahmed looked at me for a long moment before speaking. I was so sorrowful looking at him I couldn't speak.

"You bastard!" He said through clenched teeth, "You killed her. You better hope they keep you in here because if I get my hands on you, you'll pray to God to let you die."

"Ahmed, please believe me, I didn't kill Georgia. I loved her."

"You expect me to believe anything you say, you lying bastard? You raped her. You murdered her. You call that showing her you *loved* her?"

"I didn't do it, Ahmed. I would never hurt her. You know that." I pleaded for him to see the truth.

"I don't know shit. Why should I trust you? You acted like you were my friend when all the while you worked on Georgia behind my back. You were her mentor. She idolized you, trusted you, wanted to please you, and you took advantage of her."

"I deceived you. That part of what you are saying is true. For that I am profoundly ashamed and am sorry. But I never took advantage of Georgia. She got into the relationship willingly."

"That's a lie!" he said as he leaned even closer to the glass. "If that were true then why did you have to kill her? She saw through your games. She wanted out, didn't she?" He was shaking all over.

"She loved us both, Ahmed. She was tormented every day for months not wanting to hurt either one of us."

"Motherfucker, that's a load of crap! I'm not buying it. You're a liar anyway so why should I believe you now?"

"I have no more reasons to lie. I lied to protect Georgia and you, although you'll never believe it."

"That's bullshit! You lied because you were protecting your own white ass. I would have killed you if I found out and you knew it."

"I'm not afraid of you, Ahmed. I did it for Georgia."

"Fuck you. You killed her! She wanted to be with me, and you killed her! I hope you fry!" With that he stood up and left. I let out a heavy sigh. I was drained. My legs felt wobbly as I stood up to be led back to my cell.

I spent the rest of the morning lying in my cell thinking about Ahmed. It would be humiliating for him now that the word was out that Georgia had cheated on him with a white man. Baseball players were not a sensitive lot. They would give him shit about it. The loss of her was enough and now this. I didn't begrudge him his anger. I had caused that part of his pain.

Just when visiting hours were almost over the guard came back up to my cell and announced another visitor. I got up and went downstairs. Chuck was waiting for me.

"Chuck. You shouldn't be here. This is no place for a young guy like you." I said truthfully.

"Stop the father act, asshole. You've ruined my fucking life. You've ruined the life of everyone I love."

"I didn't kill her, Chuck. You, more than anyone else, should believe me. I loved her."

"Save the sentiment. I want to know one thing. Did you know that KKLA was watching you with cameras when Georgia was still there?"

"No. I just found out. Evidently, they placed security cameras around the station after we lost the phones and the other crap from the newsroom. Did you know?"

"No, but they've got you on tape treating Georgia pretty bad. Did you beat her up a lot?"

"I never beat her up. That was sex play. It looks rough, but it was something we both enjoyed."

"You never hit her?"

"No, of course not. Why?"

"I need to know. Brian is painting a picture of you to the press of a real woman hater. Lani concurs. The papers say you raped her before she died. Did you?"

"No, we made love. We had a relationship and loved each other."

"If you did beat up Georgia, you deserve what you're getting."

"I didn't beat her up, and I didn't kill her."

"You've lied to me so much, why should I believe you now?"

"I lied to protect Georgia, Chuck. That was the only reason."

"I hate you for getting involved with her. My whole life is over now."

"No, it's not! Don't say that! This will pass for you, no matter what happens to me."

"No, it won't. You don't understand me. You never have, so what else is new?" He looked so young and fragile in that moment.

"Chuck, this isn't your problem. I know it's painful for you, but you need to go on with your dreams. I'll find my way."

"Yeah, right! Thanks to you my dreams are over, man." As he got up to leave there were tears in his eyes.

Chuck's visit shook me to the core. I anticipated Ahmed's hatred, but I never realized what a profound effect this was having on Chuck. I guess I had ruined his life. I'd certainly taken away his innocence, the belief that friends treat you with integrity. Chuck views my lying to him as a gross failing in my character and feels like he is a fool for having trusted me. And he, like every man who knew her, fell in love with Georgia. If he believes that I killed her, it stands to reason that he would believe I took away something he was entitled to, a young man's fantasy. He was so troubled and confused that I felt weighted with guilt from his visit.

My long vigil had begun. Days went by slowly in an eight by six. The food was incredibly bad, but I ate it to keep my strength up. When I went to the bathroom and looked into the mirror to shave, I saw a man that was pale and drawn. I had aged at least ten years in the last week and a half. No pretty boy left to get by on his good looks. Brian would be pleased.

There were endless hours to think about Georgia and the night she was murdered. What was incredibly frustrating was I had no clues as to who did it. That drove me crazy. If she was torn inside maybe someone raped her and killed her as the police had said. But what was her phone call about. She sounded frantic. The police thought it was her calling me after a disagreement that night. They believed that I had been there for dinner, that she had called off our relationship and I left when the doorbell rang. They thought she called me because she wanted to finish talking to me, reasoning with me. But, according to the charges, I laid in wait 'til Tony Fillipi left, went in and got in an argument with her, raped her and when she tried to scream for help and called the police, I strangled her with the phone cord. A premeditated rape and murder. An open and shut case. I had nothing to defend myself with. Not a shred of evidence; I was doomed with no way out.

Every time I saw Jack, he told me the latest developments in the case. I was shocked at how all clues, all the evidence pointed to me. They had taken fingerprints of all Georgia's friends and Ahmed and me. Every fingerprint was accounted for except one lone fingerprint on the phone. One fingerprint. They had no idea where it came from. It could be anyone, a T.V. repairman, a visitor that needed to use the phone. It could have nothing to do with the murder or everything. But there were no other clues to who could have done this to Georgia except a mass of evidence pinpointing that I had been with her that night in every sense of the word.

As I endured the next week each endless day became a grim reminder of my hopeless situation. I was panicked that I could end up here or worse for the rest of my life. It began to come home to me that this could be what was left for me. I was scared beyond anything in my life. For the first time I saw my situation clearly. Reality was this cell. Reality was no alibi, no defense. Reality was I could go to the chair or spend my life on death row for a crime I didn't commit. Jack came and went, and Bix dropped by once, but I was alone more than ever. I was without comfort at a time that I needed it most. I had no one to hold me, make me feel loved and cared for. I longed to have one moment of understanding and comfort. But that was not to be. My parents stayed away, respecting my wishes. I needed them desperately, but I sacrificed myself to protect them from seeing me like this. It would kill my mother, and my dad had a bad heart. It could kill him too. I got myself into this, and I would have to find my way out.

I think the thing that surprised me most was my level of shame and humiliation. Even though I knew I didn't kill Georgia, I felt as though I had done something horribly wrong. The feeling fit what was supposed to be my crime. It was scary. I can see why prisoners sometimes confess crimes they didn't commit. The incarceration makes you guilty and ashamed. The self-hate becomes so pervasive that you begin to believe that you are getting what you deserve. My Catholic upbringing didn't help. I saw my dilemma as a just penance for my sins. It rendered me devoid of the fight I needed to defend my life.

The next week leading up to my bail hearing moved along like molasses down a glacier. Each minute took forever. Each hour lasted a lifetime. I wanted out of here. It might be my last shot at freedom.

When the day finally arrived for my bail hearing I was dressed early and ready to go. I hung on to the shred of hope that the judge would give me the chance to be free for a few months leading up to the trial. That would give me the opportunity to look for the murderer. If the police had given up and believed they had their man in me then my own investigation was my only hope. I had been an investigative reporter for years, and I know how to sniff out information that even the cops couldn't get. I had to get out.

When they came to get me to take me downstairs, I was terrified that I would be back in my cell within hours. My mouth was dry when I saw Jack. He was cordial but distant. No backslapping attorney here. I asked him what my chances were, and he honestly answered that it didn't look good. When I got into the small courtroom a bail hearing was already in progress. I looked at the poor black bastard who had robbed a convenience store and knew that the minute he got out on bail he would be back at it. Our society didn't rehabilitate prisoners, give them jobs, clean them up. We shut them away and hoped the problem would go away. Out of sight, out of mind. But the joke was on all of us. The hardened criminal only stayed locked up for a short amount of time. The prisons were over-crowded, and the prison system had to keep releasing repeat offenders. That's why little kids kept being molested and killed, people kept being assaulted with weapons and getting robbed, murders kept happening.

When it was my turn, I listened to the prosecutor make his case for not setting bail. His arguments were sound and persuasive. If I didn't know better, I would agree that I was a danger to all society from the evidence at hand. Then Jack made an equally persuasive plea on my behalf. When they had both finished, I whispered to Jack that I wanted to speak for myself. The judge said he would listen to what I had to say only if I kept it short. As I stood up, I felt tears running down my face.

"Your honor, I loved Georgia Conroy with all my heart. There is no way that I, under any circumstances, could have ever done this to her. I know the evidence looks damning, but I didn't do it. From the beginning I've done everything I could to be cooperative with the LAPD. I voluntarily came in as soon as I found out about the murder. I want the killer more than anyone can imagine. Georgia was so beautiful, so full of joy. She was the most important person in my life. If you knew her you would know that anyone that loved her could never turn and do this to her. I think it was a random killing. That's the only thing that makes sense. She had no real enemies. Please, I beg you, give me bail. I am an investigative reporter, and I'm damn good at it. I think I can be a help in finding the one who did this to her."

The judge was an older man. He looked at me with pity in his eyes. He took off his bifocals and wiped them slowly as he continued to look at me. He put them back on and began to speak.

"I've considered the statements by council and the defendant. The defendant is a well-known member of this community, has shown no inclination to flee, and I find that bail is appropriate in this case. Bail is set at $1,000,000.00, cash or surety bond."

I shook all over with emotion at the pronouncement. I didn't know how I would come up with the money, but I knew that I had to. I told Jack to contact Bix and my parents. I would have to depend on them to find a way to post my bail.

Within 48 hours I was released. Bix borrowed the money from a venture capitalist friend of his who frequented the restaurant. Bix gave him a bullshit line that I planned to write a book about my experiences, revelations of my affair with Ahmed Brooks' girlfriend, and that it would make millions. He guaranteed a big return on his investment. He bought Bix's story. I was forever indebted to my buddy Bix's creative larceny.

When I went back to my condo, I embraced the familiarity of it. It was here that I had made love to Georgia, here that we had our first fight, here that we had made our plans. My experience in the L.A. County Jail had made this feel like home to me, for the first time since I'd moved in.

Jail had terrified me. And I knew my deal with Chico was over, done, dusted, paid in full. I would be starting over in the protection game, and my cash was beyond depleted. I'd never make it.

I had a few months to find out what had really happened to Georgia or I would be back inside. The police would watch me closely. They were convinced of my guilt. I couldn't blame them. I would feel the same way if I were in their position. They didn't realize it, but I was on their side. We were allies of a sort because we both wanted justice for Georgia. My first task was to find Tony Fillipi. I had known Tony over the years as a first-rate freelancer. I wanted to know what transpired between Georgia and him after I left and not hear it through the police filter. I knew the police were holding out on me. The lone fingerprint could also mean something. They acted as if it was nothing, but it could be the clue to put the whole mystery to rest.

I found Tony Fillipi's number in the west L.A. phone book. I dialed it, and he picked up on the second ring. He said hello in a tentative way. I'm sure the media had been hounding him.

"Tony, this is Paddy McGurk. I need to talk to you as soon as possible." I started.

"I've told the police everything I know."

"Tony, you were the last person to see her alive. If it weren't for me, you'd be the man charged with murder one. Think how that would feel. I didn't murder Georgia. I'm scared. I have about two months to find out who killed her, or the murder will be pinned on me. I'm sure you've been through a lot, but I may lose my life or at best my freedom if I don't find the real killer. Please help me. I have to know every detail you can remember. The police are not sharing their information with me. You are my only hope." I pleaded my position as skillfully as I could.

He began to soften, "I feel for you, man, but why should I believe you? No one else does."

"You worked closely with Georgia. Did she ever feel threatened by me?"

"No. On the contrary. She always spoke of you in glowing terms."

"That's because she loved me, Tony, and I loved her."

Tony let out a heavy sigh. He'd had enough of all this.

"Look man, let me talk this over with my wife. I really don't want to be involved. Give me a few days." He reasoned.

"Thank you for considering my plight. I will contact you at the end of the week." He hung up without a goodbye.

My next call was to Ahmed. He picked up but when he realized it was me, he said, "Fuck off."

Before he hung up, I pleaded, "Wait."

"I have nothing to say to you. You are a liar. You murdered the only woman I will ever love."

"Ahmed, I'm a shit. I broke the "bro" code. Those are my sins. But loving Georgia came so easy. You know what I'm talking about. How many hearts did you break when you took her off the market in Sacramento? It was impossible not to fall in love with her. Surely you see that!"

"Why do you think I owe you one more minute of my life?"

"Because some creep killed the woman we both loved. Fuck, even Chuck, Red's kid, is mad at me because he says I ruined his life because he loved her so much. She was catnip to men young, old and everything in between. Plus, she was smart. Our collective dream girl. Don't hate me that I, like you, fell for her charms."

He let out a long sigh.

"It's important we find the fucker who did this. For you and me. He needs to pay. Or she." I continued.

"She?"

"There's a lot you don't know. Lani Green hated Georgia with a passion. She turned the whole newsroom against her. Georgia was a threat because she was young, beautiful and whip smart. All things Lani lacked. Plus, Lani was very fearful of being fired due to her aging. She did some really lousy things to Georgia that humiliated her beyond belief and drove her to quit."

"Wow. I thought it was Brian she quit over."

"Well, yes, she couldn't stand Brian too, but Lani really had it out for her and made it impossible for her to stay."

"I wondered why she quit her dream job, but she was impetuous to be sure and head strong, so I chalked it up to that. I was just so busy, man. In that way, it's my fault. I should have been with her and none of this would have happened, including you." He started to sob.

"Please help me even though I don't deserve it."

"I never want to see you again."

"Understandable, but just give me a few minutes to ask you some questions."

He paused. Then answered, "Shoot."

"You are a big superstar. Is it possible that any of your teammates or players from other teams might have wanted to fuck with your game enough to shake you to the core by killing Georgia?"

"Good question. I want to think about that one. Lot of ground to cover."

"Were there any white supremacists in the game that could have also wanted to derail you for having such a stunning white girlfriend?"

"It exists, but that's a pretty extreme action. They keep it well hidden. But it's there to be sure. I just don't think they would go to that level of revenge."

"Fair enough. Last question, have you ever had any threats made to you from fans of other teams or any kind of hate group?"

"The front office handles all that and unless I would be in imminent danger, I wouldn't hear about it. Hate mail and all that they just hand over to law enforcement and lawyers. It gets handled."

"Would you mind if I contacted Greg Mead? But I would need you to tell him you want him to cooperate with me. I am sure I am persona non grata at the Dodgers right now."

"Yeah, I will do it because as much as I hate you for your betrayal of me, even if you didn't do it, I still want who did to fry. I guess you will either find the killer or you are the killer and we will find out soon enough."

"Ahmed, I have betrayed you. I understand your hatred of me. I don't resent you for it. But, I don't deserve to be put away for life because of it. I would never have hurt a hair on her head. You must believe me."

"No, I don't have to believe you. But I do believe someone did it, and that is why I am giving you this benefit of the doubt. If I think of anything, I will call you. Only for that reason. We are not friends. Goodbye Paddy. Don't call me again. Ever."

We hung up, and I felt more drained than I thought possible. I had hurt this man. A man of honor. More penance for me.

I decided to call Georgia's mother. But I needed a nap first.

My sleep was troubled at best, and my brain was out of steam. My dreams were filled with conspiracy theories. Tossing and turning in my bed, fitfully playing scenarios, did not make for a restful sleep. I got up after an hour and was worse for the wear. I made coffee and sat down to speak with the mother of the woman I loved. I held my breath as I dialed.

She picked up with a reserved "Hello!"

"Hi," I started, "This is Paddy McGurk again."

"They let you out?"

"Yes, I am on bail."

"Did you murder my daughter?"

"No! I loved her more than anything in my life. I would have gladly laid down my own life to save hers."

She began to wail. A long, plaintive wail that only mothers can make with incomprehensible loss. It shook me to my core.

"I'm so sorry, ma'am."

"My baby..." She sobbed.

"I know."

"Why was I so hard on her?" She asked to no one in particular.

"You wanted the best for her." I said, hoping to assuage her guilt.

"She had it all. Beauty, brains, a fabulous career. I didn't want her throwing it away on that dumb ballplayer. Was that so wrong?"

"No. We all make judgements. But where you were wrong is he is a stand-up guy. So much more than just a ballplayer. He loved her. Adored her. Treated her like a queen. He was worthy. Trust me on that."

"She died hating me."

"No. She didn't hate you. That much I know. Moms and daughters have complicated relationships just like fathers and sons. Forgive yourself. She forgave you."

"How do you know?"

"She told me." I lied. No point in pouring salt in this grieving mother,s wounds. And I knew as Georgia matured and had her own daughter, she would come to appreciate her mother's ambitions for her and her protectiveness so this I considered a lie that even Georgia would approve.

"I read the papers. You were in love with her, too."

"Yes. I loved her, and she loved me. She loved me and Ahmed. It is possible to love more than one person. It was hard for her. Hard on her."

"I see. What do you want, son?"

"When she was in school or after she left home and took up with Ahmed, did anyone stalk her or make threats against her. Any white anger that your girl took up with a black ballplayer? Anything that scared you for her? Anything at all?"

"Oh. I have been so grief stricken I have not thought one bit about solving this once they arrested you. Let me think. Well, she had a lot of suitors, that's for sure but she was so directed, so sure footed in her ambition and studies, in achieving her life goals, she gave them very little time or thought. I mean, I guess one of them could have gotten obsessed, but I just don't even remember their names. There was no indication anyway."

"Well, give it some more thought and ask her dad as well. If something happens to jog your memory, give me a call."

"Ok, I will, son. Take care of yourself."

"Yes, ma'am. I will. And thank you."

"Thank you for loving my sweet girl." As I hung up, I heard that wail again and my heart broke into a million pieces because she was wailing what I felt inside. My silent wail. It will never end.

I decided to call Chuck. I thought he might have noticed something at the station, but I knew he was going to stonewall me. I had to give it a try. I dialed his number with a lump in my throat. I had guilt over my many betrayals, but he was so innocent, gullible, trusted me like Ahmed and Brian. I did not deserve their trust. But Chuck was different. He idolized me. Not anymore, however.

He picked up.

"Chuck, it's Paddy."

"Yeah, asshole. I heard you got out."

"Only until my trial. I have a couple of months to exonerate myself. I am guilty as hell of a lot of things, but killing Georgia is not one of them."

"Cry me a river, dude."

"Look, do you actually believe, deep in your soul, that I could strangle Georgia? That I had it in me to take her life? Do you?"

"Maybe I can believe you were not the actual killer, but it might as well have been you because none of this would have happened if you had kept your dick out of her."

His words hit me in the gut like a sucker punch. I couldn't speak because I knew he was right. I might as well have done it so maybe I deserved exactly what I was getting. I slumped in my chair and was silent.

"Are you denying it?" He drove the stake in deeper.

"No."

"Well, take your lumps, dickhead."

"Chuck, we are talking murder one. I may be every ugly name you can dig up, but I loved her, and I was a jerk for putting her in a bad situation. Had I been thinking clearly, I would have made different choices. But I was madly, hopelessly in love with her, and I made the wrong choices. That is the sin I will live with for the rest of my life. And I am sure my love of her and involvement with her might have had something to do with her murder. If it did, I am not sure I can go on. I'm sorry I called."

"Me too. Sorry you called; I mean, leave me alone." He hung up in my face.

I sat there and said to no one in particular, as I was alone as hell, "Well, that went well."

I made a little dinner and went to bed early. I vowed to try again with Tony Fillipi in the morning. He was my last shot. I just had no other ideas, and panic was setting in.

The next morning, I made some eggs and toast while sucking down three cups of coffee, pacing like a caged tiger with my nerves jangled until it was a respectable time to call. At 9AM, I dialed his number. He picked up on the first ring.

"Tony, it's Paddy McGurk."

"Hey, I've thought about it and talked it over with my wife. Man, I'm sorry, but I just don't want to be further involved."

"I understand. But my life is on the line, Tony. I've run into half a dozen roadblocks and I will be on trial for murder one before you know it."

Big sigh, "Sorry, man."

"Tony, please. I am begging you on my fucking knees, just meet with me."

In the end, he relented and agreed to meet me at Norm's for breakfast at 9AM the following morning. I spent the rest of the day pouring over all the newspapers that Bix had left for me in my apartment. I needed to be up on my case from the point of view of the jury that was reading all this crap. I went out grocery shopping because I decided to eat in as much as possible. I didn't want to be out and about with everyone whispering behind my back. I bought out the local Vons, came back and unloaded two weeks-worth of supplies into my fridge and freezer. I watched a little T.V., took a shower for at least thirty minutes and went to bed early. I slept like I had a bullet through my head. I was exhausted beyond anything I had ever experienced.

The next morning, I got up early and rode over to Norm's. I was greeted by everyone as if nothing had happened. I got a lot of hugs and plenty of reassurance that no one there believed that I had done anything wrong. They had seen me pass out when I read the paper, and a few of them, including Verna, had volunteered to make statements to the police about my shock over the headline the morning I came back from San Francisco. But the police believed that I could have staged it all. They felt that it was an act to save my ass.

Tony Fillipi showed up promptly at 9AM. I recognized him from a picture of him that was in the *L.A. Times* from a few weeks ago, right after I was arrested. He looked uncomfortable as he sat down.

"I can't tell you how much I appreciate this." I was sincere.

"Hey, I don't need the pleasantries. Let's get this over with."

"I guess you've read all the stories in the Times?" I didn't want him to think I was her killer.

"Yes. They're pretty convincing. You were with Georgia the night she died?"

"Yes, I loved her and wanted to marry her if she would have me. In fact, that's what the whole last evening was about, our making a life together. That's what makes this so painful. To lose someone you love and be thought of as the one who killed her. It's just too much and damn scary besides."

"Yeah. I bet. I think the world has O.J. fever. Now every man is a bad guy when it comes to women." He made a profound point.

"When I left Georgia the night she died, you had just rung the doorbell, and she had looked out and told me it was you. I left in a hurry out the back. At the time I left we were happy, in love and making plans. I need to know what happened next."

"I was dropping off the tickets and itinerary for our trip to Belize. I guess you knew that?"

"Yes. Did Georgia seem upset when she answered the door?"

"No, not at all. She was breezy, a little rushed and flushed you might say." When he said that I felt a warm blush spill to my groin. I had not had a sexual feeling about Georgia since she had died, but this thought of our last moments brought back the memory. I felt momentarily weak with longing and sadness.

"How long were you there?"

"About ten minutes."

"What did you talk about?"

"The trip mostly and the craziness of "the business.""

"That's all."

"That's all I can remember. Nothing earth-shattering, that's for sure. I'm sorry I don't have any answers or clues for you, Paddy. I've told you exactly what I told the police. I wish there was more. You seem desperate."

"Desperate is putting it mildly. I have no allies except a buddy from San Francisco and my family. I am fighting for my life with no lifeline."

"What about your friends at KKLA? Surely they are helping you."

"Ha! What friends? They bailed on me the minute I got into trouble."

"You're kidding! That's typical. This business is the most shallow, self-serving industry around. In fact, that's exactly what Georgia and I were talking about."

"What? What were you talking about?"

"How disgusting broadcasting is and how glad we were to be out of the mainstream and working for PBS."

"What exactly did she say?"

"She was telling me about what a creep Brian Buchanon was, and I told her that she didn't know the half of it."

"What do you mean?"

"Well, as I told Georgia, I do a lot of freelance camera work, editing and directing with all the stations. You learn a lot about the stations that way."

"What specifically do you know about KKLA that you shared with Georgia?" I was getting somewhere.

"One week when I was editing a piece for KKLA I was in the station from 11PM to 5AM, the graveyard shift, you know, the one all the freelancers get stuck with. Each night at midnight, after all the late news staff left the building, they put up a sign outside the newsroom that said, "Off-limits to all unauthorized personnel." It said something about highly dangerous electrical maintenance being done that would be an insurance risk for all but the maintenance crew. It was a pain in the ass because we couldn't get to the coffee machine or the restroom that was in the news area. We had to go upstairs for everything. Damned irritating in the middle of the night. Everyone seemed to be following the instructions and steering clear of that area, but after one night of schlepping upstairs I said, "Fuck it", and went through the taped barriers. I saw them installing some pretty sophisticated monitoring equipment in the newsroom. They were putting it in the ceilings and in the phones."

"I knew they put the cameras over the exits and the bathrooms. They were trying to catch a thief. But I sure didn't know about the phones." I said, my alarm growing.

"Don't kid yourself. They had cameras and mics all over that newsroom. Georgia asked me where exactly all of them were, but I couldn't remember. When I went by on my trips to the can they were working right in the center of the newsroom. I was there over the entire week and every night from midnight till 2AM they were there, working away."

"Jesus!"

"Yeah. Big brother is watching sort of thing. Scummy bastards! But I wasn't surprised, and neither was Georgia. She got all fired up about civil liberties. You know how Georgia was. That's what I loved about working with her. She had a lot of passion."

"Yeah. I know." I sat there looking at the man who had given me a clue, a valuable clue, and wished I could hug him. But the information he gave me made me stiff with rage. I could imagine how it affected Georgia who had a hotter temper than I did.

"Do the police know about any of this?" I asked when I regained my composure and as he finished his breakfast.

"I mentioned it briefly, not in detail, but they already knew that the place was under surveillance because of the stolen equipment. You know the cops. That's right up their alley. They love that shit. Besides, that's the business. We're just puppets on a string. If you want to work in broadcasting you have to deal with the bullshit of maniacs that run it, like Buchanon. In fact, that's what I told Georgia when she got all fired up. It's the business. It's sick and always has been. You just have to do your work and find your joy in that. The rest of it is perverse. I don't want to be a part of that game. That's why I stayed on the creative side. Leave all that bullshit to the management and power junkies."

"I can't believe it. You told the police all of this?"

"Like I said, I brought it up, but I guess Buchanon had already told them about the cameras, so they didn't spend too much time on it. Do you think it's relevant to the case?"

"I don't know but I'm going to find out."

"I'd love to see those bastards get their due. I'll help you any way I can."

"Meeting me today was a big help. I'm grateful for you giving me the benefit of the doubt."

"Hey, Georgia was a beautiful woman, inside and out. I want the killer brought to justice. If it wasn't you then the guilty party has to be found. I hope this helps."

"Thanks. I'll be in touch."

Tony left Norm's on the way to an edit. I sat in the restaurant and had a third cup of coffee. I wallowed in the familiarity of the place while deep in thought about what I had learned. Now it was clear how Brian knew my every move with Georgia. He was watching us. Georgia must have gone ballistic when she found out. Tony knew her well. She had a lot of passion. That must have been the reason she called me. She wanted to tell me. Georgia was highly agitated on the message she left. She must have been going nuts that she couldn't reach me knowing that for all those months we were being watched and listened to. Even our phone conversations, so intimate, so private were being heard by God knows who. Brian must have been the one who ordered and used the electronic devices because he was the one that seemed to know our moves before we made them. He kept his beloved control that way. Now it all seemed so clear. Brian used those minor thefts as justification to look into the private business of the entire station. That controlling dick. I decided then and there to confront him. I headed out of Norm's to KKLA.

15

THE LETTER

Pulling into the parking lot of KKLA was eerie. I had done it so many times before, but this time I didn't belong. It was more like being in a dream than reality. The cars were all familiar, the building, the trees and shrubs, my parking place with my name on it. I parked in my place for what would be the last time. I was truly surprised they hadn't attended to that detail of my elimination. I sat in the car a minute to catch my breath. I felt winded and recognized it as fear. I was still afraid of Brian, his power over me. After a moment to steady myself I left the car and walked to the building. As I got closer to the front door, I cringed at the thought that anyone might see me, want to talk to me. I was on a mission. I had nothing to say to anyone. My humiliation and alienation became too painful and all consuming. When I walked in the door the receptionist let out a whoop at the sight of me. She hopped up and ran around the desk and threw her meaty arms around me. It felt good. No one had had their arms around me in a long time.

"Lord! You're a sight for sore eyes!" Melba, KKLA's black receptionist said in greeting.

"I sure didn't expect this kind of welcome."

"I don't believe all that crap I read in the paper. You're one of the only true gentlemen that's ever been in this place. How are you, sugar? What can I do for you?"

"I need to see Brian. Is he in?"

"That asshole? No, he's not in. He's back in Birmingham buttering up the brass, sucking butt."

"Damn."

"Anyone else you need to talk to?"

"Is Red here?"

"Sure is. Let me call him for you." She went back to her headset.

I sat down to wait in the lobby of what was once my home. I picked a discreet spot in the corner and pretended to watch the monitors, but I'm sure I wasn't convincing because it was daytime TV. Reruns of I Love Lucy were on. After a few minutes Red appeared. He looked like hell. His face was bloated, and his hair was thinner. I guess this mess had taken its toll on more than just Ahmed and me.

"Red, how you doing?" I asked, wanting to know.

"What are you doing here? What do you want?" Gone was his terminally affable attitude. I guess he was enforcing the party line. Forever a company man.

"I need to talk to Brian but he's out of town. Can we go up to your office? I want some answers."

"No. You're not allowed in the station. Say what you need to and go."

"Fine. Were you aware that the entire newsroom, and for all I know, the entire station, was being monitored by Brian Buchanon through hidden cameras and illegal wiretaps?"

"You don't know what you're talking about!"

"I think I know a lot more than you want me to. Did you know about the camera's and wiretaps?"

"We put up a few surveillance camera's for security reasons. We've already shared that with the LAPD."

"That's a bunch of bullshit, Red, and you know it. It wasn't a few cameras, and it wasn't for only security reasons. There were many cameras and you tapped our phones, including mine and Georgia's. We were being watched long after the stealing stopped around here. I bet the cameras are still up. If you knew what was going on around here, Red, it was your duty to put a stop to it. That violates our civil liberties. You can't monitor employees that way. It's illegal."

"We had a security problem. We had to do something drastic."

"You're lying to cover your own ass! A few mobile phones and recorders were taken. What you spent in installing that equipment could have bought a truck load of mobile phones. What was really going on was Brian wanted to keep tabs on everyone, and *you* let him get away with it. You should be ashamed. How can you call yourself a Human Resources "director" when the only interests you protect are the ones of your employer? That's not your job, and you know it!"

"I don't need you to tell me what my job is."

"What about Georgia? What about her murder? What do you know about Georgia?"

"Maybe you should tell me. Aren't you the one accused? Besides, I don't have to answer to you. Brian Buchanon is my supervisor, not you. Now get out of this station." He grabbed my arm and tried to jerk me towards the door. I yanked my arm from his grasp and turned to him as I left.

"What's happened to you Red? I thought you were one of the good guys. But you're just a puppet. Brian owns your ass. You're pathetic, Red. That's why you look so bad. I feel sorry for you."

Red looked more flustered than he should, scared. I sensed his fear. My training as a reporter made me sensitive to his reaction. Something was up with Red. I left as Red escaped to his office.

I had all day to kill and couldn't get to Brian, so I decided to make a trip to my attorney's office. I drove over to Westwood and pulled into the parking garage of the Westwood Gateway office complex at Santa Monica Blvd and Sepulveda. I took a few moments to collect my thoughts. Jack was in his office when I stood at his door. He saw me and motioned me in. He looked slick in a plaid shirt and sports jacket. I was glad I'd taken time to dress. When he hung up, he greeted me cordially.

"Paddy! I'm surprised to see you here. What can I do for you?"

"I need to know if you are aware of the extent of the surveillance that went on at KKLA?"

"The prosecutors case mentions that they had a few cameras up. That's where they got the tape of you and Georgia outside the ladies room. I think we discussed that. It's not that unusual if there are circumstances that warrant it. Why?"

"KKLA had some mobile phones stolen and a few personal items from inside a few desks, nothing of great value. I just had breakfast with Tony Fillipi. He told me the surveillance equipment was extensive, phones tapped, cameras everywhere. A little overkill, don't you think, over an incident of petty larceny?"

"Phones, eh? I didn't hear about that. How many cameras?"

"I'm not sure, but the expense of the equipment and installation had to far outweigh the investment in new phones. I need to know if the cameras are still up, and if not, when they were taken down. I have a feeling they were put there for a much more clandestine reason than to catch a thief. Georgia found out about the surveillance from Tony. I think that's why she called me after I left and sounded so upset. I don't know if this means anything, but it could. I need your help."

"Interesting!" Jack perked up with this new info.

"I went over to KKLA after my breakfast."

"You shouldn't have done that."

"Maybe not, but Red Kelly sure was defensive when I cornered him about it."

"The old geezer who runs Human Resources?"

"Yes. He was really uptight. The prosecution believes that Georgia called me because we had been fighting. That was not the case. We had never gotten along better. This explains why she called me and sounded so upset."

"You may be right. I'll nail Buchanon and Kelly on this new detail in their depositions."

I made my way back home. It was going to be a long night. The entire evening, I went over the details that I knew of the case. I was with Georgia the night she died, so was Tony. She found out we were watched by Brian. She was agitated when she called me. Shortly after she called me, she was murdered. What happened during the hour from the time she called me at 7:30PM and she was murdered? Did someone stop by? Could she have called anyone else? A friend, some-one from KKLA? I needed her phone records.

The next morning, I got up early and took a jog and a hot shower. I needed to take better care of myself. At eight thirty sharp I called Jack. He took my call.

"Paddy! What's up?"

"Do you have the phone records of Georgia's last night?"

"Yes, I do."

"Who did she call besides me?"

"She called Brian Buchanon very briefly at 7:45PM. Then Red Kelly called her at 7:55PM shortly after she spoke with Brian, and they spoke a few minutes."

"Brian...then Red! What did she say?"

"Brian and Red both said in their statements to LAPD that she wanted their help."

"What?"

"That she needed help to keep you from harassing her."

"That's bullshit! That's utter bullshit! Why haven't I heard about this before?"

"It's a new piece of the prosecution's case. I just got this in yesterday, the revision of their case, and I've been going over it. I got to that part last night as I was reading through it. It shocked me too. Why would she say that?"

"She wouldn't. She didn't."

"You don't know that. Maybe things weren't as cozy between you as you believe."

"Whose side are you on anyway?"

"Paddy, the prosecution is going to ask you that question, over and over, so get used to it. Georgia's not here to support you. It's your word against Brian's and Red's. So, what's your answer?"

"They are lying! That's my answer. There is no way that Georgia would say that. My God, we had just finished making love for hours and committing to a future together. They are lying through their teeth, and I'm going to find out why."

"Hold your horses. You shouldn't be having contact with any of the people involved in the prosecution's case. They could turn it against you. You're leaving yourself wide open. You shouldn't have gone to see Red today. That was a mistake."

"He's lying, and there has to be a reason. I need to see him again, mistake or no mistake." I insisted.

"I'm your attorney. If you're not going to pay attention to council, I can't represent you. You are putting yourself in further jeopardy by all this amateur investigating."

"I hardly consider myself an amateur. I don't feel like I need to justify my reporting skills to you."

"I'm trying to save you from yourself, Paddy. The truth will come out in court."

"I wish I believed you. But I've already spent time behind bars for a murder I didn't commit, so I've lost my trust in the infallibility of the law, counselor."

"Paddy, cool down. Come see me when you're in a rational mood. Don't do anything till you see me. I need to finish going over the rest of the prosecution's case. I've made you a copy. You'll get it tomorrow. Read it thoroughly. There is a lot more there than the first submission we got from them. They have a strong case. Red is one of their key witnesses. We'll talk in a day or two."

My brain was spinning. Red was not the type to lie. Something was being covered up. Brian's face kept spinning around in my head. Would Brian have killed Georgia? It was too overwhelming to contemplate. Why? It may have pissed him off that I deceived him, slept with her and he didn't. But it was hardly reason enough for him to murder her. He just wouldn't do it. He was a bastard, there was no question in my mind about that, but he wasn't a murderer. I even thought of a hit man. Would Brian hire a hit man? What about Ahmed? Would Ahmed hire a hit man if Brian told him about Georgia and me? If Ahmed had anyone hit, it would have been me. There was no way he would let Georgia get hurt. I felt certain of it. And what was Red's deal? What part was he playing in all of this? He was protecting someone. The only two people Red cared enough about to lie for them were Brian and Chuck. Chuck! I couldn't believe that Chuck would do this. He loved Georgia. He was upset with me. I would be the one he would be after, not her. Nothing made sense. I was at a loss. Everyone looked guilty and innocent at the same time. I would have to turn over every stone and that night I did turn over and over every one of a hundred possibilities.

I woke up with my head pounding, and I realized that someone was pounding on my door. I looked at the clock and it was 2AM. Jesus! I felt like hell. I yelled at the insistent banging to hold on. I went and took a leak and splashed cold water on my face. When I opened the door, Chuck was standing there. His face was white with fear.

"Jesus, Chuck! What is it?"

"Oh, God. Help me, Paddy. My dad."

I brought him in to the living room and sat him on the couch. He was shaking and crying.

"Chuck, what are you talking about?"

"It's all my fault." Chuck pushed a wrinkled piece of paper into my hand as he sobbed into his hands.

I opened the crumpled paper and read a note from Red to his son.

Son,

You and your brothers and sisters mean everything to me. I've worked hard all my life to give you the things I never had as a boy. I wanted the best for you and so did your mother. It breaks my heart that in the end I have failed you and my beloved Mary so badly. Please tell everyone how sorry I am.

I always believed that I was a good Catholic husband, father and man. But sometimes, no matter how hard you try, things go wrong. I never wanted you and your brothers and sisters to see me as a murderer. I didn't mean to kill Georgia Conroy. It was a horrible accident. I had too much to drink. I couldn't think. She fought me so hard for the phone. She wanted to expose Brian. I had to stop her. She would have ruined his reputation and mine. I tried to reason with her, but she wouldn't listen. She started screaming. There was no stopping her. I got scared and panicked. Killing her just happened. Please believe me. I am not an evil man. I am not a murderer. I wanted to go to the police and tell them what happened, but Brian said no. He told me it wasn't my fault. He said it was Paddy's fault, that none of this would have happened if Paddy hadn't betrayed him. I've tried to accept that, but I can't. Although Brian has been my friend for many years and has always done right by me, I knew that I killed Georgia. I can't live with the fact that Paddy will go to jail for life for a crime he didn't commit.

Paddy came by the station today. I think he knows something. He won't stop till he finds out the truth anyway. So, you see son, it's best this way. It would tear our family apart for me to be on trial. Your shame and embarrassment would kill me. I'm a dead man either way. Please accept my decision to end my life. I've had a good life. This is my only real regret. All of you must go on knowing that I loved all of you more than life itself. That's what makes this decision an easy one. God will have to forgive me for this.

Love forever,
DAD

As I finished reading the handwritten note Chuck sobbed silently beside me. I put my arm around him, and he leaned into me like a little boy and cried harder. I let him cry until the tears began to stop. Then I gently began to ask him some questions.

"Chuck, where do you think your dad is?"

"I don't know. His car is gone."

"How long has he been gone?"

"I don't know. I was out on a date and got in a little after one. The light was on in his bedroom. I thought he must have fallen asleep watching T.V. I was going to turn off the light and stuff, so I went in. The bed was empty, and this note was on it."

"Where do you think he would go?"

"I have no idea. He's going to kill himself, isn't he?"

"Maybe. But he may change his mind after he drives around and thinks about it. Let's call the police and let them try to find him."

"No! What would we say to them? That he murdered Georgia. They'd pick him up like a common criminal."

"That's true but it's better than him being dead."

"You're right, I guess."

"Chuck, did you know about your Dad killing Georgia before you got this note?"

"Yes."

"Did he tell you?"

"No. I saw him do it."

"What?"

"I was there that night. Not in her apartment, just outside. I watched through the window."

"Why didn't you stop him?"

"I wanted to, but it happened so fast. I screamed through the window and pounded the glass to get him to stop but it was too late."

"Why were you outside?"

"It's a long story. Let's call the police and then I'll tell you. My dad could be ending his life. I want him with me, no matter what he's done."

We called the police, explained the situation, and waited for them to arrive to take a report.

"Tell me everything that happened."

"My dad and I had been out sailing all day. We'd had beers from morning till late afternoon. We were pretty hammered. It had been a great day. Lots of laughs. My dad is such a great father. The best."

He began to cry again but continued. "When we got home, Brian called and said that Georgia had called him. He told Dad to take care of it, to shut her up. Dad called her immediately when he hung up with Brian. She was spitting mad, dad said. He decided to go over and try to reason with her. I offered to drive because he had been drinking so much. But he wouldn't let me. He said he needed to go alone. I let him go, but then I started to worry. I decided to go over and make sure he was all right. That he got there safely. When I got to Georgia's I heard some shouting. I went to the window and peeked in. Georgia was literally stomping mad. She was in a fury. She was pointing her finger in Dad's face and saying she was going to tell the police and all the papers, and the tabloid shows. She was going to expose Brian and Dad for what they really were. Their lives and careers would be over once she finished with them. She ordered Dad out, but he wouldn't go. He wanted to continue to reason with her. She said she was going to call the police and grabbed the phone and started dialing. Dad tried to wrench the phone out of her hands. She started screaming hysterically for help. Within a second, he wrapped the phone cord around her neck and strangled her. I pounded on the window to get his attention, but by the time he noticed me it was too late. He didn't mean to do it. He just lost control for a few split seconds. My dad's never hurt anyone in his life. It was an accident."

"So, you've known all along?"

"Yes. That makes me an accessory to murder."

"Does anyone else know that you knew besides your dad and me?"

"No, my dad didn't tell anyone about me, not even Brian. He was so ashamed."

"What did he tell Brian?"

"He called him when we got home and told him everything, except about me. Brian went nuts. He called dad every name in the book. My dad wanted to call the police and confess, but Brian told him no. There would be too many questions. That it would ruin both of them. Brian formulated a plan of action. He decided the best defense was a good offense. That's why he gave the police the tapes of you and Georgia. He wanted a reason for why he had taped the newsroom in case it came out in the investigation. He wanted the surveillance to seem on the up and up. And he made a decision then and there to help the trail lead to you."

"Jesus! I was framed."

"And I helped them. I should have told you, but I couldn't. I had to protect my dad."

"Chuck, the police will be here in a minute. We have to honor your dad's wishes and keep you out of this mess. He is willing to sacrifice his life to save me and protect you. Don't tell the police that you saw or knew anything until you found this note tonight."

"But that's continuing to be dishonest."

"No, it isn't, Chuck. You are granting your dad his last wish. I would have done exactly what you have done if my dad had murdered someone. I'd stand by him. Chuck, you are a young man at the beginning of your life. Trust me on this one, will you? This was not your doing, and you are not to blame. You are as innocent as Georgia, and a victim just like Georgia and me. This note will give the police all they need. Enough people's lives have been ruined thanks to Brian Buchanon. Don't let yours be one of them."

"My life will be ruined no matter what."

"It seems that way now, but time heals all wounds. You have to trust me. This is the right thing to do."

"O.K."

The police came and took our statements. They read the note from Red. They put out a bulletin to all patrolman in the greater L.A. area to keep a look out for him. They even said to proceed with caution. Red as a danger was hard to imagine. But, in a moment of extreme stress, he had committed murder. After the police left, Chuck called his sisters and brothers. Each call took a lot of time. The family was in shock. Red had been their anchor and now he could play that role no longer. At about 4AM I insisted that Chuck take a sleeping pill. Whatever tomorrow would bring, no news would be good, and Chuck would need his wits about him. I made a bed for him on my sofa and within about 15 minutes he fell into a troubled sleep. I went back to bed as well but couldn't sleep. I didn't take a pill because I needed to be conscious if Chuck woke. I needed to make sure he didn't panic and do or say something stupid.

As I lay in my bed, I felt a bittersweet sense of relief. My life was saved, but many others were in jeopardy. Brian Buchanon had gone too far this time, and I silently vowed to make sure he paid for it. He had set Red up to fight his battles. Poor loyal old fool. Red's letter said it all. He was not a murderer. He had killed in a moment of fear and confusion. He did, in a split second of impulsive poor judgment, what he needed to do to protect Brian. Brian made every one of us feel as though we owed him our lives. Unfortunately, Red would now fully pay that cruel group debt.

Chuck was still sleeping when the phone rang at 9:10AM. It was Officer Wagner. They had found Red's car over an embankment in Topanga Canyon. Red was dead. His alcohol level was extremely high. Officer Wagner said Red may have passed out before the impact. They would do an autopsy to see if there were any drugs in his system. The final process had begun, but Red's pain was over. Officer Wagner asked me to bring Chuck down to the LAPD as soon as possible. He needed a more detailed statement and wanted the suicide note. As I hung up the phone in the kitchen, I heard Chuck call my name.

"Paddy?"

When I went in the living room, he was sitting up but groggy with sleep and the remaining narcotic in his system. When he saw my face, he knew what I had to tell him.

"Did they find my dad?" Chuck asked in a small voice. Gone was the bravura of our past relationship.

"He's dead, Chuck. I'm sorry." I didn't give him unexpected news. He hung his head and cried silently. I put my arm around him and couldn't speak. There were no words appropriate. The pain in the room was too great. My tears flowed freely now as well. For Georgia, for Red, for Ahmed, for Chuck and for me. Five innocent victims. The puppets of Brian Buchanon. The loss, the waste was overwhelming. I was too weak to move and so was Chuck. When I could again speak, I gave him the few sketchy details that Officer Wagner had given me. It took a long time for him to gather the strength to get up and take on the grim task of calling his brothers and sisters with the news. While he was doing this family duty, I made him some breakfast and some strong coffee. He was young and would need a every bit of strength that the ordinary elements of living could provide. When he sat down, he ate slowly and methodically, like a man who knew that to survive he had to swallow the food and drink the drink and face the worst day of his life.

I made him take a shower and I gave him one of my clean shirts and a jacket to wear. When we were both cleaned up, we headed out to the LAPD. I kept reassuring him that it was his father's wish for him be free of responsibility of this whole nightmare. He was innocent. That was clear to me. None of all that had happened rested on his shoulders. He did what any boy would have done under the circumstances. He didn't need to go through any more crap with the cops and the law.

The loss of his dad was punishment enough. By the time we reached the LAPD I extracted agreement from him that he would withhold his participation in the cover-up. No one but his priest ever needed to know the whole truth. God would forgive him too.

We walked into the LAPD together and were whisked into Officer Wagner's office. He asked Chuck and me a lot of questions. It was hard on Chuck. I was used to it. Everything was taped. Officer Wagner asked for Red's suicide note. Chuck told Officer Wagner that when they were done with Red's note that he would like it back. He wanted to keep the last loving, self-sacrificing note from his beloved father. I kept my arm around Chuck during the questioning as a reminder for him to keep his cool. The paternal feeling that welled up in me during that hour and a half left me with a profound sense that I would have a son someday and that I wanted him to grow up to be just like Chuck. He was such a genuinely good kid. I loved him that day, my fellow traveler in an unfair world, and I always will.

We got up to leave and had to steady ourselves. We were both weak with grief. As we walked down the corridor, I had my arm draped over Chuck's shoulder. We were silent on our walk out. As we were going down the steps to the sidewalk, a squad car pulled up, and two patrolmen got out. Their passenger was shaded by the smoked windows. As we reached the bottom step, they opened the back door. Brian Buchanon was looking at us through narrowed eyes. Chuck stopped in his tracks and so did I. Brian shouted out to us.

"You two losers trying to pin this on me?"

The officer grabbed Brian's arm and told him to stop. Brian wrenched his arm away. I heard a noise come out of Chuck's throat. He was trying to speak. A cry mixed with words came spilling out.

"My dad trusted you, and now he's dead. You killed him, you murderer! You killed him!" Chuck screamed.

"Your old man was stupid, kid. Nobody told him to kill that slut. You're just the stupid kid of a stupid old man!" Brian's venom spewed before the cops could stop him.

Chuck let out a long, plaintive yell as he broke free from me, bent over and charged into Brian's chest and knocked him down flat on his ass. Chuck then jumped on top of him and started beating him to a pulp while still yelling at the top of his lungs like an Indian at a massacre. The cops were trying to stop him and pulled on him as hard as they could but Chuck, in that moment possessed by a super strength, pounded Brian relentlessly. Finally, the cops and I subdued Chuck and pulled him off Brian. Brian jumped up fighting mad.

"That was assault." No one moved. "Are you fuckers blind?" Brian screamed, eyes bulging out of a blood red face, as he turned on the cops. "I demand my rights. I'm Brian Buchanon. I'm not going to be treated that way by some dead booze hound's kid."

A cop turned to me and said, "Get the kid out of here." He then turned to Brian and said sarcastically. "Keep moving. We'll worry about your rights later, Mr. Brian Buchanon." Brian shouted his profane protests as Chuck and I walked away.

The next morning, the L.A. Times front page was dominated with headlines pertaining to Georgia's murder.

"BELOVED L.A. SPORTSCASTER RED KELLY MURDERED GEORGIA CONROY!"

"PADDY MCGURK CLEARED OF ALL CHARGES IN THE DEATH OF GEORGIA CONROY"

"KKLA GENERAL MANAGER, BRIAN BUCHANON, CHARGED WITH CONSPIRACY TO OBSTRUCT

JUSTICE IN CONROY MURDER CASE"

"BRIAN BUCHANON CHARGED WITH ILLEGAL SURVEILLANCE AND WIRETAPPING OF KKLA EMPLOYEES"

"AHMED BROOKS IN SHOCK AT TURN OF EVENTS IN CONROY MURDER CASE!"

The Hollywood Reporter was breathless in their coverage of the biggest story in LA since OJ and the quake.

The New York Times covered the case in eloquent detail.

The New York Post screamed the tawdry details.

Howard Stern said to Robin Quivers, "I knew Paddy didn't do it. I knew he was framed. Yeah, he got his dick in a ringer. But, he's not a killer. He's just too god damn good looking for his own good. A problem I do not share." Robin roared.

Rick Dees and Ellen K gleefully reported my innocence. Ellen K was particularly generous as she was a big fan of my news broadcasts and had said as much to me at the cocktail parties of media gatherings.

My innocence and the ultimate story of betrayals and loss were the best gossip nugget west of Sepulveda. It told like a Jackie Susann novel. Yep, I was the party circuit tidbit of the day.

But when Sam Rubin took over the KTLA Morning News to deliver to LA the salient details of the tragedy, he was masterful. As I watched him skillfully handle the tragedy and all the players in it, I wept. I wept for all of us. Even Brian Buchanon. I knew that in my life I would never witness a greater loss, to me, and to those I had called friends and colleagues.

I was born to cover the news.

Today, and for many days to come, I would be the news.

16

FIVE YEARS LATER

Over the years since I left Los Angeles for San Francisco, I have thought back about this time in my life at least once a day. It's with me now and will be forever. Nothing before or since has equaled the passion or the pain of all that happened. But I have found a way to enjoy my new home, and my new life.

I bought a mid-century house in Mill Valley and renovated it. Each morning I made my way across the Golden Gate Bridge into the shimmering city by the Bay to do the news. I have had girlfriends, some beautiful, some charming, and some downright hot as fire, but none ever filled the giant cavern in my heart that is still filled with the feelings I hold for Georgia Conroy. Her flame shines bright inside me.

You don't get to choose who you fall in love with. Love simply takes over. I never believed in love at first sight. Seemed like a silly romance novel notion. But, the moment I laid eyes on Georgia Conroy I knew. I didn't know I'd win her over. I didn't know she would love me back. But I knew that every cell in my being was being drawn to her. I felt my heart leave my body the moment she leaned around

Ahmed's looming frame and waved hello like a shy schoolgirl. And I live without my heart fully available to any other woman. I can love, but not like that.

Recently I met a very good woman who is smart and pretty. Not a great beauty, but a great person. She is pregnant with my son. We will get married, and we will make a life together. She knows about Georgia, and we are both at peace with the life I lived a long time ago. I am so grateful that she is accepting of all that happened before her. She loves me profoundly, and I am doing my best to love her back in kind. You don't get what you want, but you get what you need. The Stones had it right. I needed this woman to heal my broken heart and take care of my tortured soul.

Chuck calls me from time to time, on holidays mostly. And once he came to see me. What a great kid. What a great man he became. Early news anchor in San Diego on an owned and operated station. He does a lot of charity work and is a stalwart of San Diego news. He got married, had three kids, and plays a lot of golf just like his dad. And he's a good man, just like his dad. Red got played. We all got played. By a man who knew no boundaries in his quest to be in control, in charge, the king of the hill. Power is heady, power corrupts, and the lines get blurred by power brokers who ignore boundaries and ignore right from wrong. Due to Brian's inability to play it straight, lives got ruined. Two got lost. And, as a result, none of us will ever be the same.

Brian served time in one of those country club prisons for rich and powerful men who do awful things. Once out, he bought a couple of radio stations under his son's name, but he ran them. It gave him something to do. He had no personal life.

Ahmed went on to break records, and then retired from playing. He bought a ranch in Montana and married a great woman who is a true earth mother. They raise their own vegetables and raise Bison. And uncomplicated life for a guy who had a lot of complications in his life. He was, I hoped, at peace.

Ahmed and I were never friends again, but others shared his story with me, and *Architectural Digest* featured his stunning home and life. I felt so good reading about his happiness. A happiness I had threatened.

But Ahmed and I will always share one thing that no one else can share with us. Our love of our golden girl, our angel, the woman of our dreams. Georgia Conroy. She left us both with memories and longing for a time never to return to us. A loss, a wound, that will never heal. We survived, but like a bird with a broken wing, we will never reach those heights again, we will never soar again. That is our shared tragic legacy that will last the rest of our lives. It marked us, now and forever.

What can never be taken from me are my memoeries. And each night, when the house grows quiet, and I am alone with my thoughts, Georgia visits me as I lie there in my dark room, holding my pillow. I see her face, her bright eyes dancing as she taunts me, teases me, pulls me to her and I feel my body respond as her skin meets mine. I can smell her, even taste her again. I can hear her laugh and feel her cry. Not one night has passed that I have not had my nocturnal visit, and I know, deep in my soul, in my next lifetime she will be there waiting for me because our story must continue.